ANIMAL MAGNETISM

"That's enough, Karic," Liane began, forcing a self-satisfied smile onto her lips. "I've seen enough."

His eyes clouded with confusion, slowly banishing the mists of passion. "Enough? What are you talking about, Liane?"

"I've seen enough of your lovemaking. Cat Men techniques seem to vary little from other humanoid species."

Karic's eyes narrowed. "Are you saying all this time you were studying me and my mating techniques?"

"And why else? I'm a scientist. I take advantage of all opportunities."

He frowned with cold fury. "I don't believe you."

Her eyes widened in feigned disbelief. "But surely you didn't think I found you attractive? You're a Cat Man, after all. I'd never mate outside my species."

Karic savagely pulled her to him. One hand tightened across her back, flattening her breasts against the hard planes of his chest.

"And what makes you think I care what you want or don't want?" he snarled.

Other Leisure Books by Kathleen Morgan:

THE KNOWING CRYSTAL

Heart's Lair

KATHLEEN MORGAN

LEISURE BOOKS ⫿ NEW YORK CITY

A LEISURE BOOK®

September 1991

Published by

Dorchester Publishing Co., Inc.
276 Fifth Avenue
New York, NY 10001

To Jean Anne. You said this was *my* book, but in so many ways it's yours as well. I couldn't have done it without your support and gentle guidance. Thank you, my friend.

And to John, my husband, science fiction consultant and research partner. You're not half bad as a hero yourself, big boy.

Heart's Lair

PROLOGUE

THEY WERE AFTER HIM.

Karic knew it though no sound stirred the deep silence of the forest, no enemy scent intruded on the damp sweetness of leaf mulch and wild violets. He could *feel* them coming, a sixth sense as innate to a Cat Man as lithe limbs and boundless stamina, a sixth sense that melded with a strong ability to cloak his presence from most humanoids. But this sol, his trackers had non-human help.

They'd pursued him for horas now, but Karic easily outdistanced them, maintaining a comfortable lead. It gave him time for a breathing space. Soon, though, he must move on—but not yet. It was still safe, and he wanted to spend those precious moments here, deep in a sunlit glade beside a water-splashed pool—watching her.

She was small, delicately boned, her ivory flesh caressing her finely sculpted frame like flowing silk.

Her long black hair, glinting like dark glass in the sunlight, fell from a center part into soft cascades down her shoulders and back. She was ethereal, serene, a fragile beauty.

Karic wanted her.

That decision had been quick, simple. His mission was twofold, and one element was to bring home a breeding female of some humanoid species. Whether he gave her to one of the other young Cat Men or kept her for himself was not the issue.

From the first moment he saw her, Karic knew he'd take the female for his own. The problem, rather, lay in the other part of his mission, and for the first time in his life Karic's sense of duty warred mightily with an equally strong sense of desire.

She did nothing to ease his conflict. In an infinitely sensual motion, the female slowly stretched her arms over her head as if reaching for the sky, her soft breasts straining against her thin blue shift. Then, before Karic could inhale another breath into his tightly constricted chest, she lowered her arms and slipped the gown from her shoulders.

It fluttered to the ground in a long, agonizing flow of cloth. Karic thought he'd never breathe again. For what seemed an eternity of heart-stopping tension she stood there, exquisitely, unashamedly naked. Then she strode into the pool.

Karic's breath returned with a painful shudder, followed swiftly by a hot, heavy tightening in his loins. Sweat beaded his brow and glistened on his powerful arms and chest. He watched her, his body little more than a quivering, knotted mass of muscles—and did nothing.

His people needed him. Too long had Agrica been at the mercy of the Bellatorian invaders, inhabitants of the distant warrior planet, Bellator. Too long had those greedy usurpers of his planet's agricultural wealth been permitted free rein, his own people the only remaining resisters on the peacefully bucolic planet. And now, even their rebellion could well be at an end if his primary mission failed.

No, there was still too much to be done. First, he must seek out the mysterious weapon fearful tales spoke of and ascertain the full extent of its powers. Then, and only then, could he return to her and take her home with him.

An eerie baying wended its way through the peaceful forest. Karic froze. It was the cry of the dreaded search canus, viciously hot on a scent—his scent.

Karic disappeared as silently as he'd come. Time enough to return for the lovely female and taste the sweetness of her. But for now, he must set his sights on the Bellatorian-held fortress of Primasedes, infiltrate its defenses and find the horrible weapon said to lie within.

CHAPTER 1

"BY THE FIVE MOONS OF BELLATOR!" LORD TERAN
Ardane exclaimed. His bearded jaw clenched in
frustrated rage. "I don't give a damn for your
explanations. They all reek of lies and deceit."

His steely glance circled the assemblage of
Bellatorian nobles and scientists seated at the huge
table in the Agrican capital of Primasedes. "Is there
no one here with the courage to tell the truth?"

Liane Allador opened her mouth to speak, then,
shaking her ebony head of hair, settled back in her
chair. She was a Sententian, she firmly reminded
herself, averting her eyes from his compelling gaze.
It was not her place to interfere in Bellatorian
politics. Her assignment on Agrica, though she'd
accepted it with some misgiving after having heard
the rumors of the planet's problems, was to assist
when requested and otherwise keep her opinions to
herself.

And Liane tried very hard to do that. Though of a Bellatorian subrace, her special Sententian gifts were not those of the more warlike Bellatorians. Instead, her people strove for attainment of peace and serenity, of learning and the development of the psychic powers of the mind. So, Liane remained silent in response to Teran Ardane's plea. It was the wiser course.

"Domina Allador." Lord Ardane's deep voice emphasized the title of respect as he addressed her.

Liane cooly turned her gaze toward him, her delicate brows arching in unspoken query. He was a commanding man, this ambassador of Bellator's High King, but his presence here had stirred only animosity and a most unsettling tension. Liane felt it strongly. No, if possible, she must stay above the rising turmoil. She dared not get involved.

"Domina Allador," Lord Ardane persisted, "you seemed about to speak a few secundae ago. What made you hesitate?"

Normally, Liane established deep mental contact by the laying on of hands, but not this sol. The power, the combined rage of this gathering, precluded the usual requirements. She could feel the assemblage turn its collective psychic force against her, mentally demanding her silence.

Their soundless commands fluttered against her skull like the wings of so many caged birds. It took all of her self-control to keep from raising her hands to symbolically protect herself. Irate demands, coupled with the innate Bellatorian compulsion to obey, warred with her more gentle, truth-oriented Sententian nature.

To betray her compatriots was unthinkable, yet was not the man seated before them also a

14

Bellatorian by birth? Liane knew the story of how Teran Ardane, with the help of the Aranean Queen Alia, had found the long-lost Knowing Crystal. Though the discovery of that famous stone of justice and power had occurred only a short time ago, the tale had spread through the planets of the Imperium like wildfire. Even Agrica, long considered a backwater planet, had heard the news.

And now he was here, with the full sanction and powers that only a master of the Knowing Crystal could possess, to begin the work of setting right the horrible wrongs and blighted leadership that had evolved throughout the Imperium in the hundreds of cycles since the Crystal's loss. He was here to help not only subjugated Agrica but Bellator itself, if only Bellator would let itself be helped.

Liane inwardly sighed, shaking aside the voices yammering in her head. Though she feared the consequences of such an act she must answer him. A Bellatorian should always obey.

She gave Teran a slow, sweet smile. "I hesitated, my Lord Ardane, in the misguided thought that I, of all assembled, knew the least about the problems. You see, I only arrived on Agrica a monate ago."

"And your assignment here, Domina?"

"Research scientist. I study the local population in the hope of finding more humane ways to control them."

A gasp of indignation surged around the table.

"My Lord Ardane," an angry male voice protested above the rising din, "she is but a scientist. She has no way with words and knows not of what she speaks. Let me explain the real truth of it."

Teran's hand rose to silence him. "And you, my Lord Necator, though Lord Commander of Agrica,

15

are but a politician. You may have a way with words, but there's rarely any truth in them. I prefer to hear the Domina's explanation."

Necator, a ferret-faced parody of a man, shot Liane one last, chilling look. "As you wish, my lord," he muttered.

Teran turned back to Liane. "You said you were sent here to study ways to more humanely control the inhabitants. Are your psychic powers utilized in this study?"

Liane nodded. "Of course, my lord. I reach into their minds and discover their innermost needs, their joys as well as fears. It is a most effective way to influence people."

He leaned forward. "Then tell me, Domina, why is it necessary to influence the Agricans? I've been informed all is well on Agrica, that the people appreciate Bellatorian assistance, that we have done much to improve and modernize this backward planet. Do you find such feelings when you examine Agrican minds?"

Liane shifted uneasily. To speak the truth now could be dangerous, yet she was sworn to it as strongly, as sacredly, as she was to obedience. And both were now being demanded by an authority higher than the Lord Commander.

She slowly shook her head, her gaze resolutely meeting Teran's. "No, my lord, the Agricans do not appreciate us. Quite the contrary. They fear and hate Bellator."

Her words seemed to hang in the dead silence, dancing tauntingly before the frozen faces of her Bellatorian compatriots. Her glance sought Necator's.

"My lord, forgive me, but the truth . . ."

The man ignored her. "Well," Necator icily said, turning his attention to Teran, "if you choose to believe a Sententian over me I suppose she has damned us in your eyes. But as you know, their race is often emotionally unstable. A few have even been found traitors."

It was Liane's turn to gasp, but she said nothing. Instead, she turned back to Teran. He smiled at her, and his gray eyes briefly warmed.

"Casting aspersions upon each other will not further the pursuit of truth," he said, his gaze slowly spanning the faces at the table. "I care not for what has gone wrong in the past, only for the righting of those wrongs. That is the true purpose of my mission here. I—"

A man burst into the room, pale and breathless. "Lord Ardane," he panted, "you are wanted in the transport chamber. A messenger has brought an urgent summons from Aranea. Your queen desires your immediate return."

Teran rose from the table in one lithe movement. He riveted his forceful gaze on the Lord Commander. "This issue is not resolved, only temporarily suspended. In the interim, I suggest you proceed with extreme caution."

Necator glared at him, then curtly nodded. His tight expression faded as Lord Ardane strode from the room, gradually transforming to a look of determined calculation.

An uneasy presentiment filled Liane. As if pulled by the invisible tendrils of her anxiety, the Lord Commander slowly turned to her. His flat, expressionless gaze filled her with a cold dread.

"Extreme caution indeed," he muttered, his voice deadly ominous. "Thanks to you, my lovely young

17

Sententian, we may all live to rue this day." His eyes narrowed to glittering slits. "And you will rue it most."

Shadows darkened the hall, the fading summer sun throwing dancing fingers of light through the tall arched windows. Necator tightened his grip on Liane's arm as he all but dragged her down the long corridor. The rapidity with which events had changed still left her reeling.

Had it been but an hora ago that Lord Ardane was here, the only Bellatorian on Agrica concerned about the plight of its inhabitants? And now he was gone, with no idea when he would return again. Once again there was no hope for Agrica and now, it seemed, little hope for her, either.

"Fool!" Necator hissed. "Did you think you'd escape unscathed by betraying me to Ardane? No matter what happened, I'd have found a way to repay you."

Liane struggled to free herself from her captor's vise-like grip. "I—I but told the truth," she gasped. "I meant no betrayal!"

Necator halted and wrenched her to him. "Well, the time is fast approaching when all must choose one side or another, though both sides be Bellatorian." He cocked a thin brow. "And which side will you choose, my sweet little Liane?"

"Neither!" She tried to ease away from his hot, smothering breath. "I wish only to do my duty, serve my people. I thought I was doing that in the assembly hall," she whispered, "but perhaps I was wrong."

"Yes, perhaps you were." Necator grinned. "You're such a lovely little femina for all your strange psychic powers. In time I had hoped to reward you with some special, most personal of favors, but now . . ."

He paused. "I'll give you one more chance to prove yourself."

Liane licked her dry lips, well aware of how close she was to losing her life. "And what might that be?"

"We've captured an Agrican, a very special one. Our new alarm system works beyond my wildest imaginings to catch one such as he. We finally have a live Cat Man to study." His grin widened into one of wolfish pleasure. "And you, my talented little Sententian, are going to read his mind."

Relief washed through Liane. "You ask but what I'm born to do, my lord. It will be as you wish."

"It may not be as easy as you think with this one."

"Not easy? But how is that possible? Few can resist a Sententian mind seek."

"And how many Cat Men have you had the opportunity of using it upon?"

Liane shrugged. "None. But they are of a humanoid species. Why should there be any problem?"

"Cat Men are only half-humanoid; their other half is pure animal. And they have purported psychic powers of their own. We know for certain they possess the ability to cloak their presence. That's why, up until now, we've been unable to capture one alive. But this sol our trackers were out with their search canus. When it became evident the Cat Man was headed for Primasedes, we had enough time to turn on our new alarm system. Though they can slip past our guards without them knowing, these Cat Men seem to have little effect on a machine. But then, thanks to the extreme secrecy of the project, this one didn't even know of its existence until it was too late."

At the mention of the search canus, Liane involuntarily shuddered. She'd heard their baying this sol as she bathed in the forest. What if that Cat Man had been nearby? What would have happened to her then? She'd heard revolting tales of their uncontrollable sexual urges.

Necator's grip tightened as he led her down the hall. "Listen closely to my instructions. I care little for the usual information you obtain from your mind seeks. All I want are specific details on where the Cat Men's lair is. I have nearly succeeded in annihilating that odious race of Agricans. If you discover their lair, I can eliminate the final obstacle to complete dominance of this planet. The Cat Men are the last of the rebels."

"Will it bring peace to Agrica?"

The Lord Commander smiled at Liane's naiveté. "Of course, my little Sententian. Isn't that what we all want?"

He and Liane stopped in front of a door marked ANALYSIS. A strange light flared in his eyes. "He's a hard one, this Cat Man. So far even our most sophisticated tortures have failed to elicit the whereabouts of his lair. Unless you can get it from him I fear he'll die with the secret. And it goes without question that you'll try your best, doesn't it, my sweet femina?"

Liane forced a wan smile. "Of course, my lord. I am, after all, a loyal Bellatorian."

Though Necator had warned her the scene in the room might be gruesome, nothing he'd said had prepared Liane for what she saw. Until now her experience, both as psychic healer and research scientist, had been directed toward compassionate restoration, not cold objectivity and torture. It required all her strength to follow the Lord Commander across the chilly, stone-tiled laboratory and up to the Cat Man.

He hung there in the middle of the room, stark naked, his wrists and ankles bound by beryllium manacles that electronically suspended him in a spread-eagled position. Two scientists worked on him, one drawing a blood specimen from a bulging forearm vein, the other endeavoring to obtain a sample of skin off the Cat Man's thigh for further microscopic study. And all, Liane thought, without any consideration of his dignity or comfort.

She was nearly overcome with the urge to turn and run from the room. If it hadn't been for her Bellatorian sense of duty, she'd have immediately recanted her earlier agreement to involve herself in this study.

Liane comforted herself with the realization that her part in the study was painless. In fact, she could easily leave the Cat Man with a temporary sense of anesthesia when she finished with the mind seek. At least for a few horas he would be free of pain, no matter what they did to him, and no one would be the wiser.

The thought motivated her to action. She turned to Necator. "I need total silence and the lights dimmed for the mind seek. And I must be alone with my subject."

Her companion's eyes narrowed. "Don't toy with me, femina."

She sighed in exasperation. "These requirements are not whim, my lord. The mind seek is a delicate art. Other thought patterns can distract from capturing those of my subject. You said this Cat Man might be difficult. Would you make my task all the harder?"

"Just be sure you succeed," he growled. "My patience is wearing thin."

"Yes, my lord."

Liane watched as the room was cleared and the lights dimmed, except for the small circle of illumination around the Cat Man's suspended form. She stood there in the shadows for a short while, preparing herself and studying him.

He was not quite what she'd imagined a Cat Man to look like. He was young. Liane guessed him to be no more than 28 or 29 cycles. Built tall, his shoulders were massive, his body tough and athletically muscular. On his fingertips she noted the sites of retractable claws.

That much confirmed the few photo prints available of the elusive species. But he wasn't as hairy. Granted, there was crisp, dark gold fur on his well-formed frame, but no more so than most Bellatorian males. And his sexual organ, Liane noted with a scientist's detachment as her eyes slid down his body, was quite the norm, if a trifle large.

His face, set off by a thick, unruly mane of sun-streaked, tawny-brown hair that fell to his shoulders, was also a surprise. His sun-bronzed skin had little facial hair other than dark brows, lashes and the shadow of a beard. That aspect of his appearance was in direct contradiction to the prints, which had always depicted a copious amount of furring extending far out from the hairline on all sides.

Though his head was lowered in exhaustion, his eyes closed, Liane was still able to catch a glimpse of his rugged features. Though his nose was slightly flattened and his browline a little more pronounced, it did little to detract from his good looks. Exotic

22

species though he was, the Cat Man was still a virilely handsome man.

Liane could admit that from a purely scientific viewpoint, trained as she was to make astute, totally objective observations. And she also knew, with the same keen sense of observation, that this was no pure-blooded Cat Man. More than the half-humanoid Cat blood ran in his veins. One of his parents had definitely been human.

But that wasn't surprising, either. Many were the tales of Cat Men abducting human females, ever since the successful massacre of most of the inhabitants of their forest lair over 30 cycles ago. A large contingent of the males had been away hunting, so the story went, when an armed Bellatorian force fell on the hapless lair.

To a man, woman and child, nearly all the Cat Men were slaughtered. Only a few managed to escape and warn the returning hunters. It was the last time the Cat Men made their lair in their beloved forest, choosing instead the cold, barren safety of the distant Serratus Mountains. And, determined to ensure the propagation of their species to carry on the unending war against the Bellatorian invaders, the Cat Men turned to other breeding females.

Harsh times necessitate harsh measures, Liane thought, but to be forced to mate with someone against your will . . . With a small shudder, she directed her attention back to the subject at hand.

The Cat Man moved slightly in his shackles, as if trying to find some position to ease his discomfort. His bruised body glistened with a fine sheen of sweat. Bellatorian tortures, Liane knew, were highly effective in their ability to incite pain that went on for horas after the initial stimulus was applied, but even their power could be measurably eased during mind seek. Liane stepped forward. Perhaps she could do little for him, but what she could do, she would do. She moved until she was but a breath away from the Cat Man and gently took his drooping head in her hands.

His lids slowly opened, and Liane found herself impaled by an intense pair of green-gold eyes. They were defiant yet at the same time probing, as if he needed something of her. She felt her resolve melting.

Liane jerked back in surprise. Well, Necator had warned her of the Cat Man's powers.

A weak smile tipped the Cat Man's mouth. "Do I frighten you?"

The rasp of his voice, harsh with pain, clawed down Liane's spine, setting her nerves on edge. Even now, without benefit of the mind seek, she felt herself merging with him, assuming his pain. There was a strong psychic link here which made her uneasy.

She shook her head, as much to discard the strange feelings as to deny his question. "No."

He cocked a dark brow. "I don't believe you."

Anger welled in her at the absurdity of the situation. Here he was, bound, weak from torture, about to have his deepest secrets wrenched from him, and he had effectively taken control. Well, pity could only go so far.

"I don't want your pity."

Liane sucked in an exasperated breath. It was obvious she'd have to guard her thoughts from him. She tightened her mental control.

Momentary confusion flickered in his striking green eyes. Then his smile widened. "Your powers are strong when you care to use them. But are they stronger than mine?"

She smiled for the first time. It was easier to rise to a challenge than be weakened by compassion. "We shall soon see, won't we?"

Her fingers moved into position on his temples and forehead.

"What's your name?"

His unexpected question both irritated and nonplused her. "What?"

"Your name. If I'm to be mentally assaulted, I thought it only fair to know my assailant's name. My name's Karic."

"I don't care what your name is," Liane hissed through clenched teeth. She closed her eyes and began to concentrate.

"Are you always such a heartless bitch?"

Liane's eyes snapped open. For the longest moment she stared at him. He was clever. She did her best work when she felt nothing for the recipient of her mind seek, neither compassion nor anger. In the course of just a few secundae he had managed to stir both emotions in her to the fullest. It had to stop.

"Do not fight me," she said, intoning the ritualistic instructions, "and you will feel no pain. Follow where I lead and it will be over before you realize . . ."

Even before he felt an insidious warmth flow into his mind, Karic knew he had lost the first skirmish and steeled himself for the far more important battle to come. He forced himself to relax his painfully tensed body, gathering all his strength where he would soon need it most. He knew what she wanted, this beauty from the forest pool. It could only be the same secret his other tormentors had so diligently endeavored to extract for the past sol, ever since they'd electronically overcome him inside the city gates. If only he'd known about the alarm system, about the incapacitating force field, he could have prepared and avoided them. But it was too late now.

He let her mind join with his, allowed her to flow through the layers of inconsequential thoughts and memories, delaying her with questions, attempting to distract. He caught the fleeting mention of her name before she clamped down on further replies and used the sound of it to tease and torment her.

Ah, Liane, so beauteous, so heartless. Why do you hate me and my people to so avidly seek our destruction? Karic mentally bombarded her. *They will kill us, wipe us from the face of this planet, if you reveal our hiding place. Is that what you want?*

She heard it all and relentlessly forged on, ignoring, as best she could, the forceful images of the man, brave, strong and proud, and his deep, abiding love for his people. It was almost too easy, his too generous permission to enter his mind, but she doggedly plummeted inward toward the deepest recesses of his being. His secret would soon be hers.

In the next instant Liane slammed into something so hard, so immovable, that it sent a psychic jolt through her body. The pain of impact made her gasp. Her eyes fluttered open to career into his. He visually held her as she stood there, suddenly pressed against him. For what seemed the longest time neither could think nor breathe.

Reality returned like the slow, sensuous movement of warm honey—heavy, sweet and thick. She'd hit his mental wall, Liane realized, and it was like none other she'd ever encountered. She inhaled a fortifying breath and began a relentless psychic hammering against him. He was strong, but her powers were stronger. She knew it was but a matter of time.

The heat between them grew. Their bodies, molded so tightly one to the other, dampened with the shared struggle, until Liane could feel every rippling muscle of his body straining against hers. Fire burned between them. A tiny ember flared to life in her mind, stoked by the insistence of the masculine intellect that held her just as firmly as she held him.

She was back in the forest, in the sunlit glade by the water-splashed pool. This time, however, she was not alone. The Cat Man, Karic, was with her, and he watched with his strange, hungry eyes, watched as she slipped the gown from her body, watched as she made her way to him.

He took her into his arms. His mouth, sensuously full and wanting, covered hers. She went mad then, her arms entwining about his neck, her fingers burying themselves into his thick mane of hair, their tongues meeting in a fierce, sweet, wild union—but the madness was but a fleeting escape from the true reality.

Liane wrenched free of his psychic manipulations and looked up into eyes hot with passion.

The angry accusations burning in her gaze elicited no apologies from Karic. "You were there as freely as I," he growled. "I felt your body respond, felt your heart quicken beneath mine. It was real no matter how much of the mind. Admit it!"

"Never!"

Before Karic had a chance to react Liane's mind seek slammed into him, forcing open a chink in his inner wall. She was half in, catching a glimpse of a distant mountain peak, before Karic shoved her out.

She fought back with all the power within her. For the longest time they struggled, neither certain who the eventual victor might be.

Pain tightened their features as one feinted then attacked the other, sheer desperation fueling Liane's assault, bitter determination upholding Karic's. Even in his physically weakened state the Cat Man managed to fend off every attack, even though he knew he had little left to give. If there'd been a way to internally kill himself or drive himself over the brink of incoherent madness, he'd have done it while he still had the strength—anything but reveal the hiding place of his people. But that small favor was denied him. All that was left was to doggedly fight on.

Liane saw it and felt his rising desperation, yet the realization failed to sweeten her sense of victory. If he'd been stronger, not so cruelly weakened by the neural torture, she'd never have prevailed this far. Yes, the victory was now within her grasp, but she knew she'd have to kill him to gain it. Only in his dying would she at last penetrate his defenses, and that knowledge was almost more than she could bear.

Never, in all her cycles as a Sententian, had she done harm in a mind seek, much less killed someone. Yet failure would be hers if she didn't kill now. Was it worth the price?

Duty and strict obedience to the will of higher authority had been instilled in her since birth and were as much a part of her as the air she breathed, the water she drank. But duty and strict obedience were suddenly of little comfort in the face of seeing a brave, indomitable man die in her arms. She didn't think she could live with herself.

The conflict grew to crazed proportions. Life . . .

28

Death . . . Right . . . Wrong. The words, mingling with the confusing pleasure of the mental moments shared in his arms, rose to a whirling maelstrom in her mind. Pain, worse than any she'd felt in her life, stabbed through Liane, sending sharp, bright, blinding shards of light into her brain.

Suddenly, it seemed too hard to go on, too hard to fight through the maze of choices. With a small cry, Liane slumped to the floor.

CHAPTER 2

HOVERING ON THE BRINK OF CONSCIOUSNESS, KARIC watched Liane being carried from the room. His bleary gaze followed, well aware it might be the last time he ever saw her. Their brief encounter, however painful, was all he'd ever have—that and the achingly sweet memory of those few moments watching her by the pool.

It wasn't enough, but there seemed little hope of surviving this imprisonment. And after catching glimpses of her fevered desperation during the mind seek, Karic wondered if Liane would fare much better. With an exhausted sigh, he lowered his head. As bitter a realization as it was, there wasn't much he could do for either of them.

"What did you do to her?"

Karic sensed Necator's approach even before he spoke. It just required too much effort to acknowledge him, even if the man had been worth the effort. He ignored the question.

A low buzzing pervaded the room. Karic felt himself lowered to the floor until he was kneeling upon it, his arms still suspended in the air. His head was wrenched back by a rough hand in his hair, and he stared up into cold black eyes.

"I'll ask you again," Necator snarled, "and I'll have the truth from you or the femina will lose her life."

A slow grin split his face at the surge of emotion that flashed across the Cat Man's features. "Just as I thought. Somehow you managed to get through to her with those sly powers of yours. You won her over, didn't you?"

Karic forced the tension to ease from his body. For Liane's sake, he must tread carefully here. He wearily shook his head.

"She's a beautiful femina; any male can see that. I don't wish her harm, but as far as what I did to her, it's simple. My powers overcame hers. You have nothing strong enough to get what you want from me."

The Lord Commander's eyes narrowed to speculative slits. "You may be right, Cat Man, but then again, you may also be a bit premature in claiming victory."

His face moved until it nearly touched Karic's. "There *is* one more thing. Perhaps you'll not do as well against a machine."

He gave Karic's hair a vicious tug. "What do you think, Cat Man? Are you man enough to go against a machine as successfully as you did a delicate femina?

"Of course," he smirked, "it's only a prototype,

still a bit cumbersome and unrefined. Perhaps it won't really be much of a challenge to you. Then again, perhaps it will turn you into a mindless, blithering idiot."

Necator turned to one of the scientists. "Bring in the Guide. It is past time we tested it on a Cat Man."

The Guide, Karic thought. That was the name reportedly given to the Bellatorian's new secret weapon. Now, not only had he gained the chance to see it, but he would personally experience its powers as well. It was an opportunity beyond his greatest expectations, if he lived to carry the information back to his people.

They rolled the metal monstrosity in with great care, a tall, heavy rectangular box studded with dials, levers and a large screen. Necator and the two scientists donned what looked to Karic to be some sort of protective hearing devices, then one of the scientists began adjusting the knobs.

A low hum filled the room, gradually rising in tone until it became a shrill, irritating whine. Karic shook his head to rid himself of the noise, but it did little good. The noise became painful, as the high-pitched sound waves relentlessly bombarded his ears.

Karic grimaced. Necator said the machine would turn him into a mindless idiot. Excruciating pain could do that to a man, but Karic doubted the Guide's purpose was quite that simplistic. There had to be a way to plumb the secret workings of the machine and divine its true abilities, if only there were time.

The effects of the Guide upon the Cat Man were not lost on Necator. He smiled in satisfaction. Things were progressing exactly as planned. The Cat

Man's mental resistance would soon be destroyed. In a matter of secundae, the prisoner would be psychic putty in his hands. Then he'd extract the whereabouts of the secret Cat lair and have his victory at last.

He had considered executing the Cat Man as soon as he had his information, but now he hesitated. The full extent of the Guide's effects on the rebels might be worth delving into. If the machine could be programed to overcome all their psychic powers, its potential would be unlimited. Why, it might even rival the purported abilities of the Knowing Crystal, and then he'd have his revenge on the arrogant Teran Ardane as well.

Yes, Necator mused, further study might well be of use. He liked the idea of delving into the soon-to-be pliable mind of the proudly defiant Cat Man, molding his thoughts and feelings into whatever form he chose. An abject slave, groveling at his feet, was a particularly pleasing image.

The fevered actions of the scientist working the Guide's controls drew Necator from his pleasant contemplation. With a frown, the Lord Commander strode over to the machine. The waves on the screen fluttered erratically and red warning lights flashed.

He grabbed the scientist's arm to get his attention. "What's wrong?" he mouthed to the man.

The scientist frantically waved at the machine, then in the direction of the Cat Man. "He's doing something to the Guide," the man mouthed back. "I can't keep it calibrated. It's like *he's* controlling it now."

With a low growl, Necator swung toward the Cat Man. There was indeed something untoward happening, for the prisoner no longer wore a look of twisted agony. Somehow, someway, he must have discovered the proper wavelength to communicate with the Guide.

Necator lifted his hearing protectors. Yes, the piercing sounds had muted to a low, almost pleasant hum. He inwardly cursed. The Cat Man had indeed found a way to manipulate the machine. Necator turned back to the Guide.

"Turn it off!" he screamed. "Shut it down before he has a chance to totally destroy it!"

The humming died as the scientist snapped off the various dials and switches. Necator wrenched away his hearing protectors, sending them flying across the tile floor to slam into the nearest wall. For a long while he stood there, his body trembling with the depth of his rage.

The Guide was useless against Cat Men. His precious machine, developed to destroy mental resistance and open its victims to reprograming, was not only useless but in danger of psychic sabotage at the hands of the one race of Agricans that Bellator had yet to subdue. And now he was no closer to discovering their secret lair than he was before. Curse them all!

He stalked over to where the Cat Man knelt, his arms still painfully suspended in the air. Once more Necator wrenched back his head. The glimmer of triumph in his prisoner's eyes nearly made him choke on his impotent rage. He jerked the Cat Man's head back so far that only the strength of the muscles bulging in the man's neck kept his spine from snapping.

"You've won nothing," Necator hissed through clenched teeth. "Nothing, do you hear me? You've only given me further reason to hasten the extermination of your race. Your people are all that stand between me and complete Imperium control. And I'll find them—believe me, I will—with or without you, that simpering little Sententian *or* my machine!"

A malicious smirk stole across his face. "Not that you'll live to see it, of course. You've more than served your purpose. At sol rise, we'll finish you off, once and for all."

The sky was a leaden gray. Dark clouds, heavy with moisture, covered the horizon like angry monoliths. In the distance thunder reverberated, jagged lightning illuminating one cloud then another with its sickly yellow brilliance. Fierce winds groaned through the trees, stampeding the electricity-charged clouds before its awesome force. The midsummer storm would be here in but a few moments, Liane realized from her place on the fortress parapets, and with it the heaving torrents of rain.

Rain, she mused, watching the scene below of a bound and drugged Cat Man being led outside the city walls to his execution. Rain would feed the thirsty land and nourish life, but that same rain would fall on a man's lifeless body—a man unjustly executed because he dared defy the enslavement of his planet. With a shudder, Liane shook off the traitorous thought.

Why should she care what happened to the Cat Man? He was an enemy to her people. That much had been evident in his crude conduct toward her. Why, he'd all but mentally raped her during the mind seek, then nearly killed her with the force of his own psychic powers. Yet the surprising pleasure of his mental touch at the forest pool lingered with a strange, aching sweetness.

Perhaps the true source of her frustration lay in

the fact that it didn't really matter what she felt or thought. He would die, and there was nothing she could do about it, except be witness to his death. She wondered if he even knew she was here—or cared.

The wind was whipping the trees of the nearby forest to a surging frenzy. Thunder boomed closer now. The Bellatorian guards swung Karic around toward the fortress of Primasedes to face his executioners. Karic thought he caught a glimpse of a slim, dark-haired femina high up on the parapet, then the press of curious onlookers on the walls blocked his view.

No matter. In but a few moments he'd be dead, seared to a smoking pile of charred remains by the lethal blaster guns. He struggled to rise through the tranquil, drug-induced haze.

Curse the Bellatorians! If he were to die he wanted to die clearheaded and defiant, not like some docile pack equs.

With an effort, Karic shrugged off the hold of the two guards, his stance widening to support his sudden dizziness. A gloating chuckle reached his ears, and his head swung up in angry recognition.

Necator had arrived to lend official witness to the execution. "Not so brave nor proud now, are you, Cat Man?" he snickered. "Most men aren't when death is but a few secundae away. Are you already regretting your decision?"

Karic glared at him.

His enemy gave a mock sigh. "Too bad. You sealed your fate when you tampered with my machine."

"You won't win," Karic rasped, "no matter what you do to me. Someone will always rise to fight you and your kind."

The wind whipped around them, nearly knocking both men off their feet. A blinding flash of lightning exploded above their heads, followed a split secundae later by thunder. The air crackled with electricity. With a wild cry, the gathering outside the walls fell to the ground—everyone, that is, but the Caṭ Man.

The sudden advent of the lightning boded his hope of salvation. He wheeled about, his heavy lethargy washed clean in the surge of excitement left in the lightning bolt's wake. Though his arms were securely bound behind his back, his legs were free.

Karic used them to full advantage. He sprinted across the open field that lay between Primasedes and the forest, agilely weaving back and forth in a zigzag fashion to avoid the blaster guns he knew would be swiftly aimed at him.

His quick reaction gained him a few precious secundae before the Bellatorians reacted to his escape. With a shout of outrage, Necator directed the guards to shoot. Bursts of blue fire exploded around him as Karic nimbly dodged his way toward the beckoning trees.

There was hope now as the forest grew ever nearer. Once within its dark safety the blasters would be useless. Once within the forest, he'd be back in his element. He quickened his pace until he thought his heart would burst from the effort.

He was almost there when a sharp, searing pain slashed through his right thigh, nearly toppling him over. Karic staggered, then righted himself, though he hardly could see where he was going. He had to make it to the trees!

Karic stumbled into a large tree trunk before he

realized he'd reached his sanctuary, and he stood there gasping, as much for air as for the excruciating pain that vibrated through his leg. If he lost consciousness now, it would all be over. Karic forced himself to limp on.

He thought he heard voices, fading fainter and fainter, but perhaps it was only the murmur of the wind-tossed trees and distant thunder. After a while it didn't matter. Time melted into a meaningless haze. The effort necessary to put one foot in front of the other, to drag his torn and bleeding leg behind him, required all his concentration.

He must go on, escape, get back to his people.

It began to rain, at first a gentle patter that intensified to large, heavy droplets and then an outright downpour. The leaves underfoot quickly slickened, and Karic slipped and fell.

This time it wasn't so easy to pull himself up, as his strength rapidly ebbed. He lay there for a time, the rain drenching him and draining the warmth from his body. Then Karic stirred. He knew he had to find a hiding place soon, or they'd find him lying here.

When he rolled over on his side to lever himself up with his bound arms, he slipped again on the wet leaves. The effort cruelly depleted him of his remaining strength. When Karic tried again, he found he couldn't rise at all.

There was nothing left. Two sols without food and water, the endless neural torture, and now the massive blaster wound to his leg had finally sapped everything. He lay there in the cold dampness of a suddenly hostile forest, until exhaustion claimed him.

* * *

A strident baying woke Karic. For a moment, he couldn't fathom where he was. Then the frigid rain, pouring down through the trees, brought it all back. He was in the forest. From the looks of it, he'd slept nearly the whole sol away.

The usual benefits of sleep had eluded him. His tightly bound arms had gone numb horas ago, the deep leg wound throbbed fiercely, and his battered body still ached with exhaustion.

Struggling to climb to his feet, he barely managed to draw his knees under him when his leg's tortured flesh sent a surge of nauseating agony through him. Karic doubled over, panting to fight back the gorge that rose in his throat.

The baying drew closer. In some detached part of his mind, Karic wondered if the Bellatorians would set their search canus on him when they found him. He'd seen the beasts tear into a dead Cat Man's body once, and the memory sent a fresh wave of nausea through him.

He'd have to hide. He couldn't go on, not yet, not without more rest. If luck were with him the incessant rain would cover his scent from the search canus, and he knew he could cloak his presence from the Bellatorians. With any luck, they just might pass him by.

A dense thicket lay to the right of him, just ten meters away. It was as good a shelter as any. He crawled over to it. The sound of voices, mixed with the excited yelps of the canus, grew nearer. He could almost make out the individual voices of his pursuers now.

Karic slid beneath the thicket's dense foliage and attempted to cloak his presence. His trackers continued to draw closer. A vague uneasiness wound its way through him. Why were they coming so near? They couldn't penetrate his psychic deception. No Bellatorian could.

The thought of Liane flashed through his mind an instant before he heard her voice.

"I cannot be certain, with all the tumult from the rain and wind," Liane called out to the soldiers behind her, "but I felt a presence over here."

From his hiding place, Karic saw her gesture in his general vicinity. His heart slammed into his gut. She had led them to him, without one shred of remorse or one moment of hesitation. An impotent rage grew in him. She was a mindless, cold-blooded Bellatorian, just like all the rest—and he was at her mercy.

She paused a few meters from him, a look of puzzlement wrinkling her brow. She was searching for him through the tumult of the storm, seeking to penetrate his protective aura. For a fleeting moment, Karic thought his deception had prevailed. Then a triumphant light flared in her eyes. She looked directly at him through the dense shrubbery.

Determined deep blue eyes collided with glittering green ones, and a battle of wills ensued. Both knew what the other wanted. Neither gave way. Yet all the while Liane never revealed his presence. There seemed to be something holding her back, a strange reluctance.

It would be so simple, Liane knew, to raise her hand and point to his hiding place. But she also realized the inevitable consequences of that action, and that knowledge filled her with loathing. Necator had given specific instructions to kill the Cat Man. The soldiers planned to turn the search canus on him. Bound and wounded as he was, Karic wouldn't stand a chance.

She shook aside the disconcerting realization that she'd come to think of the Cat Man as Karic. It only added to her confusion, and confusion, at that moment, seemed the very least of her problems.

Liane stood on the precipice of a fateful decision. If she turned from him and led the trackers away, she also would be turning her back on everything that she'd been raised to revere. But what was loyalty and blind obedience to saving a life? And the value of human life was as innate to the Sententian part of her, as blind obedience was to the Bellatorian part.

With a sigh dredged from deep within her, Liane turned to the soldiers. "I was mistaken. I led you on a false track."

She motioned back the way they had come. "Let us return to the spot where I first felt his presence. Perhaps I can pick up his aura again from there."

The voices faded as Liane led them away. Karic lay there for a long while, not daring to move or believe they wouldn't return, not daring to believe that Liane not only hadn't betrayed him but had deliberately chosen to deceive her own people in order to save his life.

That knowledge kept the pain at bay for a time. Perhaps it was the cold, seeping into his very bones as the sol waned, that finally stirred him to awareness. Perhaps it was his wound or the myriad of other insults inflicted upon his body. Whatever it was, Karic found he was no stronger after his rest than he had been before it and even more miserable.

He was going to die here, for he needed food, shelter and his wound tended, and he was powerless to obtain them. The thought angered him. Never in his life had he been so helpless.

Karic knew Liane didn't dare come back, nor did he want her to. She'd risked far too much for him as it was. It was up to him now.

The thought fueled his resolve. Suddenly, more than anything, Karic didn't want Liane's brave sacrifice to be in vain. Heedless to the gnawing torment of his leg he drove his body forward, his progress heartbreakingly slow. Time passed, the center of his existence revolving around the forward movement of abraded shoulders and tormented legs, until Karic ceased to remember any life before this moment. After a while, reflex rather than reason stimulated the progress of his body.

She found him lying on the forest floor only a few meters beyond the thicket, his feeble attempts at crawling spasming his body in an odd, rhythmic fashion. Liane stared down at Karic, so moved by his heroic determination she almost wept. Then her practiced instincts as a healer took over.

Her glance swung to the raw, gaping wound at the back of his thigh, and she winced. The blaster had done its work with deadly efficiency. The flesh was seared, the muscle torn, the sinew severed from the bone. Under normal circumstances—that is, Agrican circumstances—if Karic lived, he'd be a cripple.

But for once Bellator could help rather than destroy. She would heal him in body and mind, until he was the same strong, powerful man as before. First, however, she must get him to a shelter, where she could tend his wounds the conventional way before performing her psychic healing.

Liane knelt beside him, laying a heavy cloak over his trembling form. At the feel of the cloth Karic's struggles ceased, and he tensed.

"Karic, it's me, Liane." She tentatively touched him. "It's safe now."

"No," he groaned. "Nothing's safe for you. Go away . . . away from me . . . before it's too late."

She grasped him by the shoulders and turned him over, cradling his head in her lap. He'd begun to shiver now, great wracking spasms that shook his entire body. Only now, secure in her arms, was he at last able to let go.

The realization stirred something deep within Liane. "It's already too late," she whispered. "I've betrayed my people for you. I can't leave."

Bits of leaves and dirt caked his bruised face. Liane gently brushed away what she could. She pulled a small flask from the pocket of her cloak, unstoppered it and put it to Karic's blue lips.

"Drink, Karic. It'll give you strength for a short time, time enough to get you to my forest hut."

He looked up at her, his expression dazed. "I have no strength left, sweet femina, and you cannot carry me."

Liane knew he was dying. She raised his head and forced some of the contents of the flask into his mouth.

"Drink," she ordered, in the tone of a mother admonishing a disobedient child. "Swallow it, Karic."

He obeyed her, emptying the flask. With a deep sigh, Karic fell back.

Liane carefully laid him on the ground. It would be a short while, she knew, for the potion to take effect. In the meantime, she busied herself with removing Karic's bonds.

The coils that wound about his forearms were beryllium-impregnated and impossible to sever. She needed the key control to unlock them, which was what had taken so long to procure upon her return to Primasedes.

It had not been easy to sneak down into the analysis lab unnoticed, for it was not her assigned work station and seemed busy 24 horas a sol. As time ticked by and she thought of Karic lying wounded, perhaps dying in the forest, she'd gone nearly mad, waiting for the right opportunity. At long last, it had come.

"I'm going to roll you over and remove your bonds," she explained. "I know it'll be painful after such a long time, but I'll try to be as gentle as I can."

His nod was the only sign that he had heard her. Liane turned him over and pulled down the cloak that covered him. A small push of a button on the key control and the metallic bonds fell away. Ever so carefully, Liane brought Karic's arms down to his sides and turned him back over.

His face twisted in pain at this new addition to his torment, but he didn't utter a sound. His arms flopped limply at his sides, cold and pale. Liane took both of his hands in hers.

"I'm going to have to hurt you now, Karic," she said. "I need to massage some feeling back into your arms. Can you bear just a little more?"

"Yes," he gasped, already in the throes of that special agony of returning circulation. "Do what . . . you have . . . to do."

Liane steeled herself to his torment and began to rub life back into his arms. Never once did he utter a sound, though his strong white teeth drew blood from biting down so hard on his lower lip. He was like some wild beast, Liane realized, bearing his pain in silence, expecting neither aid nor comfort save that which he could dredge from within himself.

An urge to take on his pain, to ease a little of his torment, overcame Liane. She felt the healing aura leave her and seek its union with the one in distress. She wanted it, more than anything she'd ever wanted, for Karic.

But not now. It was too soon. First, they needed the safe haven of her hut, for her psychic healing always drained her of power. It wouldn't do for both to be sapped of their strength while still out in the forest. To control the impulse to heal spiraling within her, Liane turned her efforts to massaging warmth into the rest of Karic's body.

Through his soft domare hide boots, she rubbed his legs and feet. Little by little, Karic began to move of his own accord as the potion began to take effect. It would soon be time to help him stand. The liquid was potent, but only for a short while. Its surprising effects would be over all too quickly.

Karic levered himself up on one elbow, a quizzical expression on his face. "What was in that drink you gave me? Suddenly I don't feel any pain, and I've actually got some strength back."

Liane climbed to her feet, her hand outstretched. "An ancient Sententian remedy for what ails you. Now, come. We've little time and a long way to go. This healing is only temporary. The permanent one must wait for my hut."

He took her hand and allowed her to help him stand. When he swayed precariously, Liane quickly moved to his side, her arm encircling his trim waist. With slow, halting steps they made their way through the forest.

* * *

Liane added more tinder to the tiny flame flaring to life in the hearth and watched as it grew to hungrily lap at the logs. When satisfied that the fire had at last taken hold, she added a pot of water to heat. Conditions in the tiny hut were primitive at best, but it suited her need for some simplicity in her life.

She rose and turned toward the man lying on her bed. Thanks to him, Liane wondered if her life would ever be simple again. It wasn't because of his plight or the hard decisions she'd been forced to make to save his life. No, it went deeper than that, and in a way she'd never experienced before.

Her struggle with his mind seek had revealed too much of him. As she'd fought to delve ever deeper all aspects of his personality gradually had been exposed, like peeling away the layers of the fiery caepa fruit. She felt she'd known him for cycles, and the knowing had made him a friend—and something more.

Liane knew Karic desired her. Their mental joining at the forest pool had been too intense for her to deny that. She recognized the heated aura males gave off when they wanted to mate and had felt those same desires before, emanating from other men.

But then, they'd neither affected nor concerned her. She'd made her choice long ago to remain celibate, a choice all Sententian females had to make sooner or later. Faced with the decision to forego her psychic powers if she ever joined with a male, Liane had chosen to devote her life to others rather than herself.

It had been a simple decision in the past, but now it was no longer simple. In her heart, Liane admitted she also desired Karic. It didn't change the inevitable decision but only made it harder and much more painful. The only simple thing had been the resolve to heal the handsome Cat Man and quickly send him on his way.

She gathered up the tools she would need to cut away the ruined flesh and prepare Karic's wound for the psychic healing. The pot of water over the now crackling fire began to steam. Liane carefully removed it, carried the tools and water over to Karic's bedside, then pulled up a stool.

"Karic?" She hesitantly touched his blanket-covered shoulder.

He lay there on his stomach, exhausted, but he turned his head slightly and opened his eyes at the sound of her voice. "Yes?"

"I need to clean your wound before I heal it."

The simple statement sent a surge of anger through Karic. How could she be so naive as to think he dared trust her? He'd been fool enough to let himself believe it in the forest, but it must have been due to the pain, the cold and the danger. It had clouded his mind to all logic.

But now that he was warm and safe inside her little hut, logic had returned, and the logic of the situation was that Liane could well be trying to win him over by gaining his trust. She was a beautiful, desirable femina. Her actions *seemed* sincere, but it was far too soon to trust her. And trust meant accepting her special kind of healing.

"And how do you plan to heal me, Liane?" With an effort, Karic propped himself up on his elbows. His green eyes were shadowed with suspicion, his mouth grim.

She was baffled by his sudden reserve. "Why, by a mind healing, of course. How else would I do it?"

"In the usual manner. Cleaning the wound, then letting it mend on its own."

"It'll never mend right that way. There's been too much damage. You'll never walk on that leg again if you don't let me heal it my way."

"That's *my* choice, isn't it?"

Liane shook her head, her confusion mounting. "But why would you refuse my assistance? It doesn't hurt, and I can completely heal you."

Karic exhaled a deep breath and lowered his head to cradle it in his hands. "It's not the pain. I just don't want you in my mind."

He looked up at her, and the glance, though tinged with regret, was resolute. "Your powers are too strong. I fear I wouldn't have the strength to fight you off again if your healing turned into a mind seek. You saved my life, Liane, but I'm still not sure why."

An unexpected pain coursed through her. Didn't he know, couldn't he sense how she felt about him? Well, it was better he didn't. His powers were also strong. She was just as afraid she'd not have the strength to fight him. Each had a need to be cautious around the other.

"You think I brought you here to win your trust, then use it against you, don't you?" she demanded. "That I might be able to somehow slip another mind seek in and discover the location of your people's lair?"

Karic nodded. "If I'm wrong, I'm sorry, but I have to be careful. Too much is at stake."

He shifted to a more comfortable position. "Do you know why no one has ever captured a Cat Man alive before?"

She shook her head.

"Because we've all sworn to kill ourselves rather

than risk revealing the whereabouts of our lair. If the Bellatorians discovered it again it would be over for us. I'd be dead now, if that new alarm system in Primasedes hadn't taken me by surprise. It incapacitated me just long enough for the guards to get there."

"You must have been terrified you'd be tortured into revealing the secret."

"Yes, I was."

Liane gently brushed aside a stray lock that had fallen into Karic's eye. "But we couldn't get anything from you, no matter what we tried."

"A man doesn't know what he can bear until he's tested."

His striking eyes slowly caressed her face.

"And I'm still not safe, Liane. Far from it."

She knew his words held more than an admission that he still feared for his physical safety, but she forced any further consideration of their meaning from her mind. She couldn't let herself dwell on it—didn't dare.

Her manner became that of a psychic healer to her patient. "Your concerns are groundless, and you needlessly risk disfigurement and crippling if you persist in your stubborn refusal. I cannot mind seek when I heal. You are in no danger."

"Don't patronize me, Liane," Karic said, stung by her cool rejection of his explanation. "I'll risk the crippling and disfigurement. Under no circumstances are you to attempt your psychic healing on me. Care for my wound in the conventional way, or don't bother at all!"

CHAPTER 3

IN THE END LIANE ACCEPTED KARIC'S TERMS. SHE knew he couldn't prevail when he was unconscious, and as she worked on his wound, he tried mightily not to slip into that blessed oblivion. His fists balled in the bedclothes, his face contorted with agony, but at long last he could fight no more.

His powerful form went slack, and Liane breathed a sigh of relief. She blotted away the moisture that had dampened her brow, then wet a cloth and wiped Karic's glistening face. Pain was a part of life, Liane knew, but Karic's pain had been so unnecessary. She was glad his stubbornness was at an end. When he awoke, he would not be able to undo what she had healed.

His anger, though, might be another matter, but she'd face that when the time came. For now, it only mattered that he was wrong and she was right. She had no intention of betraying him or attempting another mind seek. She already knew him too well as it was.

It took well over an hora to complete his healing. Trembling with fatigue, Liane surveyed her handiwork. The muscle and sinew were once again reattached to the bone, the flesh perfectly aligned. A thin, angry red scar was all that remained of the terrible wound. Karic would be thankful—some sol.

She covered him with the blanket and walked away, her steps halting and awkward. He'd sleep for horas now, time enough to rest herself and replenish the strength that had drained from her during the course of the healing. Liane wearily lay down on the fur before the hearth. There was time enough to deal with the issue of what to do about Karic, time enough . . . later. . . .

Karic woke slowly, lazily, to bright sunlight shining in his eyes. He grimaced and lifted his arm to shield his vision. The presence of a normal looking hand, where only a sol before it had been swollen and mangled from Bellatorian instruments of torture, jerked him to full consciousness. He sat up in bed then fell back, a stomach-churning dizziness spiraling through his body.

Where was he? What had happened to heal his body so quickly? With a low curse, he felt his right leg. The wound had healed except for the faint remnant of a scar. It had not been a nightmare. The blasters had torn open his leg, and Liane had mended it!

Blazing with anger, his glance swung about the

room. In spite of his demands to the contrary, she had healed him. She had ignored his request and, when he was helpless, had gone ahead and done just as she pleased. Even now, the information she may have gleaned could be on its way to Primasedes.

He found her asleep before the hearth. For a fleeting instant, as his gaze swept over her slender form curled so cozily in front of the fire, Karic's resolve to seek retribution wavered. Glossy black hair spilled across her shoulders and onto the fur bed, the red glint of the dying embers catching crystalline glimmers in her tresses. The thick fan of Liane's lashes rested gently against her high cheekbones, and her mouth was tender and full in her slumber. She looked sweet, innocent, and oh, so desirable.

Karic cursed again, this time with a vengeance. Even in the face of her betrayal he wanted her still, but though the instinctual drive to mate and propagate his endangered species seethed in his groin, he was still human enough to temper it with reason. And reason told him to wait a while and discover the extent of her treachery. It was the only way to ascertain what she knew and how much of it she had already told Necator.

There were times when he cursed his human blood, believing it tainted the purity of his Cat Man lineage. His sire was Lord of the Cat Men. As his heir, Karic would eventually rule. It ate at him that he would come to that throne half-blooded, a painfully visual reminder of what they'd become in the name of survival.

But there were also times when his human side proved of more value than curse. Cat Men, for all their courage and physical prowess, reacted rather than thought, basing their actions on emotion instead of logic.

Since he'd come into his manhood and gained his rightful place on the Cat throne beside his father, Karic had tempered many a passion-laden issue with surprising wisdom and insight. He found, sometimes to his great distress, that he could be as cold-blooded as a Bellatorian when the need arose. Though the human blood ran bittersweet in his veins, Karic knew its value.

Limbs quaking with weakness, he rose and stumbled to where Liane lay, heedless of his nakedness. Sinking to his knees, he roughly shook her awake.

Liane groggily brushed the sleep from her eyes. Karic knelt there, towering over her. Though pale, his mane of hair disheveled, his eyes still smudged with exhaustion, he looked markedly improved.

Her glance swept over his muscular form, noting with satisfaction that no trace of his recent ordeal marred his body. She also noted that he was naked, and color bloomed in her cheeks.

Nudity was one thing when he was a helpless prisoner, another when he was ill and she cared for him. Now, when he was nearly well, his sexuality was too overt, too potent and too threatening. She scooted away from him.

"Karic," she murmured, "you must dress yourself." Liane motioned toward a nearby chest where there was a neatly folded pile of clothes. "Your loincloth was beyond repair. I found you some breeches and a tunic. Please put them on."

"Are you afraid of me, Liane?" he drawled with distinct mockery. "Afraid I'll rape you now that I am well? And if so, why would the presence of clothing on my body make any difference? You weren't afraid of me before when I was naked. It didn't keep you from pressing your body against mine during the mind seek."

"Stop it!" Liane sat up. "Don't talk to me like that. You make it sound so, so—"

"Loathesome?" he supplied with harsh sarcasm. "But no more loathesome than what you did to me. How dare you go against my wishes in my healing?"

Karic grabbed Liane by the arms and pulled her to him. She could feel the strength and heat of him through her gown. She swallowed a panicked sob.

"You invaded my body against my will," he snarled, his features contorting with fury. "I'd say you've more than raped me!"

Tears filled Liane's eyes. "I—I didn't mean it as such. It was for your own good. You were just too stubborn to admit it."

He couldn't bear her tears and pushed her from him. "It was still *my* body. I'll never forgive you for that."

"I don't care. I'd do it again."

Green eyes narrowed to glittering slits. "And what exactly *did* you do, aside from my healing, of course? How much more did you probe into my mind?"

"I didn't touch you except to heal." She grabbed his hand and brought it to her forehead. "If you don't believe me, look into my mind and see what I know of you. I've nothing to hide."

Karic's hand moved to entwine her hair, and he twisted her head back to expose the slim column of her throat. "And what would I find, sweet femina? Just what you wanted me to see? Do you think I'm that gullible?"

A long, lethal claw sprang out from his forefinger,

54

and he stroked her neck with its tip. "Do you know how close you are to death, my little Bellatorian? Do you know how easy it would be to slit your throat with this?"

Liane's eyes widened, and she flinched. "It wouldn't change the truth," she whispered. "I'm a healer. I'd do it again. I'd have to."

The claw resheathed itself. "Do you realize the jeopardy I put my people in by letting you live?" The question was exhaled on a ragged rasp of breath. "What am I to do with you?"

"Find it in your heart to trust me?"

Karic laughed, the sound harsh and jarring. "You'll have to do better than that, Liane."

"Then trust this." She scooted closer as if to emphasize her words. "There was a man here. Teran Ardane. He's been given power by the High King of Bellator to investigate the improprieties on Agrica and make changes."

"Is he Bellatorian?"

"Yes, but—"

"Then it won't help Agrica."

"No, Karic," Liane persisted, laying a hand on his arm. "He's not like the rest. He's a good man and will change things."

"Then where is he? Tell me and I'll go to him."

Liane sighed. "He's not here anymore. He had to return to Aranea. It was an emergency."

"And what emergency on Aranea could be of more import than the annihilation of a people?" He raised his hand to silence her when she attempted to reply. "Say no more about this Teran Ardane. His priorities are not mine. He means nothing to me."

"He's your people's only hope, Karic."

"No, *I'm* my people's only hope." The image of

the Guide and the potential of turning its powers against its Bellatorian masters flashed through Karic's mind. "I have vital information. How long before I'm strong enough to travel?"

She knew he'd have to leave. It was better this way. "With further nourishment and rest, another two or three sols. You'll feel it when you're ready."

Two or three sols! Karic inwardly railed against the feebleness of his body. Even now Bellatorians might be on their way here, if Liane had ever told anyone about the hut. He was tempted to ask her but knew she'd lie if it suited her needs. Yet each moment spent here put him in increasing jeopardy. If he weren't so damn weak . . .

His keen eyes knifed into hers. "I expect your assistance until I go."

At her nod, he smiled grimly. "It doesn't mean I trust you, Liane. Far from it. Until I leave, I'm not letting you out of my sight. We'll eat together, sleep together, bathe together. Do you understand?"

Liane wondered if she could bear the next three sols without a bath. She nodded.

"Good." Karic rose and slowly made his way over to the chest. Picking up the pile of clothing, he turned. "I'm hungry. Can you cook?"

"Yes." She stood up.

"Then please make me something to eat."

He began to dress. It was an awkward sight, and Liane was tempted several times to come to his aid but knew he'd resent it. Finally, Karic fastened his breeches and glanced up.

"One other thing, Liane."

"Yes?"

"I'll be watching everything you do. Don't try and slip some poison or sleeping potion into the food. You'd only be the one to eat it, if you did."

With an insulted flounce, Liane turned back to the hearth and angrily stoked the fire.

That nocte, she refused his offer to bathe with him and endured the indignity of being tied to the nearest tree while Karic washed in the forest pool. Her anger quickly cooled as she watched him in the water. It was hard to stay angry at a man who stirred her like Karic did.

She knew he was aware of her gaze upon him, but strangely the realization didn't embarrass her. Distance from him seemed to make all the difference—distance and the fact he'd soon be leaving, never to return. She wanted to store up memories of him for those long, lonely times in her life. He was the only man she'd ever wanted. These stolen moments were all she could ever let herself have.

He moved with a lithe grace, his long, steel-tempered thighs slicing the water like finely honed blades. His arms and chest, knotted with muscle, stretched then bunched with rippling precision as he scrubbed his body with the cleansing sand Liane had provided. Unselfconsciously, Karic turned then bent over to capture the floating container of sand, presenting Liane a tantalizing view of taut buttocks merging into long, smooth flanks. She felt her heart quicken, her mouth go dry.

The sudden surge of wanting must have been palpable. Karic turned at that moment, and his gaze shot straight to hers. His compelling eyes riveted her, eyes that changed like quicksilver from indifference to wariness to a smoldering intensity. Somewhere between hope and dread Liane watched and saw the emotion purposely flicker out. She exhaled a shuddering breath. It was better this way.

His manner was cold when he stepped from the pool, his magnificent form glistening with moisture. Neither spoke as Karic dressed, neither then nor on the walk back to the hut. There was nothing worth saying about things better left unsaid.

Karic roasted a long-eared lepus over the fire while Liane sliced bread and laid out some cheese. For dessert, there was fresh cerasa fruit. It was simple fare, but Karic ate with relish. Liane didn't have much appetite and toyed with her food.

"We'll sleep together this nocte."

What little appetite Liane had immediately fled. She raised startled eyes. "Wh—what did you say?"

He calmly stared back at her, pausing to swallow a bite of bread before answering. "We'll sleep together. I don't plan on losing track of you. Your bed is rather small, though. We'll make a pallet on the floor."

Liane gathered her plate and eating utensils and rose from the table. "I'm not sleeping with you, this nocte or any other!" she sputtered from over her retreating shoulder.

"And how do you suggest I keep an eye on you then? Tie you up?"

She wheeled around, the plate still in her hand. "This is ridiculous. I'm not going anywhere. I put up with being tied for your bath, but I am not going to sleep with you."

Karic rose and walked over to her. "And I say you will."

He was most intimidating, staring down at her from his imposing height, but an unwed Sententian female did not sleep with a male. It just wasn't done, and she certainly wasn't fool enough to lay beside a man as unsettling as he. If he touched her . . .

58

But if she refused? The look in his eyes boded trouble. Perhaps they could agree on a compromise.

"What would this sleeping together entail?" Liane cooly returned his stare, though her heart was hammering in her breast.

A quizzical expression crossed his face, then he laughed. This time it was a deep, rich sound. It skittered pleasantly across Liane's increasingly frazzled nerves, and she tentatively smiled.

"Sleep, sweet femina, and nothing more."

As he ran a finger along the line of her jaw, Liane thought she heard a note of regret in his voice.

"If I don't trust you enough to let you out of my sight, I certainly don't trust you enough to surrender my mind and body to you in the act of mating. That, I think, would leave me just a little too vulnerable."

"Oh."

"You sound disappointed."

She vehemently shook her head. "No, not at all. Those terms are quite acceptable."

He smiled wryly. "Are they now? Then let's get on with it. I'm exhausted and need a good nocte's rest. I plan to leave on the morrow."

"The morrow?" Liane felt a heavy weight settle in her chest. "You're not strong enough for a long journey yet. You need to rest at least another sol or two."

"You told me I'd know when I was ready, and you forget that you're basing your predictions on a Bellatorian male. We Cat Men are a hardier species. I'll be fine by the morrow."

She turned to hide the play of emotions that must be present in her eyes. With great effort Liane stilled her trembling hand and set the plate on the cupboard. It is better this way, she told herself.

"As you wish," she murmured. "I'll rise early and prepare food for your journey."

You'll be preparing food enough for both of us, Karic silently replied. Though you don't know it yet, you're coming with me.

He almost dreaded the coming sol. His words to Liane on his physical condition had been partly bravado. He wasn't as strong as he knew he should be, but time was the enemy now. He couldn't squander even an extra secundae for himself. If Liane had betrayed his lair to Necator, there wasn't a moment to spare. He must reach his people before the Bellatorians did.

Taking her with him would be difficult. He knew she'd fight him all the way, sapping what precious little strength he had. But what other choice had he? Killing her had never been an option.

And he still desired her, though as the half-blooded heir to the Cat Throne he could never life mate with her. He must choose a full-blooded Cat Woman to prevent further dilution of their species. The permitted temporary mating with her for several cycles would satisfy his own needs, then he'd pass her on to the others. He had planned to take her back with him for that purpose anyway, yet why did he suddenly feel such guilt over the decision?

She'd saved his life; she'd healed him no matter what her motives. Those facts were indisputable. He owed her. And abduction by another race, forced to mate with a species unlike her own, might well be an unspeakable horror for her.

Before, it wouldn't have mattered to him. The welfare of his people came first. But now, she also mattered. It made no sense, Karic raged at himself. He was mad to care for a female who probably had betrayed him, but he did, curse her cold little Bellatorian heart! He'd been lost from the first moment he'd seen her. For that reason and that reason alone, he'd try to ease her way as best he could. It changed nothing, but it was all he could do.

They made a pallet before the hearth. Though needless in the warm climate, in deference to Liane's modesty Karic left his breeches on. Until he'd the time to fashion a new loincloth from animal skins, the Bellatorian clothing would have to do. He settled onto the pallet and looked expectantly up at Liane.

She stood across the small hut beside the chest.

"Are you coming to bed, Liane? I'm tired and can't sleep until you're beside me."

"I need to change into my sleeping shift."

"Then go ahead and be done with it."

"Will you turn away while I do so?"

Karic propped himself up on an elbow. "No. Nakedness is nothing to be ashamed of. Besides, I've already seen you unclothed, bathing at the pool."

Liane colored fiercely. "So it wasn't just your imagination when we joined in the mind seek."

"No."

"I'd still like you to turn your head."

"And I said no."

She shifted uneasily, aware she was losing this battle. "You're not being fair."

"Who said I had to be?"

"A man of honor . . ."

With an exasperated sigh Karic rolled over on his back, pillowing his head in his hands. "Just be done with it, will you, Liane? I won't look."

It was more than she'd dared hope. Liane quickly shed her gown and slipped on a brief sleeping shift. It barely came to her knees, and the thin fabric was worn nearly transparent with use. She'd never noticed that before. It had always been so comfortable and cool. That was all that had mattered in the privacy of her hut, but now it was only the next step from nakedness itself.

She hesitated, half-tempted to put back on her gown and be done with it, when Karic turned to look at her. His annoyance at her dragging out this affair burned in his eyes, but one glance at her sleeping shift quickly extinguished that. His gaze boldly raked over her, missing nothing from the rosy hue of nipple thrusting through the sheer fabric to the shadow at the junction of her thighs.

A dark flush suffused his striking features, and a fire, fiercely burning and bright, sprang to life in his eyes. Liane swallowed hard and walked over to the pallet. Her gaze never left his as she lowered herself down and pulled up the blanket.

"I—I am sorry to cause you trouble," she began, not knowing what else to say in the heated intensity of the moment. "I never meant—"

"Don't say another word, Liane," Karic abruptly growled. "Go to sleep. Now. Before it's too late!"

He rolled over onto his side, his back toward her, leaving her trembling in the dying firelight.

True to her word Liane was up early, before the first rays of sol had even penetrated the forest's depths. Well aware that Karic's gaze was upon her from the first movement she made, she quickly slipped her gown over her sleeping shift and readied the fire for some baking. He rose, pulling on his tunic and tan-colored knee-high boots. Liane's eyes carefully avoided his as she gathered the ingredients for making bread.

"Do you have any boots and breeches?"

The strangeness of Karic's question stopped Liane in the process of measuring out the flour. She forced herself to meet his gaze, her brow crinkling in puzzlement.

"Yes, but what has that to do—"

He strode over to her. "You'll need them for the journey. You're coming with me."

For the longest moment Liane just stared at him, as the reality of his words penetrated her mind. Then, with a quick movement, she flung the cup of flour into Karic's face.

"No!" she screamed and ran for the door.

The flour spewed into his eyes, blinding him. He rubbed it out as fast as he could, but Liane was already gone.

Karic shot out the door after her, confident she'd not elude him for long. He was a swift runner, one of the quickest of his people, and it was an easy thing to follow her spoor. No one smelled quite like Liane with her alluring scent of wild violets. He soon saw her ahead in the trees, her long, dark hair streaming behind her in an ebony trail.

Liane never heard his approach, and so the moment of impact was doubly terrifying. She screamed when he slammed into her, turning in his arms to frantically claw at him as they fell. Karic twisted to take the brunt of their fall as they landed with a thud.

It had rained again that nocte, particularly hard, and the ground beneath the leaves was sodden. Mud oozed up to drench their backs, and the resulting struggle, as Liane fought to free herself, only added to their grime. They were quickly coated with leaves and mud.

"Let me go!" Liane cried, futilely trying to pry Karic's fingers from her arm. "I'm not going anywhere with you!"

"You have no choice," he snapped, just barely dodging a wildly flailing knee. "Stop this ridiculous struggle. You know I'll win in the end."

"You'll never win!" she screeched back at him, attempting to stuff a wad of leaves in his face. "I'll never give up, not while there's breath left in my body."

Karic lost his rapidly waning patience. He had neither the time nor energy for a protracted battle. He suddenly flipped Liane over onto her stomach. Tearing a large swath off her gown, he used it to tie her hands behind her back.

At the sound of the fabric ripping, Liane gasped in outrage. "How *dare* you? What are you doing?"

He rolled her over. "Subduing you in the gentlest way I know how."

Liane glanced down at her ruined gown. The back, she knew, was virtually gone, and as soon as she stood, the front would follow. If not for her sleeping shift . . .

She shot him a murderous look, and her temper flared. "You call this gentle? Why, you self-serving insensitive—"

"Careful, Liane. Don't say something you might later regret." Karic pulled her to her feet.

Her gown slithered to the ground.

"Regret?" She couldn't help herself. She'd never been so furious, so humiliated in her whole life.

She said the first thing that entered her mind.

"The only thing I regret is that I didn't turn you in when I had you."

Karic scowled. The set of his lips tightened, and a little muscle ticked along his jaw. He roughly swung her up into his arms and strode off in the direction they'd come.

"You'll regret more than that if you don't stop while you're ahead," he declared through tightly clenched teeth.

Liane squirmed in his arms. "Where are you taking me? What are you going to do?"

There was an undercurrent of panic rising in her voice which touched Karic, his anger quickly dissipating. He couldn't blame her for running away and fighting. He'd have done the same. There was no reason for him to treat her harshly because of it. The tension eased from his body.

"We both need a bath. It may be our last chance for a long while, and I've no intention of beginning our journey in this filthy state."

"I don't want a bath, and most certainly not with you!"

Karic shot her an amused glance. "Have you had a chance to look at yourself? Believe me, you need a bath."

She clamped down on an angry retort, knowing further argument would be futile. He was so stubborn; he wouldn't listen to her. Perhaps she could find a way to escape once they were in the pool. If only she could get him to untie her arms . . .

That request fell on deaf ears.

Karic wryly shook his head. "I may be self-serving and insensitive," he said, "but I'm not stupid. I only want a bath, not a wrestling match."

"Then how am I to wash myself?" Liane sputtered

as he strode into the pool with her still clasped in his arms.

"You aren't. I'll do it for you."

The concept was too mind-boggling for Liane to absorb. She gaped at him, speechless.

Karic stopped when he reached waist-deep water and lowered Liane to her feet. While she stood there, he proceeded to wash the grime from his hair and body, scrubbing the dirt out of his breeches as best he could. Finally he finished and turned his attention to Liane.

"Would you like your shift on or off when I wash you?"

"Neither!" She glared up at him with all the fierceness she possessed. "Don't you dare touch me!"

Karic shrugged. "Then have it your way. The shift comes off."

"No!" Liane backed away, frantically searching for some way out of her predicament, but there was none.

"No," she finally sighed, her shoulders drooping in defeat. "Please leave the shift on."

He was gentle with her, starting at her hair to accustom Liane to his touch. He could feel her gaze upon him as he worked, intently plucking the twigs and bits of leaves from her dark tresses before asking her to lower her head to rinse out the dirt. The long strands floated on the water like heavy, ebony silk. The feel of them, sliding through his fingers, was an experience like none Karic had ever known. His heart quickened in his chest.

When he was done Karic smoothed the damp tangles from her face, combing through the sodden locks with hands that had begun to tremble. He moved to her face and carefully washed away the dirt. His fingers lingered over her lips, outlining their rosy curves with soft, featherlike strokes, suddenly wishing his mouth was there instead. But never once did he look into her eyes.

Her arms, slim and graceful, felt like the petals of an arosa flower. Karic's breath came harder now, and he quickly turned her around to scrub her back. The sight of it, a sensuous undulation of bone and tender flesh, did nothing to ease the heat rising in his groin. Karic forced himself to go on.

He washed the dirt from her back, sliding his hands ever lower until they rounded the curve of her small buttocks. At his touch, she reflexively tightened. Karic thought he'd lose all control. With a supreme effort, he forced reason to return. He was here to wash her and nothing more, though he thought he'd go mad from the wanting.

She was pliant now beneath his hands, turning about to face him with only the slightest touch. Still, Karic wouldn't look at her. His fingers found the slim column of her throat, gently massaging it clean before slipping downward to her chest and the high, full swell of her breasts.

For the longest time he stared at her, fascinated by the impudent nipples straining against the thin, wet fabric. Her bosom rose and fell in an erratic fashion, the smooth, ivory skin flushed and gleaming. He felt his swollen arousal press hot and heavy against his belly. His hands moved lower still, slipping beneath her shift to ease it off her shoulders.

Liane inhaled a shuddering breath. "Karic . . . please, no."

He lifted his gaze. Liane's breath caught in her throat. His eyes had darkened to deepest jade, his pupils dilated with passion. But what captured her heart and sent it spinning was his look of hot, wild yearning. It was almost past the point of reason.

She didn't want to, her need for him so intense she could hardly bear it herself, but she had to put an end to this before it was too late. Instinctively, Liane knew her only chance was to quickly jolt him from it, and the best way was pain.

Liane swallowed back her self-disgust for the hurt she would cause. In spite of all that had happened she still cared for him and wanted him as badly as she knew he wanted her, but the preservation of her powers, her psychic healing skills most of all, was also important.

"That's enough, Karic," Liane began, forcing a self-satisfied smile onto her lips. "I've seen enough."

His eyes clouded with confusion, slowly banishing the mists of passion. "Enough? What are you talking about, Liane?"

"I've seen enough of your lovemaking. Cat Men techniques seem to vary little from other humanoid species."

He slowly pulled his hands from beneath her shift, as if still working through the implications of this latest twist in events. Karic's eyes narrowed. "Are you saying all this time you were studying me and my mating techniques?"

Liane forced herself to nod. "And why else? I'm a scientist. I take advantage of all opportunities."

He frowned with cold fury. "I don't believe you."

She faltered for a fleeting instant and knew he read it in her eyes. Kill it now, she silently cried, or you're lost.

Her eyes widened in feigned disbelief. "But surely

you didn't think I found you attractive? You're a Cat Man, after all. I'd never mate outside my species."

Karic savagely pulled her to him. One hand tightened across her back, flattening her breasts against the hard planes of his chest. The other hand clasped her buttocks, pressing her belly into the still turgid swelling of his manhood.

"And what makes you think I care what you want or don't want?" he snarled.

Before she could protest, his mouth covered hers, hard, angry and cruelly ravishing.

CHAPTER 4

TOO STUNNED BY THE FEROCITY OF HIS ACTION, LIANE stood motionless in his arms. Not until Karic's hand moved from her back to tear open the front of her shift did she rouse from her shock. She kicked, squirmed and bucked against him, but did little to deter the head lowering to her breasts, a head seemingly insensitive to pain as his mouth captured a delicate nipple.

Liane gasped, as much from outrage as from the unexpected sensations his touch sent roaring through her body. She fought back against the traitorous response. This was not the man she thought she'd known.

"Let me go!" she screamed. "Curse you, let me go! You disgust me!"

Karic lifted his head, a hard light flaring in his eyes. "It doesn't change anything."

She stared up at him with tearful eyes, desperately clinging to the image of that other man, the man she'd begun to care for. "You—you'd rape me then? Force me against my will?"

He exhaled a shuddering breath, a vestige of control beginning to replace his anger. "You were going back with me even before your mind seek, Liane. That sol I saw you in this pool, I intended to return and take you to my people. We need breeding females. If I don't mate with you, some other Cat Man will."

Karic smiled grimly at her look of horror. "Yes, I suppose it is disgusting, but you have your people to thank for forcing us to this." He stepped back from her, replacing the torn edges of her shift together as best he could. "But if I'm not to your liking . . ."

"And is that supposed to be a choice?"

His head snapped up. "I'm sorry. There don't seem to be many choices these days for any of us. It's the best I can do."

The harsh pain in his voice only goaded Liane further. "How very *kind*," she said silkily, "but I'll die before I let you or any of your friends rape me."

"You won't escape me that easily," Karic rasped, his grip tightening painfully on her arms. "I'll make sure of that."

Defiance burned in her eyes. "Will you now? We'll just see, won't we?"

Utter exhaustion flooded Karic. Now, not only would he have to drag her along, fighting him all the way, but he'd have to sharpen his vigilance to keep Liane from harming herself. By the three moons of Agrica, why had he told her his plans?

He knew he'd made it sound vile, that threat of offering her to the young males of his lair, but her words—implying that she found his race loathesome and couldn't bear the thought of mating

71

with one such as he—hurt. He had thought he knew her, thought she saw him as a man rather than some half-animal. He'd been wrong.

"Come along." Karic stepped aside and began to lead her out of the water. "The sol draws on, and we've a journey to begin. One way or another, you're still going with me."

Liane allowed him to drag her along, content to wait until a more favorable opportunity to escape presented itself. She'd seen the shadow of weariness in his eyes. Karic was not yet as strong as he'd like her to believe. There'd be time, perhaps even this nocte.

They returned to the hut and dressed in silence, Liane donning a pair of tan breeches and forest green tunic, which she fastened with a narrow domare hide belt. On her feet, she slipped a pair of loose, ankle-high boots. She twisted her still damp hair into a single braid down her back, then stomped over to resume making her bread.

Karic eased himself into a nearby chair, already battling the encroaching weariness. "How long will that take?"

She briskly stirred the liquid into the flour, not bothering to look up at him. "An hora or so. I plan to make journey bread. It takes a little longer to dry in the baking."

Hostile blue eyes were raised to him. "Have you any objections?"

It was the only kind of bread that would travel and keep well, though he had never been particularly fond of its flat, crunchy texture. Karic shook his head.

"No, none at all. What else do you have to take along? I can begin gathering it."

"No dried meat sticks, if that's what you're wanting. You'll have to catch game along the way. But there's plenty of cerasa fruit and some fermented uva wine."

"That'll do." Karic tiredly rose from the chair. "Do you have any bags to pack it all in?"

She pointed with a flour-coated hand. "Over in the bottom drawer of that chest are two domare hide bags." She resumed her forceful kneading of the dough. "Anything else?"

He caught the hostile sarcasm in Liane's voice but decided it was not worth making an issue over. She was being more cooperative than he'd dared hope, and for that he was thankful. He couldn't spare the strength for another protracted battle.

Liane slapped the dough about a few more times and then began to roll it out into a flat rectangle. She'd noticed the slump to Karic's shoulders and the absence of any spring in his step. He was tired.

She stifled a grin of triumph. Let him drag her through the forest for a sol. She'd easily escape him this nocte and make her way back to the safety of Primasedes. He wouldn't dare follow into that well-guarded fortress. After a few more horas of his exasperating presence, she'd be free of him forever.

It was near midsol when they finally set out. With her hands tied behind her and a lead rope around her waist binding her to Karic's, Liane followed behind, the lighter of the two packs on her back. The brief rest while the bread baked had refreshed him, but Liane knew its effects would not last long. She watched him closely for the first signs of weakness.

The forest was huge, a good two sols journey in any direction to clear it. Liane took careful note of the direction they were headed in, north by northwest if the sun peeking through the treetops was any indication. She would use the stars to orient herself back this nocte.

Barely an hora had passed when a wild baying floated to their ears. It came from behind them. Search canus were on their trail.

Karic swung around and grabbed Liane by the waist, pulling her to his side. "Can you run?"

She shot him a quizzical glance. "Well, yes."

"Then you'd better run—and fast."

He took off, her body tightly clasped against him. Liane almost stumbled before she could match her pace to his. They sped through the forest, nimbly dodging the trees. For a while, the baying grew fainter.

Liane valiantly tried to keep up as long as she could, but she hadn't Karic's speed nor stamina. She tired.

"Karic!" Liane panted, her lungs starving for air. "I—I've got to walk a bit."

He wanted to go on and put as much distance between them and their trackers while he still had the strength, but he knew Liane was too winded. Karic's pace slowed to an easy trot. Still, Liane could barely keep up.

"Please. I'll only slow you down. Leave me." Liane tripped over a tree root and fell.

He was barely able to pull her up before she hit the ground. He gave a harsh laugh. "You'd like that, wouldn't you?"

Karic stopped, his head cocking in concentration. All Liane could hear was the baying of the search canus, drawing near again.

"What is it?" she asked.

"Water." He turned her to the right and began a

purposeful, rapid walk through the trees in that direction. "We need to cover our scent. I hear running water."

They were near the huge Viridis River where Liane had spent many happy horas along its banks searching for herbs. It would indeed cover their scent, but crossing it, if that were Karic's intent, could be dangerous. The current in the center was strong and treacherous. At this point in the river the flow rapidly quickened, before emptying over falls into a large lake. If they got out into the middle and couldn't fight its force . . .

They halted at the edge of the river's rock-strewn bank. The flowing water was already beginning to churn into waves, as its flow met with the resistance of several boulders scattered in its path. Liane swallowed a tremor of apprehension and turned toward Karic.

His rugged features were set in a mask of determination as he studied the surging water. Liane's apprehension grew to a full-fledged panic. They were going to try to cross the river.

"Can you swim?"

The unexpectedness of Karic's question made her jump. "What?"

His eyes narrowed in growing suspicion. "Can you swim?"

She shook her head.

"By the three moons . . . !" He bit down on the frustrated curse.

In his weakened condition he doubted his own ability to make it across the river, and now he also was saddled with transporting a female who couldn't swim. It seemed one obstacle after another was being thrown in his path, and he didn't know how many more he'd be able to overcome. But what choice had he? He couldn't risk capture again. Even death in the river was a preferable fate.

Karic's gaze swept over Liane. Despite everything, he hated to risk her life. If something happened to him in the river she wouldn't have a chance, not knowing how to swim, but her potential knowledge of him was a threat to his people. There was no choice, never had been. If he died, so must she.

He eyed her with a hard resolve. "I mean to cross that river. I'll not lie to you. The crossing will be difficult, even dangerous. We might not make it. I'd like to give you all the opportunity to help yourself that I can. I'll free your hands if you swear not to fight me."

The baying grew louder, the eerie wails matching the wild pounding of Liane's heart. She didn't know how to swim. Indeed, she was terrified of water, and she knew Karic spoke the truth. He might very well not have the strength necessary to get them across.

She backed away, shaking her head. "Please, no," Liane whispered imploringly. "Leave me here. Don't make me go. I'm so afraid."

He wrenched her back to him, his green-gold eyes anguished. "Don't you understand? I can't leave you, Liane. If I could, I would."

Karic gently stroked her hair, as if to soothe her, then traced a trail down the delicate curve of her cheek to the sweet hollow at the base of her throat. His touch was sad, lingering, as if to memorize for one last time the feel of her.

"Trust me," he said, a husky catch in his voice. "While there's strength left in my body no harm will come to you."

She knew he spoke truly and would do everything

in his power to protect her, but that niggling little fear whispered that it still might not be enough. Liane clamped down hard on it. She would still escape him when she could, but not now.

She turned, her bound hands extended toward him. "Let us go. Now, before my courage fails me."

He quickly untied her and knotted the cord around his wrist. Liane understood the significance of this. If they survived she'd still be his prisoner, but she hadn't expected that to change. Karic's choices were as limited as hers.

The rope joining her to Karic's waist remained fastened, however. Liane understood that, too. If he died, so must she. It was the only way to protect his people. She shuddered at the thought but, in some deep corner of her heart, accepted it. Their fate had been bound, one to the other, from the moment she attempted the mind seek.

Karic clasped her tightly about the waist and began to wade out into the water. "Relax and don't fight me," he tersely instructed her. "If your head goes below the water, don't struggle. Hold your breath. I'll bring you back to the surface soon enough. Do you understand?"

She managed a tremulous smile. "Yes."

The surging waters closed around them. Liane momentarily pulled back, then forced herself to relax. Karic's hand slipped across her upper chest to support her head. He began to doggedly fight his way across the wild expanse of river.

Over the water's roar Liane faintly heard the bay of the search canus. She wondered if they'd make it across before the trackers found them. Blaster guns could easily reach them in the river.

For a time Karic made steady, if slow, progress.

Gradually, however, his strength began to wane. Liane could hear the rasp of his shortened breath and feel the powerful muscles begin to strain. Her heart went out to him, but there was nothing she could do but lie as still as possible and trust him.

Water sloshed over her in great waves, choking her in spite of her best efforts not to swallow it. Panic spiraled through her. She raised her hands to shield her face, but it did no good. She thought she'd drown, even before the river dragged them down.

The force of the rapids slammed them into a boulder. Only the agile movement of Karic, twisting between her and the huge rock, saved Liane from a brutal bruising. She wondered what the impact had done to Karic's weakening body.

For a few moments he clung there, one arm gripping the slippery rock, the other clasped about her waist. His head lowered to rest against the boulder, his breath coming in gasps, his body trembling with exhaustion. She silently watched him. Finally, he glanced up, inhaled a deep breath and headed back out into the river's current.

Waves engulfed them, and they were forced beneath the water. It took all the courage Liane possessed to not flail her way back to the surface, but she dared not drain Karic's strength by forcing him to fight her. She did as he'd asked; she held her breath and trusted. And he always brought her back to the surface.

They slipped downstream, the surging power of the river relentlessly beating at Karic, hampering a straight crossing. Though the added distance cruelly debilitated him, he struggled on, his strokes becoming weaker. Soon, it was all Karic could do to keep their heads above water.

"I can't make it across," he finally gasped. "We'll have to chance the falls!"

His decision came none too soon. From the far bank the sound of voices, joined by the excited wails of the search canus, reached their ears. The trackers had found them. As Karic let the churning waters drag them downstream, blaster guns were aimed and fired.

One shot narrowly missed Liane before they were safely out of range. The relief was only temporary. The roar of the falls rose to deafening intensity. In only a few moments more, they'd be going over them.

Though she knew she might die in the process, strangely enough she felt no fear. She was with Karic. He'd do all in his power to save them. There was nothing more anyone could do.

Before them the river suddenly ended. Liane briefly caught the sight of blue, cloud-strewn sky. Then they hurtled over into empty space. She clawed at Karic, attempting to cling to him, but he shoved her away. A sudden realization that his move was wise struck her. Separated, they stood a better chance of surviving.

Liane saw the advancing water. It looked hard, lethal. At the last moment she clamped her eyes shut and prayed the end would be merciful.

She hit with a force that squeezed the air out of her lungs, plunging her nearly to the bottom of the deep lake. For an instant Liane was stunned, then the instinct for survival flared, hot and strong. She struggled, fighting her way to the top, only vaguely aware her upward progress was being aided by the rope attached to her waist.

She broke the surface with an agonizing gasp,

gulping in a blessed breath of air. Beside her, treading water, was Karic. He threw back his head and laughed.

"Quite a ride, wasn't it?"

Liane blinked at him in astonishment. He'd nearly gotten them killed, and all he could do was remark on the thrill of it all? She managed to shoot him a fierce glare before she sank beneath the water.

Karic pulled her back up, slipping his arm once more about her chest. "Not impressed, hmmm?" he chuckled, as he began an easy sidestroke toward the nearest bank.

Liane clamped down on a scathing retort. What was the point in berating him? They had survived. That was all that mattered.

They lay on the grassy bank for what seemed a long while, resting, unable to summon the strength to move. Finally, Karic sat up.

"Liane?"

"Yes?" she mumbled from a place buried in her arms.

"We've got to move on. They'll be looking for us soon."

She groaned and rolled over. "I don't think I have the strength."

"Well, I *know* I don't. We'll hide behind the falls until they give up searching for us."

Karic rose, tugging her up with him. "Come on. We've got to get out of sight before they see us."

Liane followed him. There was a large cave behind the falls, with several dark tunnels branching off from it. Karic surveyed the choices, then began to lead her toward the furthest one. Pools of water dotted the rocky floor, and Karic was careful to move from one to the other.

He's determined to take no chances of the search canus picking up our scent if they follow us back here, Liane realized. Well, that suited her needs as well. Though she was still determined to escape, Liane had no desire for Karic to be cornered in here by the vicious tracking beasts. If that ever came to pass he'd be torn to shreds before her very eyes.

As they approached the black, gaping hole of the furthest tunnel Liane froze, unable to take another step forward. Karic quizzically glanced back.

"What's wrong, Liane?"

Wide blue eyes stared out of a face gone suddenly white. "I—I don't like the dark."

There was a quaver in her voice that warned Karic she was on the verge of panic. He swiftly returned to her side.

"There's nothing to be afraid of, femina," he said soothingly. "I can see quite well with only the tiniest bit of light. All you have to do is hold on to me and you'll be safe."

She shot him a tremulous little smile. "And as terrible as it seems to me, the darkness is safer than the alternative, isn't it?"

"Yes," he gently agreed.

He held out his hand. After a moment's hesitation, Liane placed hers in it. Once again, they started out.

Blackness enshrouded them, but Karic confidently strode on. She fought back against her reflexive stiffening, forcing her limbs to carry her along behind him. He *does* see in the dark, Liane thought, though the realization didn't surprise her. His admission of those powers only added further credence to what she'd already heard about the scope of the Cat Men's abilities.

Finally, Karic halted, drawing her into a deepset alcove. "Stay here," he said, before seeking a foothold on the rock wall.

A tug on the rope about her waist told Liane he'd climbed upward. She moved toward him when the rope grew taut. Karic's hand touched her head.

"Give me your pack, then take my hands. I'll pull you up."

She removed her backpack and handed it to him. Grasping in the darkness, Liane found his hands. An instant later she was dangling in midair. An instant more and she was dragged up onto a ledge and on top of Karic's body.

They lay there for a while, catching their breath, then Karic rolled her over and behind him. The ledge was narrow with just enough room for the backpacks and two bodies pressed closely together. Liane was thankful the packs at least cushioned her from the stone wall.

Karic rolled over to face her. "Give me your hands."

"What do you want my—"

"Give them to me, Liane!"

There was a sharp edge to his voice. Liane thrust out her hands, and he deftly bound them in front of her. She heard the sound of tearing cloth, then felt it cover her mouth and tied behind her head.

"I'm sorry to treat you so harshly," Karic's deep voice rose out of the darkness, "but I can't risk a struggle or sound from you until I know they're gone. And they'll check behind this fall. You can be sure of it."

His hands lingered on her head. Liane nodded into them, telling him, in the only way she could, that she understood. If she could have spoken, she'd have explained she'd no intention of betraying him and never had. All she wanted was her freedom. But he'd never believe her. Her quiet acquiescence of his apology was all she could give.

As the horas passed Liane dozed. Footsteps and snuffling sounds awoke her. She jerked into a muscular body, rigid with waiting. The trackers had arrived. A yellow searchlamp fanned the darkness ahead of them.

"I'm telling you," the raspy voice of one man rose from the blackness behind the light ten meters away, "they're not here. The fall from the river killed them both."

"Perhaps," came an equally gruff reply, "but I'm not giving up until I've checked out every angle. There's enough standing water in here to cover their scent from our canus, so we have to thoroughly search this area. Too much is at stake if we fail."

The other man chuckled. "Untold wealth *and* that lovely little Sententian. I've always had an itch for her."

Liane stiffened against Karic. A warning hand on the back of her head stilled further movement.

"We're sharing her. Don't ever forget that. Necator said she was a reward for the two of us."

"Then why does he want us to bring her back?" the raspy voice grumbled. "He gave her to us. That's one femina I'd not tire of quickly."

"Who knows?" the gruff voice replied, moving forward once more with the lamp. "Maybe he wants a taste of her himself. One way or another, the Lord Commander means to eventually kill her. You saw her this sol. She's betrayed us for that Cat Man."

It's over, Liane thought. In another secundae they'll raise the searchlamp and find us. Oh, Karic,

I'm so sorry. She touched her forehead to his chest in mute farewell.

The lamp's beam swung over them, passing by without a moment's hesitation. The trackers moved on, the hollow clunk of their boots echoing in the tunnel, growing fainter until they finally disappeared. Liane couldn't believe what had happened. How could they have not seen them?

Karic's mouth lowered to her ear, his warm breath caressing the delicate shell. "Did you forget about a Cat Man's ability to cloak his presence?" he whispered.

She smiled and slowly nodded. Of course, Liane thought. With his body in front of hers they'd appeared invisible to the trackers' eyes. She tried to sit up.

"No, lie still. We're not safe until they leave this cave."

Liane sighed and squirmed back against Karic. He was right. The trackers still had to return this way.

It seemed like horas before they retraced their steps, the thud of footsteps and snarls of the search canus heralding their approach. Though she knew Karic would once more shield them, Liane couldn't repress a small tremor. So little protected them from discovery if the search canus caught their scent.

The trackers moved on. Karic continued to hold her there for a long while, perhaps an hora or two by Liane's reckoning, before he finally pulled her down from the ledge. He removed her gag and untied her hands.

"Thank you."

His deep voice rumbled out of the darkness and

sent a new awareness coursing through Liane. She wanted to touch him, press into the comforting warmth of his male body. With an effort, she suppressed the tantalizing impulse.

"I don't understand," she murmured instead. "Why are you thanking me?"

He grasped her shoulders. "Though I had you bound and gagged you still could have moved, made a sound by kicking at the ledge with your boots. They would have heard. My cloaking can't cover sounds."

"I've never meant to betray you, Karic."

Strong fingers moved to gently encircle her throat. "Perhaps. Or perhaps your decision was made when you heard the trackers talk about what they would do to you."

Suspicion roughened his voice, turning it harsh and grating. Liane flinched and jerked away. "Yes, perhaps it was. But what does it matter? The result was the same. I didn't betray you."

He turned from her, moving to the ledge to retrieve their packs. Liane wished she could have seen his face when she'd answered him. Had her words hurt as much as his had? She hoped so.

Ordering her to wait, Karic stealthily crept into the main chamber and over to the falls. He returned after a short time.

"They're out there, camped across the lake. I don't know if they suspect something or are just bedding down for the nocte. At any rate, we'll be spending it in here."

Liane's nose wrinkled in distaste. It was dark, damp and cold in the cave. But what choice had they? Only the falls protected them from discovery from the search canus.

"As you wish," she sighed. "Where do you propose we sleep?"

"This is as good a place as any."

"Up on the ledge?" Liane asked in dismay. She didn't think she could stand a whole nocte cramped up in that hard spot.

"No. I think down here in front will be all right. That way we're close to it if we need to hide again."

"Good. Can we have a fire for heat and light?"

"No. Light from the perpetual flame box you brought is fine, but no fire. If the trackers reentered the cave, they might smell the smoke, *if* I were even able to find any dry wood in here."

It was better than nothing, Liane consoled herself, and it would just drive some of that terrible, smothering blackness away.

She squatted and began to rifle through the packs. The domare hide backpacks were virtually waterproof. If there were any dry clothes or blankets, she supposed she'd survive one nocte in the cave.

A half hora later Liane was changed into a fresh set of clothes and huddled before the perpetual flame box, wrapped in a blanket. After the numerous times that Karic had seen her naked or nearly so, she had dispensed with modesty when she had shed her wet clothing. Besides, if he wished to rape her there was little she could do about it. He neither said nor did anything, his eyes narrowing briefly before he turned away.

Karic shed his tunic but remained in his damp breeches. There was no extra clothing for him. He loosely slung the other blanket about his broad shoulders, as if impervious to the cave's pervading chill. Liane wondered at his ability to bear so many kinds of hardship without it seemingly affecting him.

His glance caught hers, thoughtfully staring at him. "What is it, Liane?"

Warmth flushed her face, and she shook her head. "Nothing. It was nothing."

His keen eyes scrutinized her, and he shrugged. "Then I have a question for you."

"Yes?"

"After what the trackers said, can I assume you now deem it safer to go with me than escape? Primasedes is certainly no longer an option."

"Are you sure?" A mocking smile touched Liane's lips. "If I truly know the location of your lair, don't I still have a bargaining piece that Necator wants? Don't you think it would buy me safe passage at least back to Primasedes?"

"You're right, of course," he growled, his eyes darkening in anger. "I'd forgotten about that."

"And if I don't know your secret," Liane continued, "my choices are virtually the same. One way or another, it seems I'm going to be raped."

"At least you won't die at the hands of my people."

The savageness of his reply startled Liane. No matter how hard he tried to hide it, her welfare mattered to him. She couldn't let it change her resolve, though.

"If I lose my maidenhood I'll die—one way or another."

"Why, Liane? Why is it so important to you? There's no shame in mating, no degradation if the loving is gentle and considerate. Most would even say it's pleasurable. What are you afraid of?"

"I'm not afraid. It's not that, Karic."

"Then what, Liane?" He pulled her to her knees, the flickering light throwing dancing shadows across his rough-hewn features. "What *is* the reason?"

CHAPTER 5

LIANE HESITATED. WHAT WOULD KARIC'S REACTION BE if she admitted that she would lose all her psychic powers if she mated? She wondered if he didn't secretly despise her for them, considering how she'd repeatedly used those powers against him. It might well prove the final excuse he needed to take her, right then and there, especially if he thought he was protecting his people.

The wise course would be to fabricate a lie, but Liane realized she'd never been wise when it came to Karic—honest, perhaps, except for her falsehood about finding him disgusting, but never wise.

She steadily returned his stare. "You may choose to believe it or not, but if I mate I lose my powers."

Surprise lifted his dark brows. "Is this unique to you, or common for all Sententian feminas?"

"For all of us."

He frowned. "Strange, but I've never heard of it before."

Liane rolled her eyes. "And do you think this is something we share with every passerby? No, it is a closely guarded secret. Our men respect it and allow us to make the choice."

"The choice?"

"Whether to mate and lose our powers or remain chaste. As strange as it may seem to you, some of our feminas prefer service to mankind over personal needs."

"And you are one of them?"

Liane nodded.

A pair of penetrating eyes studied her. "Then you are wrong, Liane. Beneath that cool, controlled exterior you're a passionate, hot-blooded femina. Your body's meant for the touch of a man, created to give pleasure as well as receive it. You've far more to offer in loving, than in the—"

"And who are you to decide that for me?" Liane heatedly interjected. "It is my life, my decision. And I have to live with the choice, not you!"

"And I say you cannot know what you're giving up until you've tried it."

She sadly shook her head. "But then it would be too late, Karic. I have to make the best choice I can with the knowledge I have. Please try to understand."

Liane tenderly stroked his face. "I am not as ignorant as you may think. I lied at the pool, when I told you I found you disgusting. The loss of my powers was the true reason."

A slow flush darkened Karic's features, then his jaw hardened. With a furious motion, he flung her hand from him.

"In one breath you tell me it's impossible to mate

90

and in the next you admit you want me? Why don't you just take a dagger and drive it into my heart?"

Tears filled Liane's eyes. "I'm sorry. I thought it would help. I just didn't want you to think I found you loathesome."

He groaned, a harsh, aching sound that filled Liane with equal portions of pain and longing. "I think you don't know what you want, except to drive me mad."

Anger stirred in her. "I know I want to remain a maiden. To do otherwise would kill me."

Karic's bitter laugh startled her. "Don't delude yourself, Liane. You're a fighter, for all your purported Sententian meekness. Since we've met there's barely been a secundae when we haven't been at odds, and you've given it back as fiercely as I've handed it to you."

He shook his head. "No, don't delude yourself in the least. You wouldn't die. Instead, you'd probably turn your rage on the man who raped you. I almost feel sorry for the poor fool."

She caught the tinge of resignation in his voice. "You mean you won't . . . ? And you won't," she swallowed hard, "give me to your friends?"

A self-mocking smile touched his lips. "No, Liane, I'll not be party to breaking your heart. If nothing else, I think it would do that. I can't promise you anything once we arrive at my lair, but I think I can convince them your healing powers are as useful as your breeding potential."

He cocked a brow. "That is, if you'd be willing to share them with us?"

She expelled a relieved breath. "Yes, oh yes! I'd be happy to help in any way I could." Liane paused, concern wrinkling her forehead.

Karic eyed her warily. "What is it now?"

"Lord Ardane. I should be there when he returns. I could do more for your people by speaking to him then by going with you."

"No."

"But you don't understand, Karic. There was something about him. He's good and brave and strong. He'll help."

He stiffened at the admiration he heard in her voice. "Are you sure you're not just in love with him?"

Liane recoiled from the barely veiled sarcasm. "What? You're mad! Does every decision you make originate from your loins? I just finished telling you I've made a vow of celibacy."

"But he's Bellatorian, one of your own kind. Perhaps a man as wonderful as you say he is might just change your mind."

She angrily jerked her blanket around her and lay down. "I'm going to sleep. There's no point in discussing this further."

He crawled over to her, dragging his own blanket with him. Lying down beside her he pulled her into his arms. She tried to squirm out of his clasp, but he only tightened it.

"Let me go!" she snapped. "I've no wish to be touched by an incoherent madman."

"I'm hardly incoherent," he snarled back. "And I still don't trust you not to run away, now that I know your true feelings about this Ardane, so lie still."

Liane bit back a jumble of insulting invectives. What was the use anyway? He was as stubborn as an elephas and not half as intelligent. The comparison brought a grim smile to her lips. Lulled by the warmth of Karic's stubborn, if stupid, body, Liane soon fell asleep.

* * *

Liane suddenly jerked awake, not sure why. She shot a sharp glance at Karic. His ruggedly handsome face was relaxed in slumber. Nothing wrong there, but something . . . !

A skulking movement, just beyond the span of the light of the perpetual flame box, caught Liane's attention. She propped herself up on one elbow, her gaze searching the darkness. A glowing pair of eyes stared back, and sheer black fright swept through her.

"Karic," Liane leaned over and whispered into his ear, "wake up!"

He was wide-awake before the words were completely uttered.

"I didn't mean to fall asleep. Damn this cursed—"

He stopped short, catching the gleam of fear in her eyes. "What's wrong, Liane?"

"There's something out there in the shadows, watching us."

Karic slowly rolled over. A warning growl acknowledged his action. The shadowy form took shape as the search canus stepped forward. Karic twisted into a squatting position.

"Stay behind me," he said. "Once I've got the canus away, climb up onto the ledge. He won't be able to reach you there."

"But what about you?" Liane's nails dug into Karic's bare shoulder. "Surely you're not going to fight him? You've no weapon."

"I've got my claws." He shook her hand from him. "Now, no argument. When the time comes, do as I say!"

He was right, of course, Liane realized. Karic had to kill the canus. If he didn't they were doomed. The beast would alert the trackers and the other search

93

canus that also might be nearby, leading them to their hiding place.

She exhaled a shuddering breath. "Yes, Karic, it will be as you ask."

The canus moved closer. It was a huge beast, easily as high as Liane's hips, shaggy, long-fanged, with small, cruel eyes. As it crept forward Liane could see the powerful muscles bunching, gathering.

With a fierce howl, the canus attacked. Karic sprang forward to meet him, his own savage growl answering that of the beast's. They collided. After a few secundae of struggle, the animal's weight was enough to topple them both to the ground. In a confusing blend of fur and flesh, the pair rolled over and over, each fighting for the advantage.

Liane backed away, her gaze mesmerized by the horrible scene. Lethal fangs slashed at Karic, drawing blood. The scent and taste of it seemed to drive the canus to an even greater frenzy. Its teeth sank into Karic's shoulder. The animal held on, tearing the flesh with vicious jerks of its head.

Karic's claws took their toll as well. Bright splotches of red stained the canus' shaggy coat. Still, the beast hung on.

Sleek, powerful muscles, glinting with sweat, strained to pull the animal's teeth loose. Finally, Karic succeeded. He shoved a forearm between the canus' jaws, wedging them open. With the other hand he clawed his way through fur and muscle to the beast's throat. Blood spurted everywhere. With a gurgling yelp, the canus was dead.

Karic lay there, the animal's body atop him, dragging in great gulps of air. Liane ran forward to kneel beside him, momentarily confused as to what to do first to help him. There was so much blood.

Steeling herself, she grasped the canus' jaws and pried them away from Karic's arm. He wrenched out his arm. Liane grimaced at the mangled flesh, then moved to shove the animal's body off Karic. Karic lay there for a secundae, then weakly pushed himself up on one elbow.

He grasped her arm with a bloody hand. "You didn't go to the ledge," he rasped. "I told you to go to the ledge."

"It doesn't matter. You killed him." Liane loosened his fingers from her arm and ran for some water and rags. She returned and knelt beside him.

She dampened a rag and began to cleanse his shoulder. Blood oozed from the deep wound no matter how hard she applied pressure.

His hand clamped down on hers again. "The other search canus. . . . He might be nearby. If he comes, swear to me you'll take to the ledge. Swear it!"

Liane winced at the pain of his grip. "How can I leave you lying here like this? To watch from that ledge while you're slowly savaged to death? And for what? So I can be captured, raped and eventually put to death?"

She laughed, bitter and low. "Don't even ask it."

Karic fell back with a groan. "You're a fool, Liane."

"And so are you, Cat Man."

The shoulder wound refused to stop bleeding. In frustration, Liane finally fashioned a pressure dressing and then tended to the rest of Karic's injuries. Aside from the forearm, which was badly torn but clotting rapidly, the rest of Karic's wounds were superficial slashes on his face and chest. They were quickly cleansed.

She turned her attention back to his shoulder.

The bandage was thoroughly soaked, and Liane made her decision.

"Karic, you must let me heal you. Now, before you bleed to death!"

His lids fluttered open. "No. I told you before—"

"Curse your stubborn hide!" Liane grabbed his face to hold it in her hands. "You have no choice. If you're dead, you can't very well protect your people from me, can you? And what other secrets are there to steal from you, if I already know the whereabouts of your lair? What possible danger is there in this healing? Presumably I've already done as much damage as I can possibly do."

His green-gold eyes, clouding over as the life blood drained from him, slowly scanned her face. "Do what you must," he whispered.

Liane's hands moved to his bloodstained bandage.

Liane gazed down at her handiwork and smiled wryly. If Karic's luck didn't change soon, he'd be crisscrossed with scars before he reached his lair. She shook her head and began to dig through one of the bags.

"What's so amusing?"

She turned back to Karic. His eyes were open, warily glaring up at her. Her smile widened. He could be so much like a young lad sometimes, with his pride on the verge of wounding.

"I thought you'd gone to sleep."

"Just resting. You didn't answer my question."

Liane shrugged. "It was nothing. I was just thinking how accident prone you are. You're fortunate I'm a healer."

"Accident prone!" Karic pushed himself up to a sitting position. "If I were any less adept, we'd be dead long ago."

He paused, noting the teasing gleam in Liane's eyes. He chuckled and eased himself back down onto the blanket.

"A few moments more of rest and we must change our hiding place. This spot is too tainted with blood to be safe. And I must dispose of the canus' body."

"Yes, in a few moments," Liane agreed, offering him a small vial of an amber-colored liquid. "But first, I want you to drink this."

Karic arched a dark brow. "What is it?"

"A potion that will renew your strength. It will make you sleep for a while, but when you awake, you'll be as strong as ever."

"And why didn't you give it to me before? I could have used it from the beginning."

"I didn't want you too strong then. If you recall, I was planning to escape."

"And now?"

"Escape is not an issue. I agreed to go with you to your lair. Now, I need you as strong as you can be."

He took the vial from her outstretched hand and fingered it consideringly. "How long will I sleep?"

"It's hard to say. Four, six, maybe eight horas. Whatever your body requires."

Karic shook his head. "Too long. It wouldn't be safe. The trackers could return." He made a motion to return the vial to her.

Liane stayed his hand. "Find us a secure hiding place and I'll stand guard while you sleep. I can rouse you if necessary. The potion won't drug you that deeply."

His gaze sharpened. Liane knew he was deciding whether to trust her or not. She didn't try to defend herself. Her actions in the past few sols spoke for themselves, if Karic cared to dispassionately examine them. She steadily gazed back at him.

Karic climbed to his feet and tucked the flask into his belt. "Let's move camp. I'm not drinking your potion until it's safe."

A soft smile touched her lips, finding a response in the sudden warming of Karic's eyes. Together, they packed their belongings. She waited until Karic returned from disposing of the canus' body, then covered the perpetual flame box. Once more she had to steel herself to follow him back into the darkness, his proffered hand and encouraging smile the only things that kept her going.

This time Karic chose to explore the first tunnel, closest to the opening of the falls. After they walked for a while, Karic finally halted.

"Uncover the flame box."

Liane pulled it from the top of her bag. Red-gold light quickly illuminated the darkness. A small pool lay before them, and beyond was the end of the tunnel. Off to one side was a small chamber. If it were deep enough, it could block them from view.

Liane glanced at Karic. "It seems secure enough."

He swung his pack off his shoulder and lay it on the ground. "I'll check it out."

With a running start and easy leap, Karic spanned the pool, landing on the other side. Liane swallowed an uneasy laugh. His catlike grace made the action appear effortless. She knew it would not be so for her. The span of water was at least five meters across. She doubted she could make it.

Karic disappeared into the side chamber, then returned to the water's edge. "The cave's deep. We can go back far enough to use the flame box without its light betraying us."

He extended his hands. "Throw me the backpacks."

Liane quickly complied.

"Now, the flame box."

She tensed, knowing she'd be in total darkness, alone on the other side of the pool. Karic's nearness and the light of the box were the only things that kept her calm in the black, smothering tunnel. If she missed the toss the flame box might be forever lost in the pool, and Karic would be on the other side.

"Throw it to me, Liane," Karic gently prodded, his voice deep and soothing. "Overthrow the pool if you must. I'll find it."

She tossed it as best she could and heard him catch it. After a moment the perpetual flame box again lit the tunnel.

Karic eyed her and the pool. "Do you think you can make it with a running start?"

"I don't know."

"Well, give it a try. I can always fish you out."

"Easy for you to say," Liane muttered under her breath as she backed away.

The leap was clean, perfectly timed, but Liane still missed the other side by a meter. With a strangled cry she sank into the pool. Karic's hands shot out, clasping her forearms, pulling her out before the water even reached her shoulders.

He laughed as his hand, placed in the small of her back, directed her toward the hidden chamber.

"What's so funny?" Liane demanded.

"I was just remembering something you said. Your unnatural affinity for getting wet rivals my tendency toward accidents."

"Unnatural! It's been unfortunate circumstances and nothing more." She paused, a slow grin spreading across her face. "Like your accidents, I suppose.

Perhaps we can both be a bit more careful in the future."

He gave her a lazy, mocking smile. "Perhaps."

They made camp again and Liane changed to dry clothes. She snuggled into her blanket and propped herself up against a stone wall. "Do you have any idea what time it is?"

"I glanced outside after I dropped the canus' body into the lake. The sky was too overcast to see the moons or stars, but I'd hazard a guess that it's a few horas before the new sol. Why?"

Liane shook her head. "Oh, nothing really—just that the potion might cause you to sleep through part of the sol."

"That doesn't matter. It would be more prudent to set out this coming nocte, in case the trackers think to wait and catch us unawares. Besides, I've the advantage traveling in darkness with my Cat's vision."

"Then you'd best take the potion and get your rest."

"Wake me if you hear anything."

"I will."

"Or if you begin to get sleepy. Someone should be on guard at all times."

"Go to sleep, Karic." Liane sighed in exasperation.

"Yes, Liane."

Karic pulled the vial from his belt. Raising it to his lips, he emptied it in one long swallow. Then he lay down, pulled the blanket over him and watched her, until he finally drifted off to sleep.

Karic slept until a little past midsol. He awoke by slow degrees, lazily stretching his long limbs to ease his sleep-stiffened muscles. He felt good, surprisingly so. Liane had said the potion would strengthen him, and he'd accepted that. After all they'd been through, all she'd done and never once tried to betray him, the time for doubting her was past. But to feel so renewed, so full of energy . . . !

"So, the rest must have set well with you."

Startled eyes swung to hers. "You were so quiet," he muttered, flushing darkly. "I'd forgotten you were here."

Liane smiled. "I've been here all along. You told me to take guard, and I did."

He frowned, remembering the danger they were still in. "Did you hear or see anything?"

"Nothing."

"Good." Karic rose and stretched again. "I'm going to check what's going on outside. I'll be back."

Liane had laid out a simple meal of journey bread and fruit by the time he returned.

"Are they still there?" She glanced up at him.

"No. Or at least no sign of them. But they could be hiding in the trees. We'll still wait them out until this nocte."

He sat down, helped himself to a slice of bread and grinned at it wryly. "This would slide down a lot easier with a slab of meat."

She didn't glance up from the cerasa fruit she was slicing. "Sorry. Nothing edible scurried by while you slept."

Karic laughed, the sound deep and throaty. "You amaze me, Liane. One moment you're the serious healer, and the next moment a dry wit. And then there's your tender heart, which is constantly at odds with your fiery temper. For a Bellatorian femina, you are really quite intriguing."

"Oh, really?" Liane paused to chew a slice of fruit. "And what is that supposed to mean?"

He chuckled. "I see I must tread carefully here or risk offending. What I meant to say was that most Bellatorian feminas, at least the ones we've captured, are docile, obedient creatures who readily accept a new master."

At Liane's angry glare, Karic quickly hurried on. "Truly, I mean no offense, but if you recall, your people are raised with a blind obedience to authority. Once they realized there was no hope of escape, your feminas quickly transferred their obedience. In many ways, it was the only practical thing to do."

Liane snorted in disdain. "They were probably only trying to lull you into a false sense of security, counting the secundae until their first chance to escape."

"But none of them ever did, Liane." At her look of surprise, he nodded. "We are not a cruel or uncaring people. I think, in time, they found happiness with us. I know my mother did."

"Your mother was Bellatorian?"

"Yes."

"I'd like to meet her."

"That won't be possible. She died over five cycles ago."

"Oh, I'm sorry. Is your father alive?"

"Yes."

"Did he love your mother?"

His full, finely chiseled mouth curved up in a smile. "Yes, very much—and she, him."

Karic frowned at the color that rose to Liane's cheeks. "Is that so hard to believe? That a Bellatorian femina would find a full-blooded Cat Man worth loving?"

Her eyes darkened with some emotion Karic

couldn't discern. "No, not hard to believe at all. I am glad they found happiness together."

Liane lay aside her fruit, suddenly warm under the intensity of Karic's gaze. It was too close, too smothering in the chamber. She wanted to leave, breathe fresh air and clear her head of the entangling emotions that threatened to choke off all logic and reasoning. But she couldn't. There was nowhere to go.

Instead, Liane gathered her blanket around her and lay down. "I am tired. With your leave, I'd like a few horas sleep before we head out this nocte."

Karic nodded, eyeing her with a sharp, glittering awareness.

Unable to bear the intensity of his gaze, Liane rolled over to face the wall.

Prickling bursts of fire coursed through Karic, warming his flesh and heating his blood. He stirred uneasily, glancing over at Liane's sleeping form. The sensations rippling through his body only intensified. With a low curse, Karic rose and began to restlessly pace the confines of the chamber.

The triple moons of Agrica were nearing their triannual alignment; they could be doing so this very nocte for all he knew. And forces, too powerful for any Cat Man to resist, would soon be set into an inevitable sequence of events. It could be a most pleasurable sequence of events, to be sure, when both participants were driven by the same impulses, but Karic knew Liane would never understand, much less willingly participate.

Once every three cycles, the Cat Men's innate urge to procreate flared to uncontrollable heights. Deeply instinctual, the compulsion overrode all conscious thought or reason, stirring needs that had to be sated. Failure to find a mating partner resulted in an agonizing death.

Karic knew that special nocte was drawing near and thought he'd be able to make it back to his lair in time, but now he wasn't so sure. A full eight sols had passed since he'd left his people's hiding place in the Serratus Mountains. Three sols journey and nearly five more had been squandered in his capture and escape. With the considerably slower pace of traveling with Liane, another three if not four were left before he'd reach the lair once more. Was there enough time left?

He should have felt the first stirrings earlier, but so much had transpired of late to override the warning signs, much less find the time to pay heed to them. And it had never been an issue before. Though breeding females were limited in their lair he'd never lacked for willing partners. But now, there was only Liane—and he'd given his word not to touch her. The vow had been made with the greatest of difficulty, as it was, and only because he rationally convinced himself there was no other choice. But this lust smoldering within him, awaiting only the combined force of the triple moons to set it into inexorable motion, was unthinking, uncaring and savage.

His long, agitated strides carried him to the edge of the pool. Better for her if he left her here and came back when the time had passed. But the time could be two, three, even four sols away. He had no way of knowing until he saw the nocte sky, a sky that had eluded his gaze for the past five sols. Perhaps this nocte he would know. Until then, time was still of the essence. He must continue his journey back to his people—with Liane.

Karic turned to the chamber. It was near dusk; he

could sense it. Time to waken Liane and prepare for their journey. They had a long nocte of travel ahead. If they were fortunate, they could just reach a farming village set at the edge of the forest before it was too light to go further. It was a farming village, Karic recalled with a growing sense of relief, wherein lived a lusty maid who'd be more than happy to bed him.

CHAPTER 6

IT WAS SOLRISE WHEN THEY REACHED THE VILLAGE. Lavender rays, tipped with rose, bathed the land in a mellow glow, illuminating the darkened forms of the villagers as they left their huts to begin a long sol's work. Karic exhaled a weary sigh and turned to Liane.

Her shoulders were slumped with fatigue, her face pale and drawn. She had kept up the furious pace he'd set all nocte, a pace only intensified by the smoldering urgency growing within him. He knew he'd been abrupt with her, taciturn to the point of rudeness during their journey through the darkened forest, but time was now the enemy. If she hadn't kept up, she risked losing more than a moment of rest for her weary limbs.

Still, Karic was deeply grateful for Liane's brave efforts and her uncomplaining attitude. Each moment he was with her yet another facet of her character was revealed, and the knowing only made him want her more.

He fiercely crushed that realization. His primary concern should be her protection, not her ravishment. With the wild, primal hunger churning within him, threatening to boil over at any moment, she was in enough danger as it was. His glance sought out the hut of the old farmer Bardic and his beautiful daughter, Devra.

She peeked through a window at that moment, no doubt awakened by the commotion Karic and Liane's arrival had stirred. With a joyful cry Devra was out the door and racing across the commons, straight for Karic. He lowered his pack and waited.

"Karic, oh my love!" Devra cried, throwing her arms about his neck and kissing him passionately. "It's been so long, so very long."

Out of the corner of his eye Karic saw Liane stiffen. Ever so carefully, he pried Devra's clasping fingers loose and turned her to meet Liane.

"Devra, this is my, er, traveling companion, Liane. Liane, this is Devra, my, er, friend."

The voluptuous woman glared at Liane and sniffed. "Say it as it really is, Karic. I'm your lover and nothing less."

Ignoring Karic's look of pained discomfort, Liane dropped her backpack and extended a hand toward Devra. "It is my pleasure to meet you. Will you be journeying with us back to Karic's lair?"

Devra's brow lifted, and she turned to Karic. "Well, my love, what about it? Will you take me back as your life mate?"

Karic bit back a groan. Devra was a hot and lusty bed partner, but until now there'd never been any mention of any deep affection, much less a life mating, neither from him nor Devra, who always had made it obvious that she wanted him for his virile young body. What had possessed Liane to ask such a question? What had flared between these two in but the span of a few secundae?

He shook his head. "This is not the time or place to discuss such things. Liane and I have been traveling all nocte. We are weary and need rest."

"You can have my bed, as always," Devra immediately volunteered, her glittering gaze assessing Liane from head to toe. "*She* can have a pallet on the floor."

Liane saw Karic's scowl and cut short his protest. "I'll gladly sleep anywhere—and as soon as possible, if that's not too much trouble."

A thin, pitying smirk touched the other woman's lips. "No trouble at all. And while you sleep, I'll see to Karic's needs, which I'm sure," she smiled archly at Karic as she began to lead him away, "are a little more complex than yours."

"I'll just bet they are," Liane muttered as she slung her backpack onto her shoulder and followed.

The hut was clean and simply furnished. Devra quickly dispensed with Liane by handing her a few blankets and pointing to a corner across the room from her box bed. After that, Liane noted with rising disgust, it was as if she weren't even present in the room.

Devra led Karic over to her bed. Combined with teasing kisses, she swiftly relieved him of his tunic and belt. Her hands were at his breeches before he had the presence of mind to stop her.

"Hold, Devra." With the greatest of efforts, Karic stilled her hands. "I meant what I said. We both need our rest."

"Let me ease your body toward that slumber, my

love," Devra purred silkily. "I well remember how you like it—slow, deep and hot."

Karic inhaled a ragged breath. By the three moons, how he needed a female! And Devra was so warm, so willing.

Until nine sols ago he'd never preferred any pretty femina over another, finding one equally as delightful as the next, but now he suddenly found he desired only one. He swallowed a savage curse. His worst fears had indeed materialized. Liane had driven him mad!

Karic shook his head. "Not now, Devra. We'll talk later, once I've rested."

A small pout pursed her lips. "Talking wasn't what I had in mind." Her glance sought out Liane, scowling at them from her pallet in the corner.

Devra's eyes narrowed. "What is she to you, Karic? Your newest love?"

"Hardly," he muttered. He gave Devra a gentle shove. "Go. I'll come for you later. I swear."

A knowing smile curved her lips. "Just be sure you do." She sauntered to the door, her hips swaying provocatively. "You won't regret it," she shot over her shoulder before leaving the hut. "I'll see to that."

Karic sighed and turned to Liane. Her face was carefully expressionless, but an angry light gleamed in her eyes. If he didn't so desperately wish it true, he'd almost think she was jealous, but that was fruitless hoping and only complicated an already difficult situation.

He walked over and squatted beside her. "Would you rather use the bed? I can sleep on the floor."

"No, thank you," Liane replied stiffly. "She made it quite clear who was to use her bed. I'm comfortable here."

"Then would you share your pallet with me? I've gotten too used to sleeping with you to now sleep alone." A lazy grin teased the corners of his mouth. "Besides, there's always the chance you might change your mind and try to escape."

Liane's heart gave a jump. All the doubts, all the anger at him, fled in an onrushing tide of relief and joy. She pulled back the blanket and scooted over, tears glistening in her eyes.

Karic crawled into bed and took Liane into his arms. Silently, she lay her head on his broad chest, reveling in the wiry crispness pressed against her cheek, the comforting strength of the hard body lying next to hers. She knew she shouldn't let herself want him, shouldn't care, but it was past the point of reason anymore. She loved Karic.

The realization filled her with a bittersweet joy. How could she not have recognized it before? What had begun as respect for a brave, strong man, devoted to his people, had quickly ripened to affection. His resolute courage, his determination to succeed against all odds, had filled her with admiration from the start. Though her mind seek had revealed amazing insights about him, the past sols and noctes together were what served to confirm that knowledge, until her life and heart had become intricately entwined with that of his.

She recalled his acute intelligence, how he'd tried to psychologically manipulate her to protect himself from her mind seek and ultimately succeeded. She remembered his wry wit, his boyish glee at the heart-stopping ride over the falls. Yet the memories that overshadowed everything else were how gentle he could be and his untiring efforts to protect her, even at great cost to himself. Combined with his animal magnetism and the hot fires he could stir in her with only a look, Liane realized she'd been lost from the start.

The admission did little to salve the raw ache spiraling through her. She may have lost her heart, but it changed nothing. She couldn't live with herself if she turned her back on her healing. To make such a decision was too terrifying, as was the possibility of living with that decision each sol. No, as great as her love and desire for Karic was, she didn't have the courage to turn her back on her life's work.

Poignant pain cut through Liane. They were both bound to courses that had the potential to force them apart. In the end, he'd turn his back on her if it meant the welfare of his people. And she couldn't blame him, just as she knew he'd not blame her for her choice.

The tears, held in abeyance until now, coursed down her cheeks. Unselfish sacrifice for a higher cause might gladden the heart at the close of one's life, but it didn't warm one's bed with a loving companion while on the journey to that inevitable end. Cycles of loneliness, cycles without Karic, stretched before Liane. Her shoulders began to shake as the long-repressed sobs shuddered through her. She wept unashamedly, the anguish rising from some deep, most personal part of her.

And all the while Karic said nothing, only gathering her to him to stroke away her sadness, kiss away her tears.

Devra found Karic late that sol, chopping wood for the village seamstress. The old woman had sewn him a soft leather loincloth, and Karic was repaying her with a split pile of logs. Devra's eyes admiringly ran up his long, muscular body, glistening with a light sheen of sweat.

"I like you much better in the loincloth," she said. "It leaves little to the imagination."

Karic lay down the ax and turned. He recognized that familiar, hungry light in Devra's eyes. Not long ago it had been more than adequate invitation to gather her into his arms and carry her off into the forest. Now, he just sighed and took her by the arm.

"We have to talk."

She resisted his gentle tug on her arm. "And why don't I like to hear you say that?" She eyed him intently. "You don't find me desirable, do you?"

"It's not that. You're still a beautiful femina. The problem is me, not you."

"I'd say the problem is that black-haired bitch in my hut," Devra hissed. "You love her, don't you?"

Karic breathed the admission on a whispered sigh. "Yes."

She cocked her head, her eyes narrowing. "Then why don't you sound happy? Doesn't she want you?"

He shook his head.

"Little fool! Shall I claw her eyes out for you?"

Karic smiled at the surge of protectiveness in Devra's voice. "No, it wouldn't change anything. She's doing what she feels is best. I can't fault her for it."

"But you're taking her back with you to your lair. How will you bear it, seeing her each sol and knowing she'll never be yours?"

His eyes darkened in pain. "I don't know. I'll deal with it when the time comes."

Devra lay a gentle hand upon his arm. "The loving's been good with you, Karic. Very good. I'll always be here, waiting, if you ever want me."

"And if some nocte I get it into my head to pay you a visit," he grinned down at her, "and find your life mate in bed with you, what will you say then, Devra?"

"Why," she fired back with a provocative toss of her long tresses, "I'll say move over husband and let an old lover in."

Karic threw back his head and laughed. "I believe you would, femina. I really believe you would."

His glance caught that of Liane's, just exiting the hut. For an instant their eyes met, and Karic's expression sobered.

He turned back to Devra. "I must speak with Liane. Do you care to accompany me?"

"And pretend courtesy to a fool?" Devra sniffed in disdain. "No, thank you." She walked away.

With a final, bemused glance in Devra's direction, Karic turned and headed over to Liane.

She gave him a tentative smile. "I woke up and you were gone."

He studied her face, still puffy from falling asleep, crying in his arms. "How are you feeling?"

"I am fine. Thank you for your patience."

"It hurts to see you so unhappy, Liane."

She inhaled a deep breath. "It'll pass. Now, no more of it. When do we leave?"

Karic's glance scanned the path of the sun. "In about five horas. It won't be dark enough until then."

"Well, at least there'll be moonlight to brighten our way. The cloudy sky last nocte blocked all light whatsoever."

At the mention of the moons, the unsettling urgency gnawing at Karic stirred anew. Curse it all! He didn't have enough to worry about with trackers on his trail and the need to get home becoming

113

more and more urgent, not to mention the distracting problems with Liane. Now, he had to face his need to mate when the triple moons came into alignment at a time that put him in a vulnerable, unthinking state that could endanger them both.

Well, by the time they set out this nocte they'd have only traveled a few horas before the moons rose. If they were in alignment he'd head back to the village. Devra, he knew, would willingly ease his torment.

"What's wrong, Karic?"

He stared down at her, momentarily confused, then he shook his head. "Nothing. Nothing at all. Come on," Karic growled, grasping her arm. "We've got supplies to gather, and I'll have to barter some service to pay for them."

Liane brightened at the thought. "And perhaps there are some ills to be healed. I, too, would like to do something to repay the villagers' kindness."

She was generous to all, Karic thought, as they headed across the commons. His people would greatly benefit from Liane's presence in their lair. It almost made the sacrifice worth it. Almost. . . .

They set out just after dusk. Their journey through open farmland was easier, but it did nothing to slow Karic's furious pace. If anything, he became more driven, more agitated as time went on. Unease spiraled through Liane.

There was something gnawing at Karic. She had sensed it growing for the past sol, a restless, churning, primitive thing, but without a mind seek it was impossible to fathom its source. And Karic would never permit even the slightest glimpse into that secret part of him. Liane squashed the rising anxiety as best she could and silently trudged on.

114

He hardly spoke or looked at her. Perhaps he was angry, she thought as they finally took a break among a small scattering of trees, angry with her for slowing him down, her presence continually placing them in situations that increased their danger. Without her, she knew he could cover distance at a much greater pace, his tall, muscular body speaking most eloquently of his strength and endless stamina.

She covertly studied Karic. The loincloth suited him and all he represented. He was a young, virile animal, simple and free. Her glance slid down his body, admiring the broad shoulders and powerful arms, the hard, flat planes of his naked, fur-matted chest, the rippling abdomen with its dark river of hair that disappeared beneath his loincloth. He stood before her, a magnificent specimen of a man, his glance averted toward the distant mountains. Then, with a low groan, he turned.

Their eyes met. Liane's breath caught in her throat. His eyes seared to the very depths of her being and stirred fires she'd thought safely controlled back to a blazing intensity. Suddenly, she felt drawn to him in a way both primal and savage.

He saw the smoldering look and knew it was a response to the fierce mating aura emanating from him. A tremor shook his tall frame. She was sensitive, just as his own mother had been to his father, but to seduce her now, in her highly emotional state, would be to take advantage of something she had no understanding and little control over. He couldn't do it.

Karic strode over to kneel beside her. "I must leave you for a time," he rasped, fiercely gripping her arms. "It is safe here among these trees. If anything prowls about while I'm gone you can

115

always climb up into them. Will you stay here? Wait for me?"

"But where are you going?" Liane searched his suddenly pain-wracked features. "What is wrong, Karic? And why can't I go with you?"

He released her with a jerk. "You can't. You'd be in too much danger. Swear you won't run away!"

Concern, mixed with growing fear, flared in Liane's heart. There was something wrong, very wrong here, and Karic refused to include her. But she couldn't deny the urgency of his request.

She tenderly brushed back a long lock of tawny brown hair that had fallen onto his face. "I swear, Karic. I won't run away."

With one last, wild look at her, he turned and sped across the rolling farm land, back toward the village they'd left behind. Liane watched until he disappeared into the nocte. Then she turned toward the mountains, to seek out what he'd seen there to fill him with such agitation.

Rising above the distant peaks were the three moons of Agrica, each in perfect alignment with the other.

Karic couldn't go on. Fire consumed his body, burning him from the inside out. His groin was heavy, a leaden weight that throbbed in unison with his pounding heart. The rapidity with which the unrequited mating urge had weakened him was surprising, even terrifying. He'd thought his strength enough to deal with it until he reached the village, but he had been wrong.

He stumbled and fell, his sweat-dampened body shivering in the cool nocte air. He struggled to his feet, took a few faltering steps, then fell again. This time his limbs failed him, and he began to drag himself along.

The pain! Karic never realized how bad the pain of denying the primal mating urge could be. It rose to blinding heights as he crawled along, the sound of the blood pulsing through his body growing louder until it deafened him. He covered his ears, writhing in agony. He was dying. It was killing him. But first, the madness would come.

He thought of Liane, waiting for him in the trees. There was nothing more he could do for her. She'd be alone now, all but defenseless, but at least he had spared her seeing him like this—turning on her.

Blood pounded through his brain, swimming before his eyes. Karic beat his head against the ground in an effort to ease the excrutiating torment. It was futile. He fell into a whirling black pit of madness, a hoarse cry on his lips.

Something was wrong. Liane climbed to her feet, her psychic powers scanning the nocte for any hint of trouble. Something was very wrong—but what? She concentrated harder, straining her abilities to their utmost capacity. A fleeting glimpse of Karic, writhing on the ground, flashed through her mind.

She choked back a cry and ran out into the moonlit nocte in the direction Karic had gone. Panic engulfed her. What had happened to him? Had some trackers found him? Were they even now torturing him to death?

The thought of what she could do to help, once she reached Karic's side, never entered Liane's mind. All she knew was that she must go to him, no matter what the consequences. To leave him out there alone, dying in the nocte, was inconceivable.

The horas wore on as Liane drove herself onward, walking when her lungs could no longer bear the demands of her rapidly churning legs. She had to reach Karic before it was too late, yet the fear it might already be so gnawed at her heart, quickening her pace.

A dark form sprawled near an outcropping of boulders caught her eye. Wild hope flared in Liane's breast. Could it be Karic? She slowed, reason gradually replacing emotion. Was he alone? She scanned the nocte for sign of others, perhaps hiding in the boulders beyond the motionless man. There was no one.

Liane stealthily crept closer. She sighed in relief. Karic's tousled mane and powerful form gave him away. She knelt and gently touched him.

A jolt of something dark and powerful shot through her. Liane jerked away. Though it had emanated from Karic, the sensation was foreign and totally unlike the man she knew—so hot, seething and frighteningly savage.

But it *was* still Karic. Liane forced herself to once more touch him and turn him over.

"Karic? Karic, are you all right?"

He groaned, his lids fluttering open.

She sucked in her breath.

Crazed eyes, eyes that gleamed with an uncomprehending light, stared back at her. Hands, fierce and clasping, gripped her arms. With a feral snarl Karic pulled her down, pressing her into his damp, heated body. A hand roved over her back, ripping at her tunic.

"Karic, stop it!" she cried, struggling to free herself from his iron grip. "It's me! Liane!"

The tunic shredded in his hand, and Liane felt the cool air flow over her back. The sensation galvanized her to more desperate measures. She slapped him, hard, across the face.

"Stop this, Karic! You don't know what you're doing!"

She slapped him again, but it seemed to make no difference. Instead, he rolled over with her, pinning her beneath his heavier weight. His hand moved with lightning speed to tear away the front of her tunic.

With a horrified cry, Liane lifted her arms to cover her nakedness. Karic wrenched her hands down to her sides, his head moving to her breasts. His lips closed around a soft nipple, drawing hard, suckling it to a taut peak. She shuddered at the roughness and the cold impersonality of his touch, something dying deep inside her. Tears welled in her eyes.

The nagging unease of the past sol crystallized with a sudden, terrifying clarity. The animal blood that flowed through Karic's veins had surfaced at last. He was blind to her except as a receptacle to be mated, an object to satisfy his bestial cravings. All the tales she'd heard whispered about the Cat Men were true. If she didn't find a way to stop him Karic would surely rape her in his unthinking, unseeing lust.

As his mouth continued to hungrily suck her breasts, his hands snaked down to her breeches. Liane desperately looked about for a weapon, a rock or stick with which to hit Karic. She squirmed a little from beneath him, frantically straining for a nearby stone, but a hand savagely jerked her back. Her breeches tore under the force of his powerful hands, ripping them down the middle to expose her.

His breath came in ragged gasps now as his knees forced her thighs apart, wedging himself between them. She stared up at him in a fleeting moment of disbelief. He freed his loin cloth, and his member sprang forth, thick and engorged. Terror surged through Liane.

"No!" she screamed. "Please, no, Karic! Don't do this! I beg you!"

A stranger's eyes glittering with a mindless light gazed back at Liane. With a gutteral growl, he lowered himself onto her. His hand slid between her thighs to her soft mound of hair, his questing fingers parting her to find her secret core.

Liane went mad then, a nameless panic gripping her. She kicked and clawed, leaving deep gouges on Karic's chest and shoulders. In his frenzied lust he felt nothing. He grasped her hips, lifting them to fit her to his need. And Liane, fighting with all the strength she possessed, could do nothing to halt the inexorable progress of his manhood as it found her opening and forced its way inside.

His hips began to move in rhythmic thrusts as he sheathed himself within her. Liane tensed, then arched in soundless agony as he rammed his way past her tight virginal passage. Her nails sunk into his upper arms.

Karic never noticed. He was unaware of anything but the hard thrust of his hips and burgeoning sense of pleasure. His breath came in low grunts now as he labored against her, his sweat-matted body brutally plunging into hers.

With each thrust, a little more of the fight ebbed from Liane. He ground her heart into a million pieces as cruelly as he ground his hard shaft into her. Her hands fell from his arms to lie limply at her sides. The tears flowed, unchecked, from her eyes.

And all the while Karic rammed himself into her. Finally, he threw back his head, the cords of his neck straining with the force of his release. A harsh, gutteral cry escaped his lips. He shuddered above her, his muscles taut and straining.

She watched him, the hatred and revulsion for his cruel act growing within her. He had taken what was most precious from her without a moment's regret or hesitation. In his bestial lust he had finally lost control, mating with her like the lowest of animals.

A rage, like none she'd ever experienced, whirled within, gaining shape and substance as the Bellatorian blood of warriors surged past the cycles of Sententian training. No man was permitted to take what she did not choose to give—not if he wanted to live. Respect for the sanctity of life shriveled and died, shattered beyond hope of reclamation in light of this nocte's brutality. She would have her revenge, and it would be a Bellatorian one.

Karic groaned and rolled off her. Throwing an arm across her body he promptly fell asleep. Liane lay there for a long while, listening to the soft sound of his breathing—listening and plotting all the ways she'd make him pay, before she finally killed him.

CHAPTER 7

KARIC WOKE TO FIND HIMSELF SPRAWLED, NAKED, ON the ground. His shoulders, chest and arms hurt. He glanced down at himself. Raw, ragged scratches marred his skin. How, by the three moons, had he gotten those?

He awkwardly sat up, blinking in the bright sunlight. What time was it? What was he doing here?

In a sickening rush, the memory of the past nocte came flooding back. Karic shook his head, struggling to clear his mind and fathom the turn of events. How was he still alive? He'd not reached the village.

Behind him came a soft moan. Karic whirled around. The sight of Liane, curled in a fetal position, her torn clothing barely covering her, was like a knife ripping through his insides. How she had gotten here didn't matter. The fact that she'd come

122

to him, and he'd repaid her by raping her, seized him with a breathless intensity. Something shattered inside Karic, splintering his heart into quivering shards of remorse. He groaned, buried his face in his hands and wept, harsh sobs that tore out of his body in great, wracking shudders.

The sound woke Liane. She drowsily glanced up and stiffened. Karic's long, powerfully muscled form gleamed in the sunlight as he lay there, fighting to bring himself under control. The realization he was weeping struck her. Strangely, its cause didn't matter.

There was nothing left with which to feel anything. Her insides had been gutted, her emotions torn away last nocte with each savage thrust of Karic's body. She sat up, pulling together the ragged edges of her tunic and breeches.

Karic must have heard her movement, for he suddenly tensed and lifted his head. Tears glistened on his face, and his anguished eyes gazed at her.

"Liane," he whispered.

She stared at him, her eyes flat, her mouth grim. "Don't say anything. There's nothing—*nothing*—you can ever say to change what happened."

He shot her a raw look, then rose and dressed. Walking over, he squatted before her. When his hand moved to touch her, she pulled back, revulsion twisting her features. Karic sighed and withdrew his hand.

"I am sorry, Liane," he huskily began. "I didn't mean for it to happen, and certainly not like that, but I had no control."

"Then that's the saddest part of all," she cried. "That you're such an animal you can't contain your primitive urges!"

"Only that one nocte, Liane. Only that one nocte

every three cycles. You know I'd never willingly hurt you!"

Liane backed away, climbing to her feet to glare down at him. "No, I don't know that, not anymore. You betrayed me, betrayed my trust, our friendship. And for what? One brief moment of lust? Do you even remember it?"

Karic averted his gaze.

"Do you?"

Her demand was low, threaded with rising disbelief. The answer to her question filled him with self-loathing, for her words were true. He had been an animal, driven by wild, crude urges, and he didn't remember any of it.

He climbed to his feet, meeting her glance. "No, I don't."

She hissed in rage and struck him, the force of the blow swinging his head around. For a long moment he held it there, the reddening imprint of her hand on his face. The action, so foreign to her Sententian nature, shocked Liane. She stared down at her hand, then back up at him.

Karic's head swung around, his eyes brimming with emotion. "Hit me again and again, Liane, if it'll help."

Pain, sharp and searing, rushed into the empty space in the middle of her chest, swirling chaotically with her fury. He hurt, she knew that, but it was not enough, would never be enough until he died from it. She was defiled and would never be clean again, mutilated at the hands of the man she'd once loved. The realization of her utter stupidity in loving him made her feel suddenly giddy.

She laughed, the sound hollow and bitter. "Nothing will help. Nothing—until I see you dead."

Liane turned to walk away. Karic's hand shot out to grasp her arm. With glittering eyes she glanced down at his hand, then back up to him. Still, Karic refused to let her go.

"None of this changes anything," he rasped. "You're still going back with me."

She shrugged. "It doesn't matter. You won't live to reach your lair."

A chill ran through him at the flat, expressionless pronouncement. Something had changed in Liane. He knew she meant what she said and knew as well, despite her special upbringing, that she was now capable of carrying it out. But it still changed nothing. She was going back with him. As much as she might hate and now dread it, it was still the safest course. He'd just have to be more careful around her.

He gently pushed her forward. "Let's go. There's no cover here. We need to get back to the trees and our packs as soon as possible."

Liane thought of the small spring sheltered by the trees. "Yes," she said, "the sooner the better. I can't wait to wash your foul touch from my body."

Karic stared after her retreating form, anguish twisting his heart into an aching, quivering mass. It was never meant to happen like this, he thought. It should have been gentle, pleasureable and oh, so loving. But in that one moment of uncontrollable lust, I've forever destroyed it for the both of us. Utter disgust for his Cat's blood filled him. With a heavy heart, Karic strode out after her.

They reached the trees about midsol and spent the rest of the sol there, hidden in the leafy shelter. Neither spoke save for what was absolutely necessary. Even when Liane prepared to bathe in the spring, she neither asked nor seemed to care if he watched.

And watch her he did, with sad, burning eyes, wincing at the sight of the bruises he'd left on her body, his heart turning to a lead weight as he saw her fiercely scrub herself, as if to cleanse all trace of him from her flesh. He watched her, sick with longing, as she rose from the water, her slender young body pink from her rough cleansing. His glance traveled down her curving form, past the pale swell of her breasts and gently flaring hips, to the dark triangle of curls and exquisitely long legs.

Liane halted, suddenly aware that Karic's glance had intensified. She scowled, visually challenging him. He met her gaze with a bleak look of his own, then swung away. Liane exhaled a breath, suddenly aware she'd been holding it. The rage boiled, once again, dangerously close to the surface.

The next few horas passed in tense silence, Liane sitting several meters away from Karic, essentially ignoring him. She was sifting through all the ways she might find to kill him, when a buzzing caught her attention. The sound grew closer. Far in the distance Liane saw a skim craft glide by. She leapt to her feet and ran toward it, screaming to gain the pilot's attention.

Karic tackled her before she'd taken ten steps, wrestling her to the ground, his hand smothering her cries. It was too late. The skim craft paused, then turned to fly in their direction.

Dragging a muffled Liane with him, Karic pulled her and the backpacks well into the shelter of the trees. He gagged her with a rag and bound her, hand and foot. Then, shoving her beneath some bushes, he lay down in front of her, firmly ensnaring her in his arms.

Liane struggled against him with all her might but, even as she did, knew it was futile. Karic's cloaking ability would shield them from view of the skim craft's pilot. Curse him! she thought. While her powers were now gone, shriveled to utter nothingness, he still possessed all of his. With a defeated moan, she relaxed in his arms.

Karic held her for a long while after the skim craft's departure, the full realization of the extent of her hatred slamming home with painful clarity. To see him dead she was now willing to risk even her own life. He'd have to watch her very carefully from now on and keep her tied most of the time. The thought sickened him, but he had no choice.

Finally, he rolled away. "That was very foolish, Liane," Karic growled. "Now I can't trust you, and I don't think you're going to like being bound and gagged."

He pulled her out from beneath the bushes to a more comfortable spot, placing a backpack beneath her head. He checked her hands and feet, assuring himself the bonds weren't too tight. Then, leaning against a nearby tree, Karic closed his eyes.

"Go to sleep, Liane. We've got several horas left of light and may as well make the most of it. We've a long nocte of travel ahead of us."

He could feel the heat of Liane's glare, raking over him with burning fingers of hatred, until, at last, he fell asleep.

They reached the foothills of the Serratus Mountains just before solrise, their journey slowed by an uncooperative Liane who had to be either dragged or carried most of the way. Karic was grateful for the shelter of a small cave by the time the sun's rays began to peek over the mountains. He untied Liane and removed her gag to allow her a brief respite to attend to her personal needs.

Before letting her go, Karic grasped her arm. "I give you this moment of privacy just this once. If you squander it by trying to escape, you'll never have it again. Do you understand?"

Mutinous blue eyes glared back at him. "Yes."

When she slipped behind a boulder, Karic listened intently but heard no sound of her trying to sneak away. In the next instant, he heard a crack of branches and a soft cry.

He was on his feet and around the boulder in a secundae. Two meters away a hole, formerly covered by greenery, lay open. Karic tensed, the sense of danger so strong he could smell it. It was a trap.

Running over, he gazed down into the pit. Thankfully, it wasn't deep, and Liane hadn't been hurt. Even now she was climbing to her feet, brushing dirt from her breeches.

"Here." He knelt and lowered his hand. "Take it and I'll pull you out. We need to be away—and fast."

Liane's gaze suddenly shifted to something behind him. Karic whirled around, agilely twisting to leap halfway to his feet in the same movement. A booted foot caught him in the side of the head, stunning him and bringing him back to his knees. Before he could recover he was flung to the ground and shackled hand and foot.

A shiver of fear rippled through Liane as she gazed up at their captors. Though she'd never seen any before this moment, Liane recognized the dreaded Atrox trackers from the horrifying tales about them. The huge, swarthy, wolfish-faced mutants were renowned for their savage cruelty and peerless tracking abilities, and for the fact their loyalty always belonged to the highest bidder. She wondered how long they'd been on their trail. She well knew who had bought their services—Necator.

Well, it didn't matter what they did to Karic. There was no hope for him now, not in the clutches of those beasts. She didn't care what happened to him anyway, except that she wished to be the one to kill him. If she could but win the Atroxes' trust . . .

Liane managed her brightest smile and raised a hand to the mutant who looked like the leader. "My thanks to you for finally rescuing me from the Cat Man. The Lord Commander will be pleased to know I'm safe."

As the other two Atroxes trained their blaster guns on her, the leader pulled Liane out of the pit. He jerked her close and sneered at her.

"And what makes you think Necator cares what happens to you, except that you're captured and suitably punished?"

She resolutely returned his stare, though her heart was pounding in her chest. "Because I've information he desperately needs. You'll be well rewarded if you take me back to him."

"And what might that information be?"

"The location of the Cat Men's lair."

At her words, Karic stiffened. The fear that she indeed carried that knowledge within her flared once more to life. It could be a bluff, an attempt to save herself, but he couldn't be certain.

The thought made him wild. This couldn't be happening, not now, not after all they'd been through, not when they finally were so close to his lair. He had to get free, to find some means of escape. Karic struggled in his bonds but did little more than abrade the flesh from his wrists and ankles.

The mutant leader noticed Karic's desperate struggles and smiled grimly. "Perhaps you do have knowledge of value. Tell me where the lair is."

"No," Liane firmly replied. "My information is for Lord Necator's ears only. It is his to do with as he wishes. You must take me back to Primasedes."

"And the Cat Man?" he softly inquired. "What are we to do with him?"

Liane shot Karic a disdainful glance. "You know as well as I that Necator wants him dead. I ask only that I be allowed to kill him."

A bushy eyebrow lifted over cruel, glittering eyes. "And why is that?"

She faltered for the span of a breath. "He—he took something from me, something of priceless value. I demand the right of retribution."

"And what gives you the right to demand anything?"

"The right of Bellatorian supremacy. It is the law. You dare not defy it."

The Atrox shrugged. "It matters not to me who kills him." He handed her his blaster. "Just do it and be quick about it. We've wasted enough time tracking you two."

Karic rolled over to face her. Liane had the gun pointed at his chest, a look of implacable determination on her face. A myriad of emotions ran through him, but the overwhelming one was of grief—grief that he'd driven her to this, that he'd never have the chance to make it up to her, and grief for the eventual fate of his people.

The memory of them and his obligation for their welfare surged through Karic, clearing his mind of remorse over Liane. Personal pain was a luxury he had no time for, not while his people were still in danger. He struggled to his knees.

"Don't do this, Liane," he pleaded, his eyes boring into hers. "Not for my sake—I don't expect nor deserve mercy—but don't do this to my people. I have to get back and warn them of the dangers. Kill me if you wish, once I've done that. I swear I won't try to stop you. But not now. Please, not now."

A warning voice whispered in her head, *Don't listen to him. Kill and be done with it.* Yet even as the thought flashed through her mind, a sickening realization twined its tendrils about her heart. One way or another, she must kill this sol, either Karic or the Atroxes, for one couldn't live if the other did. But who?

She hated Karic with all her heart and ached to see him die. He *deserved* to die, but not at the expense of his people. They were innocent, far more innocent than these mutant trackers, known to cold-bloodedly slaughter their victims for the price of a few coins. But to kill . . .

From some place deep within she summoned the courage, the sheer will power to turn against all her Sententian training, but perhaps there was nothing of that left in her now. And the Bellatorian part, the warrior blood, she knew was more than equal to the task.

Liane swung around, taking out the two other trackers in a long, fiery blast. With a cry of rage the leader leaped at her, dagger in hand. Karic flung himself into him, knocking the mutant to the ground. The Atrox stabbed wildly. Only by the quickest of reflexes was Karic able to evade his thrusts.

With a jerk, Liane roused herself from her shocked inaction. Even now, the Atrox had pinned Karic and was raising his dagger for the fatal blow. She took quick aim and fired. The mutant toppled onto Karic.

She dropped the blaster and ran to where the Atrox lay. Dragging the body aside, Liane quickly ascertained Karic was unharmed. As she dug in the mutant's pocket for the means to free him of his bonds, Karic struggled to a sitting position. His gaze met hers when she finally turned, the key control in her hand.

"Thank you, Liane."

"I didn't do it for you."

"I know."

He glanced down at the key control. "We need to get out of here. There may be other trackers."

She pointed the device at him, then hesitated. "I'll free you if you swear to let me go. I don't want to go with you, and you know I have no idea where your lair is."

"I don't know that, Liane, but it's not the point anyway. Your only safety lies in coming with me."

She gave a bitter laugh. "I've never been in more danger in my life than since I've been with you— and the only thing I have left now *is* my life.

"No," Liane fiercely shook her head, "I won't go with you. I won't spend the rest of my sols as some breeder. And that's all I have left, all that's of any value to your people."

"I won't let them use you that way, I swear it!" Karic said, a plan beginning to form in his head. "I can give you so little anymore, but I'll give you my word on that."

She sadly smiled. "And what power would you have if they decided otherwise?"

"I have some influence through my father. He's Lord of the Cat People."

"But would he back you in this? The welfare of an entire people is of more import than the wishes of one man, even if that man were his son."

"I think he'd understand."

Liane studied him for a long moment, then sighed her acquiescence. "I want the ability to leave when the time is right. I don't want to have to stay with the Cat People forever."

Karic nodded.

"And one thing more." Her glance hardened. "It changes nothing between us. I still hate you and want you dead."

He smiled, but it never quite reached his eyes. "I gave you my word. I'll stand by it."

She aimed the key control, and Karic's bonds sprang loose. He climbed to his feet. Without a word, he dragged the bodies of the three Atroxes over to the pit. After divesting them of their blaster guns and other weapons, Karic shoved them into the hole. He quickly covered them with stones and dirt, then spread greenery over the spot.

Liane watched him as he loaded the extra weapons in his backpack and slung the three blaster guns over his shoulder.

Karic noticed her quizzical look. "There's always a need for weapons. We don't have the resources to make anything too sophisticated. The blasters will be invaluable."

When had the Cat People not been at war with Bellator? Liane wondered. Neither in her nor Karic's lifetime, nor several generations before them. The loss of the Knowing Crystal had led to this situation on Agrica, and each planet in the Imperium could tell an additional tale of cruelty and chaos. Was there no end to it all? It seemed not.

She rose to her feet, utterly depressed. Were they all doomed then—the Cat People to annihilation, the Agrican planet to total subjugation and her own people to soul-rotting inhumanity? Her own problems and personal losses seemed inconsequential in comparison. Yet why did the sight of Karic, everytime she looked at him, tear her heart asunder, spilling out her life's blood until there seemed nothing in the universe more important than that pain?

Liane shouldered her pack. She was exhausted, but they were no longer safe here. She wondered if they'd ever be safe again.

They climbed for a few horas, Karic carefully covering their tracks by taking them over as much rocky terrain as possible. Once he was satisfied they had gained a safe distance, he found another sheltered area in which to rest. By dusk, they were once more on their way.

The journey through the mountains was treacherous, even with full moonlight. The triple moons had already moved slightly out of their perfect alignment, not to join again for another three cycles. Karic gazed up at them. If he'd had just two extra noctes he could have made it back in time. Only two noctes had stood between friendship—perhaps even love—and undying hatred. Angrily, he quashed the realization and strode on.

A distant peak came into view about midnocte. Liane instantly recognized it as the one from Karic's mind seek. When they paused for a short rest, she pointed toward it.

"That is all I know of where your lair lies. That is all I could gain from you in that brief instant I slipped past your mind guard."

Karic frowned. "Then you knew more than you realized. Our lair lies in the valley at the base of that mountain."

She looked at him. "It doesn't matter. I would never have revealed even that."

He stared back at her, into eyes infinitely sad and tinged with regret. But regret for what? he wondered. For what had come between them, or for having ever had the misfortune of even knowing him? For her sake at least, it would have been better if she never had.

"You always had my people's best interests at heart," Karic rasped, in a pained voice. "I know that now. I'm sorry for my distrust, but I had to be careful."

Liane stared at him for a long moment, then motioned down the mountain path. "It's best we were on our way."

Karic strode out, knowing the time for further talk was over. There was nothing personal between them anymore; the common welfare of his people was now the only thing that bound them—that and the vow he'd made to protect her from the males of his lair.

Though he had promised her, Karic knew the vow would be difficult to keep. Survival of a race was a powerful force to contend with. For the Cat Men, even one extra female was vital. Liane would see that once they reached his lair.

There were almost twice as many males of breeding age as females. With her sensual beauty and alluring form, the desire for her would be strong, and now, after what he'd done to her, the option of

Liane willingly taking him as a mate was no longer there. By right he had no further claim on her, for he'd never force himself on her again. But others would want to.

He'd have to see that never happened, and somehow, someway, bear the pain of unrequited love, a pain her presence would evoke for the rest of his life.

They reached the valley two horas after solrise. From their vantage point overlooking the lair, Liane couldn't discern any form of habitation. If not for the people moving to and fro, the children scampering about even at such an early hora, she'd have never known the valley was inhabited.

She turned to Karic. "How many of your people live here?"

A grim pair of eyes riveted on her. "All that are left of the Cat People. There are probably four hundred males, one hundred and fifty females, and about as many children. Of the females, less than one-third are of pure or half Cat blood. The rest are all captured."

"I didn't realize you had so few Cat Women."

"Only fifty Cat Women survived, out of over nine hundred, in that massacre thirty cycles ago," he bitterly said. "And even fewer children."

"I am sorry."

Liane couldn't bear the intensity of the hard gaze that held hers. She glanced away and gestured toward the valley.

"Where are your homes, your gardens? Surely you must grow food, yet I see no sign . . ."

He smiled and indicated the steep mountains that enclosed the little valley. "Our lairs are now caves, as well as our gardens. There is a special powder we add to the perpetual flames. It mimics the sun's light well enough to encourage our vegetables to grow indoors. Our fruit and berry orchards are planted outside, but in such a manner as to resemble the growth of wild plants so they draw no notice. It is the only way to hide our presence from the skim craft that constantly patrol."

Karic pointed out the guards, stationed high on the mountains. "We keep watch constantly. At first sign of intruders a warning, attuned only to our hearing, is sent out. Everyone, even the children, knows they must immediately take cover."

"A hard way to live," Liane observed.

He nodded. "Yes, but we must survive." Karic hesitated, eyeing her intently. "When we enter the lair the situation will be difficult. There may be things I say or do that might seem strange, even upsetting. I ask your trust in this."

Unease spiraled through Liane. He dare ask her to trust him after what he'd done? Yet what other recourse was there? She had agreed to come with him. For the time being at least, he was the sole conduit between herself and his people.

She exhaled a deep breath. "What choice have I? I must depend on you."

His eyes bore into her. "Everything I do is for your welfare. Remember that."

Liane nodded.

He hesitated again. "There will be times I must touch you."

She stiffened. "No."

"I must, Liane. For your safety, you must appear to be mine. If you don't, the other males will immediately begin to vie for you. I'm not asking anything except this outward sign of possession. It is for appearances only. Until I've had time to talk with my father and the Elders, it's the only way I can protect you."

She bit her lip, her anguish almost overcoming her control. So it begins, she thought—the compromise, the humiliation. Ah, but she was so weary of never having choices anymore! And Karic had done this to her!

Her gaze contemptuously raked over him. "I grow tired of your so-called protection but for a while longer, I will endure it. Just be careful how you touch me. I'll suffer no intimacies."

Though they shouldn't have surprised him, the words stung. He couldn't help it. The guilt at what he'd done to her constantly haunted him. He was exhausted from the sols of danger and endless travel. And he hurt. How he hurt!

"The intimacies, as you call them, will consist of little more than placing my arm around you and perhaps pulling you close. If you can, forewarned as you now are," he drawled sarcastically, "try not to look as though you despise me when that happens. It would help matters immensely."

She glared up at him. "Fine. That will be fine."

"Good," he snapped back at her. "Now, let's get this over with."

Liane watched Karic head out, his shoulders rigid with anger. Then, with a defiant toss of her ebony tresses, she resolutely followed.

CHAPTER 8

A CRY WENT UP WHEN THEY REACHED THE VALLEY floor. A large crowd swiftly gathered to line the path they were taking. As they passed them Liane shot quick, furtive glances at the people. In her heightened anxiety her only impression was one of the feline-flattened features and hirsute faces of some, while others bore appearances similar to that of Karic or herself. By the joyous looks, she could tell Karic's safe return greatly mattered. Though his mission, a mission she still failed to fully fathom, had been one of vital importance, she somehow sensed their relief stemmed even more from their love and concern for him.

She glanced at the man walking beside her. His eyes glowed as he scanned the sea of happy faces, waving to one, then shouting a greeting to another. The complexity of him unsettled Liane. He could be so warm, so loving when it came to his people—

and then in the next instant so savagely cruel to her. It tore at her heart to still be drawn to him yet know she could never trust him, never again bear his touch without fearing he'd turn into some wild, lust-crazed animal.

Rage grew at the realization she was weakening in her hatred. She was Bellatorian now, through and through. She'd irrevocably turned from the Sententian ways when she'd killed the Atroxes, for surely no true Sententian was capable of killing. But then Liane hastened to console herself that no Sententian had ever been forced into circumstances such as hers, either.

Confusion whirled through her. Karic was to blame for all of it, wasn't he? Or was he, too, an unfortunate victim of circumstance?

Liane fought back a spasm of panic. Now was not the time for doubts or hesitation. She was in the midst of the greatest danger of her life and needed all the strength of her convictions. And the one certainty was that Karic had brought her to this.

They halted before the opening of what appeared a particularly large cave. Anticipation trembled through Liane. Karic pulled her to him, his arm encircling her shoulders.

She tensed, then forced herself to relax when he gave her a brief, warning look. He smiled encouragingly, and she weakly smiled back.

A man walked toward them from the cave. Karic's smile widened into a grin, and the man returned it with one of his own.

He was tall and lean with a regal air about him. From the gray that heavily streaked his shoulder-length mane of dark brown hair, Liane guessed him to be in his late fifties. His eyes were green-gold and kind, and his features, though lined and much more feline, were still stamped with the look of his son.

Around his neck he wore a chain made from the precious, yellow-gold aureum, two large Cat's claws designed from that same metal dangling from it. About his shoulders was draped a cloak of royal purple. There was no doubt in Liane's mind who he was—Karic's father and Lord of the Cat People.

Karic released her and stepped forward. In one fluid motion he knelt before his lord and ruler, his tousled, sun-streaked mane bowed low. The Lord of the Cat People stepped forward and slipped a chain with one aureum Cat's claw over Karic's head.

"Rise, my son, and welcome home."

A wild cheer exploded from the crowd behind them. Karic stood up and clasped arms with his father, each gazing deeply into the other's eyes. Liane felt her throat tighten, for the love between father and son was evident. Somehow, the realization lessened her fears.

Karic pulled his father over to her. Liane instinctively tensed, her blue eyes widening.

"Father, this is Liane," his son began by way of introduction, his voice purposefully loud enough to carry to the gathering behind them. "Liane, this is my father, Morigan, Lord of the Cat People."

Karic gazed down at her, his arm once more possessively encircling her shoulders. "If not for her, I wouldn't have lived long enough to make it back to you. I ask sanctuary for her and permission to take her as life mate."

Liane swung horrified eyes to Karic, her mouth opening in protest. A sharp look and quick shake of his head silenced her. She forced a smile onto her face and turned her gaze to his father.

Morigan could not help but notice the strange interchange. A small frown wrinkling his brow, he extended his hand.

"Welcome, Liane. Sanctuary and the shelter of my lair I gladly give you. The decision of life mates can only be decided at a later date, when the Council of Elders meets." He shot Karic a piercing glance. "As well my son knows."

Liane accepted his hand, her gaze squarely meeting his. "My thanks for your kindness, my lord. I pray that you and your people have patience with my ignorance as I attempt to learn your ways."

Admiration warmed his eyes. "As you must with us, femina. Our customs may seem strange at first, but in time I'm sure you'll understand the necessity for them. Survival can sometimes be a harsh ruler."

His gaze turned to Karic. "We need to talk about what you discovered, but first, what are your needs? Food, a bath, rest?"

Karic laughed. "All that and more, Father. But let me see to Liane first, then we'll talk."

He glanced at Liane, then gestured toward the cave. "This is our lair, where my father and I live. We'd be honored if you'd share it with us."

She followed him into the chamber. In the middle of the room, lit by several large perpetual flame boxes, was a round, stone hearth, not in use now in the heat of summer. Off to one side was a wooden table with six chairs. Behind it was a vast library of books, set into shelves carved into the long stone wall. Across the room along the other wall were several chests and an assortment of weapons, as well as some farming implements. Two tunnels angled off from the room at the far corners.

Karic's eyes followed the direction of her gaze.

"Those lead to our sleeping chambers. One is mine, the other my father's."

He answered the question flickering in her eyes. "You will sleep with me."

Her mouth tightened. "Why? It's no longer necessary. I'm not going anywhere."

He cocked a dark brow. "Didn't you see the way the young males looked at you from the moment we first entered the valley?"

"No. What are you talking about?"

"They all want you."

"But you said you'd protect me. That's why you asked to take me as your mate, isn't it?"

"Yes. But that doesn't mean the permission will be granted. You heard my father. The Council of Elders decides that."

Fear and anger knotted inside her. "But you promised! Now that you're safe, does your word suddenly not matter?"

"Yes, it matters," Karic replied, trying with the soothing tone of his voice to calm her rising agitation. "I'm not telling you this to frighten you, only to explain why we must continue to sleep with each other. When the Council meets my claim on you must be the strongest. If it appears to all that we are lovers, well, it helps our cause."

"But how will anyone know if we sleep together, here in the privacy of your lair? Is it necessary to act out this charade for the benefit of your father as well? I can't hide my true feelings all the time."

"It's not my father, Liane. I'll talk to him. He'll understand and help in any way he can, but the others will be watching us, weighing the evidence, determining how best to use your breeding abilities. Sleeping next to me will put my scent upon you, as will yours upon me. It is a subtle but strong mark of our commitment to each other."

"But you are the son, the heir to the throne." Liane couldn't keep the anxiety from her voice. "Surely you can do what you wish in this matter."

Karic shook his head and sighed. "When it comes to matters of survival no one is above the law. The Council determines my mate as they do everyone else's. And by law, *as* heir to the throne, I'm required to life mate with a full blood."

"Why?"

"Our species has been diluted enough, necessary though it was. It was decided long ago that I must restore our blood to fuller strength through my heirs. I've been betrothed to the Cat Woman Kalina for several cycles now. We were to become life mates at the next Mating Festival."

"Then how can you hope—"

"The Council rarely forces an unwilling mating," Karic replied, noting her rising anxiety. "Besides, in light of all you've done for our people in rescuing me, I hope to convince them to reconsider their earlier decision. It will be difficult, I grant you, but with my father's influence . . ."

Wariness lifted her brow. "And if this mating is allowed, what will you expect of me?"

A pair of penetrating eyes leveled on her. "I won't force myself on you, if that's what you're asking."

"Even on that nocte when you supposedly can't control yourself?"

"We'll deal with that when the time comes. A lot can happen in three cycles."

"Not as far as my feelings for you are concerned," she whispered vehemently. "Those will *never* change."

Karic dragged in an uneven breath. "Then arrangements will be made to protect you that nocte. Now, no more of this. What would you like? Are you hungry?"

A heavy weariness suddenly flooded Liane. "No, just very tired. If you'd show me your bed chamber, I'd like to rest.

His gaze softened. "Come."

She followed Karic down the tunnel on the left and into a small, dimly lit room. The oversize bed, set higher than usual from the floor and heaped with furs and cushions, was carved from the side of the cave. Karic pointed out the basin of water and clean cloths set into a wall alcove across from the bed, then gave her a few moments of privacy.

When he returned she was dressed in her sleeping shift. His eyes carefully averted from the revealing garment and the tantalizing body beneath it, he lifted her up onto the edge of the bed. Liane quickly crawled beneath the furs, snuggling down into their silky warmth.

Her glance, already languid with the encroaching mists of sleep, scanned his face. "What will you do, Karic? Aren't you tired?"

He was sorely tempted to join her, to gather her softness to him, to possess her body in the only way he might be ever allowed, but first there were more pressing matters to deal with. Karic sighed and shook his head. "I must talk with my father."

A strange disappointment filled Liane which she quickly brushed aside. She didn't care if he slept with her or not; in fact, she preferred it otherwise. He had lost control once with terrible consequences. He could well do it again, without warning or reason.

It was just the foreignness of a new situation among strangers, Liane reassured herself. For the time being, as much as she hated to admit it, Karic was the one link between it all. She still needed him for that, but nothing more. And soon, she wouldn't need him for anything.

Fragile lids lowered to rest long, dark lashes upon the high hollows above her cheekbones. Liane's breathing slowed and deepened. Karic watched her for a time, fighting the yearning and the ache that burned in his chest.

He had told her he'd take her as mate and not force himself on her. Yet how would that be possible, seeing her, living with her, wanting her every sol of his life? He looked ahead to endless sols of heartbreaking hunger and unrequited desire.

His mouth twisted in a grim smile. It was irony of the cruelest kind. Though Liane had voluntarily chosen to be celibate, fate might now force that same choice upon him with a mate as beauteous and desirable as Liane at his side.

But what else could he do, if that was her wish, loving her as he did? For one last, lingering moment, Karic stared down at Liane. Then, squaring his shoulders, he strode out to find his father.

They walked among the trees that edged the valley, father and son, neither speaking for a time. Finally, Morigan halted and turned to Karic.

"What happened in Primasedes?"

"They have a new sensor system for intruders," Karic said, a bitter smile of remembrance on his lips. "It caught me unawares. I was captured and tortured. Then they sent in Liane to attempt a mind seek."

"She's a Sententian?"

Karic nodded. "Yes. I was barely able to withstand her, but I did. Afterward, the Lord Commander brought in a machine. It was the Guide."

Morigan's eyes lit with excitement. "You saw it then?"

"Not only saw it, but experienced its effects." Karic's hand clasped his father's arm. "We can fight it. Our Cat's Powers not only withstand it but control the Guide's functioning. I'm not certain what Necator has in mind for it, but I'd guess he plans to gain total control of the Imperium by using the Guide to reprogram peoples' minds."

His father frowned. "So the Cat People aren't the only ones in danger of Bellatorian dominance."

"I'm not so sure it's Bellator's decision. I think Necator and a renegade group of scientists are behind this."

"And what do you suggest we do about it?"

"Destroy the machine. Kill Necator and his scientists. Hopefully their knowledge will die with them."

Karic's brow furrowed in concern. "But whether we could successfully infiltrate a large enough group into Primasedes to carry out such a mission, especially with that new alarm system of theirs, is hard to determine. Necator has probably guessed that I made it back here. Even now he may have his scientists devising new protections for the Guide, not to mention seeking ways to override our psychic abilities to control it. It may already be too late."

"We'll have to discuss this further in Council." His father paused, arching a brow. "Now, tell me more of you and Liane. Though I sense a strong bonding, there's also deep pain and anger."

Karic averted his eyes. "She hates me."

"Really."

His son's head jerked up at the dry irony in Morgan's voice. "Really. I mated with her on the nocte of the three moons—against her will."

"You had no choice. Couldn't you make her see that?"

"I took more than her maidenhood that nocte. She lost her Sentention powers, too. She hates me above all for that."

Morgan thoughtfully stroked his jaw. "I see. And yet you still want her as mate. Most interesting."

"I love her."

His father chuckled. "I guessed that. What can I do to help you win her heart?"

"Help me gain her as a life mate. The rest is between Liane and myself."

"You know that's not possible. You're betrothed to Kalina, and the Council's decision is law," Morgan said. "Even I cannot change that. Better to satisfy yourself with this femina for a few cycles. I can probably get the Council to postpone your life mating with Kalina until then."

"I said I loved her, Father. I don't want her for just a few cycles, but for the rest of my life. Use your influence with the Council and make them see why it's so important that she be given to me."

"And why do you want a femina who doesn't want you? Yes, I know you love Liane," Morgan interjected, noting the rising frustration in his son's eyes, "but there's more, isn't there?"

Karic nodded. "I promised her she'd not be used for breeding."

"You had no right to make such a selfish decision."

"It wasn't selfish!" Karic cried. "If I'd been selfish, I wouldn't be trying to protect her at the sacrifice of my own needs."

The Lord of the Cat People stared in disbelief. "You plan to life mate with her and never breed? Are you mad, Karic? The Council will never allow such a thing."

"They don't have to know."

Morigan laughed grimly. "And you tell me this, expecting me to keep such a secret? Have you forgotten I'm lord of all, even before I'm your father?"

Karic strode over to a nearby tree and leaned back against it. The bark was rough against his bare skin, but he welcomed it. It kept him grounded in a reality increasingly hard to bear. He looked agonizingly at his father.

"I hope in time to regain her trust, perhaps even her affection. I . . . I think she was beginning to feel something for me, before . . ."

He sighed. "But even if that never comes to pass, how am I to repay all she's done for me? She rescued me from the Bellatorians," he rasped. "She healed me of mortal wounds. And when the Atrox trackers captured and were ready to kill me, she turned the blaster upon them to save my life, a blaster she'd obtained from them to avenge herself against me after I'd so savagely raped her. And now you ask me to repay her by forcing myself or one of the other males upon her?"

A defiant light flared in Karic's eyes. "I can't, I won't, do that."

"Not even if your own people demand it?"

His eyes went dark with pain. "Don't ask it of me, Father. I beg you."

Morigan strode over to face his son. "May that sol never come, my son," he fervently said. "But if it does I'll not ask it lightly nor without full knowledge of the sacrifice it entails. Will you trust me in this?"

Karic studied his father in thoughtful silence, then nodded. "You know I will, but trust this, too. I'll not go against you or our people lightly, but my feelings for Liane, for the debt I owe her, run deep."

His father smiled sadly. "I know, my son, and understand. If your mother had been in Liane's position and I in yours, my decision would be no easier." He paused. "The Council meets in six sols. Decisions for several life matings must be made then in preparation for the Mating Festival. Your petition will be added to the rest."

"Good."

They resumed their walk. Morigan glanced over at Karic, an appraising light in his eyes.

"What will you do in the meantime to win her heart?"

Karic shrugged. "I don't know. Aside from convincing her to share my bed, something she's been forced to do all along anyway, there's not much else I *can* do. My actions must speak for themselves."

A deep chuckle rumbled in Morigan's chest. "You've still a lot to learn about feminas, my son. Actions are fine, but they like words, too. Have you made her listen to the reasons for the mating urge? Made her understand what a vital part of us it is?"

"Oh, she understands all right." Karic grimly laughed. "She thinks I'm an animal, with an animal's crude, uncontrollable desires."

"Then show her your human side—the gentle, tender lover. Show her patience and consideration. And tell her, in every way you can, how beautiful, how wonderful she is."

He clapped his son on the back. "Why, you have

the perfect opportunity in the next few sols, for who else is fit to introduce her to our life here? For a time she will need you and lean on you for support in adjusting to us. Use that time to foster a desire in her that transcends dependence."

A faint hope flared in Karic's eyes. "But what of my responsibilities to you and the Council? I cannot turn my back on them to spend it picking flowers and wooing a femina."

His father smiled. "We need you, but not every moment of the sol. And there's no point in you sitting in on the minor judgments. I'll send for you for the important matters."

"Like deciding what to do about the Guide?"

"Yes, most definitely."

Morigan gave his son a gentle shove. "Get on with you. Even now you waste precious time you could be spending with your femina."

"She's asleep," Karic offered by way of protest.

"Then take her in your arms and hold her head upon your heart. Even in slumber, you can begin to convince her she is yours."

A warm, comforting closeness encircled Liane. It felt so good, so right to be there, and she snuggled deeper, sighing with contentment. A sound, low and rhythmic, thudded against her ear. She squirmed closer, easing her body between two muscular, outspread legs.

Her hand moved randomly, the crisp mat of hair threading through her fingers tickling her. Liane's lids fluttered open, then closed again. Her hand slid lower as she tried to shift herself into an even more comfortable position. Long, slender fingers grazed something, hard and swollen.

The body beneath her tensed, then jerked. A low, masculine curse penetrated her sleepy haze. Liane's lids snapped open.

Green-gold eyes, fierce, burning and bright, stared back at her. For a secundae, she was confused. What was she doing in this strange room, in a strange bed, lying atop Karic? The hand upon his chest clenched into a fist while the other moved to unconsciously curl around . . .

With a cry of horror Liane rolled away to stare down at Karic's huge arousal. Anger surged through her.

"You—you're naked!"

Karic exhaled a frustrated breath. "Yes. I usually sleep this way."

"But not with me!" She glared at him. "How dare you!"

"Oh, by the three moons, Liane!" Karic exploded. "You've slept with me for over six sols now, seen me naked probably as many times, and now you're upset because I've finally combined the two? All we did was sleep together.

"And besides," he added with a spark of deviltry, "*you* were on top of me. *You* were the one fondling me. And with that thin bit of a shift you like to wear," he said, his gaze dipping to the rounded fullness of her breasts and flat belly, "you're but one step from nakedness yourself. So, have a care who you accuse and of what."

High color washed Liane's cheekbones as her disdainful blue eyes clashed with his. "It doesn't excuse the fact that you climbed naked into bed with me. You know my feelings about you, and then you present yourself in the same condition as . . . as that nocte!"

She scooted across the bed to climb off, when an iron grip clamped around her ankle. Liane froze.

"What do you think you're doing?" he demanded in a silky, dangerous voice.

"Getting as far away from you as I can."

She threw him a wrathful look over her shoulder. "I'll sleep on the floor rather than subject myself to anymore contact with you."

A sharp tug jerked her down onto her stomach. Another, and she was halfway back across the bed. Before Liane could even gather the presence of mind to protest, she was flipped over onto her back and Karic was atop her. He captured her hands in one of his and anchored them firmly above her head.

Liane's struggles stilled. Her eyes widened. "What are you going to do?"

"Not what you imagine," he growled. "I merely want you to listen to me."

"Then free my hands."

Karic smiled. "No, I think not. Your claws can be nearly as lethal as mine."

She glared at him with glorious, defiant eyes. "You deserved that—and more!"

"Yes, that nocte I did," he calmly agreed, "but not now. I meant no harm lying close to you while we slept. And if my body reacted to yours, rubbing so intimately against mine, there's no harm in that, either. The harm would be if I forced myself on you."

He paused to eye her closely. "Have I done that, Liane?"

"No," she whispered achingly, unable to meet his gaze.

"What did you say?" Karic prodded.

"I said," Liane repeated with rising ire, "no, you didn't force yourself on me—this time."

Tears filled her eyes, but they were tears of confusion and remembrance. "Oh, curse you!" she cried. "You know I fear you now, fear the next time you lose control. I'm no match for your strength, and I can't bear to live with the dread and uncertainty of when it will happen again!"

"It won't happen again. I swear it!" Karic rasped. "If we'd reached my lair in time it never would have happened at all!"

"But it did, it did—and nothing will ever be the same!"

The tears flowed, coursing down her cheeks. Her body began to jerk with repressed sobs until the effort to contain them was more than she could bear. Pain slashed across Karic's rugged features, and suddenly Liane lost all semblance of control. Harsh, wracking sobs shook her slender frame.

She twisted free of the loose grip Karic now held her in, turning to bury her face in the furs. And still she cried, the anguish welling from deep within her.

He pulled her to him, cradling her head against his chest, her tears drenching him, her slim form shuddering with the force of her torment. He held her for a long while, stroking the rumpled head of ebony hair, murmuring soothing words. Eventually Liane's sobs lessened, easing into jerky little spasms, then small, hiccuping sounds. Finally, she was quiet.

Liane lay there beside him, the deep, even breathing of Karic's powerful body lulling her into an exhausted stupor. There was no fight left in her. When he lifted her chin to gaze down at her tear-streaked face, she let him.

"Liane," he groaned, his voice raw with emotion. "Oh, Liane . . ."

She gazed at a face twisted in a mask of agony, a face that mirrored her own pain. She gently brushed aside a lock of hair that had fallen into his eyes. Her fingers lingered, tracing a hesitant trail down the side of his face.

Karic covered Liane's hand with his. With a low, gutteral sound he turned his mouth, kissing her palm with tender abandon. The touch of his lips seared a burning path straight down Liane's arm and into her body.

"Karic?" she whispered, not even sure what she was asking.

He turned questioning eyes to her. She shyly, hesitantly touched his face again, her fingers lingering at his sensuously molded lips. Suddenly, Liane was consumed with the impulse to kiss him, to feel in reality what she'd only known in her mind before. She leaned over to cover the tiny distance between them.

Her mouth met his, and Karic went still, his breath trapped in his chest. Her soft lips, so sweet and tender, lightly brushed his. A thick, sensual haze engulfed Karic. He groaned and carefully deepened the union.

She didn't pull back, meeting his languorous kiss with a wilder one of her own. His mouth opened hungrily over hers, his tongue flicking over her lips, teasing, then urging her to part them. With a shuddering sigh Liane pressed closer, her mouth responding to his gentle probing.

Karic's mouth came down hard on hers then, his tongue thrusting inside to intimately explore her. Liane's heart pounded wildly. His tongue plunged in, then slowly retreated to plunge again and again. Her body, aching with a strange, fierce desire, arched against his, her breath coming in short, ragged little gasps.

Karic struggled with his wild passion, striving for some semblance of control. He knew he must be careful and gentle with her, prove to Liane in every way he could that he was capable of loving her with restraint and consideration. But his shaft, throbbing and hot, rose to press against that most intimate part of her.

Through the rioting mass of sensations, Liane was dimly aware of Karic's swollen sex. The touch of him triggered memories of another nocte, a nocte of degradation and pain, of savage lust and mindless bestiality.

She stiffened, wrenching her mouth from his. Twisting away, Liane pulled herself to a sitting position.

Shame, anger and bewilderment roiled through her as she wiped the taste and feel of him away with the back of her hand. She glared down at Karic with a flushed, hurt look.

"You can't help but be an animal, can you?" she whispered.

Karic lifted himself to one elbow, his face darkening. "Why? Because I responded to you like any male would? It was only a kiss, Liane."

"Yes," she said, her gaze momentarily sweeping past the hard evidence of his arousal, "but you were ready to mate with me again. If I'd let it go on a secundae longer . . ."

"I'd have lost control and raped you again?" Karic supplied the words Liane couldn't find the courage to utter. "You're wrong, Liane. I could have stopped anytime you asked.

156

"Oh, I'm not saying it wouldn't have been difficult," he said, noting the disbelief flaring to life in her eyes. "I want you, but normally I do have control. And I'd never do anything to hurt or frighten you. Haven't I demonstrated that again and again? Don't all those other times count for something, matter more than one nocte of madness?"

She lowered her head, her black mane of hair tumbling down to hide her face. "I—I don't know, Karic. You took so much from me. I don't know if I can ever forgive or forget that."

Dull, tormented eyes raised to his. "And you *do* frighten me. I can't help it, but it's true."

A sad smile touched Karic's lips, as his father's words came back to him. *Show her your human side—the gentle, tender lover. Show her patience and consideration.*

"Then what would you have me do?" he quietly demanded of her. "I don't want your fear but your trust—and maybe someday your friendship again. What must I do to win them?"

Confusion clouded her eyes. "I don't know, Karic. I don't know if I can ever be your friend again. But for now, please don't make me sleep with you. Please don't touch me. I know it complicates matters, but being near you like that only makes things worse, stirs memories I'd rather not remember. I need time, time to sort things out, time to adjust. Will you give it to me, Karic?"

He stared at her, a myriad of emotions flashing across his face. Pain, indecision and a look of smoldering desire flared then died, overcome by an expression of deep, aching tenderness. Finally, Karic sighed.

"I'll give you all the time you need, Liane," he

said, his voice hoarse with resignation, "even if that takes the rest of our lives. For all you've done, all you are to me, I owe you that much—that and so much more."

CHAPTER 9

THE NEXT FIVE SOLS PASSED IN A WHIRLWIND OF ACTIV-
ity as Liane was slowly introduced to her new home.
True to his word, Karic no longer slept with her,
making his pallet on the floor beside the bed. So
close, yet so far away, she would think as she gazed
down on his slumbering form nocte after nocte.
How could he sleep so soundly, Liane wondered,
while she spent each nocte in restless turmoil?

And Karic, listening to her tossing and turning,
lay awake as well. Only his supreme self-control held
in check the fires smoldering in his body. She had
asked for time. If the effort consumed him alive,
he'd give it to her. Yet, though the sols spent with
Liane eased some of his torment as she began to
relax a little, the noctes only stirred anew his
frustration and rising fear.

One nocte Karic awaited Liane outside their lair,

having offered to take her for a walk through the valley after supper. He stood there, anxiously anticipating her reaction to the bouquet of wildflowers he'd left on the bed. He didn't have long to wonder.

Even in the sun's fading light he could see her small, confused frown as she strode from the cave. Liane wasted no time in confronting him.

"Did you leave me the flowers?"

"Yes." His glance swept her tense face. "Did I displease you in doing so?"

"Yes . . . I mean, no," she stammered. "Why? Why did you do it?"

He smiled and shrugged. "Because you're a lovely femina and deserve beautiful things. I thought you'd like them."

"Thank you." Liane forced the words out. "They're . . . wonderful. But please, Karic, no more. Don't give me anymore flowers."

He scowled. "Why not? You act as if I offended you. I don't understand."

Liane hesitated. Too many people were about, and her next words might anger Karic. It was better if as few as possible were privy to their personal differences.

She grasped his arm. "Let's walk a ways, where there's more privacy."

Karic nodded. They were barely out of the most populated part of the valley, however, before he halted.

"What's wrong, Liane?"

She hesitated, dreading that her next words would stir the old pain anew. But Liane forced herself on. It was better he harbor no further illusions.

"I may be wrong," she began, "but I see the

flowers as an attempt to renew our friendship. Yet we can never be friends again, Karic. I told you before I'm afraid of you, can never fully trust you."

"I'm not an animal, Liane!" he growled. "And *I've* told *you* before that one nocte doesn't constitute—"

"Why do you persist in tormenting both of us?" she heatedly interjected. "Why can't you accept the fact that what was between us is over?"

"And why won't you listen to me? Let me explain?"

She blinked hard against the tears. "Because it won't change what happened, what you did to me. And because in some small part of me I *need* to hate you, if only a little, to keep the fire that is me alive.

"You almost broke my spirit that nocte." Liane forced herself to continue. "My hatred for you is the only thing that prevents me from shattering into a million pieces, never to be whole again.

"I'm sorry if that seems cruel or unfair," she whispered achingly, seeing the tormented look that burned in his eyes, "but it's all you left me, Karic. And I have to survive."

Powerful hands gripped her arms. "And do you know how that makes me feel?" Karic rasped. "Impotent, Liane. Helpless to do anything to make amends."

He gave her a small shake. "Don't you see what your hatred is doing? It not only punishes me but you as well. You've got to give it up. Let it die!"

A small, grim smile touched her lips. "And you forget I am Bellatorian. It's the only way we know how to fight."

Karic flung her away, as if she had suddenly burned him. "Curse your hard little Bellatorian heart!" he cried, his body rigid, his fists clenched at his side.

Liane quailed at the fury emanating from him, wondering at the control it took to keep Karic from striking out at her. She had deeply hurt him, but the realization gave her no pleasure. A strange kind of hatred, Liane mused, to cause pain and yet not wish to.

But she needed that emotion to protect her, to harden her heart. Her hatred and her fear of him were emotions so deep she dared not examine them. Liane shook aside the unsettling thought.

"Let it go, Karic," she said, forcing a semblance of reason into her voice. "Let it go. Please. You'll tear us both apart if you continue like this."

He threw back his head, his eyes clenched shut, his features a mask of tortured anguish. "I can't, Liane. I just can't!"

She sighed and gently took his hand, uncurling the strong, tightly fisted fingers to thread them through hers. "Then at least no more flowers, Karic. I can't bear them, not from you."

His eyes opened, brimming with tears. "If that's what you want."

"It is."

Karic's hand tightened in hers as he pulled her forward, back onto the tree-lined path they'd been walking. A heavy sense of desolation settled over him. She was determined to fight him every step of the way, he grimly realized, thwarting every attempt at reconciliation.

Fear entwined itself about his heart. Their chances for a life mating were slowly disintegrating. His father had told him to give Liane time, but time was inexorably slipping away.

Flame-haired Kalina was becoming a problem. Though a full-blooded Cat Woman, she did not possess the hirsuteness of the men, and her feline features were exotic and sensual. She was a beauty, incomparably lovely with her golden, almond-shaped eyes and lithe, graceful limbs, a beauty desired by all the young males, yet she wanted only Karic.

Before the mission to Primasedes, before he'd met Liane, Karic had accepted that he must eventually life mate with Kalina. Until he'd met Liane he'd thought Kalina a beautiful if shallow specimen of the fairer sex. Like Devra he'd enjoyed her delights, giving as much pleasure as he received, but never finding any need to give his heart.

Kalina certainly hadn't appeared to notice the lack of it. Possessing his body and eventual title was enough for her. At the time, that had seemed a fair trade to Karic—a lusty bed partner and beauteous mate, eventual mother of his heirs, for all the respect and advantages as Lady of the Cat People. A fair trade indeed—until Liane.

But Liane was different, a beguiling, an intriguing series of contrasts. The ever-developing facets of her personality captivated him. She was gentle goodness and wild spitfire, a courageously loyal friend and vulnerable beauty, trembling on the brink of passion's fulfillment. She alone had touched a tenderness and protectiveness he'd never known he possessed. And now, she was the only femina he'd ever take as mate.

Kalina, however, was just as determined that this would never be. She found ways to be with him at every opportunity, constantly interfering with Karic's efforts to introduce Liane to her new home. She was also the first to suspect that he and Liane weren't sleeping together.

Karic had just left the Council after horas spent in

fruitless discussion over what to do about the Guide. Most of the Elders were set against trying to destroy the machine and its inventors, fearing the risks too great. Since there seemed no possibility of it ever being utilized on anything but an individual scale, and as it had little power over Cat Men, they felt they were in no danger. The Elders saw no point in risking their own people for any of the other Agrican nations, who had only half-heartedly supported the war against Bellator before surrendering.

Though Karic and his father argued that the Guide's potential dangers were too great to be ignored, they were eventually voted down. Once again, the Cat Men's highly emotional nature had prevailed against logic. Too angry to bear another moment in the Council chambers, Karic had stalked out, not really caring where he was headed as long as it was as far away as possible from those narrow-minded, short-sighted old men. He walked until he reached the orchard of cerasa trees, then flung himself down against one of the gnarled trunks. For long secundae he sat there, furious and frustrated.

"And what has angered our young lord," a husky feminine voice gently inquired, "to make him frown so?"

Kalina slipped down beside him, a delicate, long-fingered hand sliding soothingly across his chest. Her musky scent wafted over Karic as she edged closer to press her body upon his. New sensations assailed him, scattering his anger on the freshened breeze that suddenly blew through the orchard. In spite of himself, his body responded to the sensuous female, cuddling so invitingly against him.

His anger ebbed, replaced by a delicious new

tension. For a moment Karic let himself savor it, closing his eyes and resting his head back against the tree. It felt so good to have a femina's hands on him again, hands that enjoyed the feel of him and wanted him. Kalina's fingers trailed lower, along the rippling muscles of his abdomen, slipping beneath his loincloth.

Karic's eyes snapped open. He quickly captured Kalina's hand and withdrew it. "No, femina," he softly said, "it cannot be."

"And why not?" she just as softly demanded. "You've enjoyed it before, were enjoying it even now. What harm is there in two healthy young animals mating?"

He returned her hand to her lap, his gaze steadily meeting hers. "Harm in letting you think there can ever be anything between us again. Harm in using you, when my heart desires another. And harm in betraying my commitment to her."

"What commitment?" Kalina snarled, enraged at his rejection. "You don't mate with her. Her scent is not on you and has never been since after that first sol you both arrived. And you never touch her when you're out together. So don't tell me there's anything of substance between you."

"We have things to work out, Kalina, but it changes nothing. I still mean to take her as life mate."

"And you're a fool if you think the Elders will allow it!" Her golden eyes glittered with a triumphant light. "Everyone has begun to talk about you two. That puny little Bellatorian doesn't even act as if she likes you, and the few times you've accidentally touched her, people have seen her pull away. There's talk it's your Cat's blood that disgusts her."

She paused to eye him consideringly. "Hardly

behavior befitting a mate of the heir to the throne, wouldn't you say?"

Karic fought against the surge of anger Kalina's words stirred in him, an anger tinged with the frustrating realization that her observations, at least in part, were true. Many were the times when Liane had recoiled from him, but he'd begun to suspect her reaction was more from fear of her own emotions than of him. But then perhaps that was his foolish heart misinterpreting everything.

Even more disturbing was the realization of how closely they were being watched, their interactions studied, and all of it to be collected as data for consideration when he came before the Council this very sol.

Kalina saw the uncertainty flicker in Karic's eyes. "You do her an unkindness to foster any hope of a life mating," she carefully pressed. "Better that you allow her to become acquainted with some of the other males, ones that the Council would favorably consider. Or else, if she desires no commitment for the time being, she might prefer to pick a temporary mate at the Festival."

The thought of Liane living with another male for the next three cycles, until the next Mating Festival, filled Karic with a wild rage. To give her up, to never know the pleasures of her body or her love, to watch another possess her, all that was more than he could bear. And what of his promise to her? He constantly had to endure the looks of recrimination, the bitter unhappiness everytime she looked at him.

"Both my brothers want her," Kalina silkily persisted. "Both good males, strong, brave and kind. Better to introduce her to them, allow her time to get to know them. It would ease her choice at the Festival."

Karic turned ravaged eyes to her. "I—I don't know."

Detecting the small chink in his determination, she quickly pursued her advantage. "You do her a disservice by selfishly keeping her at your side all the time. At least permit her the opportunity to make up her own mind. In the end, isn't her happiness of primary importance?"

Yes, her happiness means everything to me, Karic silently replied. But the thought of it not being with him was beyond comprehension, beyond bearing.

He had promised her so much—protection, as easy an introduction to life here as possible, the gratitude of his people. Yet the thing she most dreaded, a forced mating with a Cat Man, was becoming more and more of a reality. He wished he could just take her away from here to some safe place where she could begin her life anew, but that wasn't possible.

The laws of his people encompassed all who entered the valley, and once he'd brought Liane here that choice was no longer his to make. He was bound as firmly as she to the laws—hard laws, but laws necessary to their continued survival. Perhaps it *was* better to let her meet some of the other males. Perhaps there was one who'd appeal to her.

Karic sighed. "Your words have merit, Kalina. I'll give them consideration."

"Yes, give them consideration, Karic," she said as she rose to her feet, "but don't tarry too long. The Mating Festival will soon be here. She'll need time to make up her mind."

He watched Kalina disappear into the trees. Then Karic turned back to his increasingly morose thoughts, back to what to do about Liane.

* * *

"Please, Karic, I don't know if I can go through with this."

Karic turned from the carved wooden mural depicting the exploits of an ancient hero in the anteroom outside Council chambers to Liane standing nearby. Her eyes were wide with apprehension, and she could barely control the trembling that shook her. He gazed at her, never tiring of feasting his eyes upon her flawless, delicate beauty, nor of reminding himself of the goodness and determined courage that lay beneath.

He smiled at the doubt he heard in her voice and walked over. Though he yearned to take her into his arms and soothe away her fears, he held back. Instead, Karic contented himself with a wry grin.

"You bested the finest trackers Necator could send after us, rode over a waterfall and survived, and saved my life countless times," he gently teased her, "and now you say you're afraid of a group of old men? I can't believe that, Liane."

"But what will I say to your Council regarding this life mating? What do they want to hear?"

"Only what's in your heart," he replied, a soft glow lighting his compelling eyes.

Her hand tightly clasped his arm. Fear etched taut lines into her finely carved face. "But that's just it, Karic. I'm so confused. I don't know what's in my heart."

He tenderly stroked her cheek and was inordinately pleased when she didn't draw back. "Remember what we've been through," he whispered. "Remember the good times we've shared, and try, as best you can, to forget that nocte. Perhaps then you'll find the answers you need."

Footsteps squelched Liane's reply. Their gazes

turned to that of an old Cat Man, one of the Elders.

"It is time for the femina," he solemnly intoned.

Liane swung her gaze back to Karic. His lips curved into a beautiful smile, encouraging her, as he gently pried her fingers loose from his arm. He turned her toward the Elder.

"Go, Liane," his deep voice prodded. "Listen to your heart. The truth will follow."

Karic watched her leave, the brave comfort of his words turning back to mock him. He had told her to follow her heart, not even truly knowing what was in it. Though he didn't believe, as she stubbornly claimed, that she hated him, he doubted she felt any real affection for him—at least not enough to convince the Council.

And indeed, what would the Council ask? As heir to the throne he was permitted to sit in with them and offer his opinions on issues of state, but his youth and own inexperience in matters of the heart precluded life mating decisions. Though he knew his feelings when it came to Liane, Karic faced his own questioning with no small amount of trepidation. What would she find to say? Would her words condemn them both?

He angrily brushed aside the doubts. There was nothing more he could do, save tell the truth when his time came and hope Liane's words corroborated them. Tell the truth and hope the Council would have the insight and wisdom to see the love he had for her.

Liane followed the Elder down a tunnel into a large chamber lit by perpetual flames. A long table, flanked on its far side by 11 men, stood alone in the room. Her glance scanned the assemblage, coming to rest on Karic's father. She shot him a look of wild entreaty. He smiled back, his eyes warm with encouragement.

How like Karic he is, Liane thought, and felt strangely comforted. She inhaled a steadying breath and swung her gaze back to encompass the whole group.

"I have come, my lords, as you have bidden," she said, her voice ringing, clear and proud, in the hollow stone chamber. "What is it you wish to know?"

Admiration flared in Morgan's eyes. "Why do you want to life mate with my son?" he asked without further preamble.

Liane faltered at the directness of the question. What could she say that would please a father, a father who cared deeply for his son's happiness yet must also consider her fitness to be his mate? He, above all, had the right to hear the truth.

Liane swallowed hard. "What femina in this lair would not want Karic as mate? He is brave, strong and good. It—it would be an honor to be his."

Morgan's eyes narrowed, and his gaze seemed to pierce to the depths of her soul. "An honor for most, perhaps, but what about you? Do you love my son?"

A guilty flush crept into her cheeks. He knew, but then how could he not know, living in the same lair with them? But how could she tell him, admit to all the Elders, that she didn't love Karic? How could she tell them about that nocte, when his crazed violence had broken her heart and turned her against him forever?

"No, my lord," Liane quietly forced the words out, "I respect but do not love him."

"Do you think you ever can?"

Liane shifted uneasily. Why, oh why, did he

persist in this? What did he want from her? The answer suddenly struck her. He wanted what any parent would want for their child—happiness, a mate who loved them. But she could never be that mate, and she doubted she'd ever bring Karic much happiness.

She shook her head. "I don't think so, my lord. Too much has come between us for that."

The Lord of the Cat People sighed and leaned back in his chair. "I am sad to hear that, femina."

He gestured to the others. "I have my answers. Do any of you wish to ask any?"

A gray-maned Elder with cold blue eyes shook his head. "I think I speak for the rest in saying she has more than answered our questions. Karic deserves better."

He made a motion to dismiss her. "You may leave—"

Anger surged through Liane at the abruptness of her dismissal. "One moment, my lords. Will you make your decision based solely on my responses? What of Karic's desires in this? *He* wants me as life mate. Don't his needs matter?"

An irate growl emanated from the group, but Morigan quickly silenced them. He cocked his head.

"You just said you could never love my son. Why should his desires matter to you?"

"He feels a debt to me, and his need to protect me runs deep. I think it would tear him apart if he couldn't do that. I don't want to see that happen."

The hint of a smile touched the Lord of the Cat People's lips. "So, you would sacrifice yourself for him, would you?"

She shook her head. "Nothing quite that noble,

my lord. I have lost all that matters and have nowhere else to go. I have no wish to mate with anyone, but if it must be so, I'd want it to be with Karic."

"So you'd willingly breed with him? Give him children?"

Liane's heart began a dull, heavy thumping. Tell the truth Karic had said. She returned his probing stare with a defiant one of her own.

"If he gave me no other choice, yes, I would."

Morigan's mouth tightened. A clever answer, femina, he thought. A clever answer, indeed, for you and I both know Karic would never force himself upon you. But even so, there's a strong attraction between you two, an attraction you most stubbornly deny but an attraction to be reckoned with, nonetheless. But will it be enough to overcome the hurt and misunderstanding? I wonder.

He stood up. "Be assured Karic's wishes will be considered in this matter. You have my oath on that." He motioned to an alternate tunnel. "You may go, femina."

This time Liane didn't protest the dismissal. There was nothing more to say. She left the chamber with a heavy heart, convinced she'd ruined any chance for a life mating.

I should be happy that soon I won't have to endure Karic's presence any longer, Liane fiercely told herself as she headed down the tunnel that led to the outside. I should be relieved, but I'm not. What have I traded but one existence with a man I know for another with some stranger? And life here would seem strangely empty without Karic.

She reached the sunlight and ran straight for the lair she now considered home. She ran until she reached Karic's bedchamber and crawled up onto his bed. There, she'd wait, until he came for her.

Karic eyed the assemblage of Elders. Their expressions, to a man, were inscrutable. He looked at his father, and Morigan stared back.

"I am here, my lords," Karic began, resigning himself to the fact he'd gain little information regarding the outcome of Liane's interview if the Elders didn't wish to share it. "What would you know from me?"

"Why have you come here to request another, when you should be asking for Kalina instead?" Gerlic, Kalina's uncle, began. "It was long ago decided this was the cycle you would life mate with her."

Karic riveted his attention on the older man. "Decided by others, not me. I've never asked the Council for anything. Have I not the right to ask it now?"

"You have that right," Morigan said. He sternly glanced at Gerlic. "Karic's betrothal to Kalina is not the issue unless he cares to address it. There is time for that later."

Morigan turned to the others. "Proceed with your questions."

"The femina spoke of a debt you owe her," another Elder inquired. "What is that debt, and how far would you go to repay it?"

"She saved my life four times, twice with her healing powers, once when she turned against the Atroxes to rescue me and then on the nocte of the triple moons, when she came to me and I took her to save myself. When I was weakened by the Bellatorian tortures she could have forced her mind seek and torn the secret of our hiding place from me, knowing full well she would have killed me in the process. But she didn't. Even then, before she hardly knew me, she knew that would be wrong. But in making that decision Liane turned on her own kind. She cannot go back; they would kill her."

A grim smile twisted Karic's lips. "And now, knowing this, need you ask how far I would go to repay my debt—our debt—to her? I would give her my life."

"And does that life include a life mating?"

Karic nodded.

"And what of the Council's decision not to further dilute your blood?" Gerlic snarled. "Does that not matter to you?"

"In one sense I deeply regret it," Karic calmly replied, "but in another, I accept it as a hard reality of our existence. And, accepting that, why should I be punished as no other Cat Man has, by being denied the femina I love?"

"You are the heir."

"Does that preclude the consideration of my own needs? My happiness? I wish only for the right to choose my mate, not turn our world upside down."

"But she has all but admitted she doesn't want you, doesn't love you," Kalina's uncle persisted. "A lifetime of unrequited passion can be an eternity."

Karic turned toward his father who sadly nodded his agreement.

Anguish momentarily slashed through Karic and was gone. What had he expected her to say? At least now he knew what her replies had been.

"Feminas don't always love us at the start," he said, turning back to Gerlic and the others. "It was that way for many Cat Men, my father included. Why should it be any different for me?"

A murmur of agreement rose from the other

men. Karic pressed his advantage. "Liane is beautiful and strong. She will bear fine heirs. She is good and brave; all that she has done for me bears witness to that. She will be a wonderful mother. And she cared enough for the welfare of our people to willingly sacrifice all she held dear. Will her commitment, her dedication to us be any less, now that she lives among us? I think not."

He paused, as if to give further emphasis to his words. "What more could you want in a life mate for the heir to the throne? What more is wanting?"

"An assurance she will breed with you." Morigan's voice, steel-edged and commanding, reverberated throughout the Council chamber.

Karic stared at his father, disbelief widening his eyes.

"Liane's qualities are beyond dispute," the Lord of the Cat People continued in a quieter voice, "but in the end she is not a fitting mate unless she gives you heirs. Even you, my son, must fulfill your duty of procreation. It is the law, a law without which we cannot survive."

Something shattered inside Karic, squeezing the breath from his body and twisting his heart. His father had betrayed him, had used the information he'd given in confidence to turn it against him—now, when he'd needed his help most of all. And what could he say? To give his word now would negate the promise he'd made to Liane. Yet to not give it would only free her to be claimed by another.

Karic slowly shook his head. "I cannot give that oath until I've spoken with her."

"And how will that change anything?" Morigan gently prodded. "If she says no, you'll still be forced to make the decision for her. Liane must breed, whether it be with you or another. It is the law."

Wrath darkened Karic's eyes. "And you make it sound so simple. You, who have not given her your word! You, who won't have to see the pain or the look of betrayal on her face!"

Morgan leaned back in his chair. "I've seen it on yours, just now when I revealed your confidence to me. But I did it anyway, because I had to. Why should your dilemma be any less? You're my heir." His tone hardened. "You'll have to pay the price for that sooner or later."

Karic stared into his father's eyes and saw his resolve. Morgan had made his decision, however difficult it might have been. Now, he must make his.

The memory of Kalina's words drifted, unbidden, into his mind—*permit her the chance to get to know my brothers, make up her own mind. If you really care for her, isn't her happiness of primary importance?*

It seemed any chance for Liane's happiness was slowly slipping away, as both of them were dragged deeper and deeper into the complexities of life and law. There were so few choices left to either of them.

Bitterness, acrid and burning, filled his heart at the realization of his betrayal. He'd given her his word and now must break it. And break it he would, for she at least deserved to choose her own mate.

Karic's jaw hardened. His eyes smoldered with a fierce, inner intensity as he glared back at his father. "I told you once and I'll tell you again. I will not force myself on her. She is free to take her own mate at the Festival. I withdraw my petition for a life mating."

Not awaiting a dismissal, Karic turned and stalked from the room.

* * *

He stood there in the bedchamber before Liane even heard him, his face in shadows. She couldn't see his expression, but his eyes, like dying embers, were bleak and anguished.

She quashed the tide of despair that swept over her. The answer was there, smoldering in his gaze, before she even asked it.

"They refused you, didn't they?"

"No. I withdrew my petition."

Shock tore through her. "Wh—what did you say?"

"I withdrew my petition for a life mating."

"But why? Why would you do that, after you promised to protect me?"

"I can't protect you anymore, Liane. The Council was determined that you mate with some male in this lair. I had to decide between my vow to spare your becoming a breeder or forcing myself upon you."

"How very hard that must have been," she softly mocked him. "And which one did you so kindly choose for me?"

He shot her a raw look. "You made your feelings about mating with me quite evident. I thought, therefore, to at least give you a choice as to your future mate. Our Mating Festival will occur in less than a monate. Those who do not choose to life mate take a temporary mate for three cycles. It can be a trial life mating, if you will, or one that ends with the femina free to choose another."

Karic gave a bitter laugh. "In a society so short of breeding females, it's one advantage the feminas have over the males. We are chosen, not they."

"A small consolation, indeed," Liane muttered, "when one doesn't want to mate."

"It's all I have left to give you."

"*Give* me?" The words were whispered, but the tone was scathing. "When have you ever given me anything, you cursed, black-hearted liar? All you've done is take from me, torn my life apart until I've absolutely nothing left! I hate you! Oh, how I wish I'd killed you instead of the Atroxes!"

Karic turned and walked over to the weapons hung on the wall above his clothes chest. Taking down a dagger he strode back and offered it, handle first, to Liane. She looked from it to him, confused.

"What is this?" Liane asked suspiciously.

"It seems I can keep so few of my promises to you, but this one I will. You still have the right to kill me. I'll not stop you. Have your revenge."

She eyed it warily. "Don't give it to me, Karic. I swear if I get it in my hands—"

"Take it, Liane!" he ordered in a hoarse, violent whisper. "You'll be doing me a kindness, putting an end to my pain."

"Pain?" she demanded incredulously. "Tell me, Karic, what kind of pain could you possibly be feeling?"

"The pain of wanting you," he gasped, "and of never being able to have you."

"But you *have* had me. Don't you remember?"

With a wild look he shoved the dagger into her hand, curling her stiff fingers around the handle. Then he pulled the knife forward, until the blade's point was pressed against his abdomen.

"Do it, Liane. Now!"

The secundae ticked by in the tension-fraught room, Liane battling with the emotions roiling within her, Karic with eyes clamped shut, awaiting the death thrust. Her gaze swept over his face, noting the anguished features, so striking, so beautifully handsome even now.

With a heartrending cry Liane flung the dagger across the room, the blade clattering against the far wall. "For whatever remorse you may be feeling I'll not spare you even a secundae's pain!" she hoarsely lashed out, desperately grasping for any words that would hurt him, would ease some of her own torment. "Remember that, Karic, when I lie naked beneath another male, his hard, sweating body thrusting into mine! Remember then, and every sol of your life, that I hate you—and that I'll never, *ever* be yours!"

CHAPTER 10

KARIC COULDN'T TAKE ANYMORE. HE STRODE FROM the bedchamber, nearly slamming into his father who stood in the darkened tunnel just outside.

The torment, the accusation burning in his son's eyes was almost more than Morigan could bear. The ragged rasp of Karic's breathing filled the otherwise silent tunnel. Morigan's grip tightened on his son's arms.

"Karic," he began. "I am sorry—"

"Don't say anything," Karic growled. "I trusted you, and you betrayed me to them. If it had only been me I might have forgiven you, but I'll never forgive what it's done to Liane."

He pulled free and stalked away, out of their lair and across the valley to a far hiding place to lick his wounds like some injured animal—wounds that had been clawed into his heart with each word that had fallen from Liane's lips, wounds that might never, ever heal.

A soft wail from the bedchamber drifted to Morigan's ears. He tensed, as the sound became one of sobbing. With a deep sigh, he turned and walked back to the living area to await Liane.

It was several horas before she left the bedchamber, her eyes still red and swollen from her weeping. She gave a start when she saw Karic's father sitting at the table, pouring himself a cup of red liquid from a flask. Liane took a steadying breath and walked over to him.

He raised the flask as she neared the table. "Would you consider sharing some uva wine? You look like you could use a cup or two."

She nodded and slid into a chair.

Morigan poured a drink and passed it over to her. He watched Liane sip the liquid. Finally, he laid a gentle hand on her arm.

Liane glanced up at him.

"It's my fault, you know." Remorse darkened his green-gold eyes.

A frown marred the smooth expanse of her brow. "Your fault? I don't understand, my lord."

"I knew of Karic's promise not to mate with you against your will. I used it against him."

"And why do you tell me this?" she warily asked.

"Because I interfered where I shouldn't have, and now you two have been driven even further apart."

She gave a brittle laugh. "It doesn't matter. It would have happened anyway. He's lied to me from the start."

Morigan's grip tightened on her arm. "No, he hasn't, Liane. I know my son. The promises he made may have been unrealistic, but they were made in

181

good faith. Our laws of procreation are powerful, as well they should be. They allow little individual choice."

"They are cruel and evil."

He sighed ruefully at the agonized vehemence in her voice. "No more evil than your planet's attempts to wipe us out. Though at times hard and arbitrary, we try to temper them as best we can with human insight and understanding. Hence, the involvement of the Council in determining the life matings."

"Yes, I see how understanding your Council is," she mockingly replied. "But then, perhaps it was all Karic's idea. Perhaps it was his way of escaping a life mating he had no stomach for."

Morigan shook his head. "No. Despite the unreasonable terms you placed upon him, he was determined to see it through. It was I who wouldn't allow it."

Anger burned in Liane's eyes. "And why should it have concerned you? It was between Karic and me!"

"No, Liane, your refusal to mate with my son concerns us all. Your breeding abilities are priceless. We cannot afford to squander even one femina. According to their capabilities, all must give us children. They are the future, our only hope of survival."

"And where does that leave me?" she cried, jerking her arm from his clasp. "You speak of me as if I'm some walking womb. You are no better than my people. In your own way, you have cold-bloodedly subjugated an entire sex, bending them to your will, depreciating them until they're little more than a reproductive organ."

"Perhaps," Morigan sighed, "but at least we allow love to temper it all. Most life mates here have strong affections, if not love, for each other. I think that is why Karic gave you the chance to choose your own mate. You know he cares for you and wanted to keep you for himself."

"He wants my body and nothing more," Liane cried, terrified of her own fragile emotions, much less what Karic might be feeling.

"Do you really think that's all he wants, Liane?" Morigan gently prodded. "That is far from the truth, a truth that you, in your anger against Karic and our laws, are too blind to see."

He thoughtfully stroked his chin. "As the lair's newest femina, you will have first choice of all the males at the Festival. Karic will be one of them."

For an instant Liane nearly leapt at the small ray of hope Morigan seemed to offer, but it was no solution for her. Karic didn't have to force these circumstances upon them. He could have taken her away with him to a place where they both would have been safe and happy. But he had made his choice, no matter how difficult it might have been, and his choice had been for his people.

She leaned forward, forcing a look of amused disbelief onto her face. "And are you suggesting that I solve all our problems by choosing Karic? How would that help? I'd still refuse to mate with him."

"There are ways to ensure your compliance, if not active participation, until you learn to accept things. Fortunately, we rarely have to use them."

Horror widened Liane's eyes. "You would force me?"

"There are drugs, ones that act quite gently and leave no lasting effects."

"Karic would never allow it," she whispered, desperation causing her to pluck at any possibility. "He gave me his word."

"That commitment ended when he agreed to permit you to choose your own mate. He is not above the law."

Liane's head lowered, her tousled mane of ebony hair falling forward to hide her face. "I have nothing then."

Morgan rose from the table. "You have the choice of a mate. There are many fine young males here, both full and half-blooded. I suggest you start giving them consideration."

Deep blue eyes rose to carefully study him. "And how do you propose I go about that?"

An uneasy relief swept through Morgan. Had she finally accepted her fate, or was this some ploy to buy her further time? It didn't matter. Time was quickly ebbing away for the Bellatorian beauty.

"There are twenty sols left until the Festival. I'll send four or five males to you every sol until then. Spend time with each and get to know them. Perhaps it'll ease your eventual decision."

A distant look gleamed in Liane's eyes. Karic had said the Bellatorian feminas captured in the past had never tried to escape, that they'd always found happiness in their new life. Considering that, surely the guards at the lair's outposts would never be looking for a lone femina sneaking away. She'd show Karic. She'd show them all. She'd escape.

"Yes, my lord, perhaps it will." Liane paused. "One thing more. Until the Festival, is there somewhere else I may live? I cannot bear being around Karic just now."

He thought for a moment. "There's an old healer

184

who lives at the far end of the valley. She's very independent and opinionated, but she might be willing to take you in. Would that be suitable?"

Yes, most suitable, Liane grimly thought. She'd be away from everyone's close scrutiny which would only ease her plans for escape. Liane nodded. "Yes. Will you ask Karic to stay away?"

Morigan gave a sad nod. "Yes, femina. He'll stay away."

"Good. How soon can I move in with her?"

"We can go there now. Gather your things."

Liane sprang up from the table and ran from the room.

Morigan was glad Karic hadn't been there to witness the eagerness of her response. Her actions puzzled him. Were Liane's emotions really as shallow as they appeared, or was there something else motivating her?

Well, whatever it was, she was sure to reveal it in time. In her own way Liane was as strong-willed and headstrong as his son. Small wonder their relationship was as tempestuous as it was.

For the next eight sols Liane busied herself with the appearance of settling into the small cave of Agna and receiving the seemingly endless stream of ardent suitors who presented themselves. Most were very healthy, virile young specimens, and many of them, even some of the full-bloods, Liane found attractive. But she caught herself comparing each one to Karic, and each paled in comparison. For all the hurt he'd caused her, she begrudgingly admitted, he was still a man among men.

Blessedly, she was spared the discomfort of seeing him. The old healer's cave was set far away from the main part of the lair, and Karic never ventured out to visit her. Liane didn't know whether to be thankful she was spared the pain of his presence or hurt that he'd so easily cast her off.

There were times when she felt so confused she wanted to scream out her frustration. Karic had raped her, body and soul, but she still felt so drawn to him.

He was a monster within a man's body, Liane repeatedly reminded herself, a savage beast awaiting the next opportunity to show himself. Yet why were the noctes so long and lonely without him? Sometimes only her determined resolve to escape kept her from weeping her heart out.

After much surreptitious study, Liane had found a minor flaw in the security of the valley. At dusk the guards changed. The outpost at her end of the valley was the first to be emptied and the last to be refilled with fresh reinforcements. With any luck, she'd have a half hora to slip past that post before the new guard arrived. She began to hide extra food. On the morrow, Liane decided, a safe twelve sols from the Mating Festival, she would make her escape.

Aside from the young males, Liane had few visitors that sol. Kalina was one of them. Filled with uneasiness by the presence of a female who still regarded her as a rival for Karic, Liane lay down the spoon she was using to stir an herbal potion for old Agna and stood up.

"What do you think of my two brothers, Arlen and Cardow?" Kalina bluntly inquired, getting right to the point.

Liane's memory quickly flitted over the myriad of faces she'd met in the past eight sols. Glancing at Kalina's distinctive red tresses, she recalled two young males with similar hair coloring. They had said they were brothers.

She wrinkled her brow in concentration. "I remember them, but was Arlen the oldest or was it Cardow?"

"Cardow," Kalina smilingly supplied. "Did either of them suit your fancy? They are both quite taken with you."

Liane's mind raced, grasping for some tactful way out of an increasingly uncomfortable situation. "I found them both attractive. They seemed kind."

"Either would gladly take you as mate. Are you considering them?"

"Perhaps."

Kalina's gaze narrowed. "Karic is mine, you know. Since childhood, we have been betrothed as life mates."

A sensation, strangely like that of anger, began to roil in Liane's belly. But why was she angry? She didn't want Karic. Why should she care with whom he mated? She quashed the unsettling feeling.

"I know, Kalina." Liane forced a stiff smile. "I hope you'll be happy."

The Cat Woman smugly nodded. "Oh, we will. Have no doubt about that. I know how to please Karic. We've been lovers for several cycles now."

"How wonderful for you."

Kalina frowned at the heavy sarcasm. "I just wanted you to know. The Mating Festival draws near. It could be very dangerous for any femina who attempted to choose him."

I won't even be there to challenge your claim, Liane silently replied to Kalina's departing back. In twelve sols I'll be far away from this lair, headed for a life of my own where neither Necator nor Karic can ever find me. With a sigh, Liane returned to the concoction she was making for the old healer.

"Son, it's time we talked. I can't bear the animosity between us a moment longer."

Karic glanced up from the ancient book he'd been trying to read. He couldn't seem to concentrate on anything anymore. He shoved the volume aside on the table and subjected his father to a cool, appraising look.

"There's no animosity. You are Lord. Even I must obey. You once said I might have to choose between our people and Liane. Well, I chose to obey our laws; I chose our people. I hope you're proud, for I've been the dutiful son and heir."

Morgan sank down in the chair opposite him. "No one said it was easy being a ruler. Hard decisions must be made, decisions that must benefit the majority over the individual. I tried to instill that knowledge in you all the cycles you were growing. Did I fail so miserably?"

Karic's gaze lowered to his clenched hands. "No, Father, you didn't fail. Our people must come first. But I can't trust you anymore."

A sad, bitter smile played upon his lips. "I can never confide in you again for fear you might use the information against me."

Morgan leaned forward, an anguished look on his face. "Karic, you know I love you and only have your best interests at heart."

"There is nothing more important than Liane!" his son rasped. "I love her, but . . ." He sighed. "It doesn't matter. It's over, and perhaps for the better. I only pray she finds a male she can come to love. In time, I think I could find peace in that."

"Yes," his father agreed, "it would ease the pain for all of us. I am trying, you know, by sending the young males to meet her."

Karic momentarily stiffened, then forced himself to relax. "They are treating her with respect?"

"You know they are."

"Where is she?"

"Living with old Agna."

A grim smile twisted Karic's lips. "Is she faring well?"

"She seems so. Agna is teaching her some of her healing secrets. Liane shows a talent for it."

Karic leaned back in his chair and exhaled a deep breath. "Yes, she would. Perhaps it'll ease her way here. We need a healer, and when old Agna passes . . ."

Morigan nodded. "Those were my thoughts, too."

He hesitated, as if considering his next words. "You know, Karic, all may not be lost. Perhaps this time apart might work to your advantage. Liane will have ample opportunity to calmly think things through and perhaps even realize the extent of her feelings, as she meets and compares the other males to you."

"That's a wild dream, Father. The odds are greater she'll find a male who attracts her fancy."

"Nonetheless, I planted the idea in her head. I truly believe she feels something for you, but so much has happened to come between you, I think she's still confused and frightened. Give her time, Karic."

Karic's expression hardened. "I'd have given her all the time she needed, Father, if I had been given the opportunity to do so."

A flush darkened Morigan's face. "But I inter-

189

fered, is that what you're saying? No, Karic. In the end, it changed nothing. After you left the Council chambers, I was the only Elder who didn't agree that a life mating between you and Liane was impossible."

"And why was that?"

"Gerlic was adamant that you be required to honor your betrothal to Kalina. The rest of the Council was mainly concerned about the dilution of the bloodlines. They were only willing to postpone your life mating with Kalina for a few cycles to allow you time with Liane."

"That was generous of them," Karic muttered. "How do you feel about their decision?"

Morgan smiled. "About the dilution of our blood or about Kalina? Kalina's a lovely femina, if a bit calculating. She will bear fine heirs. But the choice is still yours for a time. And about the dilution of our blood? Well, we may never regain a strain of pure Cat bloodlines again. Even if we did, it would take hundreds of cycles. We've been manipulative enough with our breeding laws. I think it's an impossible task."

Karic laughed. "How ironic that the Council would permit Liane to choose me at the Mating Festival, yet not allow us to life mate. A child could come as easily from a temporary mating as from a permanent one."

"Yes," his father agreed, "but only an heir to the throne comes from a life mating. A fine point, but an important one."

"I'd take her anyway I could get her, cycle after cycle, even if the Council always deemed it a temporary mating," Karic rasped.

He shot his father a mocking look. "But then that, too, would be inappropriate conduct for an heir to the throne. You'd have to find some way to circumvent me, wouldn't you?"

Morigan considered his son. "Eventually, yes, but I'd not deny you a time with her. And who knows? It might be long enough to convince the Council to favorably reconsider the life mating. I would assist you with that in every way I could."

A flicker of hope flared in Karic's eyes. "Would you, Father? I'd like to be able to trust you in this."

"You know I would. My only concern has been Liane's refusal to breed with you. If she gave you children, you would receive my full approval. I would then use all my power to convince the Council to favorably reconsider your request."

Morigan rose and walked over to the side table that held a flask of uva wine and cups. "Let's drink to the future and the hope it brings."

Karic watched his father pour out two cups, then return to hand him one. Yes, he thought, let's drink to the future and its hope of eventual happiness. But the future will soon be upon us in a Mating Festival but twelve sols away. I only pray there's still enough time.

Liane handed the baby back to its mother and glanced up at the sun as it edged behind the mountains. Only a few horas more and she'd be on her way. Following Agna's instructions, she carefully explained the care of the child's infected foot to its mother, then handed her a small packet of healing powder which, when sprinkled into an inflamed wound, worked miracles. She'd regret not staying long enough to learn how to prepare it.

With a sigh, Liane walked over to dish up the supper meal, while Agna finished with another patient. The old woman soon joined her, easing her arthritic limbs down onto a nearby stool. They ate in silence, then afterwards shared a cup of herbal tea.

"You've a talent for the healing," Agna finally said. "My time is short, but I'd teach you all I know. The lair will need a healer when I pass."

Guilt surged through Liane at the deception she must live, but even the satisfactions of a life of healing couldn't ease the certainty of forced mating. She glanced up from her cup and managed a smile.

"I'm grateful for all you've taught me, Agna, as well as for your kindness in allowing me to stay with you."

"You've had a difficult transition to our ways," the old woman kindly said. "Has meeting the young males helped your decision any? Have you found one that attracts you?"

"No." Liane sighed. "They're all quite kind and handsome, mind you," she hastened to add, "but there's not enough time to get to know them or allow an affection to develop." She shuddered. "And the thought of mating with a virtual stranger . . ."

"I can give you a potion for that first nocte, one that would make your mate seem like one you loved. Would you like that, child?"

A look of such unutterable anguish passed across Liane's face that Agna sucked in her breath. She laid a hand on Liane's arm.

"What is it, child? Have you a pain somewhere? Tell me, and I will heal it."

"There is no potion for what I suffer, Agna, no cure except time." She forced a bright smile onto her face. "It doesn't matter. I will be fine."

Sharp old eyes scrutinized her. "It's the young lord, isn't it? His memory pains you still."

"It doesn't matter," Liane said in a strangled whisper, her head dipping like some wilted flower on its stem. "It's over. I must learn to live with it."

"Must you? Why not talk to him?"

Agna hobbled over to the fire to refill her cup of tea, then returned to sit beside Liane. "Listen to the words of an old woman who has lived a full and satisfying life. I had a mate who I loved until the sol he died, over twenty cycles ago. He fathered our four children, three of whom died in the massacre. Ours was a passionate, tempestuous mating."

She smiled softly. "Ah, the mating. It was hot and wild and oh, so loving. Not that we didn't have our battles. Yet we loved each other enough to work through our differences. And I tell you again, child. Talk to the young lord. There is still time to work things out."

"No!" Liane's head jerked up, a fierce determination blazing in her eyes. "He has betrayed me. It's far too late to work things out."

"When you love, it's never too late." Agna stiffly rose and relieved Liane of her empty cup. "Remember that, child."

Liane watched the old woman totter away, puzzled at her words. Agna's tale had touched her tender heart, but Liane knew she didn't love Karic. She'd be mad to love a man who'd treated her as Karic had. Granted, she had once thought she loved him, but that was over—dead. It was as dead as her Sententian powers, as mutilated as her maidenhood. No, she didn't love Karic.

Yet why did the thought of leaving the valley without saying good-bye to him cause such pain? Why should it matter that she'd never, ever see him again? He had betrayed her, lied to her, used her.

She must always remember that in these passing moments of weakness and stir her anger. It would give her strength for what lay ahead.

Liane watched the sun set behind the mountains in a brilliant display of crimson and gold. Then, with a weary sigh, she left Agna's tiny lair and walked into the trees where she'd hidden her supplies. It was time to leave.

It was difficult traveling through the mountains, even in the light of the full moons. She had changed into the tunic, breeches and boots she'd worn on her initial journey to the lair, but even dressed in those unencumbering clothes, Liane found the frequent climbing and sliding down steep inclines difficult. Soon she was dirty, her clothing torn in several places, her hands sore and abraded. There was no time, though, to worry over such things. Speed was of the essence.

She tried, as best she could, to travel north through the remaining mountains. Her initial destination was the large mining camp of Fodina, nestled in the foothills. There she hoped to find work for a time, long enough to afford to restock her supplies.

Then she'd set out across the high plains to the farmlands and the large city of Lyrae. She hoped to discover a new life there, far from Karic and even farther from Primasedes and Necator's evil clutches. Someday, if she were fortunate, she might even be able to find a way back to Bellator.

It was a difficult and dangerous plan, but it gave Liane hope and a sense of purpose. She would not look too far ahead or the potential problems would be too daunting. Better to break it into easily attainable steps, and the first one was to get through the mountains to Fodina.

As she struggled over rock-strewn paths and precipitous turns, Liane wondered if anyone would be sent after her. One way or another they wouldn't discover her absence until solrise, when Agna always came into her bedchamber to rouse her. More time would then probably be wasted searching the valley, for Liane had been careful to make her bed look as if she'd recently slept in it. She had left most of her belongings behind as well.

No, her plan had been well thought-out to buy as much time as possible. Now it was up to her to gain as great a lead as possible. Her trackers, if they came, would be skilled and swift. She had to make it to the safety of Fodina. It was too large and heavily guarded for the Cat Men to dare enter, especially not for just a solitary femina.

For a fleeting instant, Liane wondered if Karic would be one of the trackers sent out after her. He alone might attempt to find a way into Fodina to bring her out. The thought frightened her. The fear that he might succeed warred with an ever greater fear of the danger to him in trying.

With a fierce effort she quashed the unsettling emotions. She couldn't spare any energy worrying about him. She needed all she had for herself.

Solrise found Liane not quite as far as she hoped she'd be and much more tired than she had anticipated. The trail had been primitive, and she had lost valuable time negotiating it. She had hoped for a few horas of sleep to refresh herself, but knew now she couldn't spare it. She forced herself to go on.

About midsol she reached a small mountain stream, coursing merrily through a rockbed. She paused there for a short while to refill her water flask and refresh herself. She looked up to the top of the next peak, barren and windswept. It was all that separated her from Fodina. Finally, she shouldered her pack and headed out.

Dusk was filtering through the mountains when she reached the top of the peak. Liane paused, exhausted. Down below, perhaps a half sol journey, were the lights of the Fodina mining camp. She knew it was too dangerous to travel on in her weary condition and the rapidly fading light. From her vantage point, the path down the mountain looked treacherous. Better she find a safe place to hide and set out again at first light. Surely any trackers would not catch up with her by then.

As she stood there, surveying the area for a cave or rock outcropping to find shelter under, a high-pitched wailing drifted to her ears. It was quickly snatched away on the rising breeze, then came again. Liane froze.

She glanced up. There, even then turning into a headlong dive, was a deadly rapax. And it was plummeting straight toward her.

CHAPTER 11

KARIC SPENT A RESTLESS NOCTE. HE'D DRIFT OFF INTO fitful slumber only to be jerked awake. Something was amiss. He sensed it. Finally, several horas before solrise, he rose.

Though Karic knew he shouldn't be in the vicinity of Liane just now, something compelled him toward old Agna's lair. His presence would only upset her, but he couldn't seem to help himself. Something was wrong. The closer Karic drew, the stronger he felt something was wrong with Liane.

He halted in front of the healer's cave, his heart thudding, his mouth gone dry. The closeness to Liane was nearly palpable. To catch just one glimpse of her, even if asleep, would be enough, he told himself. It would still the niggling fears. Then he'd leave, as silently as he'd come.

Karic crept into the cave, knowing neither Liane nor Agna would ever hear him. Though the old

197

healer was full-blooded, her hearing had weakened with age, and Liane's ears weren't Cat-sensitive. He followed one tunnel off the main room and found Agna, sleeping soundly. Returning to the main room, he quickly headed to where he now knew Liane must be.

The bed was empty. Karic glanced around the room. Liane wasn't there. He stepped closer to examine the bed. It was mussed, the furs flung aside, as if she'd left it but a few moments ago. Karic felt the spot where her body had lain. It was cold, the scent of her weak. She hadn't slept in her bed.

With a low curse, Karic stalked back into Agna's bedchamber. He gently shook her awake.

"Agna, where is Liane?" he demanded, when the old woman groggily sat up, rubbing the sleep from her eyes.

For an instant Agna just stared at him, not quite believing the Lord of the Cat People's son was standing there. She blinked once, twice, and the image remained. It was he.

"Wh—what are you doing here, my lord?" she croaked. "Is someone ill?"

"No," he said impatiently. "Where is Liane? She's not in her bed, hasn't been there all nocte. Did she tell you where she was going?"

Agna shook her head. "No, my lord, she gave no hint of any plans last nocte." Her eyes widened. "Do you think . . . no, she'd never . . ."

"Think what?" Karic's hands gripped the old woman's arms. "Tell me, Agna. I care only that she's safe."

"It's of no import. I only thought, for a passing moment, that she might have slipped away to meet one of the young males. But not Liane. She'd never do such a thing."

Even the possibility Liane might be with another, lying naked in his arms and loving him, was like a hot poker ramming through Karic's gut. For an instant, the pain of it left him breathless. Then, fiercely angry, he shoved it aside.

He was the one who had given her free choice and now must live with the consequences. All he dared let matter was her continued safety, and, like Agna, Karic found it hard to believe Liane's absence was due to some lovers' tryst. She wasn't one to give her affections easily, at least not when it came to mating. He, above all others, knew that from bitter experience.

"Do you know where she might have gone? Does she have any favorite spots she frequents? There's something wrong here, Agna, and I cannot rest until I know where she is."

"Well, there's the stream that flows down from the mountains and the small forest nearby," the old healer hesitantly offered. "I've taken her there to gather herbs."

"Thank you, Agna."

Karic strode from the cave, his mind racing. The valley must be scoured immediately and thoroughly, for precious time was already being lost. A nagging feeling that Liane wasn't even in the valley began to gnaw at him.

The possibility, once recognized, rapidly grew to a full-fledged certainty. It was the only way she had to fight back against a fate no longer in her control. And fight she would, while there was still breath left in her body.

Karic cursed the folly of allowing her to slip away. If he had not been such a coward, unable to bear the silent recriminations and the pained betrayal burning in her eyes everytime they would have met, he never would have permitted her out of his sight. It was guilt, pure and simple, that had brought them to this. And now Liane was out there somewhere in the mountains in untold danger.

His pace quickened. It was a simple matter to rouse a large search party, for the Cat People were ever ready to react to an emergency.

The hunt was quick and thorough. Two horas later, as the sun's rays began to light the sky, the men regrouped before the Lord's lair.

"She's not here," Karic tersely informed his father. "We found her scent heading out of the valley. I've got to go after her."

Gerlic stepped forward. "Do not send him, my lord. She's created nothing but problems since her arrival, and Karic has already all but given her up anyway. It will ease his sacrifice if he's not forced to see her, sol after sol. A hard decision to forbid him this, but a kindness all the same."

"And what is it to you whether she dies out there?" Karic wrathfully demanded, rounding on Kalina's uncle. "You care only to pave the way for your niece's life mating. You care nothing for all Liane has sacrificed for us. But I say," he said, turning the full force of his gaze upon his father, "that our debt is not ended, not until she is safe."

His father eyed him intently. "It might be more of a kindness to kill her when you find her than bring her back. Do you realize what you'd be returning her to? She'd have to be constantly guarded. We can't afford to let her escape again and fall into the wrong hands, not with the knowledge she has about us. Is that what you want?"

"Nothing I want seems to matter anymore, Father," Karic answered, his face ravaged with worry.

"All I know is that, whether you grant me leave or not, I'm going after her."

A sad, gentle light gleamed in Morigan's eyes. "I thought as much. I will not stop you." He paused for the merest secundae. "Will you bring her back?"

Karic hesitated. He could never kill Liane, no matter how much it endangered his people. But dare he tell his father the truth? This time it would be Liane's choice, and hers alone, what would be done. It went against their laws, but that could be dealt with later.

"I don't know," he replied, squarely meeting his father's gaze. "It depends on Liane. Whatever I do, though, I'll ensure our people are not endangered."

"You may be gone for a time then."

"Yes."

Morigan extended his arm. "Safe journey, Son."

"Thank you, Father," Karic said, relief and a fierce love flooding through him.

They clasped arms. For a long moment the two men stood there, eye to eye, heart to heart, a mutual understanding flowing between them. Both knew they might never meet again. Though Karic fully intended to return once he'd seen to Liane's needs, the dangers outside the valley were as great for him as for her.

But it was the only solution to an increasingly heartrending problem. Liane didn't want to stay, and it was eating Karic alive to see her suffer. If she were forced to return, their laws demanded she submit to them once again.

For a secundae longer the two men maintained their grip. Then their hands fell away.

Lowering his head, Karic removed his Cat's claw chain and handed it to his father. "This, as well as my true identity, will once again be safer here with you."

Morgan smiled. "Until you return."

"Until I return."

Karic turned and strode into their lair. After quickly loading a backpack with provisions, he grabbed a blaster from the wall. Slinging both over his shoulder, he hurried from the cave and into the already bright sunlight. Without a backward glance Karic headed out. The farewells had been given; there was nothing more to say.

Liane had left the valley by passing the outpost near Agna's cave, and he easily picked up her spoor. Not wasting a secundae more, Karic began his climb up the mountain. His pace was swift, and a fine sheen of moisture quickly built on the hard, naked planes of his chest and shoulders.

She could have left as early as dusk, when the guards changed, Karic realized. That would give her over an eight hora lead. He quickly ascertained her course was headed north, across the remaining mountains toward the plains.

The area was sparsely populated, but the Fodina mines and its mining camp were just a little over a sol's journey away. If she reached it before he caught up with her he might never get her out of the heavily guarded compound. And that camp, lacking in femina, might be more than she bargained for.

All sol Karic traveled at a relentless pace, cursing the trail as it grew increasingly rocky and hard to traverse. He took no breaks, eating his noon meal on foot, quenching his thirst the same way. On and on he went, heavy sweat and dirt coating his body, his breath ragged, his powerful muscles cramping with fatigue.

But he drove himself on. He had to. Liane was out there somewhere ahead of him, and he had to catch up with her.

Dusk settled over the mountains as Karic wearily approached the last peak. As he neared the barren, windswept summit a series of excited howls drifted to him on the breeze. He paused, well-aware it was the cry of the half-wolf, half-bird rapax. The wildly ravenous, viciously cruel monster was known to haunt these high mountain peaks, blindly attacking whatever it came upon. He wondered what it had found.

A shrill scream pierced the sudden silence. Fear, stark and vivid, rocketed through him. Karic bolted up the mountain.

It was Liane. He knew her voice anywhere. And he also knew she'd die a horrible death, torn to shreds, if he didn't get to her soon. Somehow his muscles, already driven to the brink of exhaustion, responded.

Karic scrambled up the steep incline, his lungs burning, and all the while he felt the terror grow. For all his efforts, he still might not reach her in time.

As the rapax dived toward her, Liane wildly looked around for some place to hide. There was no shelter on the summit. She ran for the path leading down toward Fodina, hoping to find something, even a rock outcropping to slide under for protection from the monster's attack.

A series of crazed howls warned of the animal's approach. She threw a frantic glance over her shoulder. Slavering jaws and huge hooked claws were coming at her.

Before she could take another step the rapax

slammed into her, knocking her off her feet. As she fell his claws sunk through her backpack, tearing her flesh. She screamed.

Liane felt herself lifted in the air. She struggled wildly, the realization the monster meant to carry her off adding strength she never knew she possessed. The rapax hesitated in its upward ascent. His wings beat furiously to counterbalance Liane's squirming weight.

She fought to shrug out of the backpack. The animal's rank stench swirled around her, choking her. She could barely breathe. Her heart pounded in her chest, so hard she thought it would burst.

Blessedly, one arm slipped free of the pack's straps. She hung, momentarily suspended in air, by the other. Liane glanced at the ground, at least five meters below her. It was a long drop, but there was no other choice. With a quick prayer, Liane shrugged out of the remaining strap.

She fell, willing her body to remain loose and supple. She hit the ground on both feet, then rolled forward and over. The impact was hard, but Liane had little time to spare recovering from it. She was immediately on her feet, running.

Overhead the rapax howled wildly, the backpack still in its grip. It circled as she scrambled down the mountainside, growing ever closer. Then the backpack dropped from its claws. This time, it was coming in for the kill.

Panic shuddered through Liane. There was no backpack to protect her anymore. The rapax's claws would sink deep. Then it would lift off, carrying her helpless and bleeding to some lonely, inaccessible aerie—there to die, ripped apart, as it slowly ate her alive.

The shrill cry of the monster reverberated through Liane's brain, blocking out everything but the icy, numbing terror. She stumbled and fell, twisting, screaming, kicking.

Above her, a harsh blast of blue fire slammed into the beast. It halted, just meters above Liane, a smoldering hole gaping in its side. With a violent lunge Liane rolled away, barely avoiding being crushed as the rapax plummeted to the ground.

For a few stunned secundae, all she could do was stare.

Then realization filtered back. Someone had shot the creature. Liane staggered to her feet and looked up the mountainside.

There was Karic, shouldering a blaster, as he nimbly scrambled down the rocky incline. Relief surged in, making her suddenly light-headed.

With a small groan Liane sank to her knees, unable to decide if she were happy or sad that he'd found her. Her head drooped, her arms clasping her body. Harsh shudders wracked her slender frame.

Karic slid to a stop. He threw aside his gun and knelt before Liane, taking her into his arms. She cried out, tightly clinging to him. He tenderly stroked the tousled silk of her hair, fighting for control of his own wildly beating heart.

He had almost lost her.

A fierce, aching protectiveness overwhelmed him. Karic pulled Liane even tighter, memorizing the sweet feel of her, her tantalizing scent. Soon, it would be all he had. This battle between them couldn't go on.

He saw that now and accepted it. Their cultures were too different, too much at odds with each other. They had never had a chance.

Liane moved in his arms, moaning. His hand slid down her back to stroke and comfort her. Long fingers snagged in torn fabric that was damp and sticky. Karic stiffened. He lifted his hand and saw the blood.

Karic leaned over her. Two sets of slashes, deep and jagged, oozed blood from either side of Liane's back. He swallowed a savage curse.

"Take off your tunic!" he brusquely ordered, steeling himself to the pain he must cause. Climbing to his feet, Karic ran off to retrieve the backpack. Liane was still kneeling there, hunched over in agony, when he returned.

Her backpack held little of any use save a spare tunic and a leather flask of water. Swearing softly under his breath, Karic pulled the two items out. From his own backpack he retrieved a jar of healing salve that he'd grabbed along with his food supplies. Karic gently unfolded Liane's arms, now clasped about her in rising anguish. He tugged up her tunic.

Liane tensed. Her hands captured his. "No!"

He looked deep into her eyes. "I need to tend your wounds. This tunic's ruined. I'll make bandages out of it." He gestured to the clean tunic lying beside him. "You can put this one on afterwards."

Pain clouded her eyes. "I—I don't know . . ."

"Trust me. I have to care for you. You can't reach these wounds yourself."

His hands slipped from her clasp, and he carefully began to remove Liane's tunic. When Karic pulled the garment over her head, she immediately clamped her arms across her chest. For an instant his gaze lingered on her nakedness, on her slender limbs, on the sweet mounds of her breasts.

He wrenched his gaze away. Gently, ever so

carefully, Karic turned her back to him. He tore the tunic into long strips. Then, grasping the water flask in one hand and a rag in the other, he paused.

"This will hurt, Liane," he said, his voice husky with regret. "I'm sorry for that, but it must be done."

"I—I know," came the muffled reply from the bent head.

He hardened himself to her soft gasps as he proceeded to cleanse her wounds, each little sound stabbing through him like a tiny dagger. By the time he had applied the salve and was ready to bandage her back, his brow was damp with sweat, his own body wracked with the effort it took to inflict pain and watch her suffer.

Gently, so as not to cause her anymore discomfort, Karic slipped the clean tunic over Liane's head. She submitted spiritlessly this time, making little effort to cover herself. There was no hope of traveling anywhere with her this nocte, Karic realized. He'd have to find shelter.

In the deepening twilight, Karic's Cat vision scanned the mountain below him. The lights of Fodina twinkled sinisterly in the distance. He didn't like being even this close to the lawless mining camp. Karic dragged his gaze back up the mountain. Halfway there, he noted a cave.

He transferred Liane's belongings to his own backpack. Slinging his pack and the blaster over one shoulder, Karic gathered Liane into his arms. She snuggled against him, nuzzling her face into the crisp, golden chest hair. His lips moved to her forehead for a fleeting kiss. Then, summoning his remaining strength, Karic set out.

The going was treacherous, and it took two more

horas to reach the cave. Liane was already asleep when Karic gently laid her down. The hardness of the stone floor immediately woke her.

"Karic?"

His hand touched her in the darkness. "It's all right, Liane. I'm here."

She moved to pillow her head in his lap. "I missed you," she murmured drowsily. "I'm glad you're here."

The deep, even sound of her breathing soon filled the small cave. Karic sat there for several horas, stroking her hair, before sleep finally claimed him.

A metallic hum woke Karic. He was instantly alert, scanning for the location of the strange noise. It was coming from somewhere outside the cave. He gently shook Liane awake.

She propped herself up on one elbow, which brought a grimace of pain to her face. "What is it?"

"There's someone outside." He carefully slid from beneath her. "Stay here."

Karic crept over to the cave's entrance and peered out. A huge metal monstrosity, complete with two mechanically operating arms, was slowly gliding up the mountain on its cushion of air. Perched high in a windowed cabin were two faces. The drivers, Karic grimly thought.

He choked back a savage curse. It was the dreaded Fodina Sweeper, roaming the mountains in search of hapless slaves for the mining pits, and the two flying the machine were Atroxes. He couldn't cloak his presence from those non-humanoids.

Karic knew they were coming for them. His head whirled with possible plans and found only one. He must lead them away while Liane had time to escape. Together, they couldn't travel fast enough, not in her weakened condition. But alone, he knew he could lead the Sweeper a long chase before he tired enough to be captured. It should give Liane all the time she needed.

He ran back to her. "Get up! I've got to leave you. Once I'm gone, head out and don't look back. If I can, I'll find you later."

His glance, burning with a fierce intensity, lingered on her for a fleeting moment. "For what it's worth, I want you to know I would have taken you anywhere you wished to go. I wouldn't have forced you back to my lair."

Before she could reply Karic ran from the cave. Liane struggled to her feet, intending to go after him and make him explain, but he was gone. She staggered toward the entrance, each step setting afire the raw wounds on her back. The sight that greeted her immediately banished the pain.

An airborne machine was pursuing Karic down the mountain. Its jointed metal arms, complete with grasping pincers, flailed after him like long, lethal tentacles. Though the descent was rocky and treacherous, Karic managed to stay beyond its reach.

Liane ran back to retrieve the backpack and blaster, then exited the cave. She knew she should be on her way. There was a danger the machine might return to look for other occupants of the cave. But first she had to know what became of Karic.

He was maintaining his lead, even drawing away, when four skim craft suddenly appeared out of nowhere. With a sickening surge of horror, Liane realized the occupants of the big machine must have called for reinforcements. She saw Karic slide to a halt, trapped between the sweeper and the four craft spread in a semicircle before him.

For the merest flicker of an instant, she watched him hesitate. Then, with lightning speed, he attempted a feint to the left then a quick dart beneath the skimmers. The Sweeper's metallic arms, so ungainly looking when not in use, were suddenly as swift as Karic. They shot out, one clamping around his neck, the other about an ankle.

Karic was jerked to the ground. As he struggled to pry open the pincer from about his throat, he was inexorably dragged back toward the huge machine. A large door opened. As Liane watched in helpless anguish, Karic was pulled into the bowels of the Fodina Sweeper—and disappeared.

"More ale, and be quick about it!" a burly, grimy-faced miner shouted.

For what seemed the hundredth time this sol, Liane filled a mug full of foaming Moracan ale and slid it across the counter for one of the other female table servers to deliver. She sighed and brushed an errant strand of hair from her damp forehead. How many more sols must she endure this noisy, over-crowded tavern, the leers and less than gentle fondling of her body? Too many times to count now, she had barely evaded being dragged away by a drunken miner. It was a violent, dangerous camp, and Liane wondered how much longer she could avoid the inevitable.

She'd been here a full three sols now, earning her keep while healing thanks to Karic's salve, all the while trying to glean information on how to get into the mining pits. She knew Karic was in one of them, condemned to lifelong labor, extracting the precious beryllium stone. It was a life that was generally quite short, so the talk around the camp went, for if the hard labor didn't kill you the frequent explosions from the highly volatile stone eventually would.

Liane had no idea how she would find Karic once she was able to sneak into the pits, but the consideration of leaving him there never entered her mind. He'd sacrificed himself for her. Coupled with his parting words that he'd take her anywhere and not force her back to his lair, she knew she couldn't turn her back on him.

It would be certain death for him otherwise. But that was the only reason. She didn't dare examine any other motives too closely. Her feelings still smoldered too disturbingly beneath a thin layer of hurt and betrayal. Perhaps, above all else, it was that realization that drove her to stay, risking everything to see him free. Even after all he'd made her suffer, Liane couldn't leave Karic to such a horrible fate. She didn't hate him that much.

As she worked that sol and into the early nocte, Liane became uncomfortably aware of a man sitting across the room, his back against the wall, his long legs propped on a table. He'd been there for horas, nursing a single mug of ale, his dark eyes watching, taking in everything. And she was most definitely part of that everything.

He was tall, powerfully built, his dark blond hair thick and curling down the back of his neck. He had a hard, ruthless face, and his features were roughly chiseled. His dark, snug clothing only accented his commanding physique. And though the man appeared to possess no weapons, there was an unmistakeable aura of virility and danger about him.

She was suddenly aware of his gaze, assessing her

with the same frank curiosity she was bestowing upon him. She looked away, but not before she saw a dark brow arch and lips quirk in amusement. Nervously, Liane wiped a rag across the counter, wondering who he was. If he were another tracker sent out by Necator . . .

Her shift ended an hora later. Liane gratefully slipped away, her mind already intent on her impending meeting with one of the miners. He'd been badgering her all sol to go for a walk. Liane had politely but firmly told him no, until he'd offered to give her a tour of the mines. The coveted miner's pass was the only way through the gates, as well as past the force fields at the pits' entrances, and only the miners possessed them.

Liane had discovered the beryllium slaves never left the pits. They lived and eventually died down there, loading endless carts of the valuable stone barehanded and unprotected from the periodic explosions. Sometimes they were just maimed and survived to labor again, but usually the blast of the highly unpredictable beryllium killed them. Liane wondered at the cruelty of letting those hapless prisoners take such terrible risks while the miners worked, fully protected, from inside the armored mine diggers.

As she hurried to her rendezvous Liane shuddered at the thought of a life in total darkness, never to see the sun again. It struck an answering chord within her. If it were one thing that filled her with horror, it was the thought of going unseeing and alone into those pits, but she wouldn't let herself think about that—at least not yet.

One obstacle at a time, she thought, and the first was to get inside the mine. She had yet to decide how she'd get rid of her tour guide after that. Somehow, though, in the process, she needed to obtain his pass. It was the only way into the pits and back out of the mine as well.

He was waiting for her in the alley behind the tavern. A grim-faced, unkempt man, he impatiently waved her over as she approached.

"What took you so long, femina?" he growled as he pulled her to him. "I don't like being teased."

Liane leaned back from him, his ale-soaked breath nauseating her. "I came as soon as my shift was over."

She made a motion as if to go. "I'm ready to see the mine."

The miner jerked her back to him. "Not so fast, femina." A feral grin twisted his face. "A tour of the famous Pits of Fodina has a price, and I intend on collecting it in advance."

Before Liane could protest, his mouth, wet and sloppy, lowered to hers. His burly arms clamped around her, anchoring her arms to her sides. She struggled wildly, nearly smothered by his lips.

When she stomped down hard on his instep, the miner's hold loosened. Liane reared back against the circle of his arms, raising her leg in a desperate attempt to knee him in the groin. The man recognized the age-old ploy. He shoved her away, hard and viciously, and she slammed into the tavern's stone wall.

Pain shot through her as the rough rocks tore into her back, ripping fresh wounds atop the old ones. The miner's fist connected with her jaw, and she sank to the ground. Bright lights sparkled in a whirling pit of blackness, as Liane struggled against an unconsciousness that would leave her helpless before the man's lustful onslaught. Gasping for breath she fought against the darkness and won.

But it was still too late. The man towering above her loosened his breeches and lowered himself onto her.

CHAPTER 12

LIANE SCREAMED AND STRUCK OUT AT THE LEERING, greasy face. She hit him, smashing his lips against his teeth. The man yelped in pain as blood oozed from his torn lip. Surprise flashed across his face. Then he scowled, his expression darkening in rage.

"You'll pay, and pay dearly for that, femina!" he snarled. Grabbing her flailing hands, he roughly pinned them above her head.

Panic rising within her, Liane twisted and bucked against him. She'd fight until there was no breath left in her body before she'd submit to another rape, but even as she struggled, her strength ebbed. She was no match for him. And all the while he watched, holding her down, knowing it was but a matter of time.

At last she lay there, trembling with exhaustion, gasping for air. The miner's hand moved to her breeches. Sheer terror shot through Liane.

"P—please!" she whispered. "No!"

"I suggest you do what the femina asks," came a deep voice from behind them.

The miner reared around. The loosening of his grip gave Liane the chance to free her hands, and she weakly pushed herself up on one elbow. Grateful eyes sought out the man who'd come to her rescue.

It was the blond stranger from the tavern. Though she wondered at his motives for being here, considering his unsettling interest in her all sol, Liane would accept any assistance at this point.

"She's mine," the miner spat. "You know it's first come, first served. If you want her afterwards, she's yours."

"No, I think not," the tall man drawled silkily. As he spoke, a small stun gun appeared in his hand. Before the miner could even protest the stranger fired, and the miner slumped across Liane.

She shoved him off her, then turned her gaze to the blond man towering above her. She eyed him warily. "Should I thank you or prepare myself for another battle?"

He threw back his head and gave a shout of laughter. "No battle, I promise, femina."

The stunner disappeared back up his sleeve, and he offered her his hand. "I'm not particularly fond of split lips, and you seem quite adept at dishing them out."

Liane accepted his hand and was effortlessly pulled to her feet. "My thanks, then."

She grimaced, suddenly aware, once again, of the pain of her raw wounds. They felt like they were on fire. She swayed, suddenly light-headed.

Her rescuer noticed the change in her and

grabbed both arms to steady her, peering at Liane intently.

"What's wrong, femina? Did he hurt you?"

Liane shook her head. "I—I'm all right. His roughness reopened some old wounds on my back, that's all."

He swung her around, then cursed softly. "You're bleeding. What happened?"

"A rapax wanted me for supper."

She turned back around, right into his arms, and froze.

The smoky gloom of the tavern had muted his eyes, but now, up close, Liane saw they were dark brown with dancing golden lights. His cleanly chiseled jaw was shadowed with the stubble of a beard, and his skin was deeply tanned. His was the face of a coldly ruthless man, but a strikingly handsome one, nonetheless. She swallowed hard and backed away.

He smiled. "You have nothing to fear from me, femina. My tastes don't run to rape. Now, tell me, why were you out here with that miner? Don't you know all feminas who work in Fodina are considered available? As crude as this might sound, you were asking for just what you got, meeting him like this."

Liane squashed a surge of indignation. This was no time for an argument. Besides, as much as she hated to admit it, he was right. She had taken a terrible risk. There just weren't many risk-free options in a place like Fodina.

Should she trust him? There really wasn't much choice, and he did seem more decent than the rest.

"He promised me a tour of the mines," she explained. "It's imperative I get into them."

"Why?"

Her eyes searched his, looking for something, anything, to pin her trust upon. His dark gaze was imperturbable, but she thought she saw something.

"I—I have a friend in the pits. I must get him out."

A slow, lazy grin spread across his face. "A friend, eh? I don't know if I care to risk my life for just a friend."

Wild hope surged through Liane. "You'd help me? I don't have much, just what I've managed to earn at the tavern these past few sols, but I'd gladly give it to you."

"Keep your money, femina," he drawled. "I have more than one reason for taking you into the mines. I need a way to get in myself, one that won't rouse suspicion. Giving a femina a tour isn't an uncommon ploy. I'll help you if you agree to help me."

Liane's eyes narrowed. "Why do you want to get in the mines?"

"I'm a tracker. I'm looking for someone."

Her worst fears sprang to life. If he were sent by Necator . . . !

"Who?" she demanded. "Who are you looking for?"

He regarded her with lifted brow. "Why do you ask? Is your friend perhaps a wanted man?"

Trackers, Liane knew, remembering the Atroxes, sold themselves to the highest bidders. They were generally unprincipled, always on the lookout for an opportunity to collect bounties. Even if Karic wasn't who this man sought, he might haul him back to Primasedes if he knew Necator wanted him. But what could she say, now that she'd all but given it away?

She clung to the tiny bit of trust building in her for

218

the blond stranger. He didn't seem like the others. Somehow, Liane sensed he was strong and true, that his hardened, cynical exterior was nothing more than a facade. Oh, if she'd only her mind seeking abilities to verify her perceptions! But she didn't, not anymore. She'd have to trust her instincts.

Liane nodded. "In a sense I suppose he is, but through no fault of his own. You must believe that."

"Tell me who he is."

She momentarily recoiled at the hard bite to his words. "Promise me you'll not take him back."

"I can't promise that. It's up to you. Tell me or I won't help you."

There was no other choice. She had to tell him and risk the chance it was Karic he sought. But if it weren't . . .

"His name is Karic. The Lord Commander wants him."

His rigid jaw relaxed. "He's not the one I'm looking for. I'd never work for Necator, no matter the price. His policies are slowly destroying this planet. I'm ashamed to admit he's a countryman."

Liane gripped his arm, delight brightening her face. "You're Bellatorian then? So am I."

He grinned. "I thought as much. Your breeding shows. What's your name, femina?"

"Liane Allador." She couldn't help a shy smile.

It was a slow, tender movement and lit up her features, making her even more beautiful, if that were possible. The tracker inhaled a ragged breath. If he weren't on such a vital mission, if she weren't so obviously in love with the man trapped in the mine . . .

He wrenched himself back to reality. "I'm very pleased to meet you, Liane. My name's Gage Bardwin."

He extended his hand.

She accepted it, surprise filling her. Everyone had heard of the famous tracker Gage Bardwin. He worked for pay, not bounty, and lots of it. Only the wealthiest, most powerful of men could afford him. It was said he only went after hardened, dangerous criminals and always brought them back. But, as well-known and talked about as his exploits were over the cycles, she'd expected a much older man. Why, he looked to be only about 35 cycles!

"I am honored to meet you," Liane murmured, squelching the impulse to ask his true age.

His mouth quirked humorously. "Well, that's the first time anyone's been honored by my acquaintance, but thank you."

Gage's expression sobered. "Now, enough of the introductions and mutual admiration. We need a mining pass."

He squatted beside the unconscious miner and retrieved the pass from about the man's neck. Rising, Gage cocked his head, a thoughtful light gleaming in his dark eyes. "I suggest you bandage your wounds and put on a clean tunic. A blood-stained back might draw unnecessary attention to us in the mines. I'll wait for you here."

She smiled up at him. "Thank you, Gage. For everything."

With that, Liane headed back to the tavern. Gage Bardwin watched until her slender form disappeared from view. She was a naive little fool to trust so easily, he thought, especially the kind of man he'd become. With a bitter shake of his head, he found a comfortable spot to await her return.

As dusk settled behind the distant horizon they headed up into the foothills toward the Pits of

220

Fodina. "What pit is your friend in?" Gage asked as they neared the entrance to the mine. "I'll get you past the force field with the pass, then come back to let you out at a prearranged time. I need to do a little searching of my own in some of the buildings while you're occupied finding your friend."

Liane nervously averted her gaze. "I'm not exactly sure where he is."

Gage grabbed her arm, halting her. "You've *no* idea, do you? Femina, there are over ten pits in that mine. It's too dangerous to casually stroll from one to the other, peeking in, calling out to see if he's there. You've got to come up with a better plan than that, or this little adventure of yours is over right now."

"But how could I have possibly found out where he is?" Liane gazed up at him imploringly. "My only hope is to sense his presence. I had that power once; perhaps some of it still remains."

His dark eyes narrowed. "What are you? A Sententian?"

"I was."

He knew there was a story behind that simple admission, but this wasn't the time to ask. Gage sighed. "Yours is a weak, foolhardy plan."

"But you'll help me?" She couldn't hide the relieved eagerness in her voice.

"Only for a time," he said, marveling at his own foolishness in going along with it. "But if you can't identify the exact pit he's in within a half hora . . ."

Gratitude rushed through her. "Thank you, Gage. I understand. I won't endanger your mission any longer than that. I can always come back and try again."

He gave her a curious look. "You'd do better to attempt this with me and, if it fails, give it up. This is

221

far too dangerous to continue indefinitely. You'll soon end up dead—or worse."

She sadly shook her head. "If you had a friend, someone you cared for, could you live with yourself knowing he was down in those pits?"

"Loyalty is too costly an emotion for a man like me. I rarely indulge in it."

"But you're helping me," she softly countered.

His jaw tightened. "Only because it suits my needs, femina. Don't delude yourself."

"I don't believe that, Gage." Her eyes, luminous with admiration, stared up at him. "You're not that cold or hard-hearted."

"Well, it doesn't matter anyway," he growled. "We're wasting valuable time standing here."

He pulled her forward. "Let's go."

They soon reached the mine entrance. After a few lewdly suggestive comments from the guard, the man allowed them to enter. As they neared the first set of pits Liane closed her mind to any sensations save that of Karic's presence. She felt nothing, even after a time of intense concentration.

Gage was the one to rouse her from her trance-like state. His arm snaked around her shoulders, and he pulled her close, nuzzling her ear. Liane stiffened. If not for the tight grip he maintained on her she would have pulled away.

"Easy now," he breathed into her ear. "This is all part of our little act. We've been standing here long enough. It's time to move on before the watchmen get suspicious."

Liane swung her attention to the heavily armed guards patroling the area. Gage was right. There was no point lingering at these particular pits. If Karic were here, she didn't know it.

A niggling doubt eased into her mind. What if she were unable to sense his presence? What would she do then?

The possibility was too horrible to consider. If she couldn't pinpoint his exact location she'd have to go down into each pit, one by one. The thought filled her with terror. What if she became trapped in there, unable to escape?

Liane swallowed hard. She mustn't think about that. It didn't change anything anyway. If she died, she died, but she couldn't go on living if she left Karic here.

Together, they moved on to the next set of pits. There was no sense of Karic being there, either. Tension spiraled through Liane. The precious time Gage had allowed her was slipping away, and they still had three more sets of pits to examine.

They visited one more before Gage finally called a halt to her search.

"It's well past your half hora, femina," he reluctantly but firmly informed her. "I'm sorry."

Tearful eyes looked at him, and she managed a brave little smile. "I understand. You've been more help than you can ever imagine. Now, what would you like me to do to help you?"

He stared down at her, indecision flickering in his striking dark eyes. He didn't like the idea of her coming back here alone, if she even made it safely inside next time. But dare he risk trying the final two pits, knowing his own time in the mine was rapidly slipping away?

Gage dragged in a breath. "I'll take you by the last two, if you promise you'll give up and never come back here again."

"You know I can't promise that."

He scowled darkly. "Curse you, femina! You're too stubborn for your own good." His arm moved against her shoulders, urging her on. "Let's go."

As they approached the next pit a strange sensation washed over Liane. It was hauntingly familiar, heavy with the feel of experiences shared and of unspoken emotions. She knew, with a certainty that both startled and gladdened her, that it was Karic's presence.

"He's here," Liane whispered. She raised joyous eyes to Gage.

Her blond companion cocked a skeptical brow. "Are you sure you're not imagining it because you want it so badly?"

"No," she firmly shook her head. "It struck me before I even had the chance to search for it." She indicated the first pit with a surreptitious wave of her hand. "He's in there."

Gage glanced around, the casual movement of his head masking the intentness of his scrutiny. "There's no guard about just now. After I get you in past the force field, the rest is up to you. It's an hora until darkness. You've got until then to find your friend and get him to the entrance. If you can't, be back here by then. I can't linger too long without arousing suspicion."

"I understand, Gage. If I'm not back in time, go on without me."

His dark eyes narrowed. "Liane, he's either in there or not. An hora is more than enough time to find him. Promise me you'll be here in an hora."

She shook her head. "I'm sorry, Gage, I can't promise you that. If Karic's sick or hurt, I won't be able to leave him. We'll find a way out somehow, later."

"Whatever you say, femina," Gage sighed. "Just remember. I'll be back in an hora."

"I will, Gage." She hesitantly touched his arm. "Take care of yourself."

"Don't waste your worry on me. I've done this kind of thing a hundred times."

He strode over to the pit and slid his pass into a slot in the metallic archway that encompassed the entrance. The force field shut down. With an impatient wave, Gage motioned her in.

Liane never looked back, for if she did she might lose her courage. Before her loomed a blackened pit, slanting steeply downward. She swallowed hard against the gorge that rose in her throat and blanked out her fears. With a hand on the stone wall to guide her, she strode into the darkness.

Karic jerked awake. He'd been dreaming of Liane, of holding her in his arms, of mating with her. And it had been sweet, so very sweet.

Sleep was his only escape in the past sols of his captivity. It was the one release from the endless labor in the damp, nearly airless tunnels, from the miners, safe in their armored mine diggers, relentlessly driving them onward with their neural prodders, from the periodic explosions that left slaves writhing in agony, their cries echoing endlessly throughout the tunnels.

Sometimes Karic tried to imagine it all part of a horrible dream, one that he'd awaken from and find himself free, high on a windswept peak, overlooking a magnificent panorama of verdant mountains and craggy summits. Then he'd gaze up at the sky, brilliant and blue in the bright sunshine, and thank all that was sacred that it hadn't been real. But most times he faced it for what it truly was—a living death with no hope of escape.

He had tried the force field several times already, ut the electronic barrier was tamper proof. Evidently they'd worked that out cycles ago. And there was no way to slip through when the barriers were down, even cloaked, for the proper number of visitors to the mine had to be programed in, coming and going, or the barriers automatically raised. No, there was no way out of the mine. All that lay before him was the certainty of eventual death after sols, monates, perhaps even cycles of backbreaking labor in endless, heavy, smothering darkness.

Though his Cat's vision normally allowed him the ability to see, back here in the deeper recesses where the slaves worked and slept, it was pitch black even for him. It didn't really matter. There was nothing worth seeing anyway, save the pitiful, tortured faces of the other slaves.

He lay back and sighed. If only he knew Liane had made it away safely it would almost be worth it. Then he could return to the comfort of his dreams and endure, until it was finally over.

As Karic sat there immersed in his morose thoughts the strangest, most pervading sense of Liane's presence washed over him. It must have been the dream, he told himself. The eerie sense of her was stronger than it had ever been before.

Karic tried to relax and slip back into that blessed oblivion where he'd found her, but the feeling continued to grow, setting his nerves on edge. He climbed to his feet and followed the haunting attraction. The feeling became almost palpable, as if around the next bend in the tunnel he'd find her, awaiting him. Though he knew it was impossible, even the contemplation of such a thing sent his heart pounding.

Suddenly, his Cat-sensitive ears picked up a new sound, one foreign to the tunnels. Footsteps, light and hesitant, were moving toward him. He shook his head to clear it. Surely he was beginning to hallucinate, for it sounded like Liane. The soft breathing was hers, too. He'd know it anywhere.

He slammed up against the stone wall. By the three moons! He must be going mad, wanting her and missing her. It was the only explanation.

Her scent, fresh and sweet as a forest glade of wild violets, wafted to his nostrils. It was a trick, Karic tried to reassure himself, some torment devised by his keepers to break him. Yet, the certainty grew. A naked desire flared until he thought he'd scream from the psychic pain. He had to end this charade now, before it was too late.

Summoning all his will power, Karic stepped out and strode around the bend. In the dark tunnel, illuminated by light so faint as to be barely discernable, he saw the outline of a female form. Whether it was one of flesh and bone or an unsubstantial hologram, Karic couldn't discern. He stealthily crept closer.

She was alone, whoever she was, moving hesitantly through the darkness. He could hear her breathing, uneven and rasping, and he sensed her fear. It was raw, barely controlled. Suddenly, with a surety that overwhelmed him, Karic knew it *was* Liane.

With lithe agility he slipped behind her. In a quick movement Karic covered her mouth with one hand while, with the other, he pulled her back into him. She gave a small, muffled cry and began to struggle.

"Shhh, femina," he breathed into her ear. "It's me. Karic."

She immediately relaxed. He turned her into his arms, clasping her tightly to him. Liane's hands slipped around Karic's trim waist, pulling him into her soft curves. They stood there, hearts pounding, bodies clinging. Then, with a superhuman effort, Karic forced himself back from her.

"What are you doing here, you little fool?" he demanded in a mixture of joy and angry concern. "And how were you able to get this far without being caught?"

She moved back to him, her hands entwining about his neck. "I've come to rescue you," she murmured against the hair-roughened planes of his chest. "I found a friend to help us. His name is Gage Bardwin. He'll return soon to get us out."

"Good." Karic stroked her back and felt her stiffen. He remembered her wounds.

"How's your back?" he whispered. "Still paining you?"

"It was healing well until this sol. I—I had an accident, and the wounds broke open. They'll heal again."

She disengaged herself from his arms, suddenly warm and strangely light-headed. She'd felt that way more and more as the sol wore on, but now it was even worse. Perhaps the relief of finding Karic was doing strange things to her.

"I—I don't feel so well. Perhaps I'd better sit down."

"Yes, perhaps you should." Karic quietly agreed as he lowered Liane to the ground and sat down beside her. He studied her with Cat's eyes. "Are you all right?"

"Of course," she was quick to reply, banishing the unpleasant weariness with the force of her will. "It was a moment of dizziness, that's all. I feel better already."

Karic frowned. "If you say so."

He watched Liane pull a perpetual flame box out of her pocket and place it on a ledge above them. In the next instant, a soft, red glow bathed her features. "And now what?" Karic demanded, forcing himself past her distracting beauty. "Since you seem to have some sort of plan, you'd better fill me in on it."

"Gage has a miner's pass that can activate and deactivate the force field at the entrance to this pit. He had business of his own to take care of, but he promised to be back here in an hora's time. It's hard to know how long I've been looking for you, but I'd guess it to be no more than a half hora or so. We need to get back to the entrance and wait for him."

"And then what?"

She stared at him quizzically. "Why, we leave the mines as inconspicuously as possible. Gage has a stunner, just in case."

"Yes, but *then* what, Liane? Are you his femina now, this Gage you speak of? Will you go away with him?"

Did she detect a note of jealousy in Karic's voice? Before she even realized it a wild joy spiraled through her.

She fiercely shook the sweet hope from her. She didn't dare trust her feelings, didn't even want to. When all was said and done the deep fear of him, that he'd lose control again and turn into some vile, lust-maddened animal, still managed to overshadow everything else. No matter what he had told her about that nocte, Liane couldn't find it in her heart to trust that it would never happen again. She just couldn't. Whatever had driven her to rescue him—loyalty, a sense of fairness—it changed nothing.

Perhaps his reaction was from some other motive besides jealousy. Perhaps Karic had changed his mind and meant to take her back to his lair. He might still feel he owed his people her breeding services, no matter what he'd told her in the cave before his capture. Perhaps he was just trying to ascertain if he'd have to fight Gage to do so.

The thought of those two powerful men battling over her filled Liane with a sickening sense of horror. The fight would be savage and bloody, for she knew no quarter would be asked or given. But how could she, in all good conscience, set such a terrible confrontation into motion? If Karic meant to take her back she'd have to find some other way to circumvent him, other than involving Gage. She'd already caused the blond tracker enough trouble as it was.

Liane met Karic's gaze. "No, I am not his femina, and I won't go away with him." She hesitated. "I no longer need his help. You promised to take me anywhere I wished to go. Do you still mean it?"

Anguish churned through Karic. So, nothing had changed, had it? She still despised him and had rescued him only so she could make use of him. Yet, for a fleeting moment when he'd first held her, he could have sworn the utter joy he'd felt had been returned. Fool!

"I gave you my word, Liane," he rapped out in a cold, unfamiliar voice. "I'll stand by it. Where do you want to go?"

Liane recoiled from the harshness of his tone. She'd angered him. Well, if he didn't want to be burdened with her, it was fine with her. She was quite capable of going on alone.

"I journey to Lyrae." She forced her voice to sound as strong and sure as her words. "If it's too inconvenient to take me there I won't hold you to your offer."

"No inconvenience at all," he growled. "And the sooner you're safe, the sooner you'll be free of my loathsome presence."

Karic grasped her arm, jerking her into his hard, rigid body. "That *is* what you want, isn't it, Liane?"

CHAPTER 13

"THAT'S NOT THE REASON," LIANE WHISPERED IN A tear-choked voice. "I don't find *you* loathsome, just what you *did* to me."

With a fierce curse, Karic tightened his grip on her. "Then why, Liane? Why did you risk your life to rescue me? After what I did to you, surely you owe me nothing."

She couldn't meet his gaze. "I—I don't know. I just knew I couldn't leave you here, to die in this horrible place!"

"But I lied to you, betrayed you at every turn," Karic grimly persisted. "Surely I deserve to die, for that if nothing else."

"Stop it!" she cried. "You know the answer as well as I, if you cared to face it. I'm afraid to open my heart to you again. I'm terrified of that part of you that's the animal. You weren't the Karic I knew that nocte. You were someone else, and I don't ever want to know that man again. It's too late for us, Karic."

"I don't believe that," he replied. "If you truly want me, we could work it out. I'd give you time. I'd be gentle with you."

"And what of your lies and betrayal?"

"All I did, I did in good faith, for the welfare of my people."

"And will you give up your people for me?" she quietly asked. "Turn your back on your laws? It's more than just the mating. There are so many other problems between us. It's hopeless, Karic."

He groaned. "Why? Why, Liane, does it have to come to that?"

A soft, sad smile touched her lips. "Because it does. I have to know that you'll never turn on me again, like on that nocte. I have to know, though I might never ask it, that I matter more than anything else to you, that you'd give up everything for me."

She sighed. "Perhaps it's unfair, but it's what I need. It's time you accepted it."

"And would you do the same for me?"

"I thought I already had."

Karic's jaw hardened. "No, you haven't. You've fought me every step of the way, putting conditions on everything, refusing to ever completely trust me."

"And you've disappointed *me* every step of the way, betraying every vow you've ever made, save your most generous offer to let me murder you," she finished cuttingly.

"It always gets back to that, doesn't it, Liane?" he growled. "You see only the acts, not the intent."

"And *you* persist in putting your people above me!"

They glared at each other for a heated moment, then the tension suddenly eased. Karic laughed.

"What's so amusing?" Liane warily demanded.

"That two people who care so much for each other can be so determined to find every excuse to stay apart."

"I didn't say I cared."

His expression sobered. "No, you never have, have you? But I know it all the same. I think I've known it for a long while now. Though you say you fear me, the way your body responds whenever I hold you in my arms speaks more truthfully than words. Your action in coming for me alone, down into this pit, when I know you're terrified of the dark, also tells me something. And the fact you couldn't kill me, even after what I'd done to you—"

"Stop it!" Liane cried. "You're no better than I. I've never heard any words of tenderness from your mouth."

"Then hear them now, sweet femina." Karic gently took her chin in the palm of his hand. "I love you."

Her eyes widened, then, with a fierce shake of her head, she averted her gaze. "It doesn't change anything. It's too late."

"Why?" he prodded, in a deeply seductive voice. "Why is it too late?"

As he spoke his thumb moved to lightly stroke her lips, sending a delicious tremor through Liane. It so unsettled her that she suddenly couldn't seem to think straight or formulate a coherent reply. But she had to give him some answer or, by her silence, admit the truth.

"Your people. Your laws," she answered, grasping at the first thing that entered her mind. "They conspire to keep us apart."

"Yes," he gravely admitted, "it would almost seem so."

Karic hesitated. Liane didn't know the full extent of the truth, the Elders' refusal to let them life mate, yet if he told her, she'd turn from him forever. Wouldn't it be better to convince her to go back with him, choose him at the Mating Festival, and hope, in time, to change the Elders' minds? It was grasping at the only chance of happiness they had, but it was better than nothing.

Yet wasn't that exactly what she'd end up with if he once again gave her assurances he had little hope of seeing succeed? All his promises in the past had come to naught, making him appear the fool, if not the liar. He hadn't meant it to be so, but in his own way he'd been naive and unrealistic. But reality had finally forced him to face the truth. Liane's fear and mistrust of him stemmed, for the main part, from all his broken promises and unsubstantial assurances. He loved her too much to intentionally lead her astray again.

His hand fell from her sweetly beguiling mouth to lightly settle upon her shoulder. "I won't lie to you, Liane," Karic said, the words the hardest he'd ever uttered. "I love you and want you to go back with me, but it's very likely we won't be allowed to life mate."

She stiffened. "Then what would be left us?"

"A temporary mating for at least three cycles, maybe more, before they finally forced me to take another."

Liane wrenched from his grasp. "And knowing that, you can still ask me to go back with you? Why, of all the self-serving, thoughtless—"

"I know," he quietly cut in. "But at least this time there will be no illusions on either side. No sur-

235

prises. It may be all we'll ever have."

"Well, it's not enough!"

"If you loved me—"

"Love isn't enough, not in times such as these."

Though for a fleeting instant she was tempted to cast all fears aside, to grasp at even the brief time she'd have with Karic, Liane knew it was only her foolish heart speaking. In the end that same heart would be torn asunder when they were forced to part, each to become the mate of another. And that pain would be far worse than the pain of now giving him up.

She lifted resolute eyes. "I still want to go to Lyrae."

Karic's gaze narrowed. "Just like that, Liane? You can turn your back and close your heart, just like that?"

Liane gave a bitter laugh. "Yes, just like that. Will you take me to Lyrae?"

Something hardened in Karic. "Yes, Liane, I'll do anything for you—even give you up, if that's what it takes to make you happy."

She stared at him for a long moment, and the look in her eyes was unguarded, betraying the coldness of her words. Then, with a small sigh, she extinguished the flame box.

"Come. It's past time we were back at the entrance. We mustn't keep Gage waiting."

He immediately rose, pulling her up after him, and led the way through the darkened tunnel. Her warm look just before she'd turned from him told Karic everything he needed to know. Though she might be loathe to admit it, Liane loved him.

The journey to Lyrae would take three sols. There was no reason he couldn't linger a time after that to see she was safely ensconced there. His father knew not to expect him back soon.

The plan heartened him. There was time enough to convince her she was wrong about him, time enough to work through the tangled web of hurt and divided loyalties. Somehow, someway, he'd convince her to take a chance, to go back with him. He would win her heart after all.

They reached the pit's entrance and sat down to await Gage's return. Karic pulled her into the crook of his arm, and she willingly rested her head upon his shoulder. They sat there in silence. Gradually, Karic became aware that Liane seemed warmer than usual.

When he touched her forehead with the back of his hand, her skin felt hot and moist. Karic moved to get a better look at her in the greater brightness of moonlight.

Two spots of unnatural color stood out on Liane's face, and a feverishness gleamed in her eyes. She hesitantly smiled back at him.

"What's wrong, Karic? Why are you staring at me like that?"

"You look ill. How do you feel?"

"Well enough."

Karic studied her flushed face. "Your wounds fester, don't they?"

"And what if they do?" she defensively replied, pulling back from him. "It changes nothing. I must still walk out of here on my own and make my way to Lyrae. I won't let it stop me, not now, not when I'm so close to freedom and a new life."

"You're right, of course," Karic said, realizing the course of this discussion would only agitate her and she needed all her strength for the task ahead. "We'll cleanse your wounds and rebandage them once we're safely away from here. It helped before; it'll help again. I didn't mean to upset you. I was just concerned."

She sighed and wearily leaned back against him. "I know, Karic. I'm sorry if I seemed so harsh. I'm just tired, that's all. The stress of the past few sols has been great, not knowing what was happening to you, worrying about how I was going to find you, fearing the pits."

"Why are you so afraid of the darkness?" he asked, pressing his lips to her hair. "Did something happen to frighten you of it?"

"Yes," Liane replied with a small shudder. "When I was a child, two friends and I were playing in the forest. We came upon a small cave, the kind wild animals make for their den. We went in to explore and found that it burrowed deeply into the earth. My two friends were hesitant to go any further, but I, full of the excitement of discovering new worlds, mocked their fears until they went with me. The tunnel behind us caved in, entombing us behind a heavy wall of dirt. We panicked then, wasting what precious air that remained in our frantic attempts to dig our way out."

Her breath caught on a choking sob. "It was awful—the screams of my friends, the tiny, cramped space, the smothering darkness." She sighed. "Luckily, there were other Sententians nearby working in the forest. They heard our psychic cries. Unluckily, for my two friends, their bodies starved for air a few secundae before mine did. They were dead when our rescuers reached us."

"So the darkness serves to remind you of the blame you shoulder for your friends' deaths."

Her gaze met his. "Wouldn't it you? If I hadn't taunted them to follow me . . ."

"You were a child, Liane," Karic firmly reminded her. "You had no way of knowing. And though lives were lost the last time you willingly went down into a cave, this time you *saved* a life. If there was any debt for your childish mistake, I think it's been paid."

Tearful eyes studied him. "Do you really think so? It's a comfort, however unworthy I am of it. Thank you, Karic."

His finger tenderly traced the line of her jaw. "And thank you for your courage in coming into the pits for me, knowing now why you feared them so."

Karic's hand captured her chin. "You're full of courage," he said, steadily gazing down into her eyes. "If you'd just allow yourself, you could even overcome your fear of me."

Her eyes, fringed with sooty black lashes, widened as Karic lowered his mouth toward hers. "It—it wasn't courage that moved me to do it," she stammered.

"No, not just courage," he huskily agreed, his lips hovering a tantalizing breath from hers. "I know that, but you tell me the real reason, Liane. I want to hear it from you."

"Karic, I—"

"Well, I see you two haven't wasted any time renewing old acquaintances," came a deep, masculine voice from behind them.

Karic was on his feet in an instant, his claws bared. A tall, blond man calmly stared back at him, making no effort to defend himself though a hard, dangerous look flared in his eyes. Liane quickly rose and stepped between them.

"This is Gage," she hastened to explain, noting the sudden tension arcing between the two men. "He's the friend I spoke of."

Some of the rigidness eased from Karic's muscular frame, but his expression remained guarded. He retracted his claws. "Thank you for bringing Liane safely to me," he growled, emphasizing the possessiveness of the 'me'.

Gage's dark brow arched in amusement. "She'll go to great lengths for her friends, won't she, Cat Man?" he asked, his glance knowingly appraising him.

Two pairs of masculine eyes turned to Liane, and she colored fiercely. "We should be going. It's too dangerous to linger here."

Karic scowled at her, then nodded. He turned back to Gage. "What do you want us to do?"

"I'll make sure no guards are nearby," Gage said. "When it's clear I'll throw a small rock into the cave. You come out as soon as you hear it. Agreed?"

"Agreed."

They watched Gage slip back into the darkness outside the cave. It seemed an eternity before the pebble sailed in, alerting them it was time to leave. Grasping Liane's hand Karic stepped out into the nocte.

The cool air was fresh and sweet, stars twinkling in the blackened sky. He felt a wild surge of joy at being free again. They'd have to kill him before he'd ever let them drag him back down into that pit again.

When Gage motioned to them from the shadows of a nearby hut, they cautiously joined him.

"All three of us cannot stroll back across the mine together. As you Cat Men are renowned for your stealth and cloaking abilities, I suggest you let Liane and I return to the entrance the way we came, and you meet us there. You can slip out with us when the gatekeeper lets us through."

Karic nodded.

"You won't take offense, will you," Gage mockingly inquired, "if I pretend familiarity with Liane on the way back?"

"He knows it's just an act," Liane quickly interjected, noting the flare of anger in Karic's eyes. "Now, let's go."

Gage's arm encircled Liane's shoulder, and they started out across the mine, leaving Karic to glare after them. He sensed the man's interest in Liane, and something primal stirred in him. With great effort, Karic quashed the rising anger. This was not the time to battle over a female, but later, if the other man pushed his claim . . .

Cloaked as he was against detection, Karic easily made it across the mine compound and was waiting for Liane and Gage when they arrived. After a few more lewd remarks from the gatekeeper they all managed to safely leave the mine. When they were safely out of sight and earshot, Karic quickly called a halt.

"My thanks for your help," he said, offering Gage his hand in farewell. "We won't be needing your assistance anymore."

The blond tracker's eyes regarded Karic dispassionately, ignoring his outstretched hand. "Before I say my farewells," he lazily drawled, though there was a sudden coiled tension to his tall frame, "I think it only fair to ascertain if the femina is also done with me. After all, it was she who requested my help, not you."

He turned to Liane. "And what of you, femina? Have you further need of me?"

She knew, looking up into Gage's dark eyes, that his anger at Karic's high-handed dismissal was only tightly kept in check. And, though she instinctively

241

sensed the age-old basis of his animosity toward the tracker, Liane was also angry at Karic. He had no right to treat a man who'd helped them so discourteously.

But she refused to use one man to teach another a lesson. She would deal with Karic and her anger later. Liane took Gage by the arm and led him a short distance away from the scowling Karic. She smiled up at him, gratitude shining in her eyes.

"No, I've no further need of your help, Gage. My thanks, for the both of us," she muttered, shooting Karic a scathing look. "Was your mission in the mines successful?"

He shook his head. "Unfortunately, no. The man I seek has already moved on. I'll head out after him this very nocte."

"Then it's farewell."

"I'm afraid so. Your friend over there doesn't seem eager to share you."

"No, I suppose not."

The blond man grinned. "Don't let him bully you, femina."

Liane grinned back. "He never has before."

"Good." He offered her his hand. "I wish you happiness, Liane."

She ignored his hand and stood on tiptoe to kiss him on the cheek. "And you, Gage."

His gaze warmed for an instant. Then he turned and walked away, the nocte quickly swallowing him. Liane watched until Gage disappeared, then stalked over to Karic.

"What was that kiss all about?" Karic growled.

"Not one word, Karic!" Liane hissed back at him. "If you say one more word, I swear I too will walk away from you."

A pair of furious, green-gold eyes glared at her, but Karic clamped down on his angry reply. He dragged in a steadying breath, then carefully modulated the tone of his voice. "Fine. Let's get to Fodina then and take care of your back. I'm not setting out for anywhere until that's done. Do you have a place to stay?"

"Yes, upstairs from the tavern where I work," she clipped back, not quite ready to accept his unspoken offer of truce. "But you can't walk into town with me. They'll recognize you for a Cat Man on the spot."

"I'll cloak myself and follow you." He impatiently motioned her forward. "Come on. Let's get going."

She shot him a disdainful look, then turned and headed down the mountain.

Karic silently slipped into the room behind her and closed the door. He looked around the dimly lit little bedchamber and grimaced. Shabby was too kind a word for it, from the crudely made bed with its threadbare blanket to the rickety table with its chipped jug and single chair. The walls were scarred, the floor pitted and stained.

That it was scrupulously clean, Karic knew, was probably due to Liane's efforts. He hated to think of her living here the past sols while she waited for her chance to rescue him. It spoke, more eloquently than words, of her feelings for him, and that realization stirred anew his guilt at his boorish behavior toward Gage Bardwin.

He waited until she'd wearily settled into the room's only chair before he spoke. "About Gage . . ." Karic began.

"Not now, Karic," she sighed, closing her eyes

243

and shaking her head. "I haven't the strength for an argument."

"I don't intend to argue," he gruffly informed her. "I'm not very good at apologies, but I wanted to tell you I'm sorry about my conduct earlier. I only wish Gage were still here to tell him, too."

"I accept your apology, Karic. And I'm sure Gage would have, too."

"I was jealous."

"I know."

"You must think me a fool."

"No, never a fool. Stubborn, arrogant and most provoking at times, but never a fool."

"You're quite forgiving of late," he ruefully chuckled. "I don't know what to make of it."

She laughed. "Neither do I. We'll have to tread carefully here."

Karic's eyes flared with a burning, inner intensity. "Sweet femina, I'll tread as carefully as you want, if only you'll promise to be my mate."

Liane foundered in the compelling heat of his gaze, her heart commencing a heavy pounding in her breast. Karic loved her and wanted her, and a part of her loved and wanted him. That should be enough, but Karic was of royal birth and his life was not his own. He'd been raised to put the welfare of his people above everything else. That commitment could still come between them, as solidly as a wall of indestructible beryllium.

"What you ask may never be, Karic," she murmured. "You know that as well as I."

Liane couldn't bear the dark anguish that cut across his face. She lowered her gaze to begin tugging at her tunic.

"It's time my wounds were cleansed and

rebandaged," she said. "There's fresh water in the jug here," she gestured to the table, "and some bandages in the backpack."

"Do you have anymore of Agna's salve left?"

Liane shook her head and removed her tunic.

Karic grabbed the backpack and threw it onto the table beside the jug. He motioned toward her. "Turn around on the chair so I can get to your back."

Liane did as he requested, well aware the gruffness to his voice was not that of anger. Strange, she thought, how anger was frequently a camouflage for deeper emotions between them. The realization made her inexpressibly sad.

Karic touched her. Liane stiffened as he gently removed the old blood-clotted bandages. By the time he was done, her back burned, and she lowered her head to rest on the top of the chair back.

"Your wounds look bad," Karic growled from behind her. "They've already festered. We need more than water to heal them."

"But that's all you've got, Karic," she whispered. "Do the best you can."

By the time he was finished Liane was draped limply over the chair. The wounds looked little better, in Karic's grim opinion, but he'd cleansed them as best he could. He quickly rebandaged them, then gathered Liane in his arms and carried her to bed.

She stared up at him with uncomprehending eyes. "What are you doing? We need to be on our way, out of here while it's still dark."

"You're in no condition to be going anywhere right now, and you know it." He gazed down at her with tender concern. "Rest a while, and then we'll see."

"Yes, perhaps a short nap will make all the difference," Liane murmured exhaustedly. "Wake me in an hora and I'll be ready."

He watched as her lids lowered and her breathing slowly became even. Karic knew it would take more than an hora to replenish Liane's strength. She was too pale, too drawn, too drained by the infection now raging through her body.

He needed skills beyond that of his own to help her, and he doubted any lay in Fodina. Besides, to risk recapture would be foolhardy. He had few options. Lyrae might have a healer, but it was a full three sols away, even longer if he had to carry her there.

The only feasible plan was to take her back to old Agna. The lair was a good sol's travel, but the closest and best of all options. Yet Karic hesitated. To return her to his lair would be to involve her once again in the same old problems and bring her under the constraints of their laws. She'd never forgive him for that.

Perhaps all she needed was rest to replenish her strength for the journey to Lyrae, he told himself, desperately grasping at any other possibility. Give her a little time. There wasn't much left, but it was all he had to spare. With a deep sigh Karic seated himself on the floor next to the bed, and promptly fell asleep.

Liane was no better when Karic awoke several horas later. She thrashed restlessly in bed, her face hot and flushed, moaning softly. He felt her forehead and found she was burning with fever.

He cursed violently, an impotent rage tearing through him. Liane was worse, much worse. If he didn't do something quickly there would soon be no time to carry out any plan.

Karic gently shook her awake. Dazed, fever-bright eyes stared up at him.

"Wh—what is it?" Liane mumbled confusedly. "Is it time to go?"

"Yes, sweet femina," he said, tenderly brushing her tousled, ebony hair from her clammy face. "Can you stand?"

For an instant the old fire flared. "Of course," she replied disdainfully. "I'm not helpless, you know."

Her strength belied her determination, however. If not for Karic's firm hold upon her, Liane would have fallen when she rose to her feet. Karic quickly sat her back down and helped her into her tunic. Then, slinging the backpack and blaster over his shoulder, he pulled Liane once more to her feet.

"Liane, I need your help," he said, tightly gripping her arms to get her rapidly fading attention. "I can't cloak you if I carry you out of the tavern. You're going to have to walk at least that far. Look drunk, to justify my holding you up as much as I'll need to, but walk. Can you do that?"

She gazed up at him with a weak little smile. "Of course I can. Have I ever failed you, Karic?"

His whole heart was in the look he gave her. "No, sweet femina. You've never failed me."

He moved alongside her, his arm firmly encircling her waist. "Come then. We've got at least six horas of darkness left. If we leave now we can be far into the mountains before solrise."

"The mountains?" she mumbled, a small frown wrinkling her brow. "But Lyrae's toward the plains."

"I know another route that's quicker," Karic hastily replied. "Trust me in this."

She gave him a sweetly bleary smile. "You know I do."

Guilt stirred briefly in Karic at his deception. She'd finally admitted trusting him, and now he must knowingly betray her. But what else could he do? Her life was at stake. The consequences would have to be dealt with later.

Karic slowly led her across the room and out the door. They drew little attention from the tavern occupants, enthusiastically engaged in observing a sensual dance by one of the table servers undulating atop the bar counter. They were barely out the back door, however, before Liane's knees buckled. Karic quickly swung her up into his arms.

"I—I'm sorry," she gasped. "Just let me rest a moment, and I'll be able to walk a bit further."

"There's no need," Karic said, as he strode down the alley to the front of the building. "It's not that well lit here. If we keep to the shadows, we should be able to slip out of camp unnoticed."

"But you can't carry me all the way to Lyrae!"

He settled her more firmly in his arms. "Don't waste your strength arguing, Liane. When we're out of Fodina we'll see how you feel. In the meantime, you're hardly a burden to me."

Liane snuggled up against him. "If you say so," she tiredly sighed.

A wry grin touched his lips. He finally had Liane docile and obedient in his arms, but at too great a cost.

They managed to steal out of the mining camp unobserved and were soon headed up into the mountains. Though Liane tried, time and again, to walk on her own, she only succeeded in weakening herself further. Finally, Karic firmly informed her she'd be carried from here on out. With only the feeblest of protests, Liane acquiesced.

She slipped in and out of consciousness as the nocte wore on, blessedly unaware of the difficult time Karic was having in safely negotiating the steep terrain with her in his arms. He was thankful for that at least, for he knew her tender heart would never have borne seeing him struggle so hard climbing the rock-strewn mountain. Frequent rest stops were essential to relieve, at least temporarily, his painfully strained and burning muscles.

Near solrise Karic couldn't travel further. He found a shallow cave for them to take shelter in. After waking Liane long enough to force a healthy dose of water into her, he laid her down at the back of the cave and crawled in after her. Gathering her fevered body to him, he promptly fell asleep.

Muted cries, from somewhere below them, woke Karic. He cautiously climbed out of the cave and saw it was midsol by the height of the sun in the sky. He stealthily crept toward the strange sounds emanating from beyond a high outcropping of rock that overlooked the mountainside. When he reached the overlook, Karic gasped in outrage.

There, far below on a large plateau, a crowd of people huddled near the edge of a cliff. The great distance separating them made it impossible for Karic to make out any faces. Behind the people, on safer ground, were Bellatorian guards armed with blasters. But the sight of Necator, surrounded by his following of scientists and what appeared to be a greatly perfected version of the Guide, was the most chilling sight of all.

It was an experiment, Karic realized with a rising sense of presentiment, being carried out far from chance of discovery. And somehow, for some cold-blooded purpose that would surely further the Lord Commander's ambition to rule the Imperium, the hapless people on the edge of the cliff were now in the greatest danger of their lives.

CHAPTER 14

NECATOR TURNED TO THE SCIENTIST OPERATING THE Guide. "Begin the experiment."

The scientist nodded, then signaled the other Bellatorians who quickly donned their protective hearing devices. Seeing that, the crowd of frightened prisoners made a frantic surge forward. When the guards aimed their blasters, the people immediately backed away.

The little white-garbed man turned back to the Guide, punched in a command and adjusted a few dials. A low hum filled the air, rising in tone to a shrill, irritating whine.

As Karic watched from his vantage point high above the plateau, the Agricans gradually appeared to calm down. The machine's whine increased to deafening proportions, and the people slowly turned and began advancing toward the cliff.

Karic felt drawn. Only with the greatest of efforts

did he control the impulse to join his fellow Agricans. If he hadn't been so far away, he realized, if the Guide's powers weren't aimed in another direction . . .

He forced his attention back to the people below. Would Necator deem his experiment a success if he were able to halt the crowd at the edge of the cliff, or would it require sending them over to fully test the Guide? From bitter experience with the man, Karic doubted the Lord Commander would be satisfied with anything less than the death of the Agricans. Frantically, Karic searched his mind for some way to stop the mass slaughter.

He could run back to the cave and get the blaster, but it would do little good against so many armed guards. Even if he managed to damage the Guide in the process, he'd also alert the Bellatorians to his presence. He eyed the skim crafts located just behind the Guide. It would be impossible to escape pursuit with Liane in his arms.

The possibility of once more influencing the Guide flashed through his mind. Could he perhaps change its sound pattern again, negate its aural reprograming effects? It was worth a try.

Karic summoned forth all his strength and psychically directed a message to the machine, attempting to scramble its sound waves. Time passed as he hammered against it, the sweat beading his brow. For a fleeting instant, Karic thought he heard the shrill tones waver, then his concentration broke.

It was too much. The Guide's seductive pull, now more powerful than ever, had quickly weakened him.

He lay there for a few secundae, drained, his chest heaving, his body damp and trembling. Then, gathering his strength, Karic tried again. This time the sounds didn't waver, though he thought his brain would explode from the effort. The pain drove him to the brink of consciousness before he finally broke contact.

It was hopeless, Karic realized, impossible to maintain such intense effort long enough to effect any change. The now more sophisticated, highly evolved Guide was beyond his abilities of control. Indeed, he could barely resist it himself! The grave danger to all Agrica, Cat and non-Cat Man alike, was growing with each passing sol.

Fists clenched in impotent rage, Karic watched as the Agricans' mental resistance dissolved. One by one, they tumbled over the cliff. There were no cries of fear as they fell onto the rocks below. As the last victim disappeared over the edge, Necator ordered the machine shut down. The Guide was once more silent.

Karic stumbled back to the cave, horrified at what he'd witnessed. The enormity of its significance grew with each step. Now, not only for Liane's sake but for the sake of the entire planet, he must get back to his lair. This time, he must convince his people to take an active part in the destruction of the Guide and its evil creators. If they didn't, all would be lost.

Fleetingly, Karic realized that if he'd stayed with Liane in Fodina or, worse still, gone on to Lyrae, he'd never have witnessed the Guide's horrible new powers. He refused to ignore the ominous warning again. If he couldn't win the Council's support this time, he'd go after the machine alone.

But first, he must get Liane back to the lair. She was no better, he noted when he crawled into the cave. She felt hot, so very hot, and the sight of her

253

flushed face and fever-glazed eyes only increased his anxiety.

It would be dangerous to travel with Liane in sol light, but Karic knew he must get her to Agna, and quickly, or even the old healer's skills might not be enough to save her. He stared down at Liane tenderly, his eyes lovingly scanning her delicate features and slender form. Gently, Karic brushed away the ebony hair clinging to her fever-damp face. Then, pulling her into his arms, he backed out of the cave. Striding up the mountain, Karic headed toward home.

It was past mid nocte when Karic finally staggered into the lair and was met by his father. Morgan took one look at Liane and motioned for his son to move ahead.

"The Guide," Karic began as they hurried along. "Once more I've seen it, and its powers are now beyond my ability to control it. We're in the gravest danger. I must speak to the Council, convince them this time . . ."

"Later," his father said. "A few horas more or less won't make much difference, and at this moment Liane's need is greater. In the meantime, I'll speak to the Council for you."

Karic nodded and followed his father into Agna's cave.

She was up, a brisk fire already burning in the round stone hearth and a pot of water steaming over it. Her healing tools and supplies were laid out upon the table. Agna looked at Karic's grimy, haggard face.

"What happened to the femina?"

He carried Liane to the pallet laid out before the

254

fire. "Rapax wounds that had begun to heal, then broke open again and festered," Karic said. "They've been grieving her for about two sols now. Can you help her?"

The old healer poured some green liquid into a bowl. "We'll see. First, I need to examine Liane. You two leave while I undress her."

Karic hesitated. "I don't want to leave."

Agna made a shooing motion. "Get on with you. Will you waste my precious healer's time in argument? I'll call you back as soon as I've made her decent."

When they returned, Liane was on her stomach, a fur covering her from the waist down. Karic hurried over and knelt at her side.

"What do you think, Agna?"

The old healer joined him, a bowl that contained a green salve in her hand. At the sight of the swollen, pus-filled wounds, she grimaced.

"Worse than I thought. Bring me the box of rags and my cleansing water," she ordered, gesturing back toward the table.

Karic quickly complied. "What can I do to help?"

"Move to her head and hold down her arms and shoulders. And you, my lord," she said, glancing up at Morigan, "if you would, steady her hips and legs. What I'm about to do will cause her great pain, and I don't need her moving about."

She gazed down at Liane and grimly shook her head. "This must be quick and thorough, for we've little time to spare. The blood poison, even now, threatens her life."

For the next sol, Liane hovered between life and death. Karic never left her side, maintaining his vigil with her slender hand clasped in his. Early the second sol, Liane's fever broke and her fitful slumber eased.

Agna's hand settled on Karic's shoulder. "I made you a pallet." She gestured to some furs and blankets laid out against a nearby wall. "Take your rest there. She is out of danger now. You're no good to her if you sicken yourself."

"You'll call me if she wakes?"

The old healer smiled. "You know I will."

Karic rose and staggered over to the small bed. Throwing himself down, he promptly fell asleep.

It was early evening before he awoke to Agna shaking him.

"My lord? Your femina is asking for you."

Karic groggily sat up. Agna's hand stayed him when he made a move to rise.

"I'll await you outside," she said smiling down at him, "and give you time to talk with her."

Before the old woman was out of the cave Karic was at Liane's side, kneeling to take her hand in his. Intense blue eyes gazed up at him.

"Karic?" Liane murmured. "Where am I?"

He dragged in a breath before answering her. "I had to bring you back to the lair. It was the only way to save your life."

She stared up at him for a long moment, then her eyes filled with tears. "You pro—promised to take me to Lyrae. You lied."

Liane pulled her hand from his clasp and turned her face away. "You *lied*, Karic," she whispered.

Pain stabbed through him. He knew how his act in bringing her here must appear. Once again, she thought he'd broken his word. Frustration, at the unkind fate that ceaselessly threw one obstacle then another in the path of their love, rose to overwhelm him. Curse it all! It wasn't his fault!

Anger roughened his grasp, as he took Liane's chin and turned her face to him. "I didn't lie," Karic corrected her. "Don't lay that upon me, too. You'd be dead if I hadn't brought you here. There was no other choice."

She glared up at him, her anger giving her strength. "Then will you still take me to Lyrae, once I am better?"

His eyes narrowed, and a hardness settled over his features. "You know that's no longer an option. Within this lair, we are again bound by its laws."

"Then I say curse you," Liane hissed, "for you have brought me back to a far worse fate than death could have ever been. Once again you have betrayed me for your people. I hate you!"

Her anger-bright eyes never left his. "I hate you, Karic," she softly repeated.

"No, Liane," Karic rasped, "you don't hate me." He released his grip on her and climbed to his feet. "But that knowledge is more frightening than your hatred can ever be, for you won't face it, will you?"

He stared down with tormented eyes. "What else could I do but bring you back? You know I couldn't let you die. I love you too much for that. But none of that matters, does it? As hard as I try, I can't seem to make it right between us. I can't seem to do anything but cause you pain, over and over and over again."

Karic turned to lean against the mantle. "Choose me at the Mating Festival," he hoarsely said. "I will not force myself upon you, not then or ever. And when the time is right, I will take you from here, to Lyrae or anywhere else you wish to go. I will do this,

257

go against my people and laws, and have it done between us. I swear it, Liane."

"And what is this or any of your other promises to me, Karic?" she bitterly replied. "They mean nothing, *nothing* to you. You'll break this one just as surely as you did all the others. I cannot trust you. Go away," she brokenly whispered. "Just go away!"

For a moment Karic's shoulders heaved with the effort to contain his fierce emotions. Then he strode from Agna's lair.

Liane gazed after him, silence settling heavily in the little cave. Finally, the old healer tottered in.

"You must end this battle with the young lord," she solemnly chided Liane, kneeling beside her. "It is tearing both of you apart. You must accept that part of him that is committed to our people. He would not be the man you love without it."

"But it is that same part that will someday separate us," Liane whispered. "He wants me to be his mate, but he can promise me nothing. And I refuse to be a breeder, to be passed around at the whim of your exalted Council everytime they deem fit."

"Nothing is certain in this existence, child," Agna sighed. "Neither love, nor life, nor permanent happiness. I bore my children and loved my man, never guessing I'd outlive them all, but even if I'd known, I'd have done it all the same. You cannot avoid the pain of living. It will find you despite your best efforts. But you can miss the loving and the happiness, if you don't grasp it while you can."

She tenderly brushed the tangled hair from Liane's forehead. "Beware, child, that you condemn yourself to such a fate. Regret can sear the soul far worse than loss ever can."

Liane's eyes lifted to Agna. "I am so afraid."

"I know, child, I know." The old woman stroked

her, her touch strangely soothing. "Now, sleep for a time. You need to rest and heal. Time enough to deal with your heart when you waken."

Comforted by the feather-light fingers gliding down her face, Liane's eyes closed. Agna was right, she drowsily thought. The problems of her heart could indeed wait . . . just a little while . . . longer . . .

An hora later, Morigan found Karic at the communal woodpile, savagely splitting logs. He silently watched him for a time, noting the anger and immense frustration that fueled his son's forceful efforts. Finally, Karic paused, his breath coming in ragged gasps, his body glistening with sweat.

"She didn't understand, did she?"

Karic wheeled around, his fist clenching the ax handle. Fury blazed in his eyes.

"Oh, she understood well enough," he growled, burying the ax deep in an unsplit log. He eyed the tool, its handle still quivering with the force of his toss. "With that unbending pride of hers she's just too cursed stubborn to give in."

"Yes, with her pride *and* her fear of you."

Karic's head jerked up. "Yes, that, too," he sighed. "But there's nothing more I can do. If she chooses another at the Festival, so be it. It'll hurt, but I've survived worse."

He gave a bitter laugh. "Indeed, what other choice is there?"

"I'm sorry, Son. Perhaps if I hadn't interferred."

Karic sadly shook his head. "It doesn't matter. She doesn't love me enough to fight past the obstacles. It's as simple as that, and time I accepted it. Now," he continued, his features hardening in remembrance, "there's an issue of more pressing

259

import—to our people and our ultimate survival. What has the Council decided about the Guide?"

Morgan arched a graying brow, then nodded. "They are eager to know more. How can we fight it?"

"We can't, I'm afraid," Karic glumly muttered. "At least not with a frontal attack. We'll have to find a way of destroying it when it's not functioning. And we must take out Necator and his scientists, too. Anyone with knowledge of how to rebuild the machine must die."

"How do you propose we get into Primasedes with that new alarm system of theirs?"

Karic scowled. "I haven't figured that part out yet. All I know is we've no other choice. Sooner or later Necator will come looking for us with a Guide powerful enough to mentally drag us out of our lairs. It's all a matter of reprograming strength. Necator demonstrated the extent of his ruthlessness when he murdered those people. He won't stop until he's done the same to us."

"We'll need some plan to present to the Council," Morgan carefully ventured. "Something more than what you've got right now. They'll support you this time, but we dare not rush into this without a plan. We'll only have one chance at the Guide—and we must succeed."

"I know all that, Father." Karic let out a deep breath. "But at this moment I haven't any idea what that plan is." He lifted his head, a resolute gleam in his eyes. "But I will—and soon. Council support or no, I'm going back to Primasedes. *Someone* has got to take on Necator before it's too late!"

Morgan stalked his lair, nervously awaiting Liane's arrival. A full seven sols had ensued since her return and, thanks to Agna's miraculous salves and healing powders, the beautiful Bellatorian was again restored to full health. Healthy enough to attend the Mating Festival this nocte, he grimly thought, and healthy enough to choose a mate. One last time, Morigan would attempt to convince her that her choice should be his son.

Her slender form darkened the cave's entrance. Then, with a resolute straightening of her shoulders, Liane entered. Morigan motioned for her to take a seat.

"A cup of uva wine, perhaps?" he asked.

Liane seated herself. "Yes, please."

Morigan poured out two cups of the burgundy liquor and passed one to her.

"Why did you summon me, my lord?"

He leaned forward on the table. "This senseless battle between you and Karic must end. It's breaking his heart."

Liane lifted her cup for a sip of wine, betraying the sudden trembling of her hand. She locked eyes with his. "Then let me go."

"You know that's impossible."

"Then it's your laws that are breaking his heart."

Green-gold eyes glittered over at her. "You are a heartlessly stubborn femina. What are you so afraid of?"

Liane stiffened. "I am not afraid. I just don't like your laws."

"Really?" A sad smile touched his lips. "And I say you use our laws as a shield to guard your heart. Our laws have never been the real problem, have they, Liane?"

She nervously swallowed. "I . . . I don't know what you mean."

"Don't you? Is not the real issue your fear of

Karic's sexual urges, ever since that nocte of the triple moons?"

Hot embarrassment flooded Liane. She rose. "You have no right to speak to me of that. I will not stay and—"

"Sit down, femina."

The words were uttered in a low voice, but the hard command was there, nonetheless. Liane sank back into her chair.

Morigan gazed over into hostile blue eyes. He must tread carefully here, he realized, or risk losing her respect for the rest of their lives.

"Truly, I didn't mean to offend," he carefully began, "but there is much you don't understand that I would have you know. Bear with me a bit more, before you judge the impropriety of my actions."

She forced herself to relax and nodded. "As you wish, my lord."

Morigan heard the tinge of skepticism but chose to ignore it. "The nocte of the triple moons," he began, "and the wild passions it stirs has always been an event of great pleasure and anticipation, as well as one of great shame. Though we understand its significance in the continued propagation of our species, we also find it a most uncomfortable reminder of our animalistic origins. We mate on that one nocte of every three cycles like beasts, instinctively, unthinkingly."

Morigan's gaze locked with hers. "We are not proud of it but have learned to accept it in ourselves. There's no point dwelling upon what cannot be changed. Instead, we dedicate our efforts to what *can* be changed. And truly, among our own people, that nocte is one of mutual pleasure, so no real harm is done."

Liane shuddered in remembrance. "I found no pleasure in it."

"No, I don't suppose you did." Morigan's voice softened in understanding. "By the time you reached Karic, he must have been mad from the pain of fighting his urges. He was beyond rational control. And I tell you truly, Liane, if you hadn't arrived when you did, it would have soon killed him."

"I don't understand." Liane's eyes riveted on the older man. "Why would it have killed Karic?"

"The mating urge on that nocte is powerful. It cannot be denied without dire consequences. Karic left you, knowing you'd spurn his advances, hoping to make it back to a more willing femina in some village you'd passed along the way."

"Devra," Liane murmured. "He must have been going back to Devra."

"He *had* to mate with some female, Liane," Morigan persisted. "Don't you understand? Karic would have died a horrible, excrutiatingly painful death otherwise. But he didn't make it to the village. The urge struck too quickly. Unintentionally, your arrival saved his life."

The blood drained from Liane's face. Aware of her decision to remain celibate, Karic had chosen to risk his life in an effort to spare her. He had left that nocte to protect her, not knowing if he'd even reach Devra's village in time, but it had been worth the danger to him.

A hot wave of shame rolled through Liane. To think that she had called him an animal!

She raised tearful eyes. "I . . . I didn't know. He didn't tell me."

Morigan's hard stare pierced right through her. "You wouldn't let him tell you."

263

Liane's head lowered. "You're right. I didn't even give him a chance to explain. I couldn't get past my anger, nor my need for revenge."

She looked up, her smile wry. "It's the Bellatorian part of me, you know."

"It's understandable. However unintentional, my son took something of great value from you. For all your Sententian heritage, you've the heart of a warrior. It was natural you'd fight back." He paused. "But a warrior also knows when it's time to stop fighting, when to admit the battle is over, that to struggle on is only to cause more harm and gain little good. It's past time to cease your battle, Liane."

"Yes, perhaps you are right." Liane closed her eyes on the threatening tears. "But my fear of him won't as easily disappear. It goes too deep after what he did to me. I—I don't know if I can ever overcome it."

"And I cannot help you with that," Morgan quietly replied, "except to tell you how it was with Karic's mother. She, too, loathed and feared me when I first captured her."

His eyes darkened with loving memories. "Rissa was beautiful and as fiery as they came. I loved her from the first moment I saw her. But she didn't want me and fought me every step of the way, until I despaired of ever winning her heart."

"Yet you did."

Morgan nodded, his eyes gleaming. "Yes, I did. Rissa finally came to realize that, even with my half-animal blood, I was also a man, a man who loved and needed her, a man who could be gentle as well as passionate. She found happiness with me, Liane. Of that I am certain. Won't you allow Karic a chance to give you that same happiness? He loves you deeply."

Joy swelled in Liane, rising to swirl chaotically with her deep-seated fears. If only she could trust Karic, be certain he'd never hurt her and turn into that horribly mindless beast. But how would she ever know if she didn't take him as mate?

The thought both thrilled and terrified her, and, slowly, a plan insinuated itself into her mind. She'd avoided the reality of her situation for too long. She'd been a fool. She had no other choice but to choose Karic and mate with him. Then, if she forced his control to its utmost limits, she would finally have her answer. It was a dangerous gamble, with dire consequences if she failed, but one she must risk if she hoped to have any chance of happiness with Karic.

Liane rose. "But a few horas separate me from the Mating Festival. I need time to consider your words. I beg leave of you, my lord."

Morigan studied her and found no hint of any decision on her face. He sighed. Well, he had tried. "You have my leave, femina."

She hurried out of the cool cave and back into the afternoon sun. Her steps quickened as she headed down the valley to Agna's lair. It was almost too late to carry out her plan, a plan that really should have been tested before the Mating Festival to ascertain the extent of Karic's control, but there was no time left. No time left, yet so much to be learned. She certainly knew nothing of the art of loving between a man and a woman.

As the triple moons began their ascent in the blackened sky, drumbeats, rhythmic and slow, filled the air. At the sound, Karic looked at his father. A sad smile touched his lips.

Wordlessly, the two men left their lair, their long strides carrying them toward the large bonfire where, even now, the Cat People gathered. The steady beating of the drums grew louder, hypnotic and sensual in the relentless pounding, calling one and all to the ritual gathering place. It was time to once again choose a mate and renew the age-old call to join flesh and propagate the species.

As they reached the brightly lit area, sheltered on three sides by sheer rock walls and guarded overhead by sentries to preclude discovery by unexpected enemy patrols, father and son parted. Morigan strode to his royal throne set upon a lavishly decorated dais, while Karic moved to join the other males of mating age. Karic's gaze briefly met those of the others. They glowed with an excited, hungry light.

Normally, the heady anticipation of joining with a new femina would have stirred Karic as strongly, but that was before Liane, before he'd loved and lost her. Because of that, this nocte would hold only pain as he watched her go to another.

The thought of his own fate never troubled him for a moment. It mattered not that Kalina would once again choose him. He would do his duty for his people, but that was all it would be—a physical release, a joyless mating, for it would not be with Liane.

Morigan raised his hand. The drums ceased. He stood, scanning the assemblage. Then he smiled.

"Let the feminas be brought forward," he intoned the ritual words, "for this nocte the circle of life begins anew."

A hush settled over the crowd as Agna, the eldest of the lair's feminas, led Liane and the rest through the vine-twisted archway at the far end of the walled enclosure. Karic's eyes riveted on her.

Her face was pale but resolute, her lips clamped tight. She clasped Agna's hand as if afraid to let go, but she followed without hesitation. The firelight bathed her in its golden brilliance, glinting off her crimson gown. Karic's breath caught in his throat.

The fabric skimmed her body, outlining each curve from the full swell of her breasts to the gentle indentation of a narrow waist and softly flaring hips. The neckline of the sleeveless garment dipped low, for a tantalizing glimpse of the satin valley between her tenderly rounded flesh. Karic thought he'd go mad with yearning. In spite of himself he felt himself swell and thicken.

Her eyes met his, and Liane threw back her head, the luxuriant ebony mane tumbling about her shoulders. She'd seen his desire, he realized, and was angered, even repulsed by it. Desolation knotted in his chest. Would he ever be able to hide his feelings from her?

The drums began anew as Agna led Liane and the other feminas to their spot beside Morigan's throne. There they halted to face the males standing across the fire. Eyes ablaze with excitement and hot with desire glowed in the flickering firelight as each group gazed at the other—all but Liane and Karic. Suddenly, they could not seem to bear another moment of the fierce burning heat in each other's eyes.

Morigan stepped down from the dais. "Bring forward the first femina," he commanded, indicating Liane.

Agna gave Liane a quick, reassuring smile and led her over to stand before the Lord of the Cat People. Placing the younger woman's hand in his, the old healer stepped back to her place with the other feminas. Liane unwaveringly gazed up at Morgan.

"Have you made your decision?" he asked, his deep voice carrying to the furthest reaches of the gathering.

She nodded.

"Then I wish you well and hope your choice brings you happiness," Morgan solemnly replied. "Name the male who will be your mate, for this nocte and all the noctes of the coming three cycles."

Every muscle in Karic's body tightened. Blood pounded through his skull, and a fierce trembling wracked his tautly strung frame. Now, Karic thought, in bitter, shattering agony, she will choose another and have her final revenge.

Deep blue eyes slowly scanned the assemblage until they met Karic's. A soft smile played upon Liane's lips. "I choose your son, my lord. I choose Karic for my mate."

As a collective gasp swelled through the crowd, Karic thought his heart would burst from joy. He wildly searched her eyes for confirmation. The gentle acquiesance smoldering there nearly brought Karic to his knees. She wanted him! She had chosen him!

The murmuring of the people rose in volume and, from the group of feminas, Kalina stridently cried, "No, it cannot be! She is not one of us. She is not worthy of him. Make her choose another!"

Morgan sharply eyed the flame-haired Cat Woman, then quickly silenced the crowd. "The femina has made her choice, and it will stand. She has abided by our laws. We will do the same. She has chosen Karic, and so shall it be."

He motioned to his son. "Come. Your mate awaits you."

Karic strode around the fire to halt before him. Taking his hand, Morigan placed it in Liane's. "He is yours," he said, smiling down at her. "Be a good and faithful mate. Be fruitful. Be happy."

The drums pounded wildly as Karic tugged at her hand. She glanced up at him.

"Come," he said, his voice all but drowned out by the drums. "The ceremony is over for us."

Her chin lifted. "Yes, let us go. What is still between us is best dealt with in private."

Karic's eyes darkened, but he said no more. He led her across the enclosure. Behind them, Morigan's voice once more rose to fill the summer nocte's air.

"Bring the next femina forward."

They were barely inside the cave before Karic turned to Liane. "Why did you choose me?"

She steadily returned his gaze. "It's quite simple, really. I've decided to hold you to your promise."

His eyes narrowed. "You toy with me, Liane," he softly warned, "and I am near my breaking point in this."

"As am I," she calmly replied. "But it was your choice, not mine. Will you once more foreswear your vow to me?"

Karic strode to the hearth, where he stood with head bowed and shoulders taut. Then he cast an agonized glance back at her. "I told you before. I won't force my attentions upon you. I swear it!"

Her mouth trembled into a smile. "Thank you for

that. I'll not ask such a sacrifice of you, though. I'll be your mate and bear your children, for as long as they'll let us stay together."

Fierce joy flared in Karic. He closed the distance between them. His hands moved to take her into his arms, but Liane halted him.

"What, Liane?" he asked. "What else lies between us? Tell me now, and let it be done with forever."

She inhaled a steadying breath. "Foolish though it may seem, some tiny part of me fears you still—your animal side, the extent of your control. I still need to get past that, or we can never be happy together."

"What do you want from me? Name it, and it's yours."

A blush slowly stained her cheeks. "You put your life at my disposal once, when you forced that dagger into my hand. This nocte, I ask not for your life but your body. Can you not trust me in this?"

He frowned. "I trust you, Liane, but I would know what you mean to do."

Liane's courage nearly fled in the hot embarrassment that flooded her. How, in all the heavens, could she tell him, much less see this through? Agna had taught her all she could in the span of a few horas of the art of pleasuring a male, of bringing him to the very edge of control—and beyond. But now, faced with the reality of Karic's powerfully intimidating presence and her total lack of experience in such things, would she have the necessary determination to see it through?

And yet, if she didn't, some part of her would fear him for the rest of her life.

Liane stared up with gloriously determined eyes. "I want us to go to your sleeping chamber. I want you to undress and lie down upon your bed—and

270

then the rest will follow.''

A faintly wry smile touched Karic's lips. "And that is how you hold me to my promise?" He gave a low laugh. "Come, let us begin at once."

Liane hurried past him and down the short hallway to his bedchamber. Once inside she wheeled about to face him. Karic halted before her.

"Well, go ahead," she silkily commanded. "Disrobe."

CHAPTER 15

KARIC STRODE OVER TO THE BED AND SAT DOWN. IN A few quick movements, he pulled off his boots and flung them aside. His hands next went to his loincloth. He hesitated there as their eyes met.

"There's no need for false modesty," Liane said. "I'm well aware what you look like—most *graphically* aware."

With a puzzled frown, Karic rose and shed the loincloth. At the sight of him standing there, magnificent and proud in his nakedness, Liane experienced a startling rush of desire. She suddenly felt small and vulnerable, and the almost tangible heat of his presence sent a shudder of fear coursing through her. Even now there was something so elemental, so primal about Karic. The realization stirred an answering, if reluctant, attraction in Liane.

Heart pounding in her chest, she forced herself to

walk toward him. "Lie down." Liane choked out the words.

Karic scowled but turned to the bed and lay down. Never taking his eyes off her, he leaned back on his arms. A mocking smile tilted his lips.

"Well, femina? I but await your pleasure."

So, Liane thought, hearing the challenge in his voice, he doubts I can see this through. Anger stirred her resolve. She was a female, he a male. Instinct would surely guide her wherever she found Agna's instructions lacking. She walked over to the bed and lowered herself next to Karic. Propping herself on her side, she unwaveringly gazed over at him.

He stared back.

A faint sheen of moisture gleamed on his muscular torso. His thick pectoral muscles rose and fell with his deep, even breathing. Fascinated, Liane touched the aureum Cat's claw that dangled below the hollow of his throat, then slid her fingers through the tangle of dark gold hair that covered him. The satin smooth feel of his skin beneath the wiry crispness startled her. Her lids fluttered up to meet Karic's gaze.

His eyes were deep jade and smoldering.

Something hot and aching pierced her. Liane trembled. Her fingers skimmed downward to the rippling, hairy ridges of his abdomen—then lower. As she neared his manhood her hand veered away to move across his groin and down his legs. She stroked the slightly parted thighs, her fingers slipping between them to brush the sensitive inner flesh. Karic tensed, and a hiss escaped his clenched teeth.

Liane looked at his dark nest of hair where, even now, his sex was swelling. A grimly satisfied smile curved her lips. Agna had spoken true. A female's power over a male was great, and Karic was so very, very sensitive.

She looked up into his eyes, eyes hot with barely veiled excitement. "You like it, don't you, Karic?" Liane silkily purred, continuing all the while her feather-light stroking, trailing a path up his groin, then back down again.

"My body can sometimes betray me," he said, his mouth tightening in frustration at her easy effect upon him, "but I'm still in full control. You needn't worry."

"Oh, I'm not worried." Liane wound a slender finger back up his body to teasingly circle a flat male nipple. "Not worried at all."

She leaned over him then. Her lips captured Karic's nipple, and she gently laved it with her tongue. All the while, Liane watched him. He stared back at her, his face impassive save for the muscle spasming in his jaw. He could not contain the tensing of his body, however. Liane smiled and moved to tongue his other nipple to a dark, puckered arousal.

His maleness thrust boldly against her.

Her lips trailed a heated path up his chest to his strong, corded neck. She nuzzled him there, smoothing back his mane to run the tip of her moist tongue up to his ear. Karic shuddered when she delicately outlined its curves. His eyes closed.

Liane took his face into her hands, turning it to her. Karic's eyes slowly opened. Green fire burned there, igniting an answering conflagration within her. Liane felt hot, filled with a need she'd never experienced before. Suddenly, she knew she wasn't prepared to deal with it.

She risked more than Karic's loss of control. She

was treading in uncertain territory now, when it came to her own body and responses, and that loss of self-discipline loomed before her as a yawning, fearful thing. Yet the need still grew, exploding into hot, wild lust when her mouth took his.

Karic's response was just as instinctive. With a low groan, his lips parted. His tongue darted out to meet hers. He played with her, his mouth his only weapon, gently inserting then withdrawing each time she responded. And Liane matched him, thrust for thrust, kiss for kiss. But when his head moved lower, to trail his searing lips down her neck, she stiffened.

Slender fingers tightened on Karic's face, and she pulled back from him. "No," Liane huskily forced out the word. "You are not permitted even that. Do you understand?"

Sudden comprehension darkened his eyes. He fell back with a frustrated sigh. "Why are you doing this? You deny yourself as much pleasure as you do me, and by doing so, your torment will be just as great."

Renewed determination flowed through Liane. "And I say you flatter yourself." She backed off the bed to stand before him.

Karic's eyes narrowed. "What? What now, Liane?"

She smiled as she began to unfasten her brightly woven belt. "I am warm, that's all. I think I'll get more comfortable."

Liane freed the belt and let it drop to the floor. Her hand moved to the shoulder of her gown. She slid her fingers beneath the sleeveless strap and pushed it down. It fell and hung loosely on her upper arm, exposing a tantalizing glimpse of ivory-hued breast.

Karic scowled.

Languidly, Liane tarried over the other strap, prolonging the moment when its downward slide would free the garment from her body. Finally, as her eyes lifted to boldly meet his, the gown slithered to the ground.

For long secundae Liane stood there in the dim, flickering light. She could almost feel Karic's gaze sweep over her, feel the tips of her breasts tingle at his hungry, searing look. Suddenly, all she wanted were his hands on her, his mouth, the weight of his body pressed against hers. Her heart pounded wildly. She forced herself to move back toward the bed.

She climbed back over and knelt beside Karic. He tensed as her hand moved toward him, and when she touched him, her fingers curling around his thickly swollen shaft, he groaned, arching yet further into her hand.

Liane thought she'd lose all control. She could barely breathe as she began to stroke him and saw him throw back his head, his face becoming taut and strained. She continued to arouse him, kneading, squeezing, sliding up and down his smooth hard length. Karic's fists clenched in the furs, his breath a ragged rasp. Trembling spasms wracked his body, and Liane could feel him struggle to contain a wild, fierce passion. Sweat gleamed on his thickly muscled form, yet all the while he never touched her.

Liane ached for him and felt herself grow hot and wet with her own need. She lowered herself to lie beside him, leaning over to rub her nipples against Karic's rhythmically straining body. The shock of his hair-matted chest against her sensitive flesh made Liane gasp with pleasure.

Karic's lids snapped open. Liane stared into tormented green eyes, eyes surely as tormented as her own, she realized from some distant part of her mind. Her mouth lowered to his. He eagerly kissed her with hard, brutal passion, but this time Liane felt no fear. Her need was as great as his. Tongues plunged wildly, savagely, in some primitive imitation of the true coupling to come.

She moved to straddle Karic's tautly straining form, her hand ceaselessly stroking him, her mouth slanting fiercely over his. She lowered herself to meet his powerful body. His shaft, throbbing and hard beneath her fingers, pressed against her belly.

At the touch Karic went rigid, his hot green eyes impaling her. "Liane," he moaned. "Please . . ."

Fear once again shot through her. Karic was so desperately ready. What would he do if she now denied him? Go mad and take her? The consideration wasn't as horrible as she'd imagined it might be, and a tiny, most irrational part of her almost wished he would.

But reason forced its way to the surface. She must know, once and for all, what Karic's response would be if she denied him—and that moment was now upon them.

"Liane . . ." he groaned, the sound long, low and so very male in its need.

She knew what he was asking, what he wanted and craved with every fiber of his being, but for this one, final moment in her life, she hardened herself to him.

"No." The word was gritted out with the last bit of strength left in her. "No, Karic, I'm not finished with you yet."

Agony burned in his eyes as he fell back against the bed. "Then finish it, Liane," he whispered, his voice raw. "Finish it now, before I go mad."

Tears stung Liane's eyes as she forced her hand to move again, her mouth to sweetly seduce his. Karic writhed beneath her, futilely biting back the gutteral sounds that rose to his lips. His face darkened, contorting with the increasingly brutal effort it took to hold himself in check, but never once, in all that time, did he stop her. He accepted every torturous touch Liane bestowed—accepted, trusted and waited.

Finally, it was Liane's control that broke. On a broken sob, her head lowered to his chest. "Karic," she cried, her voice a mix of remorse and desire, "it's enough! I—I believe you. Oh, Karic, please, I can't bear anymore!"

With a low, animal growl his arms encircled her, pulling her to him. He rolled over, pinning Liane beneath him in a sudden movement.

"Tell me you want me," Karic hoarsely demanded. "I want to hear you say it, for after that there's no turning back. I really *will* be out of control!"

"I want you," Liane achingly whispered. "I love you, Karic. And I don't care if you lose control, as long as you always take me with you!"

An exquisitely tender look flared in his eyes. "Truly? You truly love me, femina?"

"Yes. I've loved you for a long while, buried beneath all my pain and anger. Can you ever forgive me?"

He slowly nodded. "As you forgive me."

She smiled, a sweetly tremulous movement of her lips. "Then it's done, over, behind us forever. Now love me, Karic. Join with me and let us bury all the anguish between us." Liane tenderly stroked his face. "Come to me, my love."

His head lowered. "In time, sweet femina," he thickly growled, turning her own words against her. "I'm not finished with *you* yet."

He took a soft, rosy nipple into his mouth and gently suckled it, his tongue gradually flicking the hardening tip with increasing force. Liane gasped and arched against him. His mouth moved then to nip and lick her breasts until she was moaning, moving wildly against him in frantic, panting desire.

Karic watched her, relishing his power, the same power she'd held over him, a power she still had, he wryly realized, his organ throbbing hotly against her. It was rock-hard and straining, ready to explode. His fingers moved, caressing a languid path down her body to the tangle of dense curls that guarded her femininity.

Liane tensed when he touched her there, pressing back against the furs as his hand possessively cupped her woman's mound.

"You are mine, femina," Karic whispered. "All of you. Don't be afraid. There'll be no pain this time. Only pleasure. I swear it."

On a shuddering sigh, Liane moved back to him. His hand slipped down, one finger parting the wet folds to slide slickly into her deep cleft. She trembled violently when he found that sweet, secret flesh and began to gently massage it. Of their own accord, Liane's thighs parted, instinctively granting Karic even greater access.

His mouth moved once again to hers as he continued the rhythmic caress between her legs. His kiss was fierce, hard and utterly uncompromising, but Liane's response was just as ardent. He felt the heat of her against his stiffness, felt it flame hotter and hotter. Suddenly, all Karic knew was a wild urgency to join with her, to thrust himself deeply, endlessly into her.

He grasped himself, pushing up with his other hand. For one last, delicious instant, he rubbed his swollen tip against her flesh, seeking out her velvety pink sheath. Then he thrust up, swiftly and surely.

Liane cried out as he filled her, but the sound was one of intense pleasure, not pain. She grasped at Karic, clutching his hips to her, digging her nails into his taut flesh. Her cry faded to a low moan as Karic plunged against her. Her hands were crazed, sliding over him, grabbing at his broad, straining shoulders, stroking his sweat-drenched back. She was on fire, trembling with wet heat, aching unbearably.

A wild, wondering cry ripped from Liane's throat. Her whole body was a rioting mass of sensations. She gazed up at Karic in unbelieving wonder, fighting it all the way.

He smiled down at her, holding back his own release. "Yes, my love," he growled, his deep voice thick with passion, "let yourself go. Trust me. Don't fear it. It's good, so very good."

She surrendered then, spiraling up and away from all thought, all awareness, save that of the sensual vibrations shuddering through her. Her slender body tensed, arching against his, spasming in ecstasy as Karic again and again plunged into her in an ever increasing frenzy of his own. She cried out his name, seeking him in her churning maelstrom of desire.

Karic sucked in a breath, then gasped, tensing above her. His face contorted with pleasure as his release shuddered through him. Then he collapsed against Liane, moaning her name into the tangled mass of her hair.

"Well, have I finally convinced you of the extent of my control?" Karic drowsily murmured late the next morning, snuggled tightly to Liane's softly rounded backside.

Harking back to the long nocte filled with heated passionate couplings, Liane smiled. Karic had been a skilled lover. His control, unlike her own, had seemed nearly superhuman.

No, Liane thought with a small, guilty pang. Karic had spoken true. Except for that one nocte every three cycles, he was no animal—save in the most wonderfully sensual interpretation of the word.

The thought and its accompanying memories stirred her. "Well, you've tried mightily, my love," she teased, "but I'm still not quite convinced. Perhaps one more demonstration of your prowess . . . ?"

His hand stroked the softly curved line of her hip and thigh. "You're insatiable, you know," he growled.

Karic's grip tightened, and he jerked her more tightly to him. His groin pressed against her buttocks, hot and full. Liane's smile widened. He was so sensitive, and she found she loved it that way.

She rolled over to face him. His shaft, throbbing and hard, pressed against her belly. Boldly, Liane's hand moved downward to close around his massive length. Karic shuddered beneath her touch and rose to straddle her, one leg kneeing her thighs apart. She spread herself wide, eager for him.

With both hands, he lifted Liane's hips and swiftly thrust into her.

Liane cried out. She flung her arms around Karic, wildly stroking his back, urging him on. She whimpered and arched, wrapping her legs around his hips, grabbing his taut buttocks. Her release came quickly.

She threw back her head, nearly sobbing out her pleasure. Karic groaned and drove himself into her. His pace increased now, harsh and deep. Then, with a raw cry, he collapsed atop her.

They lay there for a few secundae, Karic buried deep within, their bodies molded damply to each other. Then he rolled free and lay there, one arm flung across his eyes.

"Well, are you convinced?" he asked, his thickly muscled chest rapidly rising and falling. "If not, I fear I may soon die in the proving."

Liane moved to snuggle against him. "I'll go gently with you from now on. In truth, you convinced me long ago."

Karic uncovered his eyes to arch a dubious brow. Liane shrugged. "Can I help it if you pleasure me so well that I cannot seem to get my fill of it? Is it my fault that you have such a power over me?"

"Why, you devious little she cat!" Karic laughed and grabbed for her, but Liane nimbly eluded him, swinging down off the bed.

"Now, calm yourself," she giggled, backing away, her hands held before her as Karic quickly followed. "You just said a moment ago that you were near death. Have a care for that ill-used, exhausted body of yours."

"Have a care for *your* ill-used body, femina," he growled, grasping her wrist to pull her to him. "I'm not so exhausted I can't soon rise to the occasion."

Liane glanced down at Karic, past the hard, flat

belly and narrow hips, to glimpse the swelling of his organ. Her eyes widened. "You truly *are* an animal."

This time the words, words so fraught with past painful memories, were uttered in delighted wonder. Karic laughed, the sound rich and deep. "Yes, Liane, I suppose I am."

He crooked her chin with a long strong finger, lifting her face to his. "And, in the most wonderful of ways, so are you."

He kissed her, playing ever so softly with her lips and gently inserting his tongue. Liane rose to meet him, her own response sweetly tender. Finally, Karic reluctantly raised his head.

"You know as well as I where this will soon lead," he said, stepping back from her. "And as much as I would prefer to spend the rest of the sol in here with you, there are Festival duties to be seen to. We have just enough time for a quick bath in the forest pool, if you'd care to join me."

A slender brow quirked coyly. "And what's there to protect me from your untoward advances in the pool, as naked and helpless as I'll be?"

Karic grinned. "Only my famous control, sweet femina. I suppose you'll just have to trust me in that."

She grinned back. "Oh, I trust you, Cat Man." Her gaze raked his tall, powerfully naked form. "That's not the problem. It's me I don't trust."

The hunting party, gone to bring back game for the Festival feasting that nocte, left early. Though traditionally he went along, Karic knew his father had understood and had purposely not awakened him at sol rise. He felt a fleeting twinge of regret and then turned back to his enjoyment of Liane and the sol.

Ceremonial duties filled the rest of the afternoon, but Karic was content with Liane at his side. His people seemed to accept her presence there, as if choosing him last nocte had sealed her place in their lair. Only Kalina, murderously glaring at Liane from afar, marred the otherwise blissful sol. But Karic shoved the memory of the Cat Woman's anger into some distant corner of his mind, along with the upcoming journey to Primasedes to destroy the Guide.

The Council had unanimously accepted Karic's plan to destroy the Guide. He would take a party of about 50 men and, to avoid detection as they traveled across Agrica, divide them into even smaller groups. Each would take a different route and meet at Liane's forest hut in three sol's time. From there, Karic's plan was a little more desperate.

He gambled that he had been captured previously because of his lack of awareness of the alarm system. Hopefully he and his men's cloaking powers, combined with their ability to manipulate most machines, would this time overcome the alarms. Then, if they could reach the system and disable it . . .

But if not, Karic would sacrifice some of his men so that others could reach the Guide and destroy it. The Bellatorians could not capture all of them at once, alarm system or no alarm system. And the stakes were just that high.

The huge, shimmering sun began to set behind the western mountains, and still Morigan and the hunting party had not returned. Unease settled over Karic. It wasn't like his father to stay away at a hunt so long. The mountains teemed with game. The

Festival hunting had never required more than a half sol before. Unless, Karic thought with rising apprehension, unless the Guide was still in the mountains.

Karic angrily shook the horrible consideration aside, but the niggling fear could not so easily be discarded. What if Necator hadn't headed back to Primasedes after testing his weapon on those hapless Agricans? What if he'd remained to systematically sift his way through the mountains, searching for further humanoids to destroy—searching for them?

He bit down on a savage curse, enraged at his own stupidity. He'd been so blind, so engrossed in saving Liane's life at the time, that he'd not considered every possibility when it came to Necator and his evil machine. His people had depended on him; he was the only one who knew the Guide's full powers. And now that one slip could cost not only his father's life, but the lives of the entire race of Cat Men as well.

"What is it, Karic? What's wrong?"

Liane's sweet voice, threaded with concern, intruded on his heated musings.

"My father and the hunting party are long overdue," he gruffly explained. "I fear there's trouble."

She nodded. "I feel it, too. There's some danger about. What will you do?"

"Send out a search party. It'll be easy enough to track our own kind. Our spoors are very distinctive."

A small hand clasped his arm. "Be careful, Karic. I don't know how I know this, but I sense Necator's involvement in this."

He covered her hand with his own large one. "Are

you beginning to regain your psychic powers, femina?" he gently teased. "Your perception of the situation is very astute."

"No," she sadly sighed. "Just an educated guess, I fear. The danger from Necator has never been far from us. It's past time he intrude upon our lives again. He'll never give up until he's won or been destroyed. The craving for power consumes him."

"Yes, it does indeed," Karic grimly muttered, "and something has to be done about it before it's too late—if it's not already too late."

He took leave of her then. In but a half hora's time, Karic had raised a small search party and headed out of the valley. The going was slow in the rapidly waning light, and Karic cursed the uneven terrain that necessitated such careful traverse. The only blessing was there was little danger from the Guide in the darkness, for Necator and his men would see poorly and not easily detect their approach. If his father and the other hunters were out there, Karic knew he'd discover them long before the Bellatorians even suspected the search party's presence.

In the end, they found neither the hunting party nor the Bellatorians. The spoor of both, however, comingled in a deep ravine several horas journey back across the mountains. The evidence was clear. His father and men had been captured and most likely taken back to Primasedes.

Karic steeled his heart, locking his pain and fear behind a wall of rock-hard resolve. The high emotions of a Cat Man were more hindrance than help at a time like this. Vengeance was all he wanted, nothing more, and to gain this vengeance, to save his father and men, Karic must once again think like a Bellatorian.

"Take me with you, Karic!" Liane pleaded as she watched him fill his backpack with provisions a few horas later. It was near solrise but still dark outside. "I can be of help once you reach Primasedes."

"No."

Cold finality rimed Karic's words, as glacial as the icy resolve in his eyes.

She swallowed hard against the rising fear that he was shutting her out, not only from her assistance but also from his heart. Liane had never seen him like this—so emotionless, so mechanically disciplined, so committed to a course of action that he neither saw nor concerned himself with anyone or thing beyond it. It almost reminded her of that nocte of the triple moons, when Karic had been so singlemindedly if mindlessly committed to raping her. Only now he knew exactly what he was doing.

The realization was of little comfort. The dangers he faced were horrible. If she let him go without her he might well die in the effort. The thought of him, bleeding his life out on some cobbled street in Primasedes and her too far away to help, was more than Liane could bear.

Karic needed her, whether he had the sense to realize it just now. *She* was the one who knew Primasedes and the intricacies of the palace like the back of her hand. Of all of them, she was the only one who could pass through the alarm system without setting it off as an intruder. And one way or another, Liane was determined to pound that fact home.

She grasped Karic's arm, pulling him around to

face her. Anger briefly flared in his eyes, then was purposely snuffed.

"Liane," he warned in a low, ominous voice, "I don't have time—"

"You'll hear me out," she insisted. "You'll listen to reason for, if you don't, you'll condemn to death not only your father and his men, but you and your men as well. And you won't do that, will you, Karic? There's too much Bellatorian in you for that."

He wrenched her hand from him and turned, his shoulders taut with pain. "Now, of all times, I don't need to be reminded of that, though I'm forced to use that part of me to save my father," he answered. "And most especially not from you!"

"There is good as well as bad in being Bellatorian," Liane softly replied. "There must be, or you wouldn't have loved your mother or come to love me like you do. And as ruthless as Bellator was in its takeover of Agrica, there was much thought, much careful planning that went into it, too. I only appeal to that part of the Bellatorian in you, Karic. Ask you to accept the useful aspects of that heritage. Will you please stop for a moment, put aside your high emotions, and listen?"

For an instant, Liane feared he'd push her aside and go back to his packing. Then Karic's rigid form relaxed. He slowly turned.

Dark, intense eyes gazed down at her. "Speak," he hoarsely commanded. "Tell me your plan and quickly. We leave in one hora's time."

A lump rose in Liane's throat at the sight of him standing there, a tall, powerful young warrior and prince of his people, weighted now with the sole responsibility for their continued survival. Yet, as heavy a burden as it was, Karic could no more turn from it than cease to breathe. In that piercingly poignant moment, Liane suddenly knew it could be no other way—not for him or for her.

They were joined in this cause. It had drawn them, one to the other, from the beginning. Indeed, their love had blossomed from the fertile soil of its higher purpose, and now, at long last, it was time to reap its fruits.

"I know the city," she quietly began. "I know its thoroughfares, the quickest routes to the palace. I know where all the labs are, the most likely places where Necator may be holding your father and men. I know where the master controls for the alarm system are. And, most of all, as a full-blooded Bellatorian, I can enter Primasedes without setting off those alarms."

He studied her for long secundae, considering her words. Then Karic wearily sighed. "We've got to travel hard and fast. It'll be impossible for you to keep up."

"I'll do it. I have to." Liane struggled to keep the relief from her voice. "And you know I won't complain, no matter how hard you push on."

A wry grin twisted Karic's lips. "No, you never did complain or shy from any challenge. I well remember that, sweet femina. Your courage and dedication to our cause has never been the issue, and because I need your knowledge of Primasedes, I'll accept your presence among us. But hear me when I say—"

"We'll talk of our plans later," she quickly interrupted, "but whatever they are, I must go with you. There is no other option. If we fail, it is only a matter of time before Necator finds this lair, and you know as well as I what will happen then."

"No," he grimly corrected her, "*you* don't know, unless you've seen the Guide."

Liane's brow furrowed. "The Guide? What is it?"

"A machine and Necator's secret weapon. I assume you weren't involved in its creation then?"

She shook her head. "I worked only with my psychic skills on humanoids, not machines. I know nothing of any Guide. Tell me of it, Karic."

"It's a form of mental reprograming," he replied as he resumed his packing, explaining the full extent of the machine's horrible powers. "Our mission to Primasedes, therefore, is twofold," Karic finally concluded. "Rescuing my father and men is not the end of it. We fail just as fully if we don't succeed in destroying that weapon. People, *your* people, must die in the undertaking. Can you turn against them to that extent? Perhaps even kill in the process of helping us?"

Her lips trembled, but Liane refused to flinch from his steady gaze. "I don't want to kill. It goes against everything I was raised to revere, but my Sententian existence is over. You are my life now, Karic, and I'll do what I must—even kill—to protect what we have."

Karic smiled tenderly. "Many were the times I despaired of ever hearing those words from you." He stroked the curve of her cheek, gently lingering at the sweet line of her mouth. "I only hope now that I've finally won your heart that our happiness is not short-lived."

The going was arduous, their pace fast and furious. Karic, true to his word, drove his men hard. Liane managed to keep up for half the first sol, as the mountainous terrain forced a slower pace, but as the sol wore on and Karic continued to relentlessly drive the party onward, Liane's strength began to fade. As the sun set behind them, she began to stumble from sheer exhaustion.

"We need to travel through the nocte," Karic explained as he ignored her half-hearted protests and swung her up into his arms. "We'll be on the plains by solrise and forced to take shelter. It'll be our last chance to rest, so I want to make as much distance as we can before then. Once we cross the plains and reach the forest, we'll not stop until we reach Primasedes. So sleep. It's mostly downhill from now on, and your weight is no burden to me."

"I just wanted to go on a little further," Liane wearily murmured as she snuggled into the furry comfort of Karic's chest. "I didn't want to shame you in front of the others."

"Fear not, sweet femina," Karic whispered into the fragrant tumble of her hair. "For the past several horas my men have been shooting me angry looks for allowing you to push yourself so hard. You've more than impressed them."

"Then I won't feel so guilty," she contentedly sighed, "if I enjoy being held by you." Her lids lowered, and she was soon fast asleep.

She slumbered until midnocte and was surprised to discover they'd made it down the mountains and onto the farming plains. By solrise, they'd reached the small, forested area with the spring. It was too light to travel further without danger of detection. After a spartan breakfast, Liane volunteered to stand guard while the men slept. About midsol Karic woke, insisting she take more rest. Liane found it surprisingly easy to fall back asleep.

Karic shook her awake a little past dusk. "Here,

eat this," he said, handing her some journey bread and dried meat sticks. "We head out again in a half hora."

Liane sat up and accepted the food. "I cannot believe I slept so long."

He smiled. "There was some talk about letting you sleep and waking you when we returned from Primasedes."

"You males are all alike," Liane softly chuckled. "So totally convinced of your mighty prowess over us females."

Karic leaned forward, until he was a warm breath away. "And you feminas are all alike," he rumbled. "So conveniently short of memory when the situation calls for it. But there's ample privacy over by the spring. If there were time, I'd take you there and refresh your fading memories."

A sensual thrill skittered down Liane's spine at the suggestive growl in Karic's voice. For a secundae, she allowed herself to imagine how it would be, lying naked with him at the spring, locked in a heated embrace. His mouth would move voraciously against her throat and down to her breasts to nip and kiss her. Then he'd grab her hips and lift her up to him, swiftly, deeply burying his throbbing shaft. Oh, but it would be so good . . . !

"I see I've made my point," Karic drawled, interrupting her heated reverie. His hand moved in the darkness to stroke her hair. "Now eat, sweet femina, and save those memories for another time."

Her lips grazed his calloused palm in a loving kiss. "Yes, they can wait—for a time," she throatily murmured. "But only for a time."

Karic climbed to his feet. "Then let us hurry and get this unpleasant quest accomplished. Until my father and his men are safe . . ." He dragged in an uneven breath and looked nonplussed. "Eat, Liane. I must speak with my men."

He strode away. She smiled to herself, a soft, knowing, woman's smile. It was so good to learn that she still excited him. She had thought, in her maiden's innocence, that a male quickly sated himself and lost interest, but that was definitely not the case with Karic. His ardor for her hadn't dimmed in the least. If anything, it seemed that a few words, like just now, were enough to stir him to full arousal. Just a few words were necessary to stir her as well.

Liane bit into her dried meatstick. Karic was right, though. Their personal needs were secondary to the rescue of Morigan and his men and the destruction of Necator and the Guide. She quickly finished her meal and had just enough time to wash her face before all rose to leave.

They journeyed for the next several horas before Karic called a halt, a short distance from Devra's village and the edge of the great forest.

Liane moved to his side. An eerie silence, even for a sleeping village, hung over the land. "There's something wrong here," she whispered.

"Yes," Karic softly muttered, "there is. I neither sense nor smell anyone about."

He turned to his men. "Stay here with Liane. I'll go ahead and scout the village. It may be a trap. If anything happens, don't attempt to rescue me. Just head to our meeting place and join the others. If I can get away, I'll join you there. If not, Zorac," he said, indicating his second in command, "will carry on in my stead."

"Karic," Liane began, "don't—"

"Obey me in this!" he sharply cut in. "There's no time for discussion and, since I'm the only one of us who knows this area, few other options at any rate."

She stared up at him, fighting back the surge of fear that rose in her. If something happened to Karic in that village, if she lost him there . . . Liane straightened her shoulders.

"It will be as you ask."

He briefly eyed her, then turned and loped away into the darkness. Liane knew he'd be careful, that his Cat Man's stealth, speed and cloaking abilities would render him virtually undetectable, but she worried nonetheless. Yet perhaps the worst realization of all was that far greater dangers awaited them in Primasedes.

The unnatural quiet hung heavily on the nocte's air. Time seemed to drag with ponderous slowness as Liane awaited Karic's return. She strained for any sound of voices or struggle but heard nothing, and that absence began to fill her with rising dread. Something was very wrong, and all she could do was wait.

Finally, a tall, powerful form reappeared out of the darkness, Karic's return as swift and silent as his departure had been. Liane ran up, and he clasped her to him.

"What happened?" she demanded. "What did you find?"

"Nothing. There's no one there," Karic replied in a flat, emotionless tone. "The village is deserted."

Fear threaded Liane's voice. "Deserted? But where could they have gone? What happened to them?"

"Necator's been here," he growled, his anger bursting forth. "The spoor is weak, many sols old, but he was here with a contingent of Bellatorians. The group . . . the group of Agricans that the Guide sent over the cliff . . . They must have been Devra's village."

Chapter 16

Karic seemed like a man possessed after his discovery. They passed through the deathly silent village and into the forest without a backward glance, forging ever onward toward Primasedes—and revenge. Liane felt Karic's rage futilely beating against the iron discipline of his will. She sensed his fear that, despite the killing pace, they might yet arrive too late.

Morigan could be dead or, even worse, reprogramed into Necator's mindless slave. The Lord Commander might know the location of the secret lair and be sending troops to destroy it. And this might well be the last nocte of their lives.

The realization filled Liane with despair. The odds against them were so great, and so much was at risk if they failed. Yet what other choice had they but to journey on, to find someway through all the pitfalls and perils? Indeed, since that first sol of their meeting Liane realized her path, as surely as Karic's, led to this very moment, but she wouldn't trade it for a secundae, not to have Karic at her side. She clutched that thought to her in the darkness of the nocte, her hand clasped in his as he led her where her less acute vision could not go.

Horas passed in relentless jogging. In the bleakness of a cloudy solrise, Liane's legs at last could carry her no further. "K—Karic," she gasped, nearly sobbing from exhaustion. "P—please, I can't go on!"

Barely breaking stride he swung her up into his arms, then moved on. Liane held on to him tightly, struggling for breath. She fought back the tears as the fear, weariness and utter futility of their quest suddenly rose to overwhelm her. In the graying light the great forest loomed before her, a hideous, tangled morass of vegetation. Liane shivered. A fearful premonition filled her with a sense of death, its chilling tendrils snaking about her heart as inexorably as the fingers of the low-lying mist that wound its way through the trees.

It seemed a horrible dream, this gloomy, terror-shrouded woods—a horrible dream like the haunting specter of Karic, lying dead in Primasedes. For a time Liane clung to the warm, muscular strength that was her love, her only reality in a desperately unreal world. The steady beat of his powerful heart and the even rhythm of his breath gradually soothed her. The only moment was now, she realized. She must extract all its bittersweetness to sustain her for what was to come. She was loved. In the end, that was all that mattered.

They reached Liane's hut by solset. The groups of Cat Men who'd taken alternate routes were already there. Twilight darkened the forest. As the rest of the men assembled for a meeting, Karic took Liane aside.

"Will you prepare us a meal while I talk with the men?" Karic asked. "Afterwards we'll take a few hora's rest, then enter Primasedes near mid nocte. Our chances are greater of taking them by surprise when the fortress is asleep."

"That is probably wisest," Liane agreed. "And if you first send me ahead, to test the alarms—"

"No."

Her head jerked up in surprise. "What are you saying? You know it's safer if I—"

"You're not going with us into Primasedes, Liane. I won't have you endangered."

The flatness of his reply said it all. She girded herself for the battle to come. "You risk everything in your foolish attempt to protect me, and if you fail in this quest, I am dead all the same."

Karic stiffened. "Nonetheless, it's my decision. When you accepted our laws you agreed to obey our ruler. Until my father's rescue, I am Lord of my people. You will obey me in this, Liane."

"But you can't go on trying to protect me."

"I won't be able to do what must be done," Karic harshly cut in, "if I'm constantly worrying about your safety. Once we enter Primasedes, my mind must be totally involved with each situation that confronts me, and I won't be able to do that if I'm thinking about you or trying to protect you. I'm sorry if that seems high-handed and overbearing, but it's the truth of it. I can't overcome the part of me that's a Cat Man with my instinctive urge to protect my mate. Even if I wanted to, it's beyond my control."

"And I say those instinctive urges will be the

death of you yet," she angrily muttered. "You never meant to let me enter Primasedes, did you?"

"No, I didn't."

Liane knew it was futile to argue further. Karic would never grant her permission. She'd just have to take matters into her own hands, and as her frustration ebbed, an idea insinuated itself into her mind. If her cache of herbs were still there, hidden beneath the secret panel in her hut . . .

She sighed in apparent defeat. "Have it your way then, you stubborn male," she grumbled. "What *would* you have me do to aid in this quest?"

The merest hint of a smile teased the corner of Karic's mouth. "Tell me everything you can of Primasedes beginning with the alarm system. Where are the main controls located?"

For the next half hora Liane explained all the intricacies of the fortress, holding back nothing of even the smallest import. Though she'd resolved to slip into Primasedes before Karic and his men did and hopefully disable the alarm system, Liane knew she, too, could well be captured. If she failed to make it back, she wanted Karic armed with all the knowledge she possessed. It might well be the last advantage she could give him in a confrontation where all the odds were stacked against them.

She had decided to prepare a potion with her herbs, the same potion she'd given Karic to heal him of his wounds. Liane recalled that it had taken longer than usual to work upon him the last time she'd used it, but she dared not make it any stronger than before. It was enough that the potion would eventually make them sleep for three or four horas at least, but not so soundly that they'd not waken if there were intruders. It would be long enough for her to enter Primasedes and hopefully return. Karic would be angry, but there'd be nothing he could do after the fact, nothing except hurry to take advantage of what she'd accomplished.

While Karic held a meeting with the others, Liane busied herself preparing a meal. With all the Cat Men engrossed in discussion, she was easily able to find her herbs and mix a strong potion into their food.

After the meal was consumed, the men gathered to talk and relax around the dim light of several perpetual flame boxes—all the men but Karic. He took Liane's hand and led her into the hut, closing the door against the forest darkness. In the flickering firelight of the little hearth, she looked up at him, puzzled.

He gazed down at her, his mouth curving into a soft, beautiful smile. "It seems so long ago, cycles even, since we last were in this hut," he began, "and there were strong emotions between us even then. I mistrusted your motives in rescuing me, and then, when you forced your healing, I was so very, very angry."

His hand moved to tenderly stroke the delicate curve of her face. "But all the while, I wanted you, ached and hungered for you."

Memories flooded Liane of the sweet beginnings of their love, of Karic, proud and brave and oh, so compelling. Faint color flushed her high cheekbones, and her lips trembled into a smile.

"And I, too, was angry with you and feared you. But all the while, I burned for you though I knew I shouldn't, that the sacrifice was too great."

"Do you regret it?" Karic scrutinized her, his voice betrayingly husky. "Now, after all that has happened? Now, when we stand here, quite possibly on the last nocte of our lives?"

Glistening blue pools stared up at him. "No, never, my love," Liane achingly whispered. "I regret nothing, except perhaps that I fought you so long and hurt you. I am glad I became your mate."

"As am I, sweet femina." He paused, frowning. "I would not have our love be your destruction, though. This battle with Necator was inevitable for me, but you were dragged into it unawares."

"And I say you are mistaken," Liane ardently countered. "I knew from the start what the consequences were, from that moment I rescued you in the forest."

"It isn't your battle." Karic gripped her arms so tightly Liane winced from the pain. "Do you understand me?"

"Karic. Please. Don't deny me—"

"If I don't return," he ground out the words, ignoring her pleas, "you're not to come after me. I'm leaving Arlen, Kalina's brother, behind to guard you. If we fail in Primasedes he has orders to take you to Lyrae. You wanted to go there once to begin a new life. With some luck, Necator may never find you."

"There'll be no spot on this planet safe from Necator if you fail," Liane bitterly muttered. "I'd rather die with you."

"Well, I don't want you to die, whether I survive or not." Karic tenderly cupped her chin in his large, calloused palm. "I need to go to battle knowing you're safe, Liane, that something good will still remain, no matter what happens. I must have that hope, when all hope seems gone."

His hand fell from her face to trail down her neck

and between her breasts to her softly rounded belly. "Even now there is life within you, a child, *our* child, and therein lies my hope, the hope of our people. The children are our future. They will continue the war until we finally drive Bellator from our planet. Do you understand now why your safety is so important to me?"

"You can't know I'm with child," Liane protested. "It's too soon."

Karic bent and brushed his lips across Liane's. His breath, when he finally spoke, wafted over her in a warm, sensuous cloud. She felt herself grow hot, then cold, realizing he had knowledge he had heretofore not shared.

"You were always so sensitive, so in tune with my heart and body," Karic murmured, his voice deepening to a hoarse, aching whisper. "You were so in tune that, like the Cat Women of our lair, your womb was ripe that nocte of the Mating Festival. Believe me, sweet femina, you carry our child."

Liane's eyes widened. Surprise, then a curious, soaring sense of joy flooded her. To bear Karic's child . . . ! The realization roiled through her, bubbling up to overflow in her eyes and voice.

With a soft cry, she flung herself into his arms. "Oh, Karic, I am so glad. There's nothing I want more than to bear your child."

His powerful arms encircled her, pulling her tightly to him. Relief threaded his voice. "I was afraid you'd be angry," he hurried to explain, "and accuse me of once again manipulating you to suit my needs. But I swear, Liane, it was nothing anyone could control. It just happens when a male and female are meant to be—"

"Hush, my love." Liane pressed a gentle finger to his lips. "You have given me a wonderful gift, the consummation of our love. How could I possibly be angry with you?"

A sweetly seductive smile curved her mouth. Her fingers entwined in his gold-streaked mane. "And do your customs preclude further mating, once you've filled me with your child?"

Karic grinned. "Most assuredly not. Is that an invitation?"

The deep, throaty tenor of his voice rasped pleasantly down Liane's spine, filling her with heady anticipation. Then the corner of her vision careened off the large stone bowl on the table, the bowl she'd used to mix the herbal potion. Reality harshly wrenched her back.

She leaned against the hard clasp of his arms. "You must be exhausted. You've not slept in nearly two sols and must soon enter Primasedes. You need to rest."

"I'm still man enough to love you first," Karic growled, pulling her back to him. "And I will rest all the better for it."

His head lowered, his mouth meeting hers. He played ever so softly with her, gently easing his tongue between her parted lips. With a low moan Liane arched against him, her hands moving wildly over his thick chest muscles. She felt his manhood swell.

With swift, knowing fingers, she unlaced his loincloth and slipped it from him. Her gaze slid down his bronzed, naked body. A hot, searing need rioted through her. Liane stepped back, gently pushing Karic's arms from her.

He stood there, rigid, a thin sheen of moisture

glistening on his brow and muscled torso, stood there and watched with burning, hungry eyes as she removed her tunic and breeches. For a long moment Liane paused before him, magnificently, proudly naked, her ebony hair a riotous tumble about her shoulders, her skin gleaming golden in the agitated firelight.

Then, with a low cry, she came to him, clasping his back and grabbing his taut buttocks. Karic's mouth slanted over hers, hot, insistent, frantic. Then he tensed and jerked away.

"Liane," he groaned, throwing back his head in frustration.

She stared up at him. "What is it? What's wrong, Karic?"

"I—I wanted this to be gentle, tender, slow, but I'm already almost out of control."

"But I don't want it gentle," she whispered, pressing her body back to rub seductively against him. "I want it hard and savage and wild. I want you to take me so deep and rough that I'll never, ever forget this nocte nor the love we have for each other.

"For you see, my love," Liane continued in a tear-choked voice, "when it comes to you I'm not quite so civilized anymore. I—I'm as much an animal as you."

A tender look crossed Karic's face. "Sweet femina, you don't have to say that. It doesn't matter anymore."

"Yes, I do!" She couldn't stifle the sob. "I . . . Oh, Karic, I'm sorry I called you an animal. I think it was my way of avoiding that part in us all, in—in me."

"It's all right, Liane. I swear to you. It doesn't matter." He swung her up into his arms and strode to the little bed, pulling her down atop him.

She gazed at Karic for a long moment, smiling, then moved to straddle his thighs. Her hand encircled his erection.

Karic groaned. Her palm closed tightly around his massive length, and she guided him to her. At the first touch, Karic went wild. He drove himself into Liane, rocking his shaft as deeply into her as he could.

She cried out, arching her head back, her breasts thrust forward, plunging to meet him with all the shuddering strength of her body. He impaled her, his rhythm quickening—hard, fast, deep. Liane whimpered above him. She was on fire, trembling with a searing heat, aching unbearably, unable to bear it a moment longer.

With a sharp, keening cry, she fell atop him, lost in the throes of her release. Karic gave a harsh, gutteral moan and clasped her to him, coming violently again and again. Together, on a nocte fraught with death and danger, they were drawn into that dark, deep chasm of swirling, exquisitely poignant ecstasy.

Even as she lay there afterwards, nestled in the protective haven of his arms, Liane knew she must soon go. Though Karic was yet awake she could see the drug finally working, slowing his breathing to a deep, even rhythm, beckoning him toward sleep. Still, Liane was loathe to leave.

The nocte outside the little hut was black, filled with nameless terrors, danger and possible death. Here, lying next to the warm comfort of Karic's body, she was safe, protected and oh, so very loved. The sated drowsiness after mating teased the edges of her consciousness. Liane wanted nothing more than to sleep and forget the harsh, horrible reality that lay outside.

An irrational thought that perhaps this was all just some terrible dream struck her. Perhaps if she went to sleep she'd awaken at solrise in Karic's arms, back once again in the Cat's lair, back to a life of peace and happiness. For a brief moment more she allowed herself the forbidden luxury of dreaming, then she stirred, propping herself up on an elbow.

Karic's eyes slowly opened, eyes already glazing over with sleep. "Where are you going?" he mumbled.

She smiled down at him. "Nowhere, my love. I—I just wanted to say one thing more, then let you rest."

His lips lifted in a drowsy smile. "Then say it."

"I love you, Cat Man, with all my heart. You know that now, don't you, beyond a shadow of a doubt?"

"Yes, I know that." Sensing there was something Liane still needed to say, Karic forced back his sleepy haze. With a weary sigh, he turned on his side to face her.

His action afforded Liane a full view of tautly muscled abdomen, narrow hips and the breadth of his chest. Desire once again flared, and she nearly faltered in her resolve. But love for Karic and his ultimate safety relentlessly drove her on.

She forced herself to continue. "And you know that I've always had the welfare of your people uppermost in my heart. You know that, too, don't you, Karic?"

He slowly nodded, a quizzical frown forming between his brows. "Yes, Liane, I know that."

"And no matter what happens, you'll know that whatever I did, I did because I thought it was the right thing to do, like . . . like when I healed your leg against your will.''

Karic's frown deepened. "The only right thing left for you to do is to go with Arlen to Lyrae.'' He gripped her arm, fighting the encroaching mists closing in upon him. "And you still owe me your promise that you'll do so. Promise me, Liane!''

She heard the desperation in his drug-laced voice. She knew she must soothe him, and quickly, or his high emotions might well dispel the potion's effects. Yet to lie to him, even for such a cause . . .

"If you do not return from Primasedes," *and if I somehow survive it myself*, Liane thought, "I'll go with Arlen to Lyrae. I, too, feel a need to protect our child. If something happens to you, I'll do so as ardently as I tried to help you. I swear it!''

Karic rolled over on his back, releasing her. "I believe you, Liane," he mumbled thickly, unable to fight the drowsiness a moment longer. "And I know you'll succeed. Our child will be safe.''

She watched his breathing slow and deepen. His lids lowered to cover his striking green-gold eyes. Beautiful eyes, loving eyes, Liane thought with a bittersweet pang, eyes she might not ever see again. With the utmost care she rose from the bed, pausing only to tenderly cover him with a blanket.

Dressing was a challenge with the meager selection of clothes Liane had to draw upon. She had decided her best chance of entry and easy movement within Primasedes was to pass herself off as one of the many prostitutes who frequented the fortress, but fashioning a garishly seductive costume from her few garments was a real challenge.

She finally combined a sheer pink undertunic with a long crimson skirt, tucking a corner of the skirt up into her waistband to reveal an expanse of shapely leg to mid-thigh. Gathering her long hair high on her head to one side, she wove several colorful strips of cloth through the tresses and tied them in place.

Next, Liane turned to the task of preparing her face. She smudged her eyes with a bit of charred wood from the fire, then tinted her lips and cheeks with cerasa stain. After one last fluffing of her tousled mane, Liane gave herself a final inspection in the mirror.

Thank the five moons Karic could not see her now, she thought, for she definitely looked like an alley walker. She only hoped she possessed the nerve to see the role through, at least well enough to seduce the men guarding the alarm system. Liane shuddered at the thought of what she might have to endure in the process. It reminded her of the weapons Karic had brought along.

She moved to the table where one of the blaster guns and stunners lay. Liane hesitated over which one to take. The blaster was more powerful and deadly but was also too large to hide. She picked up the stunner. Though this version might not kill, it had several settings, the most powerful of which could disable for several horas, and she would need it to eliminate any potential resistance in her attempt to destroy the alarm system.

Liane slid the small weapon into her pocket. Then, almost of its own accord, her gaze moved toward the bed, toward Karic.

The lines of tension had eased from his ruggedly handsome face in the peaceful oblivion of sleep. Yet even now he seemed to emanate restrained power and masculine vitality. His sun-streaked mane lay about his shoulders, still tangled and windblown from the long journey. Liane suppressed a sudden urge to stroke his hair and face in tender farewell.

Her gaze lovingly moved down his body to the Cat's claw and chain he wore, symbol of his rank as lordling of his people. Even now his father might well be dead and Karic ruler, ruler of a race teetering on the brink of extinction.

Hot tears stung Liane's eyes as she took her final leave of him, his powerful naked chest, his muscular arms and strong hands—wonderful hands that had given her such joy and pleasure. Though the blanket now covered him, Liane well remembered how Karic had looked in all his magnificent, virile beauty.

With heart-wrenching resolve she turned, forcing her legs to carry her away into the forest and onto the familiar, oft trod path. She dared not look back or she'd never be able to leave. Though love strongly beckoned her in the form of the sleeping man she'd left behind, love just as strongly called her forward. The only hope of saving his life and the lives of his people lay ahead within an evil, forboding fortress called Primasedes.

Luck was with Liane as she neared the city. A small contingent of Bellatorians, recently returned from an inspection visit of one of the many agrifarms, was gathered at the main gate to be screened for entry. Tired from their long journey and excited to be home, the group was unaware of an addition to their numbers. Liane entered with them, the sensors noting only the form of yet another Bellatorian.

As soon as she could slip away, Liane took her leave. She backtracked to the main gate and the formidable building that was both guard barracks and alarm system center. Hidden in the shadows, she hesitated outside. How, by all the moons of Bellator, was she going to get past the many men milling about below?

Her ploy in the mining town of Fodina, to coax that miner to take her to the pits, had failed miserably, but that same ploy was all she had now. She would simply have to be bolder and more in control of the situation, for this time there was certainly no Gage Bardwin to rescue her. Liane smiled sadly. Her motives were still ultimately the same, though —to save Karic's life.

Liane prayed that her quest would go smoothly. Once the alarm system was out of commission, she intended on infiltrating the palace and discovering the whereabouts of Karic's father, if he were even still alive. It would aid immeasurably in his safe rescue later if Karic knew exactly where to find him.

It was a dangerous plan, fraught with potential pitfalls every step of the way, but Liane's knowledge of the lower levels of the palace, where the prison cells and labs were located, would facilitate a swifter, more unnoticed passage than Karic could. Even with his cloaking powers, Karic's ignorance of the myriad, interweaving corridors would immeasurably slow his search. And any loss of time in reaching Morigan could well be fatal for all concerned.

No, it was the only prudent course of action, Liane grimly assured herself, gazing at the guard barracks. The long, two-story building was ablaze with lights on the lower level, and the boisterous sounds of male voices, some singing, some shouting, and most already slurred with drink, floated to

Liane's ears. More the better, she thought. A drunk guard would be easier to manipulate—or, she realized with a shudder, be just about impossible to reason with.

Liane quickly discarded that thought. It was pointless to dwell on it anyway. The time had come to set her plan into motion.

With an exaggerated sway of her hips, Liane strode across the courtyard toward the barracks. A man stepped out of the doorway as she approached. Liane tensed, then forced herself to relax and smile at him.

He grinned down at her, his mouth slightly lopsided, a glazed look in his eyes. He reeked to high heaven of the famous, locally brewed ale.

"Well, well," the man drawled, "what have we here? You're a pretty little piece to be out all alone on a dark nocte."

His arm snaked out and grabbed Liane about the waist, roughly pulling her to him. "Need to couple, do you, pretty one?"

Cold fear slid through Liane. She swallowed hard against the revulsion that churned up, threatening to choke her. For Karic, she screamed to herself. Do this for Karic!

She forced what she hoped was a seductive smile onto her face. "I'm always ready for a coupling," Liane purred, "if the price is right."

"And what's your price, my pretty little piece?" the man thickly inquired. "I've gambled away all my coins this nocte and am a poor man. Do you take credit?"

"Credit?" Liane laughed. "No, never credit. But there are other ways of payment, if you've the courage."

Grubby fingers wove their way into her hair to clasp the back of her head. Inexorably, he drew her face toward him.

"Oh, I've the courage and more, my pretty one," the guard growled. "Name your price."

"I like to see new things, and I've never seen our famous alarm system. Do you possess the authority to show it to me? I especially like men with authority."

"I'm second in command of these barracks," he boasted, his chest visibly swelling. "Is that enough authority for you?"

"Will it get me in for a tour?"

"Most certainly."

Liane forced herself to press into him. "Then we have a bargain. The alarm system for a coupling. Let us go now."

"Not so fast, pretty one." The man stayed her. "I want a taste of what I'm buying first. It's dangerous showing you the alarms. You're not authorized, you know. I'll need some proof you're worth the risk."

Gazing up at his leering face, Liane was certain she'd have fled in panic if he hadn't been holding her so securely. What would it take to placate him? Would a simple kiss be enough? She fervently hoped so.

Lifting on tiptoe, Liane touched her mouth to his. With a grunt, the man pulled her into him, flattening the soft mounds of her breasts against his chest and her hips into his groin. His mouth roughly slanted over hers, his tongue wetly probing for entry. Hot tears stung her eyes as Liane warred with her revulsion, but she finally allowed his invasion. She was a whore, and she had better act the part.

But when the guard's hand groped for her breast,

Liane jerked back. "You've had your sample," she choked out. "The rest will have to wait until we're done with the tour. Shall we get on with it?"

He released her and began to pull her into the building. "Keep quiet and stay right behind me then," he snarled. "Let's get this over with. And you'd better come through with all you promised in that kiss!"

"Oh, you'll get all that and more," Liane murmured, her hand tightening around the stunner in her pocket. "That I promise."

They climbed a flight of stairs just past the entryway, the sounds of laughter even louder now they were inside the building. Good, Liane thought, it'll help cover any noise we make upstairs, especially when I fell him with my stunner.

A long corridor led off from the second floor landing. The guard led her down it to the third door, then unlocked it with the key control he wore about his neck. He quickly pulled her inside, an ominous click behind her alerting Liane to the fact he'd locked them in.

Movement at the far end of the room caught her eye. A dark-haired man, hunched before a console, swung around in his chair. His appearance, unlike her escort, was immaculate, his uniform neatly pressed, his boots gleaming. Obviously the difference between being on and off duty, Liane thought wryly. The man's eyes, however, as he slowly looked at her, were suddenly just as hungry as the guard's had been. A cold chill prickled down her spine. Now she had two problems instead of one.

"And what is this, Mardac?" the console operator asked. "Have you brought me a treat to while away the long horas of my shift?"

"You can have her when I'm finished," the man named Mardac growled. "But first she wants a tour of the alarm system."

The dark-haired man frowned. "You know that's forbidden."

Liane hastily stepped forward. "Even for the pleasure of my favors? I'll pay you for the tour the same way I plan to pay Mardac here."

He eyed her consideringly. "I suppose that would be permissible, except that you'll have to remain up here with me the rest of the nocte, after I finish watching Mardac have you first. Agreed?"

Liane forced the nausea down. There was no need to contemplate such a disgusting act. Neither would be conscious enough to carry it out, once she was done with them. She nodded.

The man motioned toward Mardac. "Well, get on with it. Give her the tour."

With an impatient gesture, her guide indicated the large set of terminals and display panels that filled the wall before the dark-haired man. "That's it. That's the alarm system."

Liane stepped over beside the console operator for a closer look. She could feel his gaze upon her, but she ignored it. "The system is very impressive. How does it work?"

Mardac moved up behind her, his hands grasping her shoulders. "Like any other machine," he irritably replied. "Now, come on. You've seen enough. Time to pay what you owe."

"Please, just a few secundae more," Liane pleaded, throwing him a beguiling smile over her shoulder. "I—I want to know how it works. I love machines. They're so mysterious, so powerful and exciting, so much like a male," she finished stroking the hands on her shoulder before pulling away.

Hot lust flared in Mardac's eyes. He motioned toward the central terminal where several lights flickered and glowed. "Those indicate the system's on," he said, his voice thick with barely restrained desire. "That button," he next indicated the one on the lower right, "switches it on and off. Those screens above the control panel can actually pinpoint where an intruder is, giving us the coordinates within a few meters of his location—and all within a matter of secundae of the intruder's entry into Primasedes. The system was recently upgraded and is now so sensitive it can even penetrate the cloaking powers of a Cat Man."

His fingers tightened on Liane's shoulders. "But enough of this. I've fulfilled my end of the bargain; now it's time for you to fulfill yours. And I've a mind to take you right here on the floor."

He turned Liane around and had only a moment to gasp in outrage before she fired her stunner. With a choking cry Mardac tensed, then jerked in response to the neural jolt before plummeting to the floor. Liane immediately wheeled around, but the console operator was upon her before she could fire again.

His face dark with fury, the man captured the wrist that held her stunner. With his other hand, he hit Liane in the face. Sparkling lights whirled before her as sharp pain shot through her jaw. Her grip loosened, and the stunner fell to the floor.

Half-conscious, she was jerked hard against her captor, one arm twisted painfully behind her. He grabbed a handful of her hair and pulled, until her head was arched back, baring the slender column of her throat. As the mists cleared, Liane found a face only millimeters from hers, ugly with rage and a cruelly calculating desire.

"You'll live to regret this nocte by the time we're done with you," the man snarled. "Nothing has changed, you know, save that now I'll have you first. And when Mardac awakens, he'll be especially angry. I'd almost pity you, if I weren't anticipating the pleasure I'll get from watching what he does to you."

His head lowered and he took her mouth, grinding his lips into hers. Liane gasped and tried to pull back, but had nowhere to go. Tears of pain filled her eyes at his cruel assault, but anger quickly rushed in to overcome that pain.

When she bit down hard on his lip, the man jerked back. It was all the opportunity Liane needed. She rammed her knee home. With a strangled cry the console operator staggered backward, then stumbled and fell. Liane dove for the stunner.

She heard a frantic yell and knew he was coming after her. She grabbed the stunner and rolled over. Even then, he was leaping at her. Liane fired.

Chest still heaving, Liane slowly climbed to her feet. She stared down at the two men, then, pocketing the stunner, she strode over to the control panel.

With a quick jab, Liane shut off the system. She glanced around for something to smash the control panel with. There was little available, save the chair the console operator had sat in. She picked it up, praying the noise she'd make wouldn't carry downstairs.

Inhaling a deep breath, she lifted the chair and brought it down on the control panel. Sparks flew, mingled with the flying shards of broken glass and the flare of burning wires. The acrid smell of smoke filled the air as she continued her single-minded destruction. Finally, the task was done.

Even with her limited knowledge of machines,

Liane knew she'd damaged the alarm system beyond quick or easy repair. She lowered the chair to the floor, her attention centered on the sounds rising from belowstairs. From all indications, the revelry hadn't diminished one wit.

The relief and sudden ebb of terror left her momentarily light-headed. She sat down on the chair, forcing deep, even gulps of air into her lungs. Her glance slowly moved to the two men. The stunner had been set on maximum power. They'd be unconscious most of the nocte, but to buy all the time she could, she decided to also bind and gag them.

The deed was quickly done. Next, she removed Mardac's key control, and after ascertaining no one was about in the corridor, Liane slipped out of the room.

So far, so good, she thought as she stealthily made her way down the hall and stairs. Now, if only her luck would hold out a while longer . . .

The outer door loomed before her like some gateway to freedom, and Liane's preoccupation with it was almost her undoing. Two men staggered from an adjoining room. She threw herself back into the shadows. For long secundae after the men passed by and out the front door Liane remained there, flattened against the wall, her heart thumping madly in her chest.

She'd been too eager, too careless, she lectured herself. She must exercise greater caution in the future, or she'd never successfully make it to the end of this dangerous mission. Liane's ears strained for sound of any further movement, then silently moved to the door and peered out. There was no one about.

The nocte quickly swallowed her in its cloaking

anonymity of darkness. Liane carefully made her way back through the streets and alleyways, this time toward the imposing stone structure of the Imperial Palace. Elation gradually replaced the tightly strung tension of the past few moments. She had disabled the alarm system and was halfway through her mission. She had secured the Cat Men's safe entry into Primasedes. She had given them a decided advantage, no matter what happened now.

The task before her, however, was far more difficult. There was no way of guessing where Necator had Morigan. It might well be a futile effort, but she had to try. Whatever she discovered would only aid Karic later.

She must hurry, though. In the excitement of getting to Primasedes and destroying the alarms, Liane had lost track of the time. She guessed it to be a couple of horas before mid nocte, time enough to get back to her hut and the sleeping Cat Men, if she hurried.

Perhaps the great success of the alarm system had lulled the fortress into a false sense of security, for when Liane reached the palace few guards were about. It was an easy task to make her way to one of the side doors without notice. Once inside, familiarity took over. She quickly slipped through the upper level and down to the subterranean area with its maze of corridors.

As Liane made her stealthy way toward the prison area, a sense of having gone back in time pervaded her. Less than two monates ago, these hallways and rooms had encompassed her whole life, her only purpose being unswerving loyalty and unquestioning obedience to Bellator as research scientist and psychic.

Now, she was no longer either. Now, her goal was

the salvation of a race alien to her with betrayal of her own kind part of the bargain. Now, she fought to preserve the life of the man she loved. Her hand slid to her belly. Liane smiled. Her man *and* child!

Strange indeed that this new life filled her with a purpose and sense of commitment she'd never before experienced, even as a Sententian. Strange indeed that this new life, though fraught with danger and complications, was so surprisingly full of joy. She had never felt so alive as she'd felt since she'd first met Karic. And, like a she cat protecting all that was dear, Liane would now fight to preserve that life with all the strength and courage she possessed.

The realization buoyed her, dispelling the lingering doubts and fears. She soon reached the prison area where two guards stood between her and the cells.

The men were seated at a small table, playing a game of Monrovian chance. Liane smiled grimly and pulled out the stunner. They couldn't be more conveniently close to each other for easy shooting. She fired at the nearest guard.

With a strangled cry, the man half-rose before tumbling to the floor. The other guard jumped to his feet, wildly glancing around. Liane fired the stunner. It was none too soon. The man's hand even then was going for his weapon.

The stunner beeped in her hand, signaling a low energy level. Liane grimaced. It would be a while before it recharged itself. She flung aside the now useless weapon and walked over to examine the two crumpled forms. The cell key control dangled from one man's belt.

She quickly retrieved it, as well as both of the guards' stunners. One she tossed onto the table, the other she slipped into her pocket. Then Liane dragged the men into the nearest empty cell and locked it. No one would hear them behind the sound proof door when they awoke.

A thorough search of the cells failed to yield any sign of Morigan or any of the other Cat Men. Frustration filled Liane. Where were they? And were they even still alive?

There was only one other place they might be— the labs. With a rising sense of foreboding, Liane headed in their direction.

Though the corridors outside the labs were quiet, work inside the rooms was going full tilt. And it was there, inside the Analysis room, that Liane found Morigan—and Necator as well.

The viewing room adjoining the lab was empty. Through its one-way glass, Liane found she could easily see and hear what was going on.

"Your people hover on the brink of final destruction now that we have at last obtained the secret location of your lair," Necator was saying to Morigan, who was electronically suspended in the air. A smugly triumphant grin wreathed the Lord Commander's face. "On the morrow, we leave for your lair. There the Guide will complete the annihilation of the Cat Men."

Morigan wearily raised his head. Beneath the utter exhaustion, a look of defiance burned in his eyes. "My son has also experienced your machine's powers. He'll find a way to stop you."

Necator laughed. "So, the young Cat Man we captured a few monates ago was your son. Well, he may well know of the Guide as it was, but not as it now is. There is no one who can stop its powers now."

A cruel light gleamed in his eyes. "I won't kill him

with the others, just permanently reprogram him to my bidding. He'll serve the rest of his sols as my abject slave, a fitting reminder to all of what happens to those who defy me."

He nodded in gloating satisfaction. "Yes, a fitting reminder indeed. The young lord of the Cat Men, the sole survivor of an entire race, and I'll grind his face beneath my heel at every opportunity. It'll make my point more eloquently than words ever could."

At that moment, Liane, filled with an image of Necator towering over Karic's prone form, wanted nothing more than to rush out of the viewing room and kill the Lord Commander—the man was crazed with his lust for power—but there was nothing she could do. Her stunner couldn't kill him, and revealing her presence would be a futile sacrifice at best. But to leave Morigan in the clutches of that evil man . . .

With cold Bellatorian logic, Liane forced herself to concentrate on the reality of the situation. Karic's father appeared in no imminent danger, and she was of more use to their cause by bringing this information back to Karic as soon as possible. It was the wiser course, she tried to assure herself, as she moved toward the door.

Just then Necator pointed a small control box at Morigan, lowering him to a kneeling position on the floor. Liane froze, watching in stunned horror as Necator shoved the box into his belt and pulled out a laser probe. With one hand he grasped Morigan's mane and cruelly wrenched back his head. With the other, he flipped forward a small lever on the instrument. A thin, eerie blue light flared from its tip.

"Of course you, my proud Cat Man," Necator

sneered, "will not live to see your son. He'll find you dead when I drag him back here, your body sliced to pieces by this most painfully efficient tool." As he spoke, he slowly raised the light beam to Morigan's face.

The crackle of laser searing flesh filled the deathly silent room. Though Morigan twisted futilely in Necator's grip, he made not a sound. But something snapped in Liane. All the hatred and loathing she'd ever felt for the Lord Commander rose in a blinding burst of fury. With a wild cry she ran into the lab, her stunner in hand. Before anyone could react, she fired at Necator.

He fell with a gurgling cry, his body spasming grotesquely. The laser probe slid from his hand, skittering across the room toward Liane. She dove for it. The lab went wild.

Scientists scrambled for cover, some running for the door, others leaping behind lab tables and computer consoles. Liane grabbed the probe and fired at a scientist reaching for the alarm button. The discordant wail of a siren filled the room, mingling with the scream of the man now grasping a hand half-severed from his arm. Rolling over, Liane fired the laser again, this time at another man advancing on her with a heavy metallic bar. He, too, bellowed in agony and toppled over, clasping his face.

The control box lay in Necator's belt. Liane grabbed it and directed it at Morigan. The electronic shackles relaxed. Karic's father slumped to the floor. She knelt and gathered him to her.

"My lord," she whispered, sickened by the deep wound the laser had slashed across his face, "we must leave!"

"Go, femina," Morigan gasped. "G—get away

before the guards arrive! I've no strength . . . would only hinder you. Get back to Karic. Warn him!"

"No!" Liane struggled to pull him to his feet, but his dead weight was too much for her. "I can't leave you. They'll kill you if I do."

"Then so be it." He gazed up at her, a tender, loving smile lighting his face. "The future lies with you and Karic now . . . and my grandchild."

Her eyes, full of hot tears, widened. "You know?"

"It was to be expected." Morigan gave her a gentle shove. "Now, go and tell Karic my thoughts were of him."

A sob rose, nearly strangling her, but Liane did as she was told. "Farewell," she whispered. She gave him a brief kiss on the cheek before standing up.

Liane made her way to the door of the now deserted room and out into the corridor. Shouts and the heavy thud of approaching footsteps echoed down the hallway. With a final glance at Morigan's crumpled form, Liane turned and fled in the opposite direction.

CHAPTER 17

LIANE RAN UNTIL THE SOUNDS OF PURSUIT FADED AND she was once more alone. She slumped against a wall, gasping for breath. The frantic beat of her heart gradually diminished, and the sheer terror ebbed.

She glanced around. Somehow, in the wild panic of flight, she'd found her way back to the upper level. She now stood inside the long hallway that led to the guest quarters. Liane peered down the length of dimly lit corridor. She saw a door at its end and sighed in relief.

Well, at least there was a way out, she thought, and the sooner she escaped the palace, the better. Once back in the winding streets of Primasedes, it would be far more difficult to find her.

As Liane made her way down the shadowy hallway, a strange sensation washed over her. She halted, confused. Her mind searched for the source of the feeling, vainly attempting to fathom its significance. Frustration welled in her.

In the past, when in full possession of her Sententian powers, the meaning of the strange vibrations would have been crystal clear, but not now, not anymore. The fact she felt anything at all amazed her. How was she able . . . ?

Her hand slid to her belly. It was the child. It had to be. Somehow, even now, the child—her daughter—was psychically sensitive and speaking to her. And she was telling her—warning her?—of some presence. But what was the significance of the message? And was the presence good or evil?

Liane's steps faltered, then stopped. The presence was near. It pervaded her, mesmerizing her. Fear spiraled, turning her hands to ice. Liane moved forward and came to an abrupt halt at the next door.

The impulse to enter beckoned with an almost uncontrollable force. There was no recourse but to face what lay within. With a resolute straightening of her shoulders, she pushed open the door.

On silent, stealthy footsteps, Liane entered the darkened bedchamber, carefully closing the door behind her. She could barely see, save for the muted recessed lighting high on the walls. She scanned the room, taking in the furnishings, the ornately stone-carved bed. Within it lay the form of a large, powerfully built man, his heavily muscled shoulders and back exposed beneath the light coverlet. A sinewy arm dangled off the side of the bed. The sound of deep, even breathing filled the room.

Stunner in hand Liane crept toward him, still puzzled as to why she'd been drawn here and who this man was. His face was difficult to discern with him sleeping on his stomach, but his hair was dark and wavy and he wore a beard. She halted, indecision overcoming her.

Should she wake him, and if she did, what would she say? At that moment what she needed was help, and most likely the only help he'd give would be to escort her back to Necator. She'd been a fool to come. She must leave, now, before he wakened, before it was too late. Liane turned to flee.

She slammed into a hard male body. With a strangled cry Liane leaped back. Before she could even aim her stunner it was knocked away, skittering across the room to strike the far wall. Powerful hands shot out of the darkness to capture her arms and drag her back.

Fear and nausea rose to choke her. Liane fought wildly, her nails rising to claw at the man's face, but he was even quicker, easily capturing her hands to pin them behind her back. He roughly pulled her to him.

"Who are you, femina, to sneak into this room? Did Necator send you to kill us?"

The voice rose out of the darkness, its deep rich timbre plucking at her memory. Liane had heard that voice before, but was its owner friend or foe?

"Answer him, femina," another voice behind her said. With a sinking heart, Liane realized it must be the man who'd been sleeping on the bed.

"No matter what that scrawny sandwart Necator has offered you," he continued, moving to stand beside Liane's captor, "it won't mean much without your life."

"And *we* control that right now," the man holding her added, giving her a small shake, "not your Lord Commander."

Recognition flooded Liane and with it a surge of relief. "Gage!" she gasped, straining to make out his features in the gloom. "Oh, thank the five moons! It's me, Gage. Liane."

He pulled her closer to the recessed wall lighting and lifted her chin to study her face. "By the . . . ! It *is* you, Liane!" Gage glanced over her shoulder. "This is the femina I told you about, Teran. The one I met—"

Liane slipped from his grasp. "My—my Lord Ardane!" she gasped, moving to stand before Gage's tall companion. "You've returned! It is I, Liane Allador, the Sententian scientist you met two monates ago."

Karic gained consciousness by slow degrees. Even as he did, the memory of his and Liane's passionate coupling filled him, heating his blood. He turned to pull her to him.

The bed was empty. Karic's eyes snapped open. He scanned the little hut and muttered a low oath. Liane was nowhere to be seen.

Flinging back the blanket, Karic swung out of bed. She's outside, he reassured himself as he pulled on his loincloth and boots. Probably standing guard, he wryly imagined, so the man could get a little rest. As he strode across the camp to the sentry's post, Karic nudged his sleeping men awake. It was time to be on the way to Primasedes, but first he wanted one last moment with Liane to say farewell.

The guard was sound asleep. Rage flooded Karic. Never had any Cat Man fallen asleep at his post. Karic roughly shook the man awake.

"My lord!" the Cat Man gasped, instantly aware of

327

what he'd done. "I—I beg forgiveness! I don't know why I slept. I fought the weariness, truly I did, but it was as if I were drugged."

Uneasiness filled Karic. Drugged! The word plucked at his heart with the sureness of a premonition. Liane had drugs, those herbal concoctions of hers, and he wouldn't put it past her to use them if she thought it would help.

Something she said flashed through his mind. ". . . *no matter what happens, you'll know that whatever I did, I did because I thought it was the right thing to do.*"

Panic wrapped itself around Karic's heart, constricting his chest until each breath was a painful effort. He threw back his head, his features twisted in agony.

"Liane!" he cried. "You little fool. You brave, crazy little fool!"

He left the sentry to stand there trembling in shame and ran back to the rest of his men. A search was quickly organized, for Karic had to be certain Liane was truly gone. And a half hora later, he knew. She had left while they were asleep. There was no doubt in his mind where she'd gone—to Primasedes.

Karic returned to the hut to retrieve his weapons. As he shouldered the blaster, he noticed a stunner was missing. Good, he thought. At least she'd had the sense to take a weapon with her. Perhaps there was some sort of plan driving her. For his own peace of mind, he had to cling to that hope.

They set out after her. As they swiftly wove through the forest, Karic numbed himself to his anguish. Emotions wouldn't save Liane nor further their cause now. Only cold, hard logic could do that, and once again Karic called upon that part of him that was Bellatorian.

A grimly amusing thought struck him. If he weren't careful, he'd soon get used to that Bellatorian part of himself after all, as often as he'd been forced to call upon it of late. The melding of two races *did* have its advantages, he reluctantly admitted. The best of both worlds, as Liane would say. Too bad those two worlds couldn't seem to live in peace with each other.

He halted the men just inside the edge of the forest. From across the wide field the lights of Primasedes glowed in the darkness. Karic turned to his men.

"I'll test the alarm system, as I'm most familiar with its effects. If it's safe, I'll signal you. If not, you'll soon know. Use the ensuing noise and confusion to scale the walls. They won't be able to detect or capture all of you. Once inside, you have your orders."

Karic didn't await a reply. There was no need for further discussion. They all knew their jobs and the utter seriousness of their mission. There would be no second chances. He only prayed that some measure of luck would be with them this nocte and that the same luck would keep Liane safe. He turned and ran across the field, his cloaking powers in full force.

It was an easy task to get past the gate guard, who continued to stare out into the blackened nocte as Karic slipped by. The man yawned widely. Karic grinned. Good, he thought. Let them find this nocte as routinely boring as all the rest—until it's too late.

Though he waited for the sirens to sound, they remained silent. It was almost more than he dared hope, but had Liane managed to disable the alarms? Karic headed toward the guard barracks she had told him housed the alarm system. Her spoor was stronger here. But how far had she gotten? And would he find her dead within?

With hard resolve, Karic banished the fears and forged on. He easily found the upstairs room. It was locked. He destroyed the locking mechanism with the blaster. The sound barely carried in the thick stone corridor, not that he cared. The noise be damned; he'd no time to waste. Even now, Liane could be dead or in Necator's clutches, her life ebbing away.

The inert forms of two men, bound and gagged, lay on the floor. Behind them was the destroyed remains of the alarm system. Karic backed out of the room, relief and grim amusement tugging at the corners of his mouth. Liane had done her job very well.

He immediately set out for the fortress parapets where he signaled his men with a high frequency whistle. When they'd all regrouped behind the guard barracks, Karic relayed the revised plan.

Cloaked from Bellatorian eyes, they'd head to the palace. Half would then set out for the labs to find and destroy the Guide. The other half, with Karic at its head, would search for Morigan, his men and Liane. Eventually, they'd rejoin and systematically comb the palace for Necator and his scientists.

Circumstances being what they were, there was no other option but a complete overthrow of Primasedes. What would transpire next, when Bellator heard of the rebellion, was anybody's guess. Perhaps the warrior planet wouldn't be so quick to punish once they were apprised of the

Guide and Necator's intent to use it for Imperium-wide domination.

But then again, Karic bitterly thought as they set out for the palace, Bellator might just as well see their rebellion as any other and mercilessly squash them. In their coldly ruthless eyes the end result was just the same. Bellator needed continued control of Agrica, and the dependency on a primary food source overshadowed other more noble though less practical realities.

Liane's spoor preceded them into the palace's lower levels. Karic wondered what her motives had been for heading down there. Had she intended on attempting to destroy the Guide? He hoped not. Necator would have had the weapon thoroughly guarded.

The party split up outside the lab area. On an impulse, Karic continued to follow Liane's trail which led to the Analysis lab. Her scent was quite strong here, no more than a half hora old. That heartened him.

The lab was in physical chaos. Two white-garbed scientists lay sprawled on the floor, one with a half-severed hand, the other with a mutilated face. Liane again, Karic realized with a twinge of pride. She was getting to be quite a little warrior.

Morigan was discovered in an adjoining room, barely conscious and secured, hand and foot, to an exam table. Karic winced at the sight of his father's seared and swollen face. He quickly freed his father and gathered him into his arms.

Morigan's eyes opened. "K—Karic?" he mumbled. "Is it really you? I—I've had so many unexpected visitors this nocte. First Liane, now you."

Karic's grip tightened on his father. "Liane. Where is she? I must find her before Necator does!"

331

"She left but a short time ago, I think. She—she stunned Necator, and they carried him away." Morigan managed a weak smile. "You've got quite a little she-cat on your hands."

"Was there ever any doubt?" Karic lifted his father into his arms. "Let's get you out of here."

The Lord of the Cat Men stayed his son. "Some of the others can assist me. You need to find Liane."

Karic hesitated. "Are you certain?"

"Quite certain."

"See to our lord," Karic instructed two of his men, "then search out our countrymen."

With a fleeting smile of farewell to his father, he ran from the room. Liane's track was more erratic now, her scent tinged with fear. She'd left the lab in a hurry, pursued and frightened. Karic followed through endless passages until her spoor finally led back to the upper level. He was drawing close to her now; he could feel as well as smell it. Her path led down a long, dimly lit corridor of what appeared to be sleeping chambers, ending at one particular door.

Karic halted before it, puzzled. Why would Liane enter someone's room? And whose was it? He doubted it was Necator's. This didn't appear to be the part of the palace where a Lord Commander would have his quarters. His hand moved to the door, when the sound of voices within stopped him.

The thick stone walls muffled the actual words, but Karic could make out two male and a female voice. The soft feminine voice was definitely Liane's. Confusion filled him, and he almost succumbed to the impulse to rush inside. Then reason returned. Cloaking himself, Karic cautiously pushed open the door and slipped into the room.

Across the span of but three meters, the broad

backs of two tall men confronted him. One was dark-haired, the other blond. Keeping to the shadows, Karic watched and listened.

"Ah, yes," the dark-haired man was saying, "I remember now. You were the only one with the courage to tell the truth. I've thought about you these past monates. Wondered what Necator would do to you because of that honesty. I am glad you're safe, Domina."

"And I am glad you have returned, my lord," Karic heard Liane reply. He tried to catch a glimpse of her, but the two men blocked his view. "We are in the direst straits and desperately need your assistance!"

"So Gage has been telling me."

Karic's gaze swiveled to the man's blond companion. Bardwin, he thought grimly. Strange that he should once again find the tracker with Liane. Uneasiness snaked about Karic's heart.

"When I arrived on Aranea and found problems of Imperium magnitude, I knew I couldn't return soon to Agrica," the dark-haired man continued, "so I sent Gage in my stead to covertly continue the investigation." He smiled over at his friend. "And only this nocte has he finally returned with the information I've been seeking."

"That runaway scientist was harder to track than some of the cleverest criminals," Gage muttered. "I almost caught up with him in Fodina, before he once again slipped away." He glanced at Liane. "That's who I was looking for in the pits, that nocte I took you there."

"And did you finally find him?" Liane asked.

"Yes, of course."

"Of course."

"My Lord Ardane," Karic heard her begin again,

"Necator has a secret weapon that reprograms men's minds. We fear he means to use it to take over the Imperium."

"Does he now?"

"Yes, my lord."

"And how do you know this?"

"The Cat Man I rescued from Necator told me of the machine. It is called the Guide."

The man named Ardane, who Karic had quickly recognized as the Bellatorian Liane had spoken so highly of, grinned at Gage. "It seems knowledge of the Guide is becoming quite common. That scientist of yours must have been determined to spread the news far and wide. We are fortunate Necator hasn't already disappeared with the weapon. This nocte is none too soon to carry out our plan."

He took Liane by the arms. "Will you help us, Domina? Gage speaks highly of your courage, and you've worked well together before. With your knowledge of the palace, we should easily find the Guide."

Anger and disbelief roiled in Karic. Was it possible? Had Liane been working with these two men from the beginning? It almost seemed so, and yet to suspect her of such treachery . . .

"I've been with you since that first sol we met, my lord," Liane breathed. "I'll help in any way I can. And there are others, not far away in the forest—"

At her words, spoken with such joyous enthusiasm, something in Karic snapped. He stepped out of the shadows. "How easily you betray us, Liane!" he snarled.

"Karic!" she cried. In the momentary confusion, she slipped between Gage and Teran.

Before she could take another step forward, Teran

pulled her behind him. He'd seen the blaster in the Cat Man's hands.

In the dim light, Karic's eyes gleamed like smoldering embers. He scathingly surveyed the tall Bellatorian who stood before Liane. "What is your purpose here?" he harshly demanded. "And what are you to my mate?"

"He is Teran Ardane," Liane frantically explained as she simultaneously attempted to squirm away from Teran. "He is the man I told you about. The one who can help your people. And Gage," she quickly motioned in his direction, "is also here."

Karic momentarily eyed Teran's hands upon Liane. "Yes, I can see how adept he is at helping," he muttered. Then his icy glance swung to Gage. "A strange coincidence, isn't it, that once again I find you with Liane. How long have you two been conspiring together?"

"There's no conspiracy," the blond tracker calmly replied, "save what you've fabricated in your mind."

Karic's face darkened. He rounded on Liane. "Have you betrayed my people to these men? Have you and Bardwin been lovers all along? Was that the price he asked for his help?"

"How could you think such a thing?"

His glance raked her seductively garbed form. "You stand there, dressed like an alley walker, plotting with two Bellatorians, and wonder how I can think such a thing? What else *would* I think?"

Liane's fists clenched at her side. "And how do you imagine I was able to get into Primasedes, you ignorant, loin-crazed male, except to play the whore? And do you perhaps also think I took on half the guard barracks to secure my way into the alarm system room? Why not lay that at my feet as well?"

Gage moved forward, all the while struggling to keep the amusement from his voice. "This reminds me of a similar discussion we had at Fodina, and once again, Cat Man, you are mistaken."

"Am I now?" Karic growled. "Well, one way or another it doesn't really matter. I can't take any chances." He cocked his blaster. "Both of you are going to die."

"Karic!" Liane's horrified voice filled the room. "Don't you dare!"

Teran turned to her. "Give me your word you'll stay out of this. Trust me. It'll be all right."

"But you don't understand. Let me talk to him—"

"Domina," Teran sharply cut in, "go stand with Gage. That's an order."

Liane choked back further protest. Her lifelong Bellatorian training effectively quelled her impulse to argue. And she did trust Teran Ardane. Her Sententian abilities had ascertained his courage and innate goodness long ago. Now, if only Karic could be made to see reason . . .

She moved to stand beside Gage. Teran shot her a brief, reassuring smile. His gaze, however, when he turned to meet Karic, was wary.

Teran eyed the blaster still pointed at him. "Do you mean to use that on me like a coward or fight for her man-to-man?"

Liane gasped.

The taunt shattered the last of Karic's control. The challenge to fight for his mate overcame his Bellatorian logic. Instinct, Cat Man instinct, took over in one wild rush of emotion. Karic tossed aside the blaster. With a low growl, he leaped at the other man.

Teran was ready for him. A past assignment on Agrica had well acquainted him with the various races and their unique qualities. He knew the highly emotional nature of Cat Men, and as a former warrior, he vastly preferred bringing disputes to a swift end, even if it necessitated the use of force. Indeed, the wiser of the two courses was to disarm the younger man in a fight, rather than risk a sudden outburst of anger and use of the blaster.

The two men slammed together, the bare flesh of chest and arms meeting in a resounding slap. For long, hard secundae the two adversaries struggled to gain the advantage. Blows fell, hard and bruising, yet neither made a sound. Teran fought with quiet determination, biding his time, awaiting the right opportunity. And, bit by bit, Karic's rage subsided, the red hot mists of high emotion clearing to a hard, bitter resolve.

In the back of his mind Karic knew he'd been goaded, but it didn't matter. Too long had he controlled the anger, frustration and sense of futility over Bellatorian domination of Agrica and Necator's increasingly bloodthirsty reign. In the absence of the Lord Commander, the bearded man he now fought represented all he hated and yearned to destroy. Liane was only part of it, this Karic knew. He fought as well for the sheer pleasure, for a release from all his long-suppressed tensions.

Sweat sheened their bodies. Breathing became ragged and panting, yet still they battled on. Liane watched with rising horror, as the realization grew that Karic would indeed try to kill Teran. She had never seen him like this—a controlled, lethal killer —and though she sensed his pent-up rage at all things Bellatorian, she couldn't allow him to make

337

this fatal mistake. To kill Teran would irrevocably destroy all hope for Agrica. But to turn against Karic!

She forced a semblance of reason past her turbulent emotions. He'd understand in the end. He had to.

Liane turned to Gage. "You've got to stop them. Karic will kill Teran."

"I know," Gage muttered, "but if I interfere, your Cat Man may go wild and use his claws. Teran could easily be slashed to death before I managed to separate them."

He strode over and picked up Karic's blaster.

"No!" Liane cried. "The stunner. Please, use the stunner!" Her frantic gaze searched the room for the weapon.

The two men were on the floor now, each fiercely wrestling to overpower the other. Liane ran across the bed chamber in the direction she'd seen the stunner fly when Gage had knocked it from her. On her hands and knees she felt along the shadowed wall, trying to block out the labored grunts of the rapidly tiring combatants.

For all Teran's commanding physique and intelligence, Liane knew Karic would eventually emerge the victor. The renowned stamina of the Cat Men was an unbeatable advantage, an advantage that gave them an Imperium-wide reputation for invincibility in hand-to-hand combat. If she didn't find the stunner soon, it might be too late.

Finally, her hand closed around the little box. She scrambled to her feet. Even now Karic was behind Teran, throttling him. With trembling fingers, Liane slid the stun setting to light stun and aimed the weapon.

Karic stiffened as the beam touched him, arching

back in soundless agony. Then he slumped to the floor. Teran, still in Karic's grip, was pulled backward on top of him. He lay there for a long moment, dragging in great gulps of air. Then he rolled off the now inert form of his opponent and staggered to his feet.

Teran ruefully grinned at Liane and Gage. "Never fought . . . a Cat Man before," he said between panting breaths. "Provoking that one . . . was definitely a bad call."

She eyed him. "He'd have killed you."

"That thought was beginning to permeate my thick skull about the time you stunned him."

"We've got to find some way to convince him to listen to you—and quickly," Liane said. "I only set the gun on light stun. He'll awaken soon."

Teran glanced in Karic's direction. "What do you suggest we do? You know him better than I."

Liane walked over to Karic. Squatting, she gently stroked his face, now expressionless in a form of neural sleep. A fierce protectiveness welled in her. He was so helpless now. If anything should happen to him . . .

She forced her attention back to Teran. "It would be wisest to bind him until he calms down enough to listen to reason."

Teran cocked an amused brow. "And how long will that take? He seems pretty hotheaded."

"Not long. His highly logical side will resurface soon enough. He's half-Bellatorian, you know."

"I gathered as much from his appearance," Teran dryly responded. He paused. "What's he doing in Primasedes? Seems like half of Agrica has free run of the palace this nocte. Necator spoke of an alarm system to keep intruders out."

"I disabled it earlier," Liane briskly interjected.

"Karic and his men must have followed a few horas later. It was all part of a plan."

"The Cat Man sent you in alone to destroy the alarms?" Gage angrily cut in. "The fool risked your life!"

"Karic knew nothing of my plan to go it alone. I drugged him and all his men. He came after me when he awoke."

Her gaze shifted once more to Karic's prone form. "He'll be very angry at me . . . later."

"Yes, I imagine he will," Gage wryly observed.

Liane smiled. "Come," she said, motioning toward Karic, "we'd better bind him now."

The two men never had a chance. The bedchamber door burst open and in streamed eight men. Backlit in the sudden brightness of a fully illuminated corridor, the face of the group's leader was indiscernible but not so his voice, smooth and smugly oily.

"Well, well, what have we here?" Necator archly inquired, motioning for the chamber lights to be turned up. "My recalcitrant young Cat Man, traitorous little Sententian and," he drawled, glancing at the tracker, "the famous Gage Bardwin?"

As the room brightened, the forms of the seven guards, all pointing blasters at them, appeared.

"And you, my Lord Ardane," Necator continued, "what cause have you to conspire with these rebels? Do you realize that even now they run amok within my palace, battling to overthrow our government?"

"So I've been told," Teran cooly replied. "I only wonder what atrocities have been inflicted to drive these people to such a dire act. And now I hear talk of some machine of yours, capable of Imperium domination. Your treason appears of far greater import to Bellator than Domina Allador's will ever be."

Necator shot Liane a murderous look. "So you told him, did you?" he snarled. "That was foolish, but no matter. Lord Ardane's death was a foregone conclusion, as is now Bardwin's. With this subversive attack upon the palace, it'll be an easy task to explain how they became caught in the crossfire."

He grinned wolfishly. "And I count myself fortunate to have found both you and the Cat Man here, too. It'll save valuable time in escaping, with you as my prisoners."

"I take it then the battle is going poorly for you?" Teran sardonically inquired.

His opponent momentarily glared at him, then catching himself, he relaxed, softly laughing. "Only for a time, Lord Ardane. A temporary setback, nothing more. Even now my men are loading the Guide into a transport craft. The Cat Men were only able to slightly damage it before we arrived. Some minor repairs and it'll again be fully functional. We'll return soon enough—and with a vengeance!"

Teran calmly eyed him. "You won't succeed, you know."

"Seems I've heard that somewhere before," Necator sneered, "and I'm still in power. But enough of this. Seize the femina. I've got special plans for her."

At Necator's words Teran tensed but controlled his impulse to leap at the guards. Liane was in the line of fire. Then, out of the corner of his eye, Teran saw Karic briefly stir. Better to buy time, Teran thought, and distract attention from the Cat Man. If fortune smiled, perhaps he would find some way to take Necator and his men unawares.

It required two guards to subdue Liane who struggled fiercely, well aware of what was to come. She had to do something or Gage and Lord Ardane would be murdered—and Karic. Karic would fall into Necator's foul clutches. Her own fate was of little import. It would not affect an entire planet like the lives of these three men would.

Her frantic efforts effectively engaged the guards long enough for them to lower their blasters. Suddenly, a flash of movement erupted from the floor. Karic flung himself at the two closest guards. It took the men by surprise. Only one managed to get off a stray gun blast before they all tumbled to the floor.

Gage tackled the other three guards, while Teran leaped at the two holding Liane. One was easily dispatched with a sharp blow to the jaw. The other, in too close contact to fire his weapon, used the butt of his blaster to strike Teran. He staggered back, nearly losing his balance. The guard swiftly took aim.

Liane wrenched the stunner from her pocket and fired. The guard toppled over. Teran grinned at her then leaped into the melee of Gage and the three guards.

It was over. Liane sagged in relief. Together, the three powerful men would easily overpower the guards. They were safe.

Necator. Where was he?

She started to whirl around when an arm encircled her shoulders. Before she could form a coherent thought, a dagger was placed against her throat. Liane froze.

"Don't move. Don't even breathe," Necator hissed into her ear.

Liane did as she was told.

"That's better, my pretty one," he purred. "Now, ever so carefully, give me the stunner—and don't try anything foolish. This blade's made of Nadrygen steel and can slice through flesh and bone like soft butter. I'd so hate to be startled into slitting your lovely throat."

CHAPTER 18

IN HORRIFIED SLOW MOTION, LIANE WATCHED KARIC, Teran and Gage climb to their feet. The guards lay scattered about them. Liane considered forcing Necator's hand and goading him to kill her, rather than surrender the stunner and put Karic and her friends in danger. If she didn't do something, all could still be lost.

She took a deep breath as her glance met Karic's. *Forgive me* was the message in her deep blue eyes.

"Don't do it, Liane!" Karic savagely snapped. "Give him the stunner. Now!"

"K—Karic," Liane stammered. "I—"

"Do as he says, Domina," Teran softly ordered.

With a sigh she handed Necator the weapon. He fired it at Karic, then Teran and Gage, all three sinking to the floor.

With a gloating laugh Necator tossed the gun aside. "That ought to put them out for the next several horas. Time enough to get safely away with you."

The guard Liane had stunned stirred on the floor, and Necator eyed the man. "You set the stunner on light, didn't you? Well, no matter. It'll be long enough to see to my original plan."

He held Liane, the dagger pressed to her throat, until the guard revived. "Use the blaster on those two," Necator ordered the man, indicating Teran and Gage, "and make sure to finish them off. Afterwards, bring the Cat Man to the transport craft. Don't tarry. We leave for the secret rendezvous shortly."

The guard nodded.

Necator's free hand entwined in Liane's hair to steady her head, effectively trapping her throat against the razor-sharp blade. It pricked her tender flesh, and she bit her lip against the pain. Warm blood trickled down to stain the thin fabric of her tunic.

"There's nothing you can do for your friends," Necator snarled. "Nothing."

Liane fought back a surge of despair. He was right, she thought, eyeing the guard who was now in possession of a blaster. But if she didn't buy them time, time enough for the stunner's effects to wear off, her friends would be at the guard's mercy.

"Come along, sweet femina," Necator murmured into her ear. "Time to go." He jerked her forward by her hair.

Liane dug in her heels. "Please, my lord," she whispered. "I beg you not to kill my friends. You've still got the Guide. You still possess the power to overcome any who stand in your way. In light of that, how can their deaths possibly matter?"

"You test my generosity in sparing you and the

Cat Man, and then you dare beg for Ardane and Bardwin?" Necator angrily demanded. "Their deaths are but another lesson to those who oppose me. And I dare leave no one alive with the power to influence the High King. Now come, before I forget my good intentions and finish you right here!"

He shoved her forward. Out of the corner of her eye, Liane thought she saw Karic move. Wild hope filled her. Perhaps, just perhaps, the stun effects were already wearing off. But had she bought them the time they needed? Had it been enough? As Necator began to drag her down the hall, Liane prayed that it had.

Karic heard the click of the blaster being cocked to fire. His head ached and his mind was still groggy from the stunner's effects, but the awareness of acute danger sharpened his Cat's responses. Before the guard could fire Karic leaped to his feet. He knocked the gun from its aim at Teran's body and slashed open the man's throat. With a gurgling cry the guard fell, blood spurting from a severed artery.

For a secundae Karic stood over the man, his chest heaving with savage emotions. He had killed yet again, and still it wasn't enough. It would never be enough to assuage the loss of thousands of his people. Even Necator's death wouldn't be enough. But if there were suddenly no satisfaction in revenge, what was there?

"Killing's never the answer," Teran softly observed, coming up behind him. "It may be a necessary evil at times, but ultimately it destroys not only the victim but his executioner as well."

Karic wheeled around, the whipcord muscle and sinew of his body straining with the effort it took not to turn the full force of his frustration upon the other man. "And what do you know about that, Bellatorian? Your people have never hesitated an instant in the senseless destruction of our people."

Teran calmly eyed him. "You are wrong, Cat Man. There *have* been a few with the courage of their convictions, who risked condemnation and exile rather than follow orders to murder your people."

He paused to help a now awake Gage to his feet. "But that's not the real issue here," Teran said. "Necator has Liane and the Guide. Let us help you rescue her and destroy that machine."

There was something in the tall Bellatorian's eyes that reassured Karic. He suddenly understood how Liane could come to trust him. Teran exuded a power and purity of spirit that bespoke of a higher calling than petty human considerations. And, when Liane had first met him, she'd still possessed her Sententian powers. She'd seen into his heart.

Karic retrieved three blasters and tossed one to Teran and Gage. "Do you know the way to the transport craft?"

Teran eyed him for a moment. "Yes."

Karic pursed his lips and silently whistled. In a few secundae Cat Men began to appear until a large group had gathered. Karic motioned toward Teran and Gage.

"These men are friends. They'll lead us to Necator and our final battle. Just have a care where you fire. The Lord Commander has Liane."

With a wave of his hand, Teran signaled them forward. It seemed an eternity of repetitious corridors and stairs before they reached the transport bay. As they paused outside the entrance, Karic stepped forward.

"Let my men and I go first. Our cloaking powers will give us the advantage of surprise. Stay behind until the battle begins. Then it will no longer matter."

Teran nodded. "As you wish." He laid a hand on Karic's arm.

The Cat Man cocked an inquiring brow.

"I wish you good fortune in your rescue of Liane."

"I'll need that and more," Karic growled, "if I'm to ever see her alive again."

Understanding gleamed in Teran's eyes. "We'll do what we can."

Gage grimly nodded his support, a fierce look of determination in his eyes.

Karic studied the two men for a brief moment more. Then, with a signal of his hand, he motioned to his men. As they crept through the doorway their forms faded from view. The warriors fanned out as they made their stealthy way across the huge bay. At that moment the transport craft's engines fired, and with a whir of sound, the exterior bay doors began to close. Take-off appeared imminent.

Karic fired his blaster at the two guards who stood outside the craft's main door, one toppling to the floor.

Suddenly the room came alive with the shouts of men and sizzling blasts of gunfire. The cloaking power could not be maintained during the heat of battle; it required too much concentration for that. Karic and his men were prime targets for the guards stationed on the overhead walkways. But they were prime targets as well.

The battle quickly rose to a fever pitch. Deafening noise and agonized screams mingled with gun blasts as bodies thudded to the floor. The stench of burning flesh assaulted Karic's sensitive nostrils. He shoved it to the back of his mind. Nothing was more important than reaching Liane, and he knew she was inside the transport craft.

The ship's remaining guard fired at him. Only a wild lunge to the side saved Karic as he dodged his opponent's blast, yet even as he fell he returned fire. The guard had his back turned, frantically pounding on the craft's opening mechanism. Karic's blaster hit not only the guard but the door opener as well.

It exploded in a burst of flame. The door slid open to be engulfed in a wall of fire. Smoke billowed into the bay as the fire quickly spread into the craft's interior. From within, Karic heard frightened cries.

There was no way to know how far or fast the fire would spread. It didn't matter anyway. He had to go in after Liane.

He backed off for a running start. His total concentration narrowed on the doorway, a doorway belching tongues of flame. Everything centered on his speed. Karic prayed the fire hadn't spread too deeply into the craft. His rescue attempt would be fatally cut short if it had.

Muscles straining to their utmost, Karic ran for the door, blinding himself to the surging flames, imagining only what he hoped lay beyond—Liane. There was a brief, prickling sensation of heat, and then Karic was through. He landed on the cool metallic floor outside the main control room. He leaped to his feet and pounded on the room's opening mechanism. The large doors slid apart.

Necator was standing near the control panel. He froze. Shock, then rising terror, widened his eyes. Karic made a quick visual search of the room. Aside from the pilot, busy readying the craft for take-off, there was no one else present.

"Where's Liane?" Karic demanded, his voice low and deadly.

Necator nervously smiled. "She is safe." As he spoke his hand moved behind him. "She'll come to no harm if you leave now."

"I'm not going anywhere without her. Tell me where she is—"

A blaster appeared in Necator's hands. Fire spewed from the gun. Karic barely lunged aside. Behind him, something exploded. Nimbly diving onto his stomach, Karic fired his own blaster. It missed Necator, taking out the pilot and the base of the control panel instead. The man shrieked, then slumped forward. With a deep, throbbing surge of the engines, the transport craft began to rise.

Without a pilot to guide it into level flight, the craft lurched unevenly, twirling about in the huge bay like some wildly drunken dancer. It ricocheted off one wall, then another, throwing its occupants about like helpless bits of debris. Karic was flung hard against a wall, the force of impact nearly knocking him unconscious. His blaster flew from his hands to slide out of sight down the hall.

Through a sparkling, spinning whirl of lights he saw Necator crawl toward him, a triumphant, evil grin on his face. In the deepening smoke he saw a dagger flash. Reflexively, Karic lifted an arm to protect himself.

Pain, deep and agonizing, tore through him. The lingering haze cleared. He saw the bloodied dagger raised high again, and an arm—his arm—spurting blood. It was an arm he barely felt, useless and limp. With a savage cry Karic kicked out with both legs, slamming into Necator's chest.

Bones snapped with a sickening crunch an instant before the man was propelled backward across the room. He struck the section of control panel shattered by Karic's blaster, his back impaling on the twisted, extruding metal. A startled look passed across Necator's face. His mouth opened in a silent, contorted scream. Then he sagged forward.

Karic staggered to his feet, clutching his bleeding arm. The blood, he thought groggily, he was losing so much blood. The transport craft lurched crazily, unbalancing him. He fell to his knees. Karic crawled over to the dead pilot. Smoke billowed in the room, choking him.

Low, he told himself. He must stay low to keep the smoke from his lungs. Karic pulled the pilot down to him. With his good hand and teeth, he tore a long strip of cloth from the man's shirt and wrapped it above his elbow to form a tourniquet. The bleeding slowed to an ooze. Ripping loose another piece of cloth, Karic made a cursory attempt at binding his wound.

There was little time for anything more. Even now, the damaged craft was in danger of exploding. Pain, deep and relentlessly throbbing, clouded Karic's mind, bathing his body in a cold sweat. He wanted to vomit. But he had no time to give in to the agony. He must find Liane—and quickly.

Time ceased as he made his tortuous way down the hall, until his whole universe centered upon the one thing that kept him going. Liane. His mate. His love.

"Liane?" he cried. "Where are you?"

"Karic?"

A soft, sweet voice rose from the darkness just beyond his blurring vision.

"Karic. Is it really you?"

He moved toward the voice, blindly, desperately. A hand touched his face.

"Liane," he thickly mumbled. "You must get out. Now, before it's too late."

351

"I can't. I'm tied."

Karic wearily lifted his head. "Where?" he rasped. "Where are you tied?"

"My hands. Here, to this post."

Karic's fingers groped for the knots, then realized he hadn't the strength to untie them, much less the use of the other hand it would require. He unsheathed his claws and tore at the thick cords.

The bindings fell free a moment before the craft again slammed into something. The collision sent Karic shooting across the room to a far wall. His wounded arm took the brunt of impact. This time Karic couldn't stifle a groan.

Liane crawled to his side. "Karic, what's wrong? Are you hurt?"

She could barely see in the smoke-filled room. She ran her hands over his body. Fear coiled within her as Liane noted his cool, damp skin and his shallow breathing. He was wounded, perhaps mortally so. She found his arm with its tourniquet and makeshift bandage. Beneath the cloth Liane's expert fingers felt the depth of Karic's wound.

Sudden terror replaced the fear. She quickly must get him to safety. Liane slid an arm beneath his shoulders.

"Karic, listen to me," she firmly instructed. "We must get out of here now. Help me get you to your feet."

He weakly shook his head. "It—it's too late for me, femina." His words sounded hollow and spiritless. "Go. Save yourself."

"No!" Liane frantically tried to tug him to his knees. "I won't leave you!"

"You must."

He turned to gaze up at her, his eyes dulling even as he spoke.

"If not for yourself, then for the sake of our child. You . . . promised . . . if anything happened to me that you'd save our child."

Tears burned her eyes. At a time like this, how could he remind her of their child, while he lay here in her arms with his life bleeding away? It was unfair to tear her heart in two opposite directions, between a fledgling sense of duty to an unborn child and her love for him.

A sudden realization tore through her. Her daughter—*their* daughter! Were her healing abilities as potent as her psychic powers? It was almost too much to hope for from such a tiny, barely developed being, but it seemed Karic's only chance. And he wouldn't need a full healing, just a little more strength to get him to safety. Liane's hand slid to her belly.

With all the power she possessed, mother called to child. For a long moment Liane felt nothing, not even the slight stirring of life she'd noted before. Then a sound, resonant and comforting, filled her mind. It reverberated through her brain until its meaning engulfed her in warmth and power.

Her hand lifted from her belly to touch Karic's face. His eyes were closed, his breathing ragged and weak. She tenderly stroked him, his forehead, cheek, neck, gradually trailing a path of healing fire down his body.

He stirred, and his lids lifted. Somewhere in the depths of his dying being, life flickered with renewed heat, flickered and burst into flame. Awareness of a dramatic change, a surge of strength, flared in Karic. He levered himself to a sitting position.

Their eyes met. "Let's get out of here," Karic said.

Liane followed him out of the room, her hand firmly clasping his to maintain transfusion of the strengthening power. Their progress was slow as they crawled down the hall. Time and again the craft crazily lurched about, flinging them against the walls. Explosions rocked them, until Liane thought the force would literally rip the ship apart, but somehow, someway, it held together.

At last the outer doorway loomed before them, blackened and gaping from the spent electrical fire. They hesitated there, waiting for the right moment to jump, as the craft constantly rose and fell to erratic heights above the floor in its wild flight about the bay.

"You go first," Liane cried. "Your strength will fade as soon as I stop touching you. If I leave before you, you might not be able to get out in time."

Karic studied her for a brief moment, loathe to risk leaving her behind. Then he nodded. There was no time left for arguing.

"Come after me quickly," he ordered. Karic gave her hand a squeeze. "Promise?"

She smiled. "I promise."

The craft dipped low. Liane shoved him forward. "Go!"

Karic leaped from the doorway, striking the floor to nimbly roll over and over before coming to a halt on his feet. Weakness immediately tore through him. He sank to his knees, his gaze fixed on the ship.

Another explosion shuddered through its metal bulk. Liane was thrown backward, disappearing into the interior. Stark terror ripped through Karic, and he began to crawl forward.

Gage reached his side and pulled him back.

"Liane," Karic whispered. "I've got . . . to go to her."

"There's nothing you can do," Gage grimly muttered. "She must get out on her own."

Karic slumped in Gage's arms. There was indeed nothing more he could do. He could barely move.

The transport craft careened off yet another wall. This time the trajectory of impact sent it barreling straight toward the open bay door.

"Liane!" Karic roared with the last bit of strength he possessed. "Jump!"

In that last moment before the tortured hulk of metal shot out to crash to the streets below, Liane leaped from the transport craft. For several secundae she lay on the floor, motionless. Then she looked about until she found Karic. She waved.

Karic waved back, then promptly lost consciousness.

Liane gazed out of the palace window upon a gloriously warm and bright morn. She was happy, content.

She looked at Karic, propped up in the huge bed, his arm swathed in bandages and sling. He had improved so much in the past few sols. At first, there had been doubt if they could even salvage the limb. When Karic wasn't unconscious from the pain, it required the strongest drugs of the palace healer to control his agony.

Ultimately they had saved the arm, and though the healer had said only time would tell if Karic would regain full use of it, Liane knew he would. Their child had told her.

Drained as both were from the horrible events of the palace overthrow, neither Liane, as conduit of power, nor her child had the psychic energy left to heal. To even attempt to do so might risk both their lives, so Liane had not even brought up the possibility to the others. Time enough to explain it all to Karic later—about his healing, their daughter . . .

"Liane?"

With a smile she turned from the window to the man who was her love. "Yes, Karic?"

"I have a pain," he began.

Her smile faded, and she reached for the vial of narcotic on the nearby table. "Here, let me give you—"

"The pain is of the heart, sweet femina," Karic laughingly interrupted her, "not the body. I need you beside me."

She shook her head in tender exasperation, but willingly joined him. With his good arm, Karic pulled her down to lie against his chest. His lips gently caressed her forehead.

"My father and men leave for the lair this morning," he said. "I wish we were going with them."

Once more, the memory of Morigan's earlier visit stirred Liane's unease. "Your words to your father," she finally began. "You would never return to your lair if they refused to accept me as your life mate?"

"I meant what I said, Liane."

She lowered her head. "But you might come to hate me some sol for such an act and regret our love."

At the thread of tortured uncertainty in her voice, Karic slipped his hand from her grasp. Taking her chin in his palm, he gently lifted her eyes to his.

"Never. Do you hear me?" he hoarsely whispered. "Never will I hate or regret loving you. And I will never give you up, either. You have proven your loyalty, your courage and your fitness to rule at my side. Nothing anyone can do will change that."

His grip tightened on her jaw. "Do you hear me, Liane? Do you understand what I say?"

She smiled through a sparkling blur of tears. "Yes, Karic, I hear and understand."

"Good." A smug grin tugged at his lips. "It's past time anyway that you learned to obey your lord and master."

Liane gasped in mock outrage, but before she could respond Karic pulled her down to him. Even the strength of his one good arm was enough to subdue her half-hearted struggles. With a contented sigh, she relaxed against him.

"My poor, unfortunate mate," she chuckled. "You can barely control one femina as it is. What will you do when there are two?"

Karic nuzzled her tumbled ebony mane. "Two? There is no other femina but you in my life. Why do you speak so—?"

He paused and turned her face to his. A dark brow cocked quizzically. "Our child *is* a male, isn't he?"

"*Is* he, my lord?"

Karic scowled. "Liane, if you know something . . ."

She laughed. "We're to have a daughter, my love. A daughter who possesses all of my former powers."

"Then it was she who gave me that surge of strength in the transport craft," he said, after a moment of thoughtful consideration.

"Yes."

He lapsed into silence.

"Are you displeased?"

"About what?"

"That our firstborn will not be a son."

357

"Ah, yes," he lazily drawled, shooting her an amused glance. "And it equally displeases me that I'll have a daughter as lovely as her mother, with psychic and healing powers that will aid her people. A daughter who'll be wise and kind and good, as her mother is. A daughter who'll adore her father, just as her mother does. A daughter—"

"Oh, hush, Karic." Liane lay a silencing finger upon his lips, her deep blue eyes sparkling in exasperation. "I think I get your meaning."

The teasing light in Karic's eyes faded. "I love you, sweet femina. It matters not to me whether our child is a son or daughter. As long as you're happy, and never stop loving me."

A firm knock sounded at the door.

Karic sighed. "Enter!"

Teran and Gage strode in. Liane quickly struggled to a more upright position. Though Karic allowed her to do so, he refused to relinquish his grip.

She smiled to herself. Even now, knowing how much she loved him, Karic still couldn't overcome the Cat Man's instinctive possessiveness of his mate, but she didn't really mind. It was nice to be cherished and protected, and most times Karic was quite amenable to reason.

Teran pulled up a chair and sat down, Gage standing behind him. "I've business of vital importance to discuss with you," Teran began without further preamble.

"And I with you," Karic quickly interjected. "By your leave, I'd like to speak first."

Teran hesitated, then shrugged. "As you wish."

"First," Karic firmly declared, "I'd like to apologize for my crude behavior and unreasonable accusations that nocte in your bedchamber. I was acting the fool."

He turned to Liane. "And I am equally sorry as well for what I said to you. I felt betrayed, nothing more."

She steadily returned his gaze, her eyes warm with love and forgiveness. "I understand."

"As do I." Teran extended his hand.

Karic eyed it for a moment, then grinned and accepted it. "I'm not certain I'm worthy of such quick forgiveness, but I'll do my best to be so."

He then turned to Gage. "And you. Not only is there the matter in the bedchamber but also my conduct at the mines. My jealousy overrode what should have been my deepest gratitude toward you."

"Liane's a femina any man would treasure," Gage smilingly replied. "I won't deny I wanted her, but I also wasn't blind or stupid. You are the only man for her. So," he sighed, his glance briefly swinging to Liane's, "I'll content myself with her friendship, as I will with yours, if you're willing."

Karic chuckled and grasped Gage's outstretched hand. "I'm willing." He turned to Teran. "You mentioned having something to discuss. What would that be?"

Teran leaned forward. "Has Liane had the chance to finish the story of all that transpired since Necator's death?"

"No." Karic shook his head. "Only this morning did I begin to feel more like my old self."

"As I gathered from Liane's reports," Teran dryly observed. "So you don't know that the Guide was totally destroyed when the transport craft crashed?"

Karic glanced at Liane, a look of relief flaring in his eyes. She gave him a quick smile, then turned to Teran.

"And what of the scientists who designed the Guide?" she inquired. "What became of them?"

"Some were killed in the palace overthrow and most of the rest were captured. Unfortunately, a few escaped."

"That could create a problem." A worried light flared in Karic's eyes. "If they carry knowledge of that machine . . ."

"Gage is leaving this very sol to begin tracking them," Teran said, "but from all I could gather, no one scientist possessed total knowledge. Each was responsible for a finite aspect of the Guide's construction. Apparently it was Necator's way of maintaining total control."

"And hopefully that all died with him," Liane offered. "What will you do with the captured scientists?"

Teran's expression hardened. "They are traitors to Bellator *and* the Imperium. They've already been sent back to Bellator for a memory purge. They'll soon recall nothing of the Guide. After that, they'll be transported to Carcer for rehabilitation."

Liane couldn't help but shudder at the mention of the Imperium's infamous prison planet. Few managed to survive on its barren wastes longer than six monates.

Teran noted her reaction. "We have plans to return Carcer to its former sols of benevolent rehabilitation. The task is large, this dream of bringing the Imperium out of its downward spiral into total chaos, but there is finally hope."

He directed the full intensity of his gaze back to Karic. "Which brings me to the purpose of my visit."

Karic studied him impassively. "Go on."

"Agrica needs a new Lord Commander."

"So we're to remain a colony of Bellator." Anger ignited in Karic's eyes.

"For the time being," Teran calmly replied. "My planet was never one to accept rapid change. It's our rigidly disciplined military system, you know. But the High King seems amenable to a gradual return of Agrican power as the inhabitants appear ready for self-rule. It's all part of our master plan—I and my mate, Queen Alia of Aranea—to restore law and order to the Imperium."

Karic thoughtfully contemplated him. "That's an impressively large task. You'll need help."

Teran nodded. "The right man as Lord Commander would help immensely. I want you for the job, Karic."

Liane gave a small cry and turned to Karic, who had stiffened in surprise. "Did you hear that, my love? You as Lord Commander! Oh, it is a perfect choice. You're a brave and resourceful warrior. As one of the most well-known rebels and leader of Necator's overthrow, the people will easily accept you. And with your half-Cat Man, half-Bellatorian blood, you are a living symbol of the best of both worlds!"

Amusement tugged at the corner of Karic's sensual mouth. "And you lack only a detailed description of my prowess in bed to complete your glowing recommendation."

"But aside from that accounting," Teran dryly interjected, "I totally agree with Liane. You *are* the perfect choice." He paused. "Will you accept the position?"

"Possibly," Karic hesitantly replied, "but I must first ask my father's permission. And I couldn't work with just any Bellatorian in this. My trust in them will take a time to grow. It would have to be you, Teran."

Teran laughed. "Then it's decided. I spoke with your father yestersol. He gave his whole-hearted approval. And, as I'm already the High King's ambassador to Agrica, you'll be working with me until you sicken of my face."

"Then it's decided." Karic lay back against his pillows. "The sol is yet new, and already my life has completely turned around. I need time to ponder this."

"Take all the time you need," Teran said, standing up. "Rest, regain your strength, enjoy your mate. The palace and its servants are at your disposal. I'll return in a monate and we'll talk again."

"Where are you going?"

"I, too, have a mate whom I've had precious little time to enjoy. Perhaps I'll bring her here for a short visit upon my return, if I can tear her away from her royal duties." Teran chuckled at some private thought. "I think you would like her, Karic. She's a courageous little spitfire, a lot like Liane."

Karic lovingly glanced at Liane. "Then I'm sure I would. I look forward to meeting her."

Teran bowed to Liane, who flushed prettily. "Until then, Domina Allador, I leave my new Lord Commander in your most able hands."

"Until then, my Lord Ardane," she murmured.

He grinned, then turned and strode with Gage from the room.

Liane made a move to climb off the bed when Karic tightened his hold. "Where do you think you're going?"

"I only thought to allow you to rest. You must be exhausted after all that's transpired this morn."

Karic's lids slid closed, but he didn't let go. "Yes, I am, but I want you here where you belong—at my side."

Liane most willingly snuggled down against him, laying her head upon the firmly muscled expanse of his chest. "I'm so very happy," she murmured, her fingers making circular whorls of his dark gold chest hair.

"Really?" Karic drowsily inquired. "And how so?"

"Why, I have it all—a mate I love, our child growing within me, and the hope for a bright, wonderful future."

He cocked one eye open to stare down at her. "So, you've truly no regrets? You admit giving up your Sententian powers ultimately was for the best?"

"I've no regrets," Liane replied, hastening to soothe his lingering doubts. "Though how you could have known the eventual outcome is a mystery to me."

"I didn't. All I knew was that you were a passionate, loving femina and had more to offer in joining with me than remaining chaste." He gave her a smoldering look. "I knew that from the moment we first mind-bonded."

Hot color flooded Liane. She propped herself up on his chest to face him. "That was never the intent of my mind bond!"

Karic stirred beneath her, the last vestiges of weariness gone from his face. His gaze, hot and hungry, raked her slender form. "Perhaps not *your* intent, sweet femina, but certainly mine."

Warmth, wholly unlike her former embarrassment, surged through Liane. She leaned over to gently graze his lips with hers, gradually deepening the union until their tongues met. Against her belly, she felt his shaft swell. A knowing, seductive smile spread across her face.

"You always *did* think with your loins," Liane purred, as her fingers began to lightly stroke him. "But then, what can one expect—with such an animal for one's mate?"

Dear Reader,

I hope you enjoyed *HEART'S LAIR* as much as I enjoyed writing it. It was certainly difficult for me to say good-bye to Karic and Liane. But the tale of the Knowing Crystal must unfold, and it is time for Brace and Marissa's story to be told.

CRYSTAL FIRE, the third in my Knowing Crystal series, will be a Summer, 1992, release. It is the tale of Brace Ardane, Teran's younger brother, and Marissa Laomede, a young member of a militant society of outcast women. Compelled to join forces in what initially appears a simple rescue of Marissa's twin sister, their quest quickly evolves into a desperate battle to save the Imperium from a power-crazed criminal and a Knowing Crystal gone awry.

I love hearing from my readers. Please write me (enclose a self-addressed, stamped envelope) at P.O. Box 62365, Colorado Springs, CO 80962.

Kathleen Morgan

Kathleen Morgan

CONNIE MASON

"Ye cannot kill the devil," whispered the awestruck throng at the hanging of the notorious Diablo. And, indeed, moments later the pirate had not only escaped the noose, but had abducted Lady Devon, whisking her aboard his ship, the DEVIL DANCER. Devon swore she would have nothing to do with rakishly handsome captor. But long days at sea, and even longer nights beneath the tropical stars, brought Devon ever closer to surrender. Diablo was a master of seduction, an experienced lover who knew every imaginable way to please a woman — and some that she had never imagined. Devon knew she would find ecstasy in his arms, but dare she tempt the devil?

__2958-8 $4.50